The Perfect Wife

Katherine Scholes was born in Tanzania, East Africa, the daughter of a missionary doctor and an artist. She has fond memories of travelling with her parents and siblings on long safaris to remote areas where her father operated a clinic from his Land Rover. When she was ten, the family left Tanzania, going first to England and then settling in Tasmania. As an adult, Katherine moved to Melbourne with her film-maker husband. After working there for many years, writing books and making films, they returned with their two sons to live in Tasmania.

Katherine is the author of the international bestsellers *The Rain Queen*, *Make Me An Idol*, *The Stone Angel*, *The Hunter's Wife* and *The Lioness*.

katherinescholes.com

Praise for Katherine Scholes

The Lioness

'An incredible saga . . . a spellbinding book filled with the essence of Africa and soul-searching lessons on motherhood.' *Chronicle*

'A great summer read . . . It made me want to jump on the next plane to Tanzania.' *Bookseller + Publisher*

'An exotic setting, a superbly crafted narrative and more than a passing look at what makes us human.' *Weekly Times*

The Hunter's Wife

'Captures the very essence of East Africa . . . one of Australia's most respected women's fiction authors.' *Courier-Mail*

'*Out of Africa* meets *White Mischief* in this classy romance . . . A bittersweet, entertaining mix of Hollywood, obsessive love and the unbearable longing for what is not possible.' *Australian Women's Weekly*

'Beautifully written and a crowd-pleaser.' *Herald Sun*

The Stone Angel

'Scholes crafts her fiction with such care and subtlety.' *Weekend Australian*

'A truly absorbing book filled with secrets and conflicts.' *Woman's Day*

'A beautifully descriptive read and a soul-searching take on human relationships.' *New Idea*

'Full of passion, fine writing and interesting observations . . . Wonderful stuff.' *Australian Women's Weekly* 'Book of the Month'

'*The Stone Angel* touches the senses with its rich descriptions of coastal Tasmania and emerges as a lovingly crafted account of a home we can never run away from.' *Good Reading*

The Rain Queen

'A big, sensuous, splendid novel.' *Overland*

'Moving and inspiring.' *Australian Good Taste*

'Utterly bewitching.' *The Independent* (France)

'A magnificent portrait of a passionate woman, a superb romantic saga.'
Elle (France)

'An intense vision of grief, solitude and the comfort of strangers.'
L'Express (France)

'Disturbing and enthralling – an authentic African voice, exotic and
magical. An amazing book.' *Madam Figaro*

'This most moving book, whose every breath is a love-song for Africa
and her people, is a faultlessly woven cloth.' *Le Monde*

'Three out of three stars.' *Le Tribune*

'Beautifully written, lively and sympathetic.' *Bookshow* (Germany)

Make Me An Idol

'Filled with surprises.' *Mach Malpause* (Germany)

Book of the Week *Dei Zwei* (Germany)

'A superb novel.' *Cote Femme* (France)

Make Me An Idol
The Rain Queen
The Stone Angel
The Hunter's Wife
The Lioness

Katherine Scholes

The Perfect Wife

MICHAEL JOSEPH
an imprint of
PENGUIN BOOKS

MICHAEL JOSEPH

Published by the Penguin Group
Penguin Group (Australia)
707 Collins Street, Melbourne, Victoria 3008, Australia
(a division of Pearson Australia Group Pty Ltd)
Penguin Group (USA) Inc.
375 Hudson Street, New York, New York 10014, USA
Penguin Group (Canada)
90 Eglinton Avenue East, Suite 700, Toronto, Canada ON M4P 2Y3
(a division of Pearson Penguin Canada Inc.)
Penguin Books Ltd
80 Strand, London WC2R 0RL England
Penguin Ireland
25 St Stephen's Green, Dublin 2, Ireland
(a division of Penguin Books Ltd)
Penguin Books India Pvt Ltd
11 Community Centre, Panchsheel Park, New Delhi – 110 017, India
Penguin Group (NZ)
67 Apollo Drive, Rosedale, Auckland 0632, New Zealand
(a division of Pearson New Zealand Ltd)
Penguin Books (South Africa) (Pty) Ltd
Rosebank Office Park, Block D, 181 Jan Smuts Avenue, Parktown North,
Johannesburg, 2196, South Africa
Penguin (Beijing) Ltd
7F, Tower B, Jiaming Center, 27 East Third Ring Road North, Chaoyang District,
Beijing 100020, China

Penguin Books Ltd, Registered Offices: 80 Strand, London WC2R 0RL, England

First published by Penguin Group (Australia), 2013

1 3 5 7 9 10 8 6 4 2

Text copyright © Katherine Scholes 2013
The moral right of the author has been asserted

Cover design by Nada Backovic © Penguin Group (Australia)
Cover photographs: Woman/background: Mark Owen/Arcangel
Tree ©Galyna Andrushko/Shutterstock.com
Suitcase © Patricia Hofmeester
Typeset in Fairfield Light 12/18pt by Samantha Jayaweera, Penguin Group (Australia)
Printed and bound in Australia by McPherson's Printing Group, Maryborough,
Victoria

National Library of Australia Cataloguing-in-Publication entry
Scholes, Katherine, author.
The perfect wife / Katherine Scholes.
9781921901706
Man-woman relationships – Fiction.
A823.3

For Jonny and Linden, with my love

ONE

Kitty shifted impatiently in her seat. The journey seemed to have dragged on forever but now at last the end was near. Soon, she would be reunited with her husband. They were going to make a fresh start together, beginning their marriage over again. With the past left safely behind them, everything would be new, clean, undamaged. She couldn't wait for the plane to land – and her life in Africa to begin.

To distract herself, she straightened her jacket and brushed away crumbs from her cream linen skirt. Then she rested her head against the seatback, closing her eyes. They felt gritty and hot – she'd hardly had any sleep in twenty-four hours. Somewhere between Rome and Benghazi the flight crew had made up beds for the nine passengers, but even though Kitty had been comfortable enough she'd found it hard to relax. The throb of the propellers, coming straight in through the unlined metal of the fuselage, was distracting. And there was the awkwardness of lying down in the midst of a group of men who'd been complete strangers to her before this journey began. Kitty felt she'd only just drifted off to sleep when the crew had returned to fold up the beds and serve breakfast.

Opening her eyes, she turned to the passenger beside her. Paddy showed no sign of being tired. He was sitting up straight, reading a well-worn paperback with pages bent at the corners. As though sensing Kitty's gaze, he looked up.

'Not long now. Bet you can't wait to see that husband of yours.'

Kitty nodded. 'Six weeks feels like forever.'

'That's true love, then.' He gave her a cheeky grin.

Kitty smiled back. Paddy had none of the constrained manners of the English. She couldn't imagine him standing about like Theo always did, waiting for a lady to sit down before he could do the same. In that way, the Irishman was like an Australian – perhaps that was why she felt so comfortable with him. There was also the fact that he was short and plump, with a demeanour that reminded her of a friendly puppy. It was impossible to imagine him posing any kind of threat.

'Got to finish this before we get there.' Paddy fanned the remaining pages of his novel. 'I've got the feeling we're going to be busy.' He resumed reading, moving his finger over the page to find his place.

Kitty thought back to the draughty hangar at the airstrip outside London where she'd first encountered Paddy, along with the other passengers who were to set off with her to Tanganyika. The war had been over for three years, but the men still identified themselves by military rank as well as names. They were all engineers and mechanics, bound for the Kongara Tractor Workshops. Standing in a little group, suitcases at their feet, they'd begun talking about the Groundnut Scheme – what they'd heard, what they knew . . . Kitty had listened in, storing up every piece of information. She wanted to be well informed when she arrived, so that from the very beginning Theo would be able to come home each day and discuss his work with his wife.

Paddy had arrived late, puffing and red in the face. He had a kit bag hanging from one shoulder, crumpled travel documents in his hand. The official from the Ministry of Food looked torn between annoyance at Paddy's lack of punctuality and relief that the last name could now be ticked off the embarkation list. He began shepherding his charges towards the hangar door.

As she stepped outside, Kitty held the fur collar of her coat close around her throat; the country was in the grip of a cold snap. The concrete was icy, and she kept her eyes on her feet as she made her way across the runway – so she heard rather than saw the man who came striding up beside her.

'My name's Paddy O'Halloran.' He gave her a cheerful smile. 'I didn't fight in the war.'

Kitty raised her eyebrows, taken aback by his direct, almost teasing manner. 'I'm Mrs Hamilton.'

'Indeed you are,' he said. 'I know all about you.'

Kitty's step faltered, alarm tingling through her body. In a flash of memory, she heard Theo's voice, tight with anger.

My wife, it seems, is famous.

Then the slap of a newspaper dropping onto the table, teacups rattling in their bone china saucers.

Kitty swallowed, bracing herself for whatever was going to come next. But Paddy's tone remained casual. 'You're going out to join your husband. Wing Commander Theo Hamilton. Manager of Administration. They told us at the briefing that you'd be on board.' He winked at her. 'I think they wanted to make sure we all behaved ourselves. Some of the fellows are not used to having a lady around.'

Before Kitty had a chance to respond, she felt one shoe begin to slide on the ice. Paddy grabbed her arm and held it. 'Bloody slippery. Take care, now.'

As they neared the aircraft, he pointed up at the line of square windows running along the body. 'It's a converted Lancaster bomber, you know. Let's just hope they added seats as well as windows!'

'My husband flew a Lancaster.'

'How many missions was he on?'

'Forty-nine,' Kitty said proudly.

Paddy whistled between his teeth. 'Must be immortal.' He stood aside to let Kitty go ahead up the metal stairs.

She gripped the railing, a chill reaching in through her kid gloves. She tried to ignore the feeling that the Lancaster was a huge beast, about to consume her. Newsreel scenes flashed through her head. She heard the frantic clatter of crippled engines. She saw cockpits bursting into flames and dark trails of smoke streaming out behind planes that looked like toys, falling against the sky, then plunging into the sea. During the three long years that Theo had been on active service, she'd lived in fear that sooner or later he would be lost to her this way. It had almost happened: his plane had been hit during a night bombing raid into Germany. He'd managed to bring the Lancaster back to England, crash-landing in a field – but he'd been the only one of his crew to survive the flames that engulfed it. The next day, he'd returned to duty. The nightmare had gone on and on – his friends dying, one after another. Kitty had almost begun to feel it would be a relief when she finally received the telegram that brought her fears into reality.

Reaching the top of the stairs, Kitty paused to take a deep, calming breath. Against all the odds, Theo had survived. The war was in the past. And today, the might of the bomber was being turned to a different use.

The flight crew helped the passengers take their seats, stowing away coats, bags and newspapers. Paddy had picked the spot next to Kitty.

'First time in the air for me,' he'd commented. 'I'm more at home on a boat. What about you?'

'I've been in a small plane quite a few times,' Kitty replied, 'but it's not the same.' It wasn't just the Lancaster's link with the war that Kitty found unnerving: the sheer scale of the bomber was daunting. The pilot and the controls were so far away. It was nothing like being in the Tiger Moth with Theo sitting behind her only just beyond her reach.

'Don't you worry,' Paddy had said. 'We'll all be fine.' Kitty had the sense he was comforting himself as much as her.

In the long hours that had passed since then, there had been bouts of turbulence when the passengers clutched their armrests and sick bags were passed around. When the flying was smooth, people began to tell stories or make jokes about the food. There were even quips concerning the lavatory, though Kitty knew she was not meant to have overheard them. During refuelling stops in Italy, Libya, Uganda and Kenya, they'd waited together in ex-military sheds that stood in for reception halls. With the smell of fumes in their lungs, they'd drunk warm Coca-Cola and cups of over-brewed tea. At the last stop, in

Nairobi, they'd eaten delicious snacks called *samosas*. They'd all made a mess, scattering flakes of pastry, licking their fingers shamelessly. It was not surprising that each time they'd returned to their places in the cabin, they'd felt more and more like friends.

Now, with the journey nearly over, Kitty looked around the cabin at her companions. They were going to spend their days in the workshops repairing heavy machinery, and would be accommodated in the single men's quarters. Kitty knew she would be living in a proper house – the delay in renovations being carried out was the main reason she'd had to wait behind in England for all those weeks after Theo had come here. But beyond that, she didn't know what to expect. Along with the excitement of being reunited with Theo, Kitty felt an undercurrent of tension. She comforted herself with the thought that Kongara was not such a big place – she'd at least cross paths with these men now and then. It would be good to see some familiar faces in the midst of so much that was new and strange.

Kitty ran her fingers through her hair, pushing untidy strands back from her face. The fashionable bob was new. She was still shocked by the sudden nothingness below her chin-line; she missed the long dark hair that had draped over her shoulders for as far back as she could remember. She hadn't wanted to cut it all off – the new look had been part of the deal she'd made with Theo. He didn't want to risk anyone recognising her. Neither, of course, did Kitty. But as her long hair had disappeared snip by snip, she'd watched the mirror through a blur of tears. She knew that, in truth, the transformation had more to do with Theo reclaiming her than anything else. Her new appearance was an acknowledgement that she really was ashamed of what she'd done – who she'd been. She shook her head, feeling the tickle of hair brushing her cheeks. Shorter hair was a sensible choice, she told herself. It would suit the hot climate.

Picking up her handbag and clicking it open, she took out her powder compact. She was about to flip up the lid when she paused, staring uneasily at the gold embossed monogram. She was meant to have left behind everything that linked her to Katya, but the compact was one thing she'd been unable to relinquish. Now, she began to think she'd made a mistake. She should get rid of it as soon as possible, before anyone saw it. But as she held the case in her hand, feeling the smoothness of the tortoiseshell, a nub of resistance formed inside her. Theo would be unlikely to notice it. And as for anyone else – the initials *YKA* were so ornate they were almost impossible to read.

In the small pink-dusted mirror she examined her lips, coated in matte ruby red. Then she glanced over her eyebrows, plucked thin and lined with pencil. As with her hair, she wasn't used to the new style yet. She felt she was looking at a stranger.

There was a slight shine on her nose and forehead. Kitty's hand hovered over the powder puff. She could almost hear Theo's mother expressing her views on the kind of woman who would powder her nose in public. It was just one of the many small crimes Louisa had warned the Australian girl about. Kitty closed her eyes briefly, wanting to block out the memory of Louisa impressing upon her the need to keep a refined distance from the common world.

A lady's name appears in the newspapers three times in her life. When she is born, married and buried.

Because of what had happened later, the words had grown large and daunting in Kitty's mind. As if she could make amends in some tiny way, she gave up the idea of powdering her face. She knew that even the walk to the lavatory, with all those male eyes watching her, would have an unseemly quality to it. She closed the powder case and slipped it into her bag.

Beside her, Paddy put down his book, then left his seat to look out one of the windows. He stood with his legs apart, but still had to stoop in order to peer downwards.

'See anything yet?' Kitty called to him.

He shook his head.

She sighed. She thought of getting out her *Teach Yourself Swahili* book and doing some practice translation. Janet, the retired missionary who'd given Kitty language lessons before she left England, would have approved of that – she'd stressed that every spare moment should be devoted to learning lists of vocabulary. But Kitty didn't feel able to concentrate. She gazed idly down at her shoes. Though they were a bit dusty, they still looked smart. She studied the way the leather hugged the contours of her feet. And how the high heels made her calves appear long and elegant. She just hoped the extra height wouldn't mean she'd stand taller than her husband.

Paddy suddenly straightened up, calling over his shoulder. 'There it is! Come and see!'

Kitty went to stand beside him. During the last four or five hours, there had been only wilderness below – the kind of unremarkable countryside that reminded her of home. But now, as she pressed her face to the glass, she caught her breath in surprise.

The ground below had been transformed. The surface layer of bush, grass and trees had been stripped away revealing bare red earth. The cleared land, stretching away into the distance, was broken up into huge sections by a grid of straight lines. They were roads, Kitty guessed; they reminded her of the tracks that traversed the wide paddocks of her father's farm back in Australia. Looking more closely, she could see the wavy lines of windrows marking the earth. She wondered if they were there to prevent wind or water erosion, or both.

'Just look at the scale of it.' Paddy whistled through his teeth. 'Each of those plantations is a hundred times the size of most English farms.' He smiled at Kitty. 'I was listening carefully at the briefing. They told us the Tanganyika Groundnut Scheme is to be nearly two-and-a-half million acres. Half the area of Wales. Apparently a hundred thousand ex-soldiers have already signed up to it.' He grinned. 'So that's us – the Groundnut Army.'

The other passengers gathered at the windows. The magnitude of what lay below made them stare as well.

'You know how all this began?' Kitty recognised the voice of Billy, an engineer from the Middlesex regiment, who still had a limp from a shrapnel wound. 'The Minister of Food, Mr Strachey, got the idea during the war while he was watching trucks setting off to the front. He dreamed of seeing another kind of convoy. Ploughs instead of arms, bound for Africa.'

Everyone was watching Billy now. He had told plenty of jokes during the journey, but now his tone was almost reverent.

'That's what this is,' he continued, 'a chance to do something good, to make up for all the destruction and death. That's what we're all a part of. A war on hunger.'

Kitty swapped looks with Billy and Paddy, and then with all the others – Nick, Jimmy, Jamie, Robbie, Ralph and Peter. The sense of a shared mission was almost tangible. Kitty felt all her concerns about what lay ahead at Kongara fall away. Her new life was going to be busy and exciting, her days filled with purpose.

The men stood back, letting Kitty disembark first. As she stepped out onto the metal stairs that had been wheeled up to the plane, she was met by a rush of hot, dry air – the kind of heat she'd grown up with. Amid the aircraft fumes she picked up the familiar smell of the bush: dust, cow dung and the musky scent of leaves. Her gaze darted over the small crowd gathered below her, searching for Theo's red-blond hair, or for a figure with his distinctive stance – the body leaning forward a little as if pushing into a headwind. There was no sign of him. She frowned, checking again. There were some men standing together, dressed smartly in suits, shirts, ties and hats. There was another group wearing khaki shirts and baggy shorts, walking socks and boots. None of them looked like Theo.

Raising her hand to shield her eyes from the afternoon glare, Kitty peered further afield. The only other white person she could see wore blue overalls and appeared to be part of the airstrip staff. She fought against a fear that Theo was ill, or had been involved in an accident. She tried not to think about the fate of the man he'd come out here to replace; what had happened to him had been so terrible that Theo would not even describe it. But it had been a freak accident, she knew. Her husband's job was not normally dangerous in any way. She walked down the steps. Behind her, she could hear the heavy beat of Paddy's boots. She lifted her chin, determined not to let her anxiety show. She told herself there would be some simple, ordinary reason why Theo was not here to greet her.

The moment she set her foot down on the tarmac, one of the men in suits stepped forward. He presented her with a bunch of flowers wrapped in cellophane.

'Welcome to Tanganyika – and welcome to Kongara.'

As she accepted the bouquet, Kitty searched his face for some hint that he had bad news.

He held out his hand. 'Private Toby Carmichael, your husband's assistant.'

'I'm pleased to meet you,' she replied. She was struck by his pale skin – it didn't look as if he spent much time outside.

'Most unfortunately, he's been called away. Urgent matter. Unavoidable, I'm afraid.' Toby had the shortened vowels of a Midlands accent but his choice of words reminded Kitty of Theo. 'He's down at the Units. He'll be back by the end of the afternoon.' He gestured towards a girl standing nearby holding a clipboard. Kitty took in a young plump face, red lips and elaborately styled hair offsetting a plain khaki skirt and blouse. 'I've arranged for Lisa to take you to the house. Mr Hamilton will join you as soon as possible. I trust your journey was not too exhausting – though it is, of course, very long.'

'Where did you say Theo has gone?' Now that Kitty knew Theo was not ill and hadn't met with an accident, she felt let down by his absence.

'There's been some trouble with the Irish contractors down at the Units.' Toby lowered his voice, like someone giving out confidential information. 'Absolutely nothing to worry about.'

Kitty pushed her hurt feelings aside. Work had to come first. That was why they were here. The war on hunger.

'Did you say "the Units"?' she queried.

'That's what we call the plantations.'

She stored the term away. She'd already discovered that roads were called 'traces'. The OFC was the Overseas Food Corporation. The UAC was the United Africa Company, which provided contract labour to the OFC. And of course 'groundnuts' was just another name for peanuts.

'Now,' said Toby, 'let's do some introductions.'

The exchanging of name and rank, the smiling and shaking of hands, seemed to go on for ages, with Toby turning from one person to another and back. Kitty stifled a yawn, covering her mouth with her hand. But then, movement at the edge of her vision made her instantly alert. A car was coming fast towards them over the tarmac. A big shiny sedan, the same blue as the sky.

As it drew nearer, Kitty recognised it as a Daimler – there were two of them garaged in the stables at Hamilton Hall. This one was a more recent model, but it still had the old-fashioned grandeur of huge wheel arches and a wide, low-slung chassis.

The car came to a halt just a few feet away. Close up, Kitty saw there was an African at the wheel, his dark features almost lost behind the shine of the windows. She peered towards the rear of the vehicle, expecting to see Theo there. He'd escaped from his work! He couldn't bear to miss her arrival.

Sitting in the back was a woman in sunglasses, wearing a large lemon-yellow hat.

The driver jumped from his seat and came around to open the door; though he looked middle-aged, he wore an outfit that resembled a sailor suit.

A white high-heeled shoe was lowered to the tarmac, followed by another. A pair of stocking-clad legs appeared. Then, the woman emerged. She wore a yellow dress to match her hat, and white gloves to match the shoes. After pausing for a second, surveying the scene, she removed her sunglasses.

'Damn. I knew I'd be late.' She looked accusingly in the direction of her driver. Then she turned to Kitty, fixing her with a pair of grey-green eyes, carefully made up with eyeliner and shadow. 'You must be Theo's wife.' She had the same refined English accent as Theo, but it was overlaid with a languid drawl. 'I'm Mrs Richard Armstrong. My husband asked me to come and meet you, since Theo was called away.'

'How kind of you to come,' Kitty said.

There was no hint in the woman's manner as to whether the task was a pleasure or a chore. She offered the rest of the group a half-smile, before turning to address Toby. Kitty saw him draw up his shoulders, almost standing to attention. 'Please arrange for Mrs Hamilton's luggage to be sent to the house. We'll go ahead.'

'Yes, of course.' Toby threw a glance at Lisa, the one with the clipboard. She appeared disappointed at having her role so abruptly snatched away.

Kitty searched her memory for the name Armstrong. Was he Theo's superior, the General Manager? Or perhaps his offsider, the Manager of Agriculture?

The woman turned back to Kitty. 'You can call me Diana.'

'Thank you. Please call me Kitty.'

Diana's eyes travelled over Kitty's face and figure. She was glad now that she'd kept her promise to Theo about changing her appearance. Under Diana's scrutiny, the skirt and jacket outfit seemed much too plain and even the new shoes uninspiring – but at least her haircut and eyebrows were up-to-date.

'Let's go, then,' said Diana.

Kitty glanced around, seeking out Paddy. He gave her an encouraging grin along with his farewell wave. She was about to follow Diana towards the car when a sudden gust of wind sprang up. Men grabbed their hats and hunched over for protection from the stinging dust. Papers flew, swooping and flapping, from Lisa's clipboard. As Kitty screwed up her eyes she stole a look at Diana. The woman stood there, tall and unflinching. She just lowered her gaze, mascara-layered eyelashes making dark crescents against her skin. One gloved hand rose to grasp the brim of her yellow hat.

The Daimler left the airstrip, driving along a newly made road – a neat ribbon of gravel cutting through a swathe of cleared bush. The two women were sitting side by side in the back of the car. Diana kept her eyes fixed ahead. Close up, her skin was still flawless – powdered to a flat, even tone and touched up with rouge.

'You're Australian.' Diana spoke without shifting her gaze.

Kitty eyed her uneasily. Theo wouldn't have told her this, which meant Diana must have picked up an accent. The elocution teacher had assured Theo's mother that her daughter-in-law's origins were virtually undetectable. Talking to Paddy must have lured Kitty's buried accent out of hiding. Perhaps it had crept back to the surface while she was telling the Irishman stories about growing up on the outback farm.

'Yes, originally,' she said finally. 'But I've been living in Britain for years. I moved over just before the war.'

Diana made no further comment. She rested her head against the seatback, seeming exhausted, as if she'd just undertaken a difficult task. As the silence lengthened, Kitty looked out of the side window. The red soil was rich enough, but the vegetation quite sparse. Everything appeared very dry. Her father had spent his life battling with country like this, struggling to draw out an income that was barely sufficient to support his family. Yet this was the area that had been chosen as the site of one of the world's most ambitious farming projects. Perhaps it was just the time of year, Kitty told herself – the effect of extreme tropical seasons; things she didn't yet understand. She glanced around her at the interior of the car with its polished woodwork, gleaming nickel fittings and mulberry-red leather seats. It belonged in a completely different world to the scene outside.

The road led on into an area where the cleared bush was dotted with outcrops of rock. The Daimler wove its way between mounds of pale stone crusted with bushes, before emerging again into the open. At the same time, the road took a sharp turn. Kitty sat up, her lips parting in surprise. A range of mountains rose up ahead – abruptly, as though they'd been dropped there by accident. She hadn't seen them from the aircraft during the approach to the landing strip; they must have been on the other side. She traced the outlines of steep pointed peaks made of rugged stone, piled up tall. They were perfect pyramids, like images from a children's book.

She turned to Diana. 'Those mountains . . . They're beautiful!'

Diana lifted her shoulder in a half-shrug. 'I'd call them hills. I think of mountains as a place to ski.'

There was more silence then, broken only by the smooth hum of the motor. In contrast to the mountains, the close-up landscape looked even more unremarkable. Then, in the distance, some kind of settlement came into view. Kitty peered ahead, trying to make sense of what she could see. As they drew nearer, the odd shapes and colours began to make sense.

It was a sea of tents stretching away into the distance – identical dirty-white triangles laid out in dead-straight rows.

'What's this place?' Kitty asked Diana. There were lots of high wire fences as well, and parking bays marked with white painted stones. 'It looks like an army camp.'

'This is Kongara.'

Kitty hid her confusion. From Theo's comments after his briefing in London, and the two letters he'd sent back from Tanganyika, she'd formed a picture of a small town consisting of buildings that were simple but solid. There had been mention of a club with a swimming pool, and a row of shops. *You'll love our new home*, Theo had written. *It's been fully furnished by the OFC, right down to pink towels in the bathroom.*

'The Africans call it *Londoni*.' Diana gave a short laugh. 'That's Swahili for London – though you'd hardly know, the way they pronounce it. The name has rather caught on. We all use it, now. Not for the whole area – just the town.'

Kitty repeated the word in her head. Lon-*do*-ni. The middle syllable was drawn out, making the name sound melodic and intriguing. She scanned the rows of tents. She noticed, among them, some groups of round huts with mud walls and canvas roofs. Then she saw a long narrow building with a verandah. One end was painted white and had a sign over the door that read *DINING ROOM*. The other end was built from plain wood and was labelled *MESS*. In front of both sections were fences surrounding what could have been gardens except that nothing was growing. She recognised a few Nissen huts – the long, half-cylinder tin structures had become a familiar sight in England during the war. There was an outdoor cinema with a screen and rows of seats.

The car slowed almost to walking pace as they reached an area of larger tents. Quite suddenly, it seemed, there were people everywhere. Fair-skinned Europeans, Africans, a few Indians – they were all dressed in shades of khaki, adding to the atmosphere of an army camp. The vast majority were men, but Kitty saw a few young women in shirts and skirts, like Lisa. Everyone moved around briskly. A man in a tropical suit checked his watch, then broke into a run.

'Head Office,' Diana said.

Outside the largest tent was a flagpole. A Union Jack hung limply at the top. Nearby was a black Rolls Royce. An African soldier wearing a smart belted jacket, a maroon fez on his head, stood to attention beside it. Kitty craned her head, hoping to see inside the tent. All she glimpsed was a large desk, a typewriter and a crooked pile of folders.

The car rolled on, passing hundreds more of the small tents, before entering an area occupied by lines of wooden bungalows.

They were identical, and looked as if they contained just a couple of rooms. Most had washing lines erected to one side. The laundry hanging there consisted mainly of khaki work clothes, with the odd bright splash of a dress, blouse or child's pyjamas.

'And this,' Diana said, 'is known as the Toolsheds.'

'Is this where you – we – live?' Kitty asked tentatively.

'Good Lord, no.' Diana responded. 'It's for the field assistants, medical staff – people like that.' She pointed further on towards the mountains, where a band of green marked the foothills. 'We live up there – on Millionaire Row. That's not the real name, of course. It's Hillside Avenue. The grandest address in Tanganyika.'

Kitty detected a mocking tone in Diana's voice. She was trying to frame the right response, when Diana's face suddenly froze. Her hand shot out, reaching towards the driver's shoulder. 'Look out!'

The car came to an abrupt halt, throwing both women forward against the seats in front. There was a dense quiet. Then came the sound of a child laughing.

'Praise to God,' the driver said. 'She was not hit.'

A little girl ran from the road, blonde plaits swinging behind her as she chased a bouncing red ball.

The two women regained their seats. Kitty sighed with relief. But beside her, Diana remained rigid and wide-eyed.

'It's all right,' Kitty said. 'She's fine.'

Diana nodded, but seemed unable to catch her breath. Sweat broke out over her face. She snatched off her hat, tossing it to the floor, revealing crimped auburn hair. Then she covered her face with shaking hands. Kitty caught an impression of polished nails, fingers laden with rings, before turning tactfully away.

In the rear-vision mirror, Kitty met the concerned gaze of the driver.

'Let's go,' she instructed him. 'Mrs Armstrong might like a glass of water.'

He let off the brake, easing the car forward. They left the Toolsheds behind, heading on towards Millionaire Row.

Gradually, Diana's breathing grew more even. Finally, she lifted her head, peeling a strand of damp hair from her brow. 'I don't know why people can't look after their children properly.' She leaned to pick up her hat, smoothing dust from the brim, and resting it carefully on her knees.

Kitty nodded politely, then averted her gaze once more. She was uncomfortably aware that she'd witnessed something she shouldn't have – Diana had been exposed in a way that was deeply embarrassing. From both their points of view, it had not been a good start.

TWO

The Daimler turned into a sweeping driveway, tyres crunching the gravel. Kitty searched eagerly for the first glimpse of the house. After the tents and bungalows, she was prepared for disappointment, but the building that came into view was solid and large, and strikingly modern. A central verandah jutted forward from the façade. The walls, made from concrete blocks, were freshly painted white, and the tin roof had an elegant pitch. There was a spacious garden in front of the house, bordered by a white picket fence. Bougainvillea bushes grew there – most of the flowers were a strident purple, like the ones in Australia, but there were also pastel tones of pink, orange, mauve and white. An attempt had been made to train the plants into arches, but unruly shoots sprang out in all directions.

The driver honked the horn. Within moments, two African men dressed in white shirts and shorts emerged from the front door. They were joined by another two men in khaki uniforms. The four flanked the entrance, a pair each side, standing to attention. Kitty was reminded of scenes at Hamilton Hall before the war. Whenever one of the family returned after more than a week or so away, the whole staff – at least twenty of them – would be assembled to form a welcome party.

Diana climbed out of the car, leaving her hat behind on the seat. She was perfectly calm now – the incident with the child and the ball might never have occurred. She led Kitty up onto the verandah. Crossing a polished concrete floor speckled with tiny stones, she stopped in front of the Africans.

'Your cook, your houseboy, gardener, guard.' She paused by the last man, waiting pointedly until he removed his cloth cap.

Kitty tried to offset Diana's dismissive manner by smiling warmly. She even gave a greeting in Swahili. '*Hamjambo.*'

The men stared at her as if they did not understand, even though Kitty knew her greeting was correct. She could almost hear Janet's firm tone, drumming it all in: '*Hujambo* is used when saying hello to one person. For two or more, it is *Hamjambo,* to which the reply is *Hatujambo . . .*'

Kitty tried again. '*Habari gani?*' How are you?

Still no answer came.

'How sweet of you to learn some Swahili.' Diana sounded bemused. 'But they speak perfectly reasonable English. Cynthia was very particular about her staff.'

Kitty was about to move on when the man described as her houseboy reached for the bunch of flowers in her hand.

'I can put them in a vas-ie, Memsahib,' he said.

'Vase.' Diana corrected him, rolling her eyes. 'They've got this thing of adding "i" on the ends of words. Tractori. Londoni. It's awfully annoying. Sounds like they're making a joke of everything.'

Kitty decided not to explain that all nouns – and all names – in Swahili must end in a vowel. Refusing to be put off by the apparent rejection of her language skills, she gave a friendly smile to the houseboy. He now stood to attention, the flowers held upside down by his side. He looked about the same age as her – late twenties, early thirties perhaps. At Hamilton Hall, Kitty had become used to being waited upon by grown men. But it felt stranger here, somehow. Tanganyika was their country, not hers.

Diana led Kitty on into the house, stripping off her gloves and dropping them into her handbag. Her heels rapped smartly against the floorboards as she entered a large sitting room. There was a slight smell of fresh paint, even though a pair of French windows stood wide open. It was late afternoon now, and the sun made pools of light on the varnished floor. Kitty took in a three-piece suite upholstered in green velvet. Matching curtains draped the windows. There was a bookcase with sets of leather-bound novels on its shelves. A drinks trolley stood nearby, loaded with bottles and decanters, glasses and a silver soda siphon. There was even a potted palm, draping frayed fronds onto a coffee table. The place reminded Kitty of a picture from a magazine. It looked rather unreal, but she was pleased and impressed.

Diana took a packet of cigarettes from her bag. She shook it until two poked out. 'Cigarette?'

'Not at the moment, thank you.' Kitty decided to postpone declaring that she didn't smoke.

'You should find everything you need.' Diana spoke from the side of her mouth as she lit her cigarette. 'Otherwise send a note to Supplies. If they don't have what you want, keep asking. If there's anything you don't like, just send it back.'

Moving into a hallway, she opened the door to another spacious room. 'The master bedroom,' she announced. 'The houses are all the same. So I know my way around.'

There was a double bed with a cream candlewick cover and mosquito nets hanging from a canopy. The rest of the space was dominated by a vast dressing table with a scalloped-edged mirror. Kitty searched the room, a puzzled frown on her face. Theo was meant to have moved over from the single men's quarters weeks ago, as soon as the painters had left. Yet there was no sign that he was sleeping in here. Kitty left the room quickly, wondering if Diana had noticed this as well.

Further along the hallway, Diana moved past a closed door. The smell of kerosene and cooking oil emanated from behind it.

'I never set foot in my kitchen if I can help it, but Cynthia liked to make regular inspections.' Diana looked at Kitty as if expecting to hear which approach she favoured. Kitty gave an equivocal shrug. She wasn't sure which woman she should be agreeing with.

'Anyway,' Diana moved on, 'the good news is that we finally have decent fridges. Electrolux. They only arrived last week. So we have cold tonic at last. And plenty of ice.' She smiled back over her shoulder – the first proper smile Kitty had seen. One of Diana's front teeth was slightly crooked, but the flaw only enhanced the perfection of her other features.

'Lavatory. Study.' Diana pointed out some other rooms. 'The bathroom. I'm afraid you'll find pink towels in there. Lord knows where they got that idea.' She paused, tilting her head thoughtfully. 'Some of the wives believe the people in London chose the colour on purpose, since everything turns pink in the end out here, because of the red dust in the water.' She shook her head. 'But that seems unlikely to me. Far too sensible for the OFC.'

Kitty wondered what was meant by this last remark. So far, everything she knew about the workings of the Overseas Food Corporation (picked up from Theo, and from her own experience of the travel arrangements) formed a picture of order and precision – just as one would expect with all the ex-army, navy and air-force people involved.

Diana flicked ash into the sink, then left the bathroom. She gestured towards another closed door. 'That was the children's room. There were two.'

Kitty assumed they'd inspect the space together as they had done all the others, but Diana hung back. She examined her fingernails, picking at a cuticle. Kitty decided to take a quick peek, regardless. As she pushed open the door, she faltered in surprise. On a small table she recognised Theo's hairbrush. On the floor by a narrow single bed were his slippers. His blue dressing gown was draped over a chair. For a moment, Kitty's pleasure at seeing these familiar possessions was overridden by confusion. It seemed odd – inexplicable – that her husband had set himself up in the spare room. But then it came to her. Theo was just being thoughtful. He had waited for her to arrive before occupying the master bedroom. From the very beginning it would belong to them both.

She looked around the sunlit space. Another happy thought came to her. One day, her children would sleep in here. There would be at least two, hopefully three, but no more than four. (Theo had been a lonely only child, and for her part, Kitty had watched her mother worn out by too many offspring.) They hoped to start their family soon; Kitty was nearly twenty-eight, and Theo was older. During the war the couple had endured frequent separations. When they had been able to see one another, they took careful precautions. It was no time to bring a child into the world. And then, life afterwards had not proved to be very much easier. But now, it was time. Kitty smiled as she scanned the room. She would enjoy choosing bright curtain fabric and bedspreads. She might even have the walls and window frames repainted. Lemon, perhaps – to suit both girl and boy.

Kitty found Diana waiting for her in another large room. She'd located a glass ashtray and was carrying it around.

'What are the schools like here?' Kitty asked her.

Diana drew deeply on her cigarette. 'I'm not the one to ask. I don't have any children.'

'Oh, I'm sorry.' Kitty bit her lip, wishing she could take back the thoughtless question. At least there was no emotion in Diana's eyes – it seemed she wasn't one of those women who'd been unable to have children and became upset when they were mentioned. It occurred to Kitty that Diana could even be content to be childless. There was nothing motherly about her.

In the short silence Diana took another long pull on her cigarette. Kitty moved around the room, skirting a heavy dark table surrounded by dining chairs. She stopped by a glass-fronted cabinet. It was stacked with crockery. Along with the usual plates, bowls, cups and saucers, there was a cake stand, a butter dish, a salt pot and a pepper shaker.

'I thought crockery was on the list of personal items,' Kitty said, feeling puzzled. After checking the document sent to her by the

OFC, she had purchased a new set – plain white, sturdy – especially to bring with her.

'It is,' Diana confirmed. 'Cynthia left hers behind. She didn't want to go to the bother of having it packed up.' She raised her eyebrows enquiringly. 'You do know who she is – Mrs Wainwright?'

Kitty nodded, lowering her eyes respectfully. Cynthia was the widow of the previous Manager of Administration, Major Wainwright. Theo had inherited both the man's house and his job. Ever since she'd learned of the situation, Kitty had been uncomfortably aware that she and Theo had benefited from someone else's heartbreak. She looked up at Diana, wondering if she was going to make any comment on the tragedy. But Diana was already crossing to the table.

'This belonged to her as well.'

From the patina on the wood, Kitty guessed it was generations old. It was solidly built with thick legs, square edges – out of place in this modern house with all the finely formed, pale pine furniture.

'She bought it from some Foreign Service fellow who finally got a transfer home, after being stranded here the entire war,' Diana said. 'Cynthia asked me to give this to you, personally.'

Kitty unfolded a piece of paper, finding a handwritten recipe for furniture polish. At the top was the instruction: *To be applied under supervision, twice a day, after meals.*

Kitty trailed her hand along the surface of the dining table – so silky smooth, the tone rich and dark. It was beautiful, but she already felt the burden of being responsible for it. She pictured dents, scratches, stains and watermarks.

Over in the cabinet, she could see Cynthia's crockery with its pattern of pink roses, embellished with gold. The handles on the cups were delicate and ornate. Kitty knew they'd be hard to hold securely – especially while remembering to stick out that little finger, dead straight. The cups were so fine she'd fear biting a piece out of the lip. The narrow base meant it would be almost impossible to pass them across the table without causing them to rattle on their saucers.

Diana stubbed out her cigarette, then put down the ashtray. 'Well, I'll leave you to settle in.'

Kitty gathered herself, remembering that she was now the mistress of this house. 'Would you like some tea before you go? I could check . . .'

'No, thank you. I should go home and prepare for the evening. I'll collect you tomorrow at ten. We'll go to the Club. There's a coffee morning.'

She trotted down the steps, high heels tapping on the concrete. When she reached the driveway, she walked on tiptoes so that her heels wouldn't sink into the gravel.

Kitty waited on the steps as the Daimler pulled smoothly away. Then she spun around, striding eagerly towards the front door – *her* front door. She couldn't wait to walk back through the house looking properly at each room. At last, she and Theo had a home of their own. The rooms they'd rented after they married, near the air base in Skellingthorpe, didn't really count; they were only there together when Theo managed to get some leave. And when Theo was de-mobbed they'd moved back to live with his parents in Hamilton Hall. Kitty had felt they were only visitors there. The rooms they'd been given bore the stamp not only of her mother-in-law's taste, but that of generations of Hamilton ancestors. Everything was sacred – the pair of china dogs with their gold-painted ears; the child's highchair that held a life-sized baby doll with black glass eyes; and the medals, admiral's hats and other military memorabilia. Then there was the portrait of a girl in a red dress – some distant relative of Theo's – whose haunted eyes seemed to hold a premonition that she would die before reaching her seventh birthday. Each of the rooms they'd used had been heavy with history. Theo referred to their sitting room as 'the schoolroom', because he'd had lessons in there as a child. Their bedroom was really 'Gran-Gran's room'. No single space was blank and fresh.

But here in Kongara, it was different. The house was almost brand-new. It was nothing like the grand old establishment Theo was used to. In fact, Kitty found it hard to picture him living here – but then, he must have been aware that adapting to different conditions would be part of the job he'd taken on. She smiled as she gazed around her. The house was utterly unlike the run-down weatherboard homestead she'd grown up in. To both her and Theo, it was a completely new setting. There was only the impersonal hand of the OFC to be shaken off. Cynthia's crockery could be packed away; the precious table covered with a cloth. Kitty stepped back over the threshold, hugging herself with silent pleasure. She'd been married to Theo for almost seven years. The first five had been disrupted by the war, and the next two overshadowed by what had come next. It had been a long wait. But now heart and home were at last coming together.

*

Kitty stood for a moment outside the closed door to the kitchen. She raised her hand to knock, then let it drop – it was her own kitchen, after all. Instead, she pushed the door open slowly, giving the servants warning of her presence.

The houseboy jumped up from the back doorstep, scattering peanut shells from his lap. The cook turned from the stove. Within a second or two both men were standing in front of Kitty, heads held high as if ready for inspection.

Kitty eyed them, feeling awkward. She addressed the cook. 'What is your name?'

'I am Eustace.'

Kitty saw that his tight-curled hair was sprinkled with grey. There were deep lines around his mouth. He was probably old enough to be her father.

'And you?' She looked at the houseboy.

'I am Gabriel.'

Kitty was tempted to ask how they'd acquired these unusual English names – ones ending in consonants, which they would find difficult to pronounce. But she made do with introducing herself.

'You may call me Memsahib Kitty.'

Eustace made no response at all. Kitty took a breath. She was determined to make use of her Swahili.

'*Chakula cha jioni pangu gani?*' What is your plan for the evening meal?

The men exchanged glances, but said nothing. Kitty was about to repeat herself, when Eustace responded.

'Today is Monday.' He spoke in English, forming his words carefully as though Kitty might have difficulty understanding him.

'We are cooking corned beef, mashed potatoes, white sauce and beans. For pudding we are cooking Bakewell tart.'

He pointed towards the wall, where Kitty saw a page from an exercise book pinned up. Even from a distance she recognised the handwriting displayed there. It was from the same hand that had penned the recipe for furniture polish. She moved to take a closer look. Monday's menu was as the cook had described it. Under 'Tuesday' was listed cold beef with potato salad and boiled vegetables, followed by rice pudding. Wednesday was roast chicken. Thursday, meat loaf. It was just the kind of food Theo liked – along with the rest of his family. Yuri used to laugh at them, saying they'd never grown out of eating boarding-school fare. He wouldn't have contemplated adopting a set menu. Most of the time he didn't even eat proper meals. He just foraged in the kitchen, collecting bread, cheese, pickles, smoked sausage – whatever the housekeeper had bought for him. In her mind, Kitty saw him crouched by the open fridge, silver hair falling forward over his brow. Stripped to the waist, in spite of the chilly air; a paint rag dangling from his trouser pocket. His upper body lean and trim for a man of sixty.

'We will eat like peasants, Kitty,' he'd say. At the same time, he'd be opening a bottle of French vintage wine, dusty from the cellar. The food would be dumped on a table spotted with candle wax, sharing space with whatever had accumulated there – a half-formed maquette, a pile of old letters, a jar of wilting flowers.

Banishing thoughts of Yuri, Kitty turned back to the cook. She took a moment to prepare what she wanted to say in Swahili. 'And Bwana Hamilton – he is happy to have the same meals each week?'

'Yes, Memsahib. The bwana is very happy.'

Kitty knew he would be. Since the war, Theo had liked things to be predictable. Who could blame him when he'd spent years knowing there was a good chance he'd not be alive by the next morning?

Kitty walked around the kitchen, pretending to be interested in the row of large canisters labelled as flour, sugar, salt, oats, biscuits. There was a tin of Keen's curry powder set beside bottles of HP Sauce and Tabasco. She sensed this was a moment when she should ask a question, or criticise something – assert her authority as the new memsahib. Crossing to the stove, she lifted the lid from a large pot. Her eyes widened at the sight of a huge piece of meat, bobbing in a sea of boiling stock.

'Where did you get this meat?' she asked, abandoning using Swahili. She hadn't seen a cut of beef this size since she was on the farm back in New South Wales. In wartime England the hunk of flesh in this pot would use up the weekly allowance of several large families – if it could be purchased at all.

'From a cow,' the cook answered.

Kitty searched his gaze but detected no sarcasm. She made do with nodding her approval. She was about to leave, but then realised she was thirsty. 'I would like to have afternoon tea.'

'Where shall I bring it?' asked the houseboy.

'The sitting room,' Kitty replied. 'Black tea. With a slice of lemon. And a biscuit.'

'Yes, Memsahib.'

'And Eustace – I believe the beef is boiling too fast. It will get tough.'

'Yes, Memsahib.' The cook smiled broadly as though pleased his mistress was finally behaving correctly.

As she left the room, Kitty congratulated herself. She felt she'd handled the exchange well. But when she reached the end of the hallway, she stopped. From behind the closed door to the kitchen she heard muffled laughter. She recognised Eustace's voice, calling her name in a dramatic tone. 'Kitty! Come here, Kitty!' Then came the sound of mewing, high and fake. More laughter broke out as Kitty walked slowly away.

A large leather suitcase stood in the middle of the bedroom floor. Though old, with stains and scuff marks, it was of fine quality. Like the travelling trunk, it had been donated by Theo's mother.

'Take our luggage,' Louisa had said. 'My son won't want his wife turning up looking like a refugee.'

She'd watched while Kitty removed the suitcase from a massive teak wardrobe in one of the spare bedrooms. Faded hotel labels were clustered around the handles; stickers from shipping lines – the Orient, the Union Castle – were slapped across the top and sides. Together they formed a picture of the life the Hamiltons had led, at least up until the war. There was an oval sticker with a grand crest in the middle and the words 'Ritz Barcelona' in gilded letters. Another identified Stateroom Baggage from the RMS *Queen Mary*. There was even a luggage label marked 'Aloha Hawaii' with a dark-skinned man on a surfboard.

Louisa had sighed deeply, taking a seat on a chair covered with a dust cloth. She looked old and tired, her body thin beneath the fuzz of her cashmere cardigan. A rope of pearls hung heavy around her neck. Kitty had pretended to study the suitcase, but she had still felt the woman's accusing gaze. Louisa had almost lost her husband to a heart attack, brought on by acute stress. The family name was irreparably damaged. Now her only child had gone off to Tanganyika. Louisa blamed all these disasters on her daughter-in-law. And Kitty was not in a position to disagree.

Now, on the floor of her bedroom, Kitty knelt beside the suit-case. The hotel and cruise ship emblems had been covered up by the no-nonsense black-and-white labels of the OFC. She glanced at the bedroom door, which was firmly shut. When her luggage had arrived from the airstrip, Gabriel had carried it inside. The trunk was still in the hallway, but she'd asked him to take the suitcase to the bedroom. He'd lingered in here, clearly keen to help unpack, but Kitty had sent him away. She didn't want him laughing about her possessions later on, behind her back.

Unbuckling the leather straps and opening the metal clasps, she raised the lid. The smell of stale lavender and camphor escaped. And there was something else there, too. She leaned over the case, drawing it in. The pine-needle tang of turpentine. She'd brought no paints with her, no brushes; not even a sketchbook – but the smell must have hidden in her clothes, clinging to the fibres like the proof of a crime.

She took out a pile of blouses, expertly folded by Lizzie, Louisa's maid; then she unpacked some dresses, skirts and jackets. They would all have to be ironed in due course, but for now she planned just to put everything away. The wardrobe doors were wide open, and she'd pulled out all the drawers in both the dressing table and the tallboy. As she lifted up each item of clothing she exam-ined it critically. If the other ladies in Kongara dressed like Diana,

Kitty would be very out of place. Her clothes were either old-fashioned – cast-offs from Hamilton Hall – or else made to the strict utility designs enforced by the British government during the war: narrow skirts, tight sleeves, no extra pockets or wasteful decorations. But Kitty reminded herself of the women she'd seen from the car, moving busily around Head Office. Their clothes were plain and practical.

Kitty rummaged through the case until she found her own version of a khaki outfit. The shirt and skirt were looser in fit than the ones she'd seen earlier that day, and had more pockets, but they would be just as useful. Kitty ran her thumbs over the soft-worn cloth. There were darned holes here and there, along with old stains that looked like blood, and others that might have been grease from an engine. Kitty recalled the photograph of Janet wearing these very garments. She'd been a young missionary then – on her first tour to Africa – but still recognisable as the person Kitty had met at the village church near Hamilton Hall. Janet's eyes were hidden behind the round discs of her spectacles, but you could tell from her posture that she was determined; even a bit fierce. Kitty had felt that glare when she stumbled over her Swahili lessons.

'Get it right,' Janet had admonished. 'How can you expect to have any authority if you speak like a toddler?'

Kitty laid the old clothes in one of the drawers, then turned back to the suitcase. From among the last layers, she lifted out a flat bundle about the size of her hand. At the dressing table, she unwound the slippery lengths of a satin nightdress, revealing a leather picture frame. Theo's face, formed in shades of black and grey, gazed out at her. The photograph had been taken soon after he joined the RAF. A studio light played over his face, throwing his features into contrast and making him even more striking than he was in the flesh. His posture was upright, his chest showing off the wings embroidered above his pocket. His gaze was level and firm.

Louisa had a copy of the photograph too. She'd placed it on the sitting room mantelpiece – set at a tactful distance from the image of Theo's father, Admiral Hamilton, and the portraits of all the other Hamilton men who'd served in the navy before him. Their peaked caps were white with a black visor; their coats double-breasted. Theo's airman's cap was grey with a matching visor and his jacket had just one row of buttons. He was like an interloper from a different tribe.

Kitty stroked the picture with her fingertips. For years, she'd slept with it under her pillow on nights when she and Theo were apart – first while he was being trained, and then when he was on active duty. Lying alone, far away from him, she used to watch the sweep of searchlights pass over the darkened window of her room, waiting anxiously for the air-raid siren to sound. She'd push one hand under the pillow and grasp the leather frame. Just the firm shape was reassuring. And if she pulled it out, she was immediately comforted by the image of Theo, so brave and stalwart in his uniform.

Looking at the photograph now – halfway across the world from where she'd been then – Kitty suddenly felt differently about the picture. She wished she had one that reminded her of the old Theo – the man she'd fallen in love with; and the man she hoped he would become again, in this new setting. Before the war he'd been lighthearted and funny, with a head full of dreams and plans. He'd flown not to serve his king, but for the love of air and cloud and sky. Kitty smiled to herself, thinking back to the day – nearly ten years ago – when they'd first met, in the lush green of the English countryside. It was 1938, the year before the war began.

Frost lingered in the shadows beneath the blackberry bushes, even though the morning sun was bright. Kitty blew on her hands, puffing small clouds into the air, then rubbed them together for warmth. With her basket hooked over one arm, she eased further into the tangled mass of leaves and thorns and branches. It was late in the season, but there were still plenty of berries left. The purple-black fruit glistened with dozens of tiny polished orbs. She plucked a few, plump and round, dropping them into the basket. The next one she ate, closing her eyes in pleasure as the juice burst over her tongue. She'd make a fruit crumble later on, with rolled oats, sugar and butter – one of the few recipes she'd learned off by heart from her mother.

Twice as much flour as fat, or it won't hold together . . .

The fruit that lay beneath the crunchy topping marked the seasons of her childhood – apple for most of the year, rhubarb as well; strawberries only in summer, blackberries stretching into autumn. Each member of the family had their favourite. Kitty pressed her lips together as visions of life at Seven Gums brimmed up, potent and painful. She missed her parents and little brothers so much. A whole year had passed since she'd left the family farm, travelling to Sydney and then on to England, and she longed for news from home. Had Jason stayed on at school or left to get a job? Had

Tim's broken leg finally healed or did he still have a limp? Did they manage to find homes for all of Tabitha's kittens? Had her mother finished making the new curtains or was she still waiting to borrow a sewing machine? Though Kitty had written several times, giving a return address, there had been no reply. But what did she expect? Her father had made his views quite clear. And Kitty had made her choice.

She fumbled, dropping a berry into the shadows. Reaching for another, her finger was caught by a thorn. As she snatched her hand back, the spike dug in deep and then tore. The stinging pain blended with her feelings of loss. As she sucked the blood away, tears ached behind her eyes. She made herself focus on the scene before her: the lush green field with a copse of bare-limbed trees. Stone walls made up its boundary. Each rock had been fitted like a jigsaw piece into the right spot. She tried to imagine how many years it must have taken to build. But this thought only brought up more pictures of home. Kitty saw herself standing in a sheep-scarred paddock, sun beating hot through her shirt. She held the heavy head of a mattock up against a wooden fence post, bracing it while Jason hammered in staples from the other side. Some of the posts were so weathered the taut wire was all that held them up. There were no neat rock walls at Seven Gums – they had fifty thousand acres to deal with. Maintaining the fences was an unending task.

'Like painting the Sydney Harbour Bridge,' Kitty's father liked to say.

Pushing the raw memories away, she returned to picking berries. She concentrated on their shape, their colour, as an artist would – noting the dots of reflected light, the many shades of purple-black. This was better. It made her think of Yuri, at work in his studio just across the field. He was not family, and she had only known him for a matter of months, but their friendship was already strong. At his age, Yuri could almost have been her grandfather, yet he seemed young and full of life. He had taught her so much already. And she had so much more to learn. That was why she was here, she reminded herself – why she'd left the farm behind.

She had almost picked enough berries when a faint buzzing sound came to her ear. It grew louder, overtaking the murmur of the stream nearby. Kitty searched the sky. A raven flapped in an empty expanse of blue. But then, another black shape appeared in the distance. It came steadily nearer, bigger. She saw the silhouette of a small plane with two wings mounted one above the other. Much closer, its true colour could be seen. A bright, strong red.

The plane flew towards her, dropping height. Then the engine changed pitch, slowing down. It was going to land, Kitty realised, right here in the field. Now, as she scanned the meadow, she noticed an area of grass had been mowed to create a landing strip. She wasn't sure if it was new, or if she'd just not seen it before. She guessed the pilot would be someone connected to Hamilton Hall, the mansion that rose up beyond the line of ancient oaks. The aristocratic family that lived there – the Hamiltons – owned the fields, along with the hills, the woods and even the little house Kitty now shared with Yuri. They owned everything, as far as the eye could see.

Hastily, she plucked the last few berries that she needed. The plane bounced over the grass. Then it wheeled in a wide arc and headed straight towards her. The engine sputtered into quiet, leaving just the thudding sound of the propeller. Kitty measured the distance from the bush to the stone wall. It was too late for her to hurry off now – she would look like some common trespasser, running away. And the pilot may not even have noticed her. From the corner of her eye, she saw a man lever himself from his seat, then step onto the wing, before jumping down to the ground.

Kitty bent over the blackberry bush, letting her long hair fall forward to hide her face.

'Hello there!' A man's voice came from behind her.

She pretended not to have heard anything.

'You're picking blackberries.'

Kitty leaned further into the bush as if seeking a prize berry. She didn't want to have to explain who she was. She wasn't sure what Yuri would want her to say . . .

'You're trespassing.'

She turned around reluctantly. She found herself looking into the face of a young man with friendly eyes and a teasing grin.

'No, I'm not,' she began. Then she swallowed, lost for words. The man's eyes were clear and blue, his teeth even and white. His nose was straight, his brow wide. The leather helmet served as a frame for a face so classically handsome that it could have belonged to one of Yuri's statues. Kitty gathered herself, gesturing towards the walled garden that lay beyond the main buildings of the Hall. It was just possible to see the gable of the Garden House set into the wall at the far end. 'I live over there.'

'Then we are neighbours. Allow me to introduce myself.' The man removed a pair of leather gloves. 'Theo Hamilton.'

It took Kitty a few seconds to realise he was watching her right hand. She remembered Yuri telling her that in England a lady must always initiate a handshake, unless she wishes to keep her distance. She thrust her hand forward. 'I'm Kitty.' Too late, she saw that her finger was still oozing blood. She snatched it back.

'You've cut yourself!' Theo took a handkerchief from the pocket of his jacket – clean and white, ironed into a square. He wound the cloth around her bleeding finger.

Kitty stood rock-still. He was standing so close to her that she could smell the oiled leather of his jacket, and feel the warmth coming from his body.

'Thank you,' she managed to say.

In a single movement, he pulled off his helmet and goggles. A lock of red-blond hair fell forward over his brow. He swept it back with one hand, then peered into her basket. 'Looks like a good crop. I used to pick them when I was a boy.' He grinned at her again. Then he nodded in the direction of the Garden House. 'Has our Russian friend moved out, then?'

Kitty shook her head. 'I am Prince Yurievitch's guest.' When she said the name she used her best Russian accent, rolling the 'r'. She hoped she sounded like the kind of person one might expect to find staying with royalty. Not that Yuri was all that typical of a prince, as far as she could tell.

'How is he?' Theo enquired.

'Very well, thank you,' Kitty answered – even though, at this moment, Yuri was in bed with a cold. He'd worn himself out last night, working late on a large canvas. Kitty had begun by holding a resting pose for 'Sleeping Girl with Shawl', but had soon been truly asleep. When she woke, it was nearly dawn and the painting was almost done. It was strange to think of the long hours that had passed, with Yuri studying every detail of her skin, her hair, the folds of the velvet gown, while she was lost in dreams.

'I haven't seen him for months,' said Theo. 'I've barely been home.'

'Where do you live?' The question slipped out. She couldn't imagine why anyone would want to move out of Hamilton Hall.

'I'm at Oxford. Reading Classics.'

Kitty smiled vaguely. She knew Oxford was a city with a famous university, and she thought he was making a reference to his studies – but could not be certain. Wanting to change the subject, she turned towards the plane. 'Did you fly all the way here from Oxford?'

'It's not far. Have you ever flown?'

Kitty shook her head. When she'd investigated travelling to England, she'd discovered it was possible to fly between Sydney and London, but the tourist-class ticket on an ocean liner had been cheaper. Consequently, the only time she'd been anywhere near an aeroplane was one year at the Wattle Creek Agricultural Show. A shiny new plane with just one seat for the pilot had landed on the football oval. The farmers had examined it longingly, talking of how it would be if they could check their whole properties in hours rather than days. But who'd trust it to stay in the air?

'Would you like to?'

Kitty stared into her basket as she considered her reply. She didn't know if Theo was making light conversation or if his query was serious. Either way, she felt a sudden desire to appear brave and worldly – as he no doubt was. She tossed her hair back, looking up into his face. 'Of course.'

'Well, let's go up, then.' As he said the words, he sounded almost surprised at himself.

Her pulse quickened. 'You mean – now?' She eyed the plane doubtfully. The front was propped up on two small wheels that could have come from a wheelbarrow. The wings seemed to be held in place by wires.

'Why not? It's a perfect day – and I have to fly back to Oxford tomorrow.' He smiled. 'Come on. It's a very safe little plane, I promise.' Theo was already putting his helmet back on. He began walking away.

Kitty remained where she was, clutching the basket. She couldn't possibly go off in the plane with him. All she knew about Theo was that he was a Hamilton, from Hamilton Hall. He was friendly – but perhaps too friendly. He was probably used to being admired by women just because of who he was. And what would it say about Kitty, if she were prepared to accept such an invitation from a complete stranger?

'Actually,' she called to him, 'I think I should go back. Prince Yurievitch will wonder where I am.'

Theo turned around. Kitty saw a shadow of uncertainty in his eyes. He seemed suddenly at a loss. She could easily imagine him as the boy who'd picked blackberries in this field. 'I'm sorry,' he said. 'I don't mean to be pushy.'

There was a moment then, when everything hung in the balance. Kitty could see that Theo felt he'd been too forward; now he was afraid of rejection. She still wasn't sure she should accept his offer. But it was as if a current had formed between her and this stranger, drawing them towards one another.

'We won't be long,' Theo added. 'Please come. You'll love it.' Along with the pleading note in his voice, there was an edge of challenge. He might have been inviting her to take part in a childhood game of chicken – and she didn't want to lose.

'All right, then.' Dropping the basket, she strode after him before she had time to change her mind.

At the plane, Theo took her hand, pulling her up to stand on the wing, then guiding her into the front seat. She faltered in confusion at the sight of an instrument panel there.

'This plane has dual control,' Theo explained. 'But the pilot usually takes the rear.'

He found a second pair of goggles and a helmet, and helped her put them on. Then he reached down beside her, locating the safety straps. As he arranged the harness over her body, tightening the belt, clipping it in place, she avoided looking at his face in case he saw how his touch unnerved her – how his hands, though gentle, seemed to leave their imprint behind, patterning her skin.

Theo eased himself into the seat behind her. Turning back, Kitty watched his head moving from side to side as he made checks of the aircraft. She couldn't begin to imagine how he made sense of all the dials and switches. Finally, the propeller kicked into life again, speeding up to a blur. Then there was a wait – several long minutes – before the aircraft rolled forward, picking up speed.

Kitty felt the instant when the nose lifted. Then the wheels left the ground. The aircraft swayed and wobbled in the air. She swallowed hard, her stomach knotted with fear as she stared ahead at the empty sky. Soon, the motion began to feel less strange. She was able to look down over the side, past the red slab of the lower wing, to the field below.

They flew over the Big House with its many wings, the clock tower and the lofty barns that edged the farmyard. As they passed the walled garden and the quaint little Garden House, Kitty glimpsed her own washing hanging out on the line. Then they left Hamilton Hall behind.

They came to a river edged with trees. It curved like a snake over a landscape where every piece of ground was carved up by fences and walls. Even the woods were hemmed in. After they'd been flying for a while, Theo attracted Kitty's attention, then pointed to the right side of the plane. Following his gloved finger, Kitty saw a large bird – a stork or egret – flying almost at their height.

They came upon a lake – a silver shape with smooth curves, a small pool beside it reminiscent of a child hovering close to its mother. As the plane swooped down, birds rose from the water, running and flapping along the surface before breaking into flight. Kitty looked around to Theo, wanting the share the moment. As their eyes met, a smile spread across her lips. Words were not possible – the engine was too noisy. And they were not needed, anyway. She knew exactly why he'd brought her here – what it was that he wanted her to see.

She saw that the shape of a hillside was like a woman lying down, her hands resting at her waist.

She understood how the green moss creeping over exposed rock was like a fine soft carpet.

She felt the freedom of being able to move in three dimensions, defying gravity.

The plane, Theo, herself – they were like one creature, riding the wind.

As they flew back towards the landing strip she looked down at the Garden House again, wondering if Yuri had glanced up and seen the red plane. If he had, what would he think when she told him she'd been inside it? From what Theo had said, it sounded as if the two had met. Perhaps they were even friends. She couldn't wait to ask Yuri to tell her everything he knew about Theo Hamilton – and what he thought of him . . .

When they landed, she was breathless with excitement. As Theo helped her down from the cockpit, she found that her legs were shaking. She stumbled away from the plane, almost losing her balance. But suddenly, he was by her side, his hand at her waist, holding her up.

The ground beneath her gradually became firm again, her steps steady. But Theo remained close to her.

'That was wonderful,' she said. The comment was paltry, but any words would have fallen short of what she wanted to express.

'I love the freedom. You feel you can escape from everything.' As he spoke, Theo's eyes turned in the direction of Hamilton Hall.

Kitty wanted to ask why he yearned to escape the luxurious life of the Big House. Living with Yuri, she'd caught glimpses of a whole troop of servants, and seen guests in shiny black cars arriving for weekend parties. There were lots of dogs of different breeds – none of them built to work. The gardens alone would require all the care of a farm.

She undid the chinstrap and pulled off her helmet. Her hair tumbled loose around her shoulders. Theo lifted a strand away from her cheek, tucking it back behind her ear. Then they just stood there, looking into each other's eyes. A smile ran between them. It felt bright and strong, like a beam of light brought back from the sky.

*

Kitty paced in a slow circle around the sitting room, trying to decide where to put the framed photograph. Eventually, she chose a spot at one end of the sideboard, towards the corner of the room. She knew Theo would want his picture to be displayed, but in a way that was discreet. War service was to be acknowledged, not shown off. When she'd set it down, tilted to the right angle, she toured the room again, examining each item of furnishing that had been provided by the OFC. She wondered idly if the company had hired a wife to make the selections, or if one of the men on staff had done it. Or perhaps they'd left it up to the people in the furniture shops. Her footsteps were muffled as she trod on the mat that filled the centre of the room, then became loud again as she ventured onto the polished boards. Someone had been walking around with heels that were too spiky, she noticed. Areas of the wood were quite deeply pitted. Perhaps it had been Cynthia, perhaps a guest – whoever she was, she'd concentrated her steps around the drinks trolley, and crossed to the French windows more than once.

Passing the sofa, Kitty trailed her fingers along the back, making a furrow in the velvet pile. Then she stood still, listening for the sound of a car. But all she could hear was a rooster crowing in the distance and the clatter of pans coming from the kitchen. She checked her watch again. It was nearly five o'clock and Theo had still not arrived. She'd unpacked her luggage and moved Theo's things from the single room into the master bedroom. Then she'd had a long relaxing bath before changing into a red-and-white spotted dress with a broad sash that showed off her trim waist. After that, she'd tried reading one of the novels in the bookcase, but found she couldn't concentrate.

Kitty sighed as she ran her hand over her hair, ensuring that all the strands lay smooth. Bringing her wrist to her nose, she checked that her eau de Cologne was not too strong. Theo hated overpowering perfumes, not just before midday, but in the evenings too. She picked up the framed photograph of him from the sideboard where she'd put it earlier – trying it in a new position, then returning it to where it had been in the first place.

She went out to stand on the verandah. Past the picket fence, and beyond the foreground trees and shrubs, the settlement of Kongara was spread out for her to see. In spite of the neat placement of the tents, it was untidy and rather ugly. Viewed from up there, the lines of painted stones were crooked. The pale gravel roads had ragged edges; drainage trenches dug into the red earth were like long scars. Powerlines made black slash marks, seemingly at random. The few trees that remained looked lonely and unhealthy.

She listened again. This time, she heard the faint drone of an engine. Peering along the driveway, she saw the boxy shape of a small truck, or perhaps a jeep, like the ones the American soldiers drove. It might not be Theo, she warned herself. It could be Toby, or even Lisa, coming with a message.

But moments later, she saw him, sitting in the front passenger seat – his profile, his hair; so instantly familiar to her. With the vehicle barely at a standstill, he flung open the door and jumped out. He wore the khaki work clothes Kitty was now accustomed to seeing – the baggy shorts, the socks pulled up to his knees. Kitty felt a thrill of pride. He looked busy and efficient. He wasn't just some desk-bound administrator who spent his time being driven around in a smart car. He'd been down at the Units, dealing with a serious problem.

He strode across to the house, waving up at Kitty, an eager smile on his face.

She waved back, then clasped her hands over her chest, trying to contain her impatience. When he reached the verandah she hitched up her skirt and ran towards him.

He raised his hands to ward her off. 'I'm dusty from head to foot.'

'I don't care.' Kitty threw her arms around him. As she hugged him close, she felt his arms enfolding her.

'I've missed you so, so much.' Theo's voice seemed to come from deep inside his body.

'Not as much as I've missed you.'

They held one another at arm's length. Kitty looked into her husband's eyes. His gaze was clear and bright. He had the beginnings of a suntan, which made him look healthy and relaxed. She could feel the change in his body as well. He was his true self again – light and happy.

His gaze lingered on her face, her hair. He made no mention of her new, fashionable look. Kitty didn't know if this was because, deep down, he preferred her how she used to be, or if he wanted to avoid thinking back to how he had instructed his wife to make the change, and why.

She pushed the uneasy thought aside as Theo led her towards the French doors. At the threshold, he paused. Kitty guessed he was going to kiss her again, but instead he placed one arm behind her shoulders, and with the other he swept up her legs and carried her inside.

Kitty buried her face against his neck, smelling traces of soap beneath the dust. Joy and relief flooded through her. Theo loved her again. He had forgiven her.

Theo stood by the drinks trolley. He'd washed and changed into a cream linen suit. His jacket hung open but he wore a shirt and tie. Beside him, Kitty felt her spotted dress was too informal. He picked up a hand bell and gave it a good shake. A tinny clanging broke the stillness of the room. A short while later, Gabriel appeared. He wore a red fez and a long white gown.

'Yes, Bwana.'

'Pour some drinks, please. Gin and tonic for the memsahib. Don't forget ice and lemon. A whisky soda for me.'

Gabriel set about preparing the drinks, whipping the lid from a bottle of tonic and using a small pair of tongs to lift ice cubes from a silver bucket. The chink of ice and glass was mesmerising. The late sun, reaching into the room, added its glow to the golden tones of the whisky, brandy and sherry set out in matching decanters.

Kitty's drink was completed first. 'Thank you,' she murmured as the man placed the glass on a side table, positioning it on a coaster. Gabriel returned to the trolley, expertly angling the soda siphon, pulling the trigger. Then he selected another ice cube.

'What are you doing?' Theo sounded annoyed.

Gabriel turned to him, eyes wide with alarm. The ice cube dripped onto his tunic.

'I don't want ice, for heaven's sake,' Theo said. 'And make it a double.'

'Yes, Bwana.'

When Gabriel was gone, Kitty picked up her drink. The slice of lemon was in fact lime, as had been the case with the afternoon tea she'd been served. She watched the rind bobbing in the bubbles. It was such a pure, almost translucent tone of green. Taking a sip, she savoured the fresh, exotic tang. Beside her, Theo gulped down his drink and stood up to pour himself another.

'How was your flight?' he asked.

'It was long, of course. Very tiring.'

'No problems with your luggage?'

'None at all.' Kitty felt a sudden fear that the magic of their reunion was about to vanish under a blanket of banalities. Then she remembered something interesting to say. 'We flew over El Alamein. Three of the other passengers were in the second battle of the campaign. They pointed out the places they'd fought. You could still see some burnt-out tanks and the remains of an aircraft. And there was a line on the ground – maybe a trench. Something to do with the Australians —'

'Do you like the house?' Theo gestured at their surroundings.

'Yes, it's very nice.' Kitty hid her confusion at his blunt change of subject. Back in England, Theo had always been ready to discuss the war. He didn't talk about his personal experiences, but was almost obsessed with analysing military strategies. He spent hours talking to the Admiral about it; they had something in common now, skirting their disagreement about Theo's defection to the air force, and focusing instead on the atrocities committed by the enemy and the all-round superiority of the Allies. Kitty thought Theo would have been keenly interested in her anecdote about El

Alamein. Then it occurred to her that perhaps he'd decided it was finally time to let it all go, as part of making a fresh start – though that wouldn't be very easy; the Groundnut Scheme seemed to be staffed largely by ex-servicemen. She glanced across at the photograph on the sideboard. When she had the chance, she thought, she'd quietly put it away.

Theo stared down into his drink. He shook it slightly, making a sloshing sound.

'Diana showed me around.' Kitty spoke brightly, wanting to retrieve the light mood of before. 'She introduced me to the staff.'

Theo raised his eyebrows. 'Diana?'

'She met me at the airstrip and brought me here.'

'Did she?' Theo sounded impressed. 'She's very busy, you know. Being the wife of the General Manager, she has a lot of responsibilities.'

'She's . . . very nice.' Kitty let the comment hang in the air. She wasn't sure she should mention how oddly Diana had reacted to the near-accident with the child, or the fact that Kitty found her manner quite difficult to read.

'She'll be a great help to you,' Theo stated. 'If you need any advice, information – just ask her. She sets a terrific example to everyone.'

Kitty twisted her hands around her glass. Was there something pointed about this last remark? Or was he simply paying a compliment to the wife of his boss? She bent her head, wishing she could still hide behind her long hair. The blunt-ended locks fell forward like broken wings to each side of her face.

'I'm so glad you're here.'

She looked up at Theo's words. There was a faint crack in his voice that made her heart jump. In this new place, he was relaxed and in control. He was an important man with a big job to do. Yet he still needed her.

Rising from her chair, Kitty moved to stand in front of him. She looped her arms around his neck and pulled him close. For a moment, he seemed to collapse against her, making her take a short step back. Then he drew himself up, tall and straight. Kitty rested her face against his chest, breathed out slowly, and closed her eyes.

THREE

Kitty stirred and stretched, waking slowly. She was confused at first by the white gauze that surrounded her and the lightness of the single cotton blanket covering her body. Then she remembered where she was. Even half awake, she was conscious of the luxury of having Theo right here with her. She reached out for him, her fingers ready to meet his warm skin. But his side of the bed was empty.

Looking around her, she saw that the top drawer of the tallboy was open. This was where she'd put Theo's collection of khaki socks – at least a dozen pairs, rolled into balls. The wardrobe door was slightly ajar as well. He must have risen early and dressed quietly, not wanting to wake her after the long journey.

She lay still for a while, memories of the night before coming back to her. It had been late when they'd finally come in here – after escaping the attentions of Gabriel, who'd insisted on serving coffee after dinner, though neither of them wanted it. Alone at last, they'd felt suddenly shy; they were like strangers caught together in this unfamiliar room. The modern furnishings were intimidating. Kitty's pot of face cream and single bottle of perfume looked abandoned on the vast dressing table. She felt like a child in a grown-up's place. Theo had removed his tie, tipping his head back as he always did. Then he shrugged off the jacket and put it on the chair. Kitty slipped off her shoes and peeled down her stockings. Every sound they made seemed loud, each gesture exaggerated. Half undressed, they stood facing one another as if at a loss as to what to do next.

Theo turned off the main light, leaving just the one by the bed. The orange lampshade cast a coloured glow. Everything was different now. Shadows hid the details of the room, creating mystery. The two figures were painted with firelight. Theo unzipped Kitty's dress and let it fall with a swish to her ankles. Then he lowered the straps of her petticoat and bra. He pressed his lips to her shoulders, tasting her slowly, then with growing hunger. He pulled off her underwear, his hands rough with wanting. Taking her hand, he led her to the bed. In one movement he swept off the bedspread and flung it in a heap on the floor.

Now, sitting on the bed, bathed in morning light, Kitty smiled. She laid her hands over her belly, cradling the softness there. Maybe even now, at this moment, it had already happened. She imagined her body swelling into a mound, the skin stretched tight. A baby on the way.

Her attention was caught then by the distant drone of voices. Swinging her legs to the floor, she cocked her head to listen more closely. She recognised Theo's low tone, and the higher note of Gabriel's voice. It came to her suddenly that she might have slept in so late that Theo was leaving for work.

From the wardrobe, she grabbed a dressing gown – a silk embroidered kimono that Louisa had given her because it had a tear at the hem. As she tied the sash, she checked her appearance in the mirror. Her hair was a little tousled, but her eyes were clear, her cheeks rosy. She bit her lips to bring out the colour. Then, pushing her feet into her slippers, she hurried from the room.

Theo was sitting at one end of Cynthia's dining table, which had been spread with a fresh white cloth. His head was bent over a newspaper. For an instant, Kitty felt alarmed – but then she reminded herself that the crisis with reporters was over. No one was still thinking about her. She padded into the room. After a few steps, she faltered in surprise. The cup and saucer in front of Theo were from Cynthia's crockery set. So was the teapot, sugar bowl, milk jug – even the little pot of salt with its tiny spoon. Yet, when Kitty had supervised the unpacking of the trunk the day before, she'd told Gabriel to stack the Royal Doulton away in a box. She'd made it clear the plain white crockery was to be used in its place. And, last night at dinner, it had been. The white plates and dishes, set out on the white tablecloth, had created a look of simple elegance, set off by a posy of red and orange hibiscus flowers picked from the garden. Kitty had been disappointed Theo had made no comment – but then, there'd been a lot to talk about.

The Scheme had faced many challenges, it seemed. Though large tracts of land had been cleared, a great deal more had to be achieved. The process had proved unexpectedly difficult. Ordinary bulldozers were not up to the task. The best progress so far had been achieved by dragging huge chains between tractors. But it was all too slow, and hopes were now pinned on a new machine that had been made especially for the Scheme: a converted army tank crossed with a tractor, called a Shervick. The first shipment of them was due to arrive any day from England, but things were often delayed. The conversation had continued in this vein. It had taken all evening for Theo to give Kitty a full account of how much hard work and inventive thinking had been required for all the problems to be overcome.

Kitty approached the table, silent in her slippers. She took in a silver rack containing triangles of white toast, a glass dish of marmalade, a napkin ring. Here they were in Africa, yet this could have been breakfast at Hamilton Hall.

Theo glanced up, then rose to his feet. 'Good morning, my darling.' He stayed half bent over, indicating that he expected to sit down again very soon. Kitty hurried to pull out a chair opposite him.

'Good morning.' She smiled. 'I can't believe I slept in so long!'

'You must have been tired.' Theo smiled back at her. Then his eyes passed over her face and body, pausing on the neckline of her gown. Kitty felt heat rise in her cheeks. She guessed he was remembering last night – how urgently they'd made love, as if they were only just married. And how they'd done so a second time later on, relishing one another's bodies, their desire fuelled by the knowledge that there would be no more separations, no more gloom, no more fear. She was about to comment on it, when Theo gestured towards Gabriel who was waiting by the far doorway. He spoke in an undertone. 'One normally dresses for breakfast.'

Kitty wrapped her gown more closely. 'I was afraid I'd miss you.'

'You very nearly did. I've got a meeting in a quarter of an hour.' He closed the newspaper. 'Just ask the boy for breakfast.' He nodded again at Gabriel. 'Tell him how you'd like your eggs. It's not like England, by the way. There are no shortages here. Obviously there are things you can't get, but all the basics – eggs, milk, meat, vegetables – you can have as much as you like!' There was a boyish enthusiasm in his voice. He could have been discussing a midnight feast in the school dormitory.

Kitty smiled again. 'You're making me feel hungry!'

He grinned back at her, his eyes locked on hers. Reaching across the table, he squeezed her hand. 'What's on for you today?'

'This morning I'm going to a club of some kind, with Diana,' Kitty said. She'd see Theo at lunchtime, but after that – she had no idea. She had yet to discover what would occupy her days. The sense of the unknown filled her with excitement. She remembered the words of the old missionary, Janet: *The need is so great . . .*

'Oh, good. You'll enjoy that.' Theo stood up, looking at his watch. 'I'd better see if the driver has brought the car around.'

He headed for the French windows. Kitty followed him, taking small steps in her tightened kimono. When she reached the verandah she could see, parked in the driveway, the khaki-green vehicle that had delivered Theo the day before. A man in a green uniform and a peaked cloth cap was flicking the bonnet energetically with a feather duster. The paintwork gleamed in the morning sun.

'What do you think?' Theo asked. 'It was a wonderful piece of luck. Someone ordered it from England, but by the time it turned up they'd been transferred back to London.'

Kitty frowned in surprise. He'd actually chosen this vehicle for himself! A traditional car like next door's Daimler was much more his style. Unsure how to respond, she shrugged, spreading her hands. 'I've never seen a brand-new jeep before.'

'Jeep?' Theo's voice rose to a squeak. 'That is a Land Rover – the first one in Africa.' As Kitty came to stand next to him, he put his arm around her shoulders. 'It's an absolute triumph. You see, the idea was to make a civilian, peacetime, go-anywhere vehicle – something that could be produced in the factories where they'd built Spitfires during the war. They're made of aluminium, you see – like the aircraft.'

'Ah.' Kitty nodded, still taken aback by his enthusiasm for something modern.

'Two ranges of gears – four high and four low. You can see the winch there, on the front. They've got waterproofed wiring, too. Ideal for a place like this.'

As she listened to him speak, it dawned on Kitty that his choice to buy a Land Rover was part of his commitment to the new life they'd come here to make together. She smiled encouragingly, trying to think of something to say that would show she understood. She pointed at the closed-in cabin made of canvas. 'I suppose you can remove that and sit in the open.'

'You certainly can,' Theo agreed. 'It's called a "rag-top", by the way.' He turned to Kitty. 'I'm afraid you won't have the use of it. Not like Diana with the Daimler. Richard spends his days in Head Office, but I can get called out to the field at any time. Anyway, she never learned to drive, it seems – so she needs his driver.'

Kitty thought of the long dusty road from here to the heart of Kongara. Presumably that was where the shops, the Club and other facilities were. She wondered how she was going to get about.

'I'm looking into buying a second car – one you can drive yourself,' Theo announced, as if reading her mind.

'Thank you!' Kitty grinned at him, grateful and excited.

'It won't be anything special,' he warned. 'A Hillman, perhaps. Just something small.' He eyed the Land Rover lovingly. 'This'll be the end of jeeps. They've been well and truly left behind.'

The driver ran the duster over the bonnet and headlights one last time, and then climbed into the front seat.

'Time to go,' Theo said, giving her shoulder a pat. 'I'll see you at lunchtime.'

'Bye.' Kitty knew her voice sounded small, so she paired it with a solid smile. She was disappointed he had to go so soon, and annoyed with herself for sleeping in and missing the chance for them to share breakfast on this, her first morning.

Theo gave Kitty a kiss on the cheek, then strode away across the verandah. Reaching the steps, he turned and waved. As he climbed into the Land Rover, Kitty waved back. With her other hand, she touched her cheek in the spot where he'd planted his kiss. Warmth stirred inside her. This simple gesture – the husband kissing his wife goodbye and heading off to work – swept away the feeling of being abandoned. Kitty had seen the ritual played out in films, on television and in real life, but she'd never taken part in it before.

Back in England, Theo hadn't had a job since being de-mobbed from the air force. At first, he'd thrown himself into the task of helping his family reinstate their old way of life at Hamilton Hall after the disruption of the war. When that was done, he had seemed at a loss; there was no talk of returning to Oxford or finding work. Often, he spent the whole day in the Hall library. He picked from the shelves at random – odd titles like *Naval Tactics* and *The British Soldier*. He read doggedly, but without passion. Or he fell asleep. He was permanently exhausted, as though the stress of the war had left him so depleted his energy could not be rekindled. It had taken the events following Yuri's death – the scandal that could not even now be mentioned – to shake Theo from his malaise. But the strength he found then had been fuelled by anger, humiliation and betrayal. It burned away, leaving nothing but ashes.

When the letter from his old RAF colleague had arrived, containing the offer of a senior position in the Groundnut Scheme in faraway Tanganyika, it had felt like a miracle. A chance to escape to a new world. But Kitty had been concerned Theo might not be up to the task. Now, she could see she need not have worried. Clearly, he was passionate about his work here, his spirits high. This morning's goodbye kiss seemed to symbolise the transformation that had taken place. As she headed back indoors, Kitty smiled at the thought that this ritual would be repeated day after day, building up the edifice of their married life, holding them close and safe inside.

Kitty laid out a choice of outfits on the bed. She tried to concentrate on deciding what to wear, but her thoughts kept returning to the dining room, where she could hear the distant sounds of Gabriel clearing away the breakfast she'd just eaten. The food lay heavy in her stomach and her jaw was tense as she replayed her interchange with him. She'd waited until he'd set out her eggs, toast and tea, then she'd looked him in the eye, and spoken to him in plain English.

'Why did you take out these plates and cups? I told you very clearly that we would be using the white ones. You must listen to me!'

'Yes, Memsahib.' He bowed his head submissively, but there was an odd expression on his face. He adjusted Kitty's cutlery, straightening her knife. 'But the bwana, he does not like your white ones. He instructed me to use the others.'

There was a moment of silence while Kitty absorbed his words. 'Oh.' She traced the pattern on the egg cup with her finger.

'The problem is with the cups. They are too fat.'

Kitty looked up. 'Fat?'

Gabriel picked up one of Cynthia's teacups and pointed to the rim. He frowned, lost for the right word. '*Maskini*.' Skinny.

'I see.' Kitty kept her face blank, though she felt a flash of anger that Theo had undermined her like this – he must have known what he was doing. But then, she told herself, she had made a mistake by not discussing the crockery with him – after all, Theo had been using this set during the weeks he'd been living here alone. She rubbed her temples with her fingers. Why did it even matter what plates and cups they used? She pictured Yuri rolling his eyes. He used to drink his tea from whatever came to hand – a jam jar, a cream jug, or a bone china cup with no handle. He'd long ago banned saucers as being nothing more than a nuisance.

Gabriel had hurried back to the kitchen, clearly eager to report his evidence of a tiny rift between the bwana and the memsahib. Left alone, Kitty had turned to the newspaper. It was time, she told herself, to overcome the near phobia she'd developed about the press. Ignoring the tension that ran through her body, she'd scanned stories about austerity measures, lingering rationing and unemployment among ex-servicemen. The gloomy articles were juxtaposed with stories about rebuilding a better world, the Olympic Games in

London, and even fashion designers taking on the task of making the world a prettier place. She'd made herself keep going, turning the pages, until the act of reading a newspaper almost began to feel normal. Only then had she left the table, coming here to the bedroom to get changed.

Kitty selected one of the frocks – a plain blue one with white piping around the neck and sleeves, which she thought was the least likely of the four to draw any attention. She crossed to the tallboy to find a pair of gloves. As she picked them out, she couldn't help thinking of Theo's vests and underpants folded away in the neighbouring drawers. He'd been surprised, almost annoyed, to find that Kitty had transferred his possessions from the spare room. Apparently, he'd planned to keep them in there until the space was needed for some other purpose. He liked the idea of having his own things in his own room. Now and then, he'd commented, he might prefer to sleep on his own as well.

When he'd said this, Kitty had stared at him in confusion. In their flat in Skellingthorpe and then in the suite of rooms allocated to them at Hamilton Hall, there had been only one bedroom, so the question of ideal sleeping arrangements had never come up. But last night Theo had explained to Kitty that in English families of his class it was normal for husbands and wives to have separate rooms. His own father had one, and made visits to his mother. If heating had not been an issue due to post-war fuel rationing, Louisa would have offered her son a room to himself when he and Kitty moved in. When you had such a large home, it made sense. Women liked to fill their bedrooms with clothes and perfumes and ornaments; a man had simpler tastes. And one liked one's personal space.

Kitty had quietly nodded agreement, even though she struggled to understand. Surely if you loved someone, you'd want to be close to them all the time? To hear the sound of them breathing as you drifted into sleep, and be greeted by their warmth when you awoke? Of course, not all married people were in love. Courtesy was the closest thing to affection she'd seen pass between Louisa and the Admiral. Kitty wondered if sleeping separately was the cause or the effect of the distance between them. Her own parents had always shared one bed and one small room – weathering sickness, pregnancy and night feeds for babies. Her father's snores after a bout of drinking were loud enough to disturb the whole household, yet his wife always remained at his side. (There was nowhere else for her to go, unless she climbed in with one of her children.) The constant proximity didn't seem to have sparked any deeper intimacy, though. There were plenty of babies, but in the spheres of daytime life – kitchen, sitting room, farmyard – Kitty had seen no more fondness displayed by her parents than she'd detected between Louisa and the Admiral.

Kitty gazed at the tallboy, still feeling confused – and if she was honest, hurt and disappointed – about the exchange she'd had with Theo. But then she pulled herself together, picking up the blue dress. She eased it carefully over her head, avoiding messing up her hair. Sucking in her belly, she did up the zip. Then she retouched her make-up and added another burst of hairspray, before strapping on a pair of high-heeled sandals.

Facing herself in the mirror she felt suddenly doubtful about the dress. She was about to reach for the zip when the doorbell rang. Seconds later, she heard the front door being opened. Kitty lowered her arm as she heard Diana's heels come tapping down the hall. She picked up her carry bag, quickly checking that she'd packed her swimming costume and towel as Diana had instructed. Then she took a deep breath and walked out to meet her neighbour.

'Welcome to the Kongara Club,' Diana announced as the Daimler rolled to a standstill outside a dull grey building. It was no more than a long half-tube of corrugated iron with a flagpole erected at the front. Kitty concealed her surprise – the converted Nissen hut was more in keeping with the tent settlement and the Toolsheds than with Millionaire Row.

'Awful, isn't it?' Diana said. 'We keep complaining. They've promised to build a new one.'

In a large gravelled area to one side of the building were dozens of cars, parked in groups wherever trees offered shade. There was a mix of styles – ranging from jeeps to large saloons – but nothing anywhere near as grand as Diana's Daimler.

Diana got out of the car and led the way towards a red door set in the bricked-up end of the tube. She was quiet this morning – not impolite, but distracted. Her dress was simpler in style than the one she'd worn yesterday and made from plain pink cloth, but with her sunglasses and heavy gold necklace she still looked very glamorous. Kitty checked that the back of her skirt was hanging properly as she followed Diana towards the entrance.

When they reached the door, a teenaged boy jumped to his feet, pushing over a low stool. His black skin blended with a dark shirt and trousers. He ushered the women inside.

Diana set off at a brisk pace along a line of carpet that ran down the middle of the building. Her skirt was narrow and she swayed her hips as she moved. Kitty followed, trying to take in her surroundings without appearing to stare. The large, lofty space was filled with armchairs and couches set around low tables. There were several potted palms on wooden stands, and Persian rugs scattered on the floor. There was a grand piano, being played rather amateurishly by a man in a shirt and tie; Kitty recognised the tune of 'The White Cliffs of Dover'. Even with these touches, though, the place had a sombre atmosphere. It didn't help that the windows set at intervals in the curved walls were small and placed too high up to give a view outside. Kitty could imagine how morning, noon and night would all feel the same in here.

Cigarette smoke hung blue in the hot, still air. There was quite a large number of people – men and women of all ages. They were gathered into different groups. Mothers with children were in one area (most were accompanied by young African women in white starched uniforms, who Kitty guessed were nannies). A good distance away was a section occupied by isolated figures – all male – their faces hidden behind upheld newspapers. Here and there were small clusters of men sitting in chairs pulled up around the tables. Most of them were dressed in business suits, a few in khakis. They leaned towards one another, deep in conversation, pausing only when they caught sight of Diana parading down the room. They looked at Kitty as well – giving her frank appraising stares. She wondered why they weren't at work.

Further on, there was a noisy gathering of young women dressed in khaki shirts and skirts, all wearing bright lipstick. They reminded Kitty of Lisa and the others she'd seen bustling around Head Office.

They didn't stop talking as the newcomers passed, but Kitty could feel their eyes following her. She was glad now that she'd worn the plain blue dress. She was attracting enough attention as it was.

The bar stood towards the rear of the building. It was made of dark wood, highly polished in a way that reminded Kitty of Cynthia's dining table. Here, at last, the glittering rows of glasses and white bar towels gave the mood of the place a lift.

'Good morning, Memsahib.' The African barman was a towering figure, both tall and heavy. He wore a white tunic and a red fez.

Diana inclined her head. 'Good morning, Alfred.' She led the way on towards a pair of Japanese-style folding screens that closed off the back corner of the room. In the enclave beyond, half a dozen women sat together reading magazines and smoking cigarettes, with tea or coffee cups at their elbows. The effect of Diana's appearance on them was immediate. Cups were put down, magazines slapped shut. Every eye turned to her, ready and alert.

Diana directed all the attention to Kitty. 'Ladies, this is Mrs Theodore Hamilton.' She introduced the women in turn, beginning with the one furthest away. 'Mrs Nicholas Carswell.'

Kitty recognised the name of the Manager of Agriculture. His wife was mousy-haired with a small, sharp nose. Next to be named was a Mrs Neil Stratton – plump but pretty, with a large mouth.

'Unit Manager,' Diana added in an undertone.

Mrs Jeremy Meadows followed. Senior Medical Officer. Frizzy orange hair.

Kitty tried to remember all the names and faces – but it was an impossible task, even without the heat and the smell of smoke and perfume. When Diana had named the last of the women, she gave an airy wave. 'So, now we've done with all that . . .' She aimed her finger again towards each of the women in turn. 'Alice, Audrey, Evelyn, Sally, Eliza, Pippa.'

Alice gave a polite nod, but all the others smiled warmly.

'And I'm Kitty. I'm very pleased to meet you all.'

'Kitty arrived yesterday from England,' Diana explained. 'But she's from Australia originally.'

'Australia!' exclaimed the Medical Officer's wife. 'My sister lives in Melbourne. Perhaps you know her.'

'It's a big place,' Kitty said. 'And I was out in the country on a farm.' She had a sinking feeling that the red-haired woman was going to continue with her questions. Kitty knew how it would play out. She'd end up saying that her father's farm was over fifty thousand acres – bigger even than one of the Units here in Kongara. As well as the main house, there were barns, sheds and farm workers' quarters. Her listeners would be picturing a place a bit like Hamilton Hall. And – as had happened with Theo and his mother – Kitty would not be brave enough to explain how the land was half-barren, the cattle skinny, the sheep grey with dust, their fleeces flyblown and daggy. How the house was made of wood, which was peeling and cracked. How the tin roof was patterned with rust.

Fortunately, there was no chance for the conversation to take place. Alice picked up a notepad from a basket at her feet. 'Let's start the meeting, ladies – now that we're all here.' She glanced pointedly at her watch.

'I simply must order coffee first,' Diana said. She addressed Kitty. 'What about you? There is only Nescafé. Apparently we're waiting for a percolator to arrive from London.'

'Well, if you're having some – yes, please. Except that . . .' Kitty felt herself blushing. 'I don't have money with me.'

Diana was confused for a second. 'Money? Heavens – no one has money. We just sign on our husband's accounts. Theo has one.'

'Oh yes, of course.'

Diana turned to Alfred, who was already hovering at her shoulder, ready to take her order. 'Coffee for two. And something to eat. Small, and not too sweet.'

'Yes, Memsahib.'

Close up, Kitty saw deep purple scars on the man's cheeks – lines, and rows of dots. She'd seen faces with tribal markings like this in one of the Hamilton Hall library's books, *Percy's Africa Sketches*. The primitive look was eerily out of place beside the barman's spotless uniform. It made his submissive manner seem fake. Kitty thought of Eustace and Gabriel. Was there a veiled hostility in all the African staff, running just beneath the surface? Or was it only Kitty's lack of familiarity with the place and the people that made her think this? Diana certainly didn't appear to have any concerns about this man. She waved him away as rudely as if he were an annoying fly.

Alice stabbed her pencil into her notepad – a restless staccato beat. 'Let us begin. Our next charity event is the pot-plant sale.' She turned to Kitty. 'We're raising money for the missionaries. Sister Barbara has grown the plants. We just have to sell them.'

'You mean *buy* them,' said Evelyn.

Alice gave her a tight smile. Then she turned to Diana. 'May I put you down for writing out price tags? I've already allocated some of the other tasks.'

'Absolutely. I'd love nothing better,' Diana said sweetly.

Alice narrowed her eyes suspiciously. Kitty realised she wasn't the only one who found Diana hard to read: what Diana had just said was beyond reproach, but there was a false tone in her voice. With a faint sigh, Alice turned back to her notepad. 'The stall will be set up right outside the main door so we can catch people as they arrive or leave. Now, we need some eye-catching posters. Along with the words, we need drawings of pot plants, flowers . . . It would make all the difference.' She turned to Kitty. 'I don't suppose you're an artist? That would be too perfect!'

Kitty's face stiffened as she searched Alice's face. Was the question just a coincidence? She shook her head, setting her hair swinging. 'No. No, I'm not. I'm sorry.'

Alice looked sympathetic. 'I'm sure you're good at something.'

A woman with blonde hair piled up in an elaborate coiffure raised her hand. 'I can probably draw a flower or two.' She smiled self-consciously.

'Thank you, Pippa.'

As the meeting continued, the women took discreet sips of coffee, leaving lipstick marks on white cups that had *Kongara Club* in loopy red script on the side. In the distance, the pianist turned to a new song. Diana shifted restlessly in her chair. Then Alfred finally arrived bearing a loaded tray. Along with two cups of coffee was a plate piled with iced pastries. They were big, and looked very sweet.

Diana was not perturbed by the discrepancy with what she'd ordered; in fact, she seemed pleased. She put two of the pastries on a side plate, which she balanced on her knee.

Alfred handed Kitty her coffee. It remained dark and strong even after she'd added lots of milk. She was still learning to drink the pungent brew, to keep Theo company. He'd become almost addicted to it during the war; it was a well-earned luxury for the pilots who flew by night as well as day. Kitty lifted the cup to her mouth, avoiding breathing the smell of the steam. As her lips closed on the thick rim, it suddenly came to her why Theo didn't want to use the white crockery she'd chosen: such utilitarian ware belonged in a club or a hotel, not in a home on Millionaire Row. She felt a slump of discouragement; it was so easy to fail.

Diana ate hungrily, scattering crumbs over her dress. As soon as she finished one of the pastries, she began on the next. There was a disconcerting intensity about the way she consumed the food. There was even a slight tremor in her hands. Kitty noticed that none of the other women watched Diana as she ate; they kept their eyes on the floor, on their own drinks, or on Alice.

'At our next coffee morning,' Alice was saying, 'we will begin work on our major event. The Caledonian Charity Dinner.'

She went on to talk about haggis and kilts and bagpipes. Diana finally put down her plate. After brushing away the crumbs from her lap she sat forward, fixing her attention on Alice. Now she looked like a model student in class. Audrey raised her hand to ask a question about timing – there was a birthday and a christening to bear in mind. Alice explained that no other date was possible. Kitty listened quietly, struck by the refined English accents of all the women who spoke – and puzzled as to why they were holding a Scottish dinner.

The meeting wound on, punctuated by the erratic beat of an electric fan with a bent arm. Eventually, Diana raised one manicured hand to cover her mouth and yawned loudly. 'I need a swim or I'll fall straight to sleep.'

A ripple of enthusiasm ran through the group, and Alice reluctantly put down her notepad.

As Kitty picked up her bag, she was torn between looking forward to cooling down and dreading getting changed. She knew, without any doubt, that her costume would be an embarrassment. It was a pretty strawberry colour, but the rubber was beginning to perish, the skirt had lost its shape and she'd had to replace the straps with lengths of ribbon. She'd found it in the bathing pavilion at Hamilton Hall, where it had been abandoned by a guest years before. That had been back when Kitty's presence at the Big House was, officially, as Yuri's guest. Louisa was wary of the young woman's friendship with her son, but had not yet begun to fear that the worst would happen.

'You can swim, can't you?' Diana asked.

Kitty nodded her head. She'd been able to swim for as long as she could remember. At last, she thought. Here was something she knew she could do well.

In the damp heat of the bathing hut, Kitty stood alone. The other women had already left – they'd slipped into their suits and organised their clothes with the efficiency born of familiarity. Diana had been the last to get changed, having disappeared somewhere briefly after they'd all left the lounge.

Kitty hung her dress on a hook and placed her sandals side by side on the floor. Then she sat down on the narrow wooden bench. A wave of emotion swept over her, taking her by surprise. She felt acutely lonely, homesick – but she couldn't say what, or who, she longed for. She pressed her hands against her eyelids to prevent tears gathering. She was tired, she realised. The journey had been long and everything was so new and strange. Raising her head, she stared into the shadowy corners of the windowless room. The sounds of distant laughter, voices, coming from outside seemed far away. She had the frightening sense that she could remain in here – entombed, alone forever.

She heard the sound of someone approaching – the slap-slap of rubber thongs, or flip-flops, as Theo called them. She lifted her head as Pippa came in, smiling brightly.

'Forgot something – as usual.' She foraged in a bag, then turned around wearing a pair of sunglasses with big round lenses.

As she left the room, Kitty stood up. If she didn't go out soon, people would wonder what she was doing.

After the gloom of the hut, she squinted in the bright sun. No one was in the pool; sunshine bounced off the still water and shone silver in the puddles that lay on the concrete surrounds. Kitty scanned the sets of tables and chairs, shielded by green-and-white striped umbrellas that were dotted around the pool. People were sitting alone or with friends, reading or drinking. The women Kitty knew had taken over two tables next to one another. They sat in upright wrought-iron chairs, except Diana, who was stretched out on a wooden lounge. She wore a pink costume that showed off a fine suntan. Her midriff was daringly exposed. Even from here, Kitty could see that it was slender and well toned.

The other women all had towelling bathing gowns, but Kitty had to make do with tying her towel around her waist. She held it in place as she walked towards them. The concrete was hot beneath her bare feet (she hadn't thought to bring a change of shoes, and she could hardly walk around in a bathing suit and high heels). During the years of living in England, her feet had become tender, always encased in shoes. She moved quickly, veering onto patches of wet ground where she could.

Kitty headed towards a vacant chair at the closer of the two tables. As she neared the group she saw there was a man in their midst – an old fellow with a long grey beard and a walrus moustache. There was a pith helmet on his head. His safari suit had the well-worn, old-fashioned look of Janet's missionary clothes.

When Kitty came to a standstill, Audrey introduced her to him. 'Kitty, this is Bowie. Bowie, this is Kitty.'

Bowie didn't get to his feet, but saluted Kitty instead. 'Delighted to meet you.'

While Kitty took her chair, Audrey touched Bowie's sun-blotched arm. 'Kitty's husband is the new Manager of Administration. You know . . .' Her tone became hushed. 'He replaced Major Wainwright.'

Bowie shook his head. 'Terrible business. Awful way to die. I'd rather face a herd of buffalo than a swarm of African bees. And that's saying something!'

'He was killed by bees?' The question slipped from Kitty's lips.

'He certainly was,' Bowie replied. 'Didn't have a hope. They fastened onto him and just stung him to death. There's nothing you can do when they strike. Nothing.'

Kitty felt her stomach contract as she formed a mental picture of his words. She saw a figure staggering in agony, every bit of his skin black with bees.

'We've had a few deaths from bees on the Scheme,' Bowie said. 'Bulldozer drivers have pushed over trees and broken up hives. But this attack was rather odd. A man from Head Office visiting the Units is hardly in the frontline of work. There was talk of the vet deliberately taking him off somewhere —'

'Bowie is a professional hunter.' Alice cut him off bluntly. She turned to Kitty. 'When the OFC started work here, he was employed to protect people from wild animals.'

Her tactic was successful. Bowie forgot about the bee attack and sat forward, fixing Kitty with his faded blue eyes. 'It's hard to believe it was only a couple of years ago. Things were so different back then.'

He went on to explain how the Kongara plains had been teeming with game, big and small. No one was safe, day or night. But then the heavy machinery had been brought in.

'It was quite a sight, I can tell you, watching a long line of tractors – sixty of them, maybe more – driving across the plains, side by side, like an advancing army. The dust clouds spreading behind. And all the game running for their lives ahead of them, never to return. We've had the odd elephant roam in since then. A rhino attacked a bulldozer once, but I believe it was provoked. We've seen a lion or two – but nothing much. So I get to spend my days here at the Club, keeping all you ladies entertained.' He flashed a smile, showing teeth like old ivory. 'Can't believe my luck.' He spoke brightly, but as Kitty met his gaze she sensed an undercurrent of sadness. He'd much rather be out on the plains, she guessed, his gun on his shoulder, a pack on his back. This idle life was all that he had left.

Kitty rested her elbows on the solid tabletop. It was made of the same speckled concrete as the floor of her verandah. Last night, Theo had told her it was called 'terrazzo'. When Kitty had commented how odd the word sounded, he explained it was Italian. He'd spoken with that overly patient tone he used these days whenever his wife exposed her lack of knowledge of the world. Kitty cupped her chin in her hands, letting the memory slide away. By moving her chair a little to the left she'd escaped the shade of the umbrella. She relished the touch of the sun on her bare back and shoulders. It had been so cold in England, she felt the chill was still there, deep in her bones. Kitty lifted her face to the sun, letting it play over her closed lids. She could hear Bowie telling Pippa he was planning to travel to the Swahili coast – but there was something in his tone that made Kitty think he would never actually go. She tried to place his distinctive accent, but couldn't. Perhaps he was South African. She knew they had an odd way of speaking; in England she'd been mistaken for one herself.

Eventually, sweat broke out over her face; a trickle ran down her back. Opening her eyes, she saw that the pool was still unoccupied. The water was inviting, but no one seemed keen to swim. Away in the corner of the grounds, beside a set of swings and a slide, was a paddling pool – a small shallow version of the big one. From there came squawks of delight and the sound of splashing. Kitty turned to watch. A handful of children played in the water with a rubber ring and a striped beach ball. Parked nearby were a couple of prams draped with white nets to keep out flies. The only adults over there were African nannies, four of them, their white uniforms hanging limply in the heat.

'Those two are mine.' Kitty turned to see Audrey pointing to a girl and a boy, both with the same orange frizzy hair as their mother. 'Dickie and Fiona.'

'They look lovely,' Kitty said.

Audrey smiled, pleased by the remark. 'They can be a handful for their *ayah*, though.'

Kitty looked at her blankly.

'That's what we call nannies out here,' Audrey explained. 'Apparently it's the name they used in the British Raj – in India.'

Kitty stored the term away for later use, wondering how it was spelled. Noticing that Audrey's little girl was now waving, she lifted her hand to respond.

'Oh, dear.' Audrey frowned. 'Now she's coming over.' Jumping to her feet, she hurried towards the paddling pool to head off the child's advance.

Kitty watched her, puzzled. It was strange that mothers came here to relax, but kept a distance from their children. She guessed the joy of being a parent wore off in time. And here in Kongara, African nannies were probably quite affordable. One thing was for sure: she and Theo would not be handing their children over to be cared for by others. Kitty recalled Theo's wistful stories of his child-hood. He'd virtually lived in the nursery and then the schoolroom. Louisa was always keen to send him off with his nanny. He'd made it clear he wanted something different for his children. They'd eat with their parents every night. His sons could make friends with whoever they liked, and choose their own careers.

Theo's beliefs about the ideal family life had been one of his favourite topics of conversation when he and Kitty first met. They seemed to have so much time to talk back then. In that year before the war really began, Theo would escape from his studies whenever he could and take Kitty flying in the little red plane. Landing on the private airstrip of some friend of his, they would walk to a hilltop or other scenic spot. They'd spread out an old travelling blanket, embroidered in the corner with the initials of one of Theo's fore-bears, and unpack a picnic. As they ate and talked, they laid out their dreams for the future. Theo's plans never included Hamilton Hall. He regretted that he was going to disappoint his parents so deeply, but he didn't approve of inherited privilege. People should make their own way and there should be opportunities for all.

Kitty used to listen, mainly. Her own experiences of life were so different – so limited – that she had little to contribute. Sometimes she talked to Theo about her family and what it was like growing up in Australia. But since she'd already told him how desperate she'd been to escape from her life on the farm, he found it hard to see why she now talked of what she missed. She tried to describe to him how she longed to be part of the early-morning bustle at Seven Gums – her mother trying to get the boys washed and dressed for school, the cats getting under everyone's feet, the warm smell of porridge on the stove. Someone burning toast and throwing it out the window. Missing shoes. Ripped shirts. Lost buttons. Kitty's father running in from the yard to get something he'd forgotten, clipping a pair of wrestling boys over the ears as he passed. All the small details of family life . . . She wanted to be part of it, yet she didn't want to go back. It was hard to explain. It was much easier just to sit quietly, absorbing Theo's ideas about the world. She loved to watch how his whole face lit up as he shared his beliefs.

His almost childlike passion, clothed in the authority of a man of conviction, was irresistible. But he had changed so much since then. So many things had happened. Now, as Kitty eyed the nannies with their charges, she felt a twinge of uncertainty. She and Theo hadn't talked in recent times about how they would raise their children. His views could well have altered – and if that were the case, Kitty knew she would have to engage an *ayah* for her family whether she wanted to or not.

As Kitty watched Audrey trying to coax her daughter to remain with her *ayah*, her eye was drawn towards the edge of the grounds. A high wire fence marked the perimeter. The inside world of concrete, water and bright umbrellas was in stark contrast to the dusty bushland beyond. There was a tree growing close to the fence, not far from the paddling pool. Two African children sat in its branches. They gazed, transfixed, in through the wire.

'Those poor children,' Kitty commented. 'They must wish they could swim.'

Alice summoned a waiter who was standing near an outside bar. She didn't say anything to him – just gestured at the fence. The waiter strode towards it, waving his arms and making shooing noises. The children scrambled from the tree and ran off.

Pippa took that moment to announce she was going to have a swim.

'Me too,' Sally said. She began tucking her hair into a bathing cap.

'Are you coming, Kitty?' Pippa gave her a friendly smile.

Kitty hesitated. She felt guilty, picturing the wistful faces of the children who'd just been banished.

'Come on,' Sally said. 'Take the plunge!'

Kitty stood up. She'd have to get used to situations like this, she told herself – it was part of living in Africa.

Pippa and Sally led the way over to the shallow end of the pool where there was a set of concrete steps. As they lowered themselves into the water, Kitty moved away to the deep end. She always preferred to jump in. If the water was cold, she liked a brief shock rather than a slow immersion. In a hot setting like this, she enjoyed the sudden coolness.

She dived in, making a neat splash, then let herself glide forward, long and streamlined. Breaking the surface, she moved straight into a strong crawl. She'd forgotten the joy of pulling her body through the water, losing herself in the rhythm of turning her head, breathing in, then blowing out a stream of bubbles. She didn't stop until she reached the end of the pool. There, she stood up, sweeping back the hair from her face, wiping the water from her eyes. After a few seconds, she froze. Everyone was staring at her. She checked the ribbons that held up her top, but they were still secure. She couldn't guess what was wrong. At a loss as to what else to do, she swam another length, then another. After five laps, she stopped again. It was only then that she saw Pippa and Sally. They were swimming sedately along, heads held high out of the water, arms and legs moving in a gentle breaststroke.

Kitty swung herself out of the water with her arms and sat, panting, on the side. She gazed down at the image of her face, fractured by ripples. She knew she'd made an exhibition of herself. People on the other side of the pool were still looking at her. Even the African *ayahs* had shifted their attention from their charges. Kitty turned around to gauge Diana's reaction. She was surprised to see that Diana was the one person not looking in her direction. Instead, she was watching Alice, who was standing nearby, lips pursed, arms folded across her chest. On Diana's face, there was no sign of the disapproval or dismay Kitty expected to see. Rather, there was a glint of amusement in the grey-green eyes, a twist of satisfaction on the crimson lips. Diana appeared to be enjoying the upset caused by the Australian. Kitty turned back to the water, now feeling puzzled as well as embarrassed. Diana was the most senior wife, who Theo claimed set a 'terrific' example. Yet right now, she looked just like a mischievous child relishing the sight of someone causing trouble.

Near midday, there was a sudden outbreak of activity at the tables by the pool as women, children and *ayahs* prepared to go home for lunch.

Diana levered herself into a sitting position and stretched lazily. Instead of standing up, though, she reached into her bag and took out a magazine. 'I'm going to stay.' She flicked open the cover. 'I'm not hungry. And Richard is bound to be running late. He can fend for himself.'

Kitty frowned at her in alarm. Theo was expecting her home. And she was looking forward to seeing him.

'Don't worry,' Diana said, as if picking up her thoughts, 'James will take you back before he collects Richard.'

'Thank you.' Kitty smiled with relief.

'I'm sure your husband will be glad to see you,' said Alice primly.

'There's a lot to talk about,' agreed Kitty.

Diana raised her eyebrows but made no comment. She called over a waiter and instructed him to summon her driver.

Outside the Club, Kitty stood in the shade of a bougainvillea the size of a tree. Several different plants had combined to form the huge mass; there were purple, apricot and white flowers all mixed together. Kitty looked across to the car park, where people were piling into their vehicles. No one else had a driver, like Diana. Kitty watched women manoeuvring with caution, grating the gears. She thought smugly how she had learned to drive around the farm before she'd even left primary school. She hoped it wouldn't be too long before Theo bought the second car. Then she shook her head, surprised at herself. How quickly she'd become used to the idea of having a car of her own!

James drove faster than he had when Diana was present. As they bumped along the rutted road Kitty saw an object rolling around on the floor by her feet. Reaching down, she picked up a glass bottle full of pink pills. She read the label, written in loopy red script, in much the same style as the words on the Kongara Club crockery. *Dr Newman's Safe Effective Blood Tonic*. Kitty rested the bottle on her lap. She wasn't sure what to do with it. If she placed it on the seat beside her, Diana would know she'd seen the pills. But on the other hand, at least they would be found. In the end, Kitty put the bottle back on the floor.

As they drove on, she felt it there, nudging her foot. There was something sinister about the bright colour and round shape of the pills. They were like sweets to tempt a child. Kitty knew she shouldn't speculate about what might be wrong with Diana – ill health was a private matter. But she couldn't help thinking of her

Auntie Madge, who was said to suffer from nerves. She behaved in odd, unpredictable ways; no one knew where they stood with her, or what she might do next. Madge took a blood tonic as well – not pills like these, but a blue syrup that reminded Kitty of horse medicine. Kitty glanced down at the bottle of pills. It made sense to her now – how Diana had reacted to the shock of the child nearly being run over, and how strange she'd been at times this morning. Diana was unwell. She had a disorder of the blood. Yet she looked so healthy and strong.

They soon reached the busy hub of the settlement. As they approached Head Office, Kitty searched anxiously for Theo's Land Rover – she hoped he hadn't gone home already and found his wife absent. She was relieved when she saw the smart, boxy shape with the canvas top parked outside the main tent. A black Rolls Royce stood next to it. When they drew near, Kitty peered at the car. It was bigger than the Daimler, the sweep of its contours even more extravagant. But it was older, the paintwork dull. There was even a dent in the bumper bar. Kitty guessed it belonged to the Manager of Agriculture – Alice's husband. A picture of the world of Kongara was beginning to form in her head. Diana, wife of the General Manager and resident of number 1 Hillside Avenue, was at the top of the tree. Kitty was at number 2. Presumably Alice lived next door, in the third house. Kitty was pretty sure their husbands were on an equal footing. That meant she and Alice were on the same rung – but with the complication of Kitty having the better address. Part of Kitty wished she could have been an ordinary resident of Kongara – someone who just worked hard and was barely noticed. With a pang, she thought of Paddy and the other engineers. She wondered how they were settling in, and when she would have the chance to see them.

Without any warning, James slowed the car to a walking pace, steering off the road onto the bushy verge. Kitty heard grass brushing the undercarriage. Before she had the chance to ask what was happening, she saw a vehicle coming towards them. It was neither jeep nor truck nor tractor, but a bizarre combination of all three. It had narrow, old-fashioned tyres and bulbous headlamps set close together. The cabin was like an open-sided shed with a timber frame, the steering wheel fixed onto a section of fence. The dented bonnet – once red – was covered in a thick coating of dust. There were several Africans sitting in the back, and a fair-skinned man at the wheel. In front of him, mounted on the bonnet, was a wooden box. Kitty's eyes widened. There was a naked child crouched there, clinging on with two hands. She caught her breath, shocked. Then she saw it was a monkey.

The vehicle was close now, the rough noise of its engine cancelling the purr of the Daimler. Kitty took another look at the driver. He was in old bush clothes, like the ones Bowie had been wearing, but he had no hat; unruly hair stuck out from his head. He was much younger than the hunter. He gripped the wheel as if fighting to keep control. For an instant, she found herself meeting his gaze. Even at a distance his eyes were striking, his expression impenetrable yet strangely intriguing. As he was passing, he gave a salute. Kitty quickly raised her hand in reply. But just as promptly she dropped it, realising the gesture had not been directed at her – the man was acknowledging James for giving the road over to him.

Kitty leaned forward. 'Who was that man?' She wondered why James deferred to him. Perhaps he wanted to make sure the Daimler was safe; the kind of person who drove such a contraption might well be a reckless driver.

'Bwana Tayla.'

It was an unusual name, Kitty thought, until she guessed it was probably 'Taylor', with the second syllable shortened to sound like a vowel. 'Does he work for the OFC?' Even as she asked, Kitty thought it was unlikely. He was far too scruffy. And there was something about the way he handled his vehicle – as well as the interaction with James – that suggested a longer history in this country.

'He does not,' James confirmed. 'Londoni people – they do not like him.'

'Why?' Kitty asked.

The driver shook his head. 'I do not know why.' The tone in his voice suggested he was not prepared to elaborate.

Kitty looked over her shoulder. The vehicle lurched along the road, receding quickly. Black smoke came from the exhaust. It was burning oil, Kitty knew, like her father's old Chev truck. Thinking of the trusty workhorse evoked a wave of pain and guilt, dragging her thoughts from the present. She hoped the truck was still going – she didn't want to think about what would be happening if it wasn't. Her father had intended to replace the Chev when his mother-in-law finally died, using the inheritance. He'd also drawn up plans to rebuild the shearers' huts. He reckoned he'd tolerated his mother-in-law's visits for years, putting up with her airs – her insistence that she be called Gloria, for example, not Grandma like any other grandmother – and this would be his reward. However, the old woman had secretly changed her will.

She'd left some jewellery to her daughter, and various possessions to be shared between her grandsons. But she'd left all her money to Kitty.

This shocking fact had been revealed at the reading of the will in the solicitor's office in Sydney. To the family's astonishment, Kitty had been required to attend. Mr Walker had explained the situation in a calm, unrelenting voice. The instructions he'd been given were very clear. It was the prerogative of the deceased alone to make choices about his or her estate – and his client had decided to make her granddaughter her main beneficiary. Kitty had sat in the corner of the office, grasping the carved wooden arms of her chair while her father expressed outrage and disbelief. Her mother had joined in. Mr Walker had remained unmoved.

'It's just mischief,' Kitty's father had declared eventually. 'It won't make any difference to how the money's spent.'

'Of course it won't,' his wife had agreed. 'We're all family.'

But Mr Walker had pointed out that the money was to be held in trust until Kitty turned twenty-one, in three years' time. The only purpose for which it could be used before then was for Kitty to travel or study.

'Travel? Study?' Her father had almost choked. 'What on earth does that mean?'

'Gloria wanted me to go to England,' Kitty had explained. 'She wanted me to become an artist.' It had sounded mad, even as she said the words. But it was true. Ever since Kitty had emerged from childhood and been able to meet her grandmother on more equal terms, Gloria had been telling her stories about her life as a young woman in England – the museums, the art galleries, the artists she knew. When Kitty won first prize in the Agricultural Show for a drawing of a horse, Gloria had declared that her granddaughter possessed a gift for drawing. It had to be nurtured.

'One day, you'll go to England and become an artist.' Her voice had been clear and firm, stating a fact. 'This place is too small for you.'

Kitty had drunk in the praise, never imagining that the vision would one day become reality. When she looked back, she saw that during her visits Gloria had spent her time dropping tantalising clues to another world – far from this harsh, sorry place the Miller family called home. Kitty always gave up her bedroom to the visitor, and for days after her grandmother had gone, she could smell perfume – not the plain scent of rose or lily of the valley, but a rich, spicy fragrance that had been made in Paris. Sometimes there was a silk shirt or a pair of stockings left behind. And there was always a novel. They were not classics of the kind Kitty sometimes borrowed from one of the school teachers, but newly published books ordered from abroad with titles like *Gone with the Wind, The Snows of Kilimanjaro* and *Tender Is the Night*. They were all stories of faraway places – of lives that were interesting and glamorous. That the heroines very often endured heartbreak didn't prevent Kitty wishing she could swap places with them. Now, whenever she thought of the books, they were linked in her mind with the smell of wool and sheep manure. She had read them in the shearing shed when it was not in use, careful to keep their existence a secret, especially in the weeks after each visit. Kitty's mother claimed she liked having Gloria as a guest, and she was polite and cheerful during the visits, but afterwards she'd be edgy and brittle – tough on the boys and Kitty; even rude to her husband. It was not a good time to carry out a task carelessly – or to be caught wasting time with a novel or sketchbook.

Kitty gazed past James's shoulder at the road ahead. With the red dust and sundried bush she could almost have been back in New South Wales. She tried to imagine what life was like now at Seven Gums. At least she knew all of her family had survived the war. She'd managed to contact an old schoolfriend via the Wattle Creek School; a kind teacher had sent Kitty's letter on and Myra had replied. Myra didn't know the Miller family well, but she had been able to convey the wonderful news that they were all alive and in good health. Farmers were engaged in essential work, and so her father had never enlisted. Jason had joined the navy and fought in the Pacific, but had come safely home. Tim was declared unfit due to his weak heart, the result of having had rheumatic fever. The other boys were too young to be involved. Kitty had nearly wept with relief as she'd read the letter. She wrote straight back to Myra, begging for more information – any little scrap or titbit about them. But she didn't get a second reply.

Before leaving England to join Theo, Kitty had sent a letter home explaining that she was moving to Tanganyika. She'd made it clear that any mail addressed to *Mrs Theodore Hamilton, Kongara, Tanganyika Territory, East Africa*, would reach her. But she expected this letter to be ignored like all her others. An envelope bearing her handwriting would probably not even be opened. She'd shamelessly put herself first. The fact that she had – as it turned out – been able to live out her grandmother's dream for her was neither here nor there. She'd chosen against the family – and she did not expect to be forgiven.

*

Resting her hands on the verandah railing, Kitty gazed out over Kongara. Theo was standing nearby. They'd carried their drinks outside to watch the sunset.

'They call it a sundowner here,' Theo commented, raising his glass. Kitty watched his profile as he tipped back his head and drank. He looked deeply familiar to her, and yet foreign at the same time. When he'd come home at lunchtime, running late and loaded down with a heavy briefcase, their greeting had been polite, even slightly awkward. On his return from work a short time ago, the same reserve had been there. Kitty felt an odd sense of dislocation from her husband that she suspected he shared; it was as if their hearts hadn't quite caught up with their bodies. They were together, yet still apart. But then, Kitty had only just arrived. And it was a big adjustment, being reunited here in Africa. In no time, she felt sure, they would settle in with one another and relax.

The red globe neared the horizon, sinking fast. Suddenly, the view was transformed. The ugly rawness of the encampment blended into the landscape. In the far distance, the vast scar of the plantations was softened into a rose-tinted plain. Then, the sun disappeared and there was just deep velvet blackness. Kongara was a sparkling veil of lights, alluring and mysterious. Out at the Units there were lights as well.

'That's the accommodation for the workers and contractors,' Theo explained when Kitty asked what was there, down on the plains. 'They have everything – shops, bars, tennis courts. There's no reason for them to come into Londoni. They even have a club with a swimming pool, and a Catholic church.' He shook his head admiringly. 'It's such a huge undertaking. The plantations themselves are just a part of it. We have to provide everything that people need.'

'It's extraordinary,' Kitty agreed. 'The scale of it . . .'

'And we've a big job to do with the local people – the Wagogo. That's the name of the tribe, believe it or not. Apparently one native on his own is called an Mgogo.' He smiled, looking pleased with his knowledge. 'Anyway, the thing is, we're bringing them from the Stone Age into the twentieth century in one big step. We have to, if we're going to change the way they use the land.'

'It looks rather barren,' Kitty said carefully. 'More like sheep country than a place for plantations.'

Theo waved his cigarette dismissively. 'We can change everything with modern equipment and methods. But there's no point tinkering around the edges – they tried that in Jamaica. If we're going to provide margarine for the housewives of Europe – and we're talking long-term; decades, not years – we need an agricultural revolution.' He spoke boldly into the gathering darkness. 'And that's just what the Groundnut Scheme is going to bring about.'

'Are all the peanuts going to be exported to Europe?' Kitty asked. She remembered Billy, the Middlesex engineer, giving his speech on the plane about the war on hunger. Surely vegetable oil was needed here too.

'Well, yes – it's all for export,' Theo said. 'But the Scheme offers lots of opportunities for the Africans – employment, for a start.' He turned to Kitty. In his smart clothes, his jaw clean-shaven, he was the epitome of a civilised Englishman. 'And they'll inherit it all one day. When they're ready, Britain will hand over Tanganyika to the Africans. That's what we're working towards for them. Independence.'

Kitty looked at him in surprise. 'Will Australia stop being a colony as well?'

Theo laughed. 'Of course not. It's not the same. These people are black!'

'Are all of them black?' Kitty knew she sounded like a schoolgirl, and Theo her teacher, but she couldn't help being curious.

'A lot of Indians have been here for generations and consider themselves Tanganyikans. There are some Europeans who've been around for a long time too: Germans left over from when they were in charge here; some Greeks and Italians. There are even a few Englishmen, born and bred out here – odd types, most of them, I imagine . . .'

Kitty remembered the man who'd driven past the Daimler in the half-timbered vehicle, the monkey sitting on the bonnet. Perhaps he was one of these misfits . . . When she described the encounter to Theo he almost spat the man's name.

'Taylor!'

'Who is he?'

'He's *persona non grata* around here, to put it mildly. The original naysayer. He wrote a report early on assessing the proposal for the Scheme. He's some sort of local farmer. He questioned its viability – but it turned out he was just trying to protect his own interests. He's had to eat his words now, of course.' Theo shook his head. 'He's a nasty piece of work.'

Kitty could feel the tension emanating from Theo; his voice had a strained edge. She regretted having mentioned Taylor at all.

'Don't worry,' Theo continued, 'you won't have to cross his path. He's been banned from the Club. If we had our way, he'd be banned from the whole bloody place.'

Kitty rested her hand on his arm. 'See all those lights – they make Kongara look like a fairyland.'

Theo breathed out slowly. Finally his expression softened. 'Yes, they do.' He turned back towards the house. 'I'm quite hungry. What's today?'

Through the windows, Kitty could see Eustace placing Cynthia's serving dishes on the dining table. Cold beef, vegetables, potato salad. She gave a wry smile. 'It must be Tuesday.'

FOUR

Kitty glanced over her shoulder as she walked past the vegetable plot towards the end of the garden. There was no sign of Eustace and Gabriel; they were safely preoccupied in the pantry. Kitty had discovered them there after breakfast, crouched over the rat-proof bins that contained dry foods. Apparently, they were carrying out the monthly inventory of supplies, following some complicated procedure Cynthia had devised. Two weeks had passed since Kitty had become their new mistress, but the pair still ran the house as if the previous memsahib was in charge. The gardener, on the other hand, happily took instructions from Kitty. But he worked so inefficiently that the results were barely evident. He was out of sight as well, pruning bougainvillea at the front of the house.

The rear boundary was bordered by a tall hedge of a leafless, succulent shrub that the gardener called *manyara*. Lines of the plant marked out spaces all over Kongara – the edges of car parks, roads, gardens and even the small fields that were called *shambas*. Kitty walked along until she found a section that was sparse enough to push through. Shouldering her way between the shrubs, she snapped a branch. Milky sap oozed from the cut ends. Kitty shrank away from it; she'd been warned that if it got in your eyes, you went blind.

She checked her shirt for sap. It was the old one Janet had given her. As soon as Theo had left for work that morning Kitty had changed out of the cotton frock she'd worn at breakfast, dressing instead in these bush clothes, and putting on a pair of pull-on riding boots she'd brought with her from Australia. She'd felt guilty about deceiving Theo, but it was easier than explaining to him that she just didn't want to go to the Club, the tennis courts or the shops today. She was tired of listening to talk of face creams that prevented shine, or the strips of tape you could wear between your eyebrows while at home, to train yourself not to frown. She was worn out with the task of either responding to Diana's erratic ways, or discreetly ignoring them. She just wanted to be on her own.

On the other side of the hedge, Kitty crossed a strip of untidy ground that was neither tame nor wild. She found the remains of an abandoned maize plot, a few clay shards from a broken pot, and a tree trunk with all the smaller branches hacked off. Picking a path towards the brow of a low hill, Kitty took her bearings carefully. She knew better than to walk off into unknown territory without making a plan to find her way home – she'd grown up with stories of children getting lost in the bush, never to be found again. Janet had assured her that lions, elephants, rhinos – even buffaloes – normally left humans well enough alone unless they were taken by surprise or provoked. Snakes were a much more serious danger. As Kitty wove her way between thick clumps of grass, she kept her eyes fixed on her feet. Only when she reached the crest of the hill did she stop and look up.

She caught her breath, stunned by the beauty of the land spread out in front of her. A flat plain stretched away towards the foothills. Between patches of bush were wide swathes of bare earth – deep orange-red. Clumps of grass glowed golden against it. Here and there were giant baobabs with broad fluted trunks and strange twisted branches with no leaves. Each of them stood alone, as though the sheer power of their presence required separation from one another. Lifting her eyes to the hills, Kitty saw a carpet of soft green, scattered with ochre boulders. Beyond were the mountains with their steep rocky peaks. And above, a sky of flawless blue.

It was an artist's landscape. The sky was pure ultramarine. *Terre verte* – 'green earth' in French – would make a perfect grey-green for the leaves, whose pastel shades reminded Kitty of the drought-proof gums and wattles of New South Wales. The shadows on the fluted tree trunks were a deep purple. (Not black, of course. There was no such thing as black.) To get the right tone for that, you'd use the same blue as the sky, plus a dab of red – Alizarin Crimson. Even the name of the paint was exotic. The pigment came from the root of a plant in the madder family. Humans have been using it since ancient times. A fragment of cloth dyed with madder was found in Tutankhamen's tomb. The same dye was used to make the famous jackets of the Redcoats. Yuri had taught her this.

'You have to understand your paints,' he'd told her. 'How they are made, what they can do. The artist must know the whole story.'

Kitty shook her head, pushing the memory away. She knew she shouldn't be thinking about Yuri, or about her life as an artist. That was the deal she'd made with Theo – and with herself.

Certain parts of the past were not to be discussed. They were not even to be remembered.

She walked on a short way towards where a large boulder. It had a flat top, almost as if it had been sculpted as a seat. She sat down, propping her elbows on her knees, resting her chin in her hands. As her gaze travelled over the plains she felt her thoughts beginning to wander again. In the house on Millionaire Row she found it easier to keep her memories boxed up, packed away. And if they did escape, it was not too hard to rein them in – she could feel Theo's presence in the air, watching over her even when he was at work. But out here it was different. The land was so vast and open, with nothing to hide. Beside the power of the mountains, the strength of the massive tree trunks, and under the endless skies, Kitty felt small. Who she was, what she had done, meant nothing. It didn't seem necessary, or even possible, to put up walls in her mind, dividing now from then.

As she sat there in her stone seat, she gave in to the memories that crowded at the edges of her mind. They rose up, vivid and detailed as the scene spread before her – carrying her back to another time. It was before the war. Before she'd met Theo, even. She'd only recently arrived in England, a young Australian abroad. One of the biggest adventures of her life was just about to begin . . .

On the steps of the British Museum, a pigeon pecked at some scattered grain. There were a few seeds near Kitty's feet. She watched the bird move boldly up to her, then jab its beak towards the grey stone. It was midday and the sky was clear, but there was no heat in the sunshine that gleamed on the bird's silky plumage. Kitty leaned against one of the massive columns that stood along the façade of the building. Cold seeped in through her coat and the soles of her shoes. But she barely noticed it. Her mind was full of images, impressions, of all that she'd just seen. She'd only walked out of the museum moments ago – the hushed air of the place had barely left her lungs – but already she was looking forward to revisiting the grand galleries full of art.

The scale of the paintings had struck her first: the sheer size of the canvases with their ornate gold frames. Then the colours – so rich and deep compared to photographs of masterpieces she'd seen in one of Gloria's books. But it was the texture of the paint that had captured her attention the most. She'd leaned as close to the works as she was able, attracting dubious stares from the attendant standing in the corner. She saw how the pictures were made up of thousands of individual brush strokes. Yet when she stood back, everything came together into a single image. It was like a miracle.

The pigeon flapped away, drawing Kitty's eye. It settled again, further down the steps. A young woman with red hair stood there, accompanied by two men. Kitty recognised the trio from inside the museum. They'd been examining the paintings as well, pointing to different parts of the canvases. The woman had even taken out a book and scribbled a few notes. Kitty had watched them from the corner of her eye, keeping very still, as if they were a species of wildlife that might easily be prompted to take flight. She'd studied the way they dressed, the way they behaved. The woman had an oversized coat that she might almost have borrowed from her grandfather. Snatches of bright red were visible at the neck and sleeve. Her hair was piled on her head in a messy heap, with strands hanging loose. The men wore tweed jackets, patched at the elbows, and soft collared shirts. One had a paisley scarf with sparse remains of fringes on the ends. They were at ease in the gallery, talking quietly but freely, undaunted by the frowning attendant.

Out here on the steps of the museum, they were even more relaxed – chatting and laughing together, the men smoking. Then an earnest look came over the woman's face, suggesting a more serious conversation. She used her hands to add emphasis to what she was saying. The men nodded with enthusiasm.

Kitty watched the interaction, unable to hear any words, but picking up on the shared interest that flowed between the three. She felt a wave of envy, backed by acute loneliness.

Two weeks had passed since she'd left the home of the Harris family. They were distant relatives of her grandmother's solicitor, Mr Walker. When he'd learned that Kitty's parents – while stopping short of obstructing their daughter getting a passport – had made it clear she would be travelling abroad without family support of any kind, he had stepped into the role of advisor. He'd told Kitty where to stay in Sydney while she was preparing to leave, and had helped her book her passage on the ship. He'd even come to the wharf to wave goodbye, smiling at the young woman's excitement over her tourist-class cabin – the place she'd call home for the six weeks of the voyage.

Mr Walker had arranged for Kitty to stay with the Harrises when she arrived in London, for as long as she needed. They were polite and kind, and seemed happy to have Kitty as a guest. But the house was very quiet. Mr Harris spent a lot of time at his club; Mrs Harris rested for much of the day and listened to the radio in the evenings. Kitty went out on a few excursions – visiting the Tower, and going to see Picadilly Circus and Big Ben. Aside from that, she spent many long hours in her room. She set herself drawing tasks – a draped scarf, a wilted flower – and read some books borrowed from Mrs Harris. The solitude Kitty had longed for, after living with four noisy brothers, did not feel like a luxury any more. Her basement room had a barred window, set at pavement level. When she sat by it, watching the passing parade of feet – shoes and boots, delicate and sturdy, old and new – she felt she was in a prison cell. Flipping back through drawings and paintings she'd made on the voyage – chaotic impressions of the Port of Bombay, dreamy watercolours of ocean sunsets – made her current situation feel even more dreary.

When she could stand it no longer, she made plans to leave. She thanked Mr and Mrs Harris for their hospitality and gave them a sketch she'd made of their house. She'd stood in the park opposite while she worked on it, resting her sketchbook on the wrought-iron fence. Using shading to highlight contrast, she'd made the building look dramatic, standing out from its neighbours. The couple had been surprised and pleased. Whether they were happy or dismayed that their guest was leaving, Kitty could not tell. As she left in a cab, having been vague about her destination, they wished her well.

When the cab reached central London she sat forward, looking out for the first glimpse of the famous Savoy Hotel. As the grand façade came into view, she felt a shiver of excitement. It ran through her whole body, a tingle in her blood. A man in a smart uniform opened the door of the car. Stepping out onto the forecourt, she squashed a sense of panic. Coming here was such a mad, extravagant gesture. She felt like a young woman in a story by F. Scott Fitzgerald – Bernice, Honoria, Josephine – or even the author's real-life wife, Zelda. They all stayed in places like this. But that was not why Kitty had chosen it. The Savoy was Gloria's favourite hotel. Kitty was certain her grandmother would have approved of her coming here.

Trailed by a porter carrying her scuffed old suitcase, she walked with her head held high – mimicking Gloria's confident posture. The old woman had always pulled herself up to her full height when preparing to make an entrance, whether to a shearing shed, church or the general store. Kitty suspected that the doormen, so smart in their top hats, knew she was an interloper, but they displayed impeccable courtesy. When she was shown to her suite – the cheapest available – she'd been silent with awe.

'Is there something wrong, madam?' the bellboy had asked.

She'd shaken her head, still lost for words.

For a week she'd stayed there, taking lunch and dinner in the dining room, and breakfast on a tray in her suite. In the foyer she chatted to other guests – the ones who were friendly. She found their questions about Australia amusing and confusing by turn. Did she have a pet koala? Could she whistle on a gum leaf? Had she seen an Aborigine? Kitty had to consider how to answer that last one. She felt sure these English people were not picturing someone like Gunja, the itinerant farmhand who turned up to work at Seven Gums when it suited him. He had black skin and a mop of wild hair like Aborigines in picture books, but he wore ordinary clothes and carried a rifle instead of a spear. She made do with vague remarks about boomerangs and corroborees, hoping not to be asked for details.

Each morning and afternoon, she wandered in the nearby streets. She found interest in everything, from the luxurious shops to street carts, from ladies dressed in daytime furs and jewels, to a litter of stray kittens. The British Museum was only a few minutes' walk away. Sometimes she went there just to look at the building itself. It was like a vast Roman temple with its row of fluted columns topped by a frieze depicting ancient figures dressed in robes. She felt there was a connection between this icon of London and the gold statue of a Roman soldier that was mounted over the entrance to the Savoy. The act of coming and going between the two places made her feel as if she belonged here – that she'd made this corner of London her own.

By the time she'd paid her bill, the funds in the bank account Mr Harris had opened for her were alarmingly depleted. She carried her own suitcase from the foyer and hurried past the doormen, shaking her head at the cab drivers. She set off for a place she'd noticed on one of her trips to the museum. There was a hand-drawn sign in the window of a soot-stained townhouse: *Rooms Available. Cheap*.

Since moving in there, she'd been truly alone. Her landlady showed up only to collect the rent, and her fellow lodgers hardly ever appeared. At least one of them worked at night and spent the days asleep. For companionship, Kitty had to make do with odd smiles or brief words exchanged with people she met in passing – while handing in her coat at the museum, or paying for food in the little pie shop she discovered. She asked herself what she'd expected, setting off on a journey by herself. Of course she was going to be lonely. The truth was, she'd pictured experiencing London as Gloria had – taking part in a whirl of parties and gatherings, meeting artists and authors, making friends and maybe even falling in love. But Gloria had been a sophisticated, educated woman who knew how to form connections. Kitty was just a simple girl from the bush. Even when she dressed up in some of the clothes she'd inherited from her grandmother – like the cream silk shirt, or the tailored dress and jacket that Gloria had declared to be timelessly stylish – she didn't feel she carried them off. And when she wore her homemade skirts and shirts, or the hand-knitted cardigan given to her by Mrs Harris, she felt old-fashioned and boring.

Kitty peered along the museum steps to where the red-haired girl still stood chatting with her two friends. In that big overcoat, someone else would look like a tramp – yet on her it was almost glamorous. Perhaps style was something you were born with, Kitty thought – or else it went with your address. If either were the case, she had no hope of making an impression on anyone.

While Kitty was still watching, the woman pulled back her heavy sleeve and consulted a wristwatch. The men put out their cigarettes, grinding the butts under their heels. Then the three walked off down the steps towards the street.

Kitty could almost feel the warm aura of their camaraderie fading as they moved away. After only a moment's hesitation she found herself heading after them. She didn't intend to say anything. She just wanted to watch them a little longer. If they went to a teashop, she might go in there too. Or else, after a short while, she'd just let them go. She wasn't ready yet to return to her small, cold room, where the curtains, the bedding – perhaps even the wallpaper – smelled of stale cigarettes, fried sausages and mould.

She walked just behind the woman, observing her blood-red shoes. Their style was a perfect mix of glamour and practicality. Unlike the coat, they were brand-new.

Before long, the three turned smartly onto a concrete path that led across a stretch of lawn. They were joined by other young people, walking in groups, in pairs or by themselves. Up ahead was a big stone building with grand pillars and a rounded portico. Kitty assumed it was another museum.

She kept her gaze fixed on the woman's shoes as she followed her up a set of steps and in through a high, wide doorway. In the middle of a large lobby, Kitty faltered. The place didn't seem quite like a museum. People were walking around too quickly, talking and laughing loudly. They carried too many bags and books. There were several marble sculptures on display – ancient-looking statues of male and female nudes. But they were grimy with dust. And the finely formed figure of a man, occupying an alcove near the entrance, had a tartan scarf tied around his waist. Kitty was aware of the three friends disappearing down a corridor. A man in uniform hovered by a desk. Kitty pretended to study one of the other sculptures while she decided what to do. On the wall next to her was a glass-fronted cabinet containing a noticeboard. Kitty glanced over a series of papers pinned up inside. She scanned them quickly, taking in phrases like *Memorandum to All Students* and *Notice of Referral*. There was one that kept recurring, both in headings and small print. She stared at the words as if they contained a rare magic.

The Slade School of Art.

After just a few moments' hesitation, she turned on her heel and marched down the corridor, pretending she knew exactly where she was going.

There was no sign of the three people she'd followed in here. She walked steadily, her footsteps loud on the bare floor. Ranged along the corridor on both sides were banks of locked cupboards with numbers painted on them. Each one belonged to a student, Kitty guessed. There must be other corridors with other lockers, because the numbers she saw were in the three hundreds. There were more grey-white sculptures. A faint, elusive fragrance – like pine needles – drifted on the air.

Reaching a door that stood partly open, Kitty slowed her step. On tiptoes she crept up to it. Peering inside, she saw a dozen or so figures – mostly men but a few women too – standing at easels, painting. They were ranged around a central dais, which was the focus of attention. A woman sat there on a wooden chair, completely naked. She gazed out over the room with vacant eyes, while the students scrutinised her body. Her breasts were heavy; her nipples were round circles of dusky pink. Kitty took a step back. The image of a dark triangle of pubic hair stayed with her. She knew artists worked from life – just today she'd seen an oil painting of a man at work in his studio, with a naked woman as his subject. But still, she was shocked.

She moved cautiously to the doorway again. Keeping her eyes well away from the model, she looked at the students. Dressed in loose smocks that were densely patterned with paint marks, they all held a palette in one hand and a brush poised in the other. On each of the canvases was a painting in progress. Even Kitty could see that the works were of varying standard. Some showed clumsy shapes, lumpy and heavy. Others were made up of lines that were timid and weak. None had come close to truly capturing the softness of skin, the moulded muscle beneath, and the deeper strength of bones. Kitty hugged herself with her arms, as if holding in a secret joy. What a huge task it would be to learn how to achieve this! But what a wonderful quest to undertake.

A silver-haired man with an upright figure roamed between the students. Even at a glance, he was impressive. There was a sense of authority in the way he moved, and though he must have been in his sixties, he was still handsome. Kitty saw how the students stiffened as he came near, leaning back from their canvases, eyeing his face. She watched them taking in his words: a middle-aged woman struggling against despair and humiliation; a young man smiling with raw delight.

Kitty studied the students in turn, wondering who they were and how they'd got the chance to be in a place like this. She thought of the red-haired woman with her careless manner and extravagant shoes. Envy gripped her in its vice. These people had everything – paints, canvas, easel, model, teacher. They had a place to work, and the gift of time as well.

She pushed the door further open to see more of the studio. The hinges creaked loudly. The teacher turned around. As his eyes found her, Kitty froze. For a second, he too was immobile. Then he took a step towards her. Kitty jumped back out of sight. She made herself walk calmly away down the corridor. She'd done nothing wrong, after all. But she quickened her pace as she heard the door creak again, then footsteps coming behind her.

'Wait! Please.'

Reluctantly, she stopped. She didn't want to be pursued into the lobby, to be confronted by the man in uniform.

She turned to face the teacher. For a long moment, they just looked at one another. He wore a silk shirt, open at the neck, and a brown scarf. Silver hair grew from a receding hairline, falling to each side of his face, fanning out around his ears. He was like someone from the past, a character in a play. As he lifted his hand, rubbing his face, Kitty noticed a ring with a turquoise stone – the first she'd ever seen on a man. It repelled her and intrigued her at the same time.

'Do not go,' he said. It sounded more like a command than a plea. 'I want to talk to you.' He had a strong foreign accent.

Kitty eyed him in silence. He was studying her intently. His eyes were a bright blue, untouched by age. His brows were raised slightly in surprise. Kitty wondered if he had mistaken her for someone he knew.

'Are you a student here? I have not seen you before.'

'No, I'm sorry. I just came in . . . for a look.'

The man held out his hand – long-fingered, lean, with traces of paint in his nails. 'I am Prince Fyodor Yurievitch. People call me Yuri.'

As Kitty took his hand in hers, she wondered briefly if she'd heard him correctly. She recognised his name as Russian, from reading *Anna Karenina*. It fitted with his accent. But why would a prince be teaching at a London art school? It occurred to her that he might not be telling the truth. On the other hand, there was something about him that suited the idea of royalty. The students were almost reverential towards him. His personality seemed to fill the air, making everyone else look pale and short of space. 'My name's Kitty.'

'Kit-ty.' He said her name slowly, stretching out the two beats. 'Kitty,' he repeated. 'I want to paint your portrait.'

The girl stared at him, shocked. She thought of the chair in the studio, the naked woman.

'You will keep your clothes on, of course,' Yuri said quickly. 'I should have said that straight away. Just your face. Neck and shoulders. Nothing more.'

Kitty shook her head. 'I couldn't possibly.'

'Not here. Come to my house. It's only just outside London. I'll send a car. Bring a friend if you like.'

She laughed incredulously. Then she searched his face. He was completely serious. 'I don't even know you!'

'All of London knows me.' Yuri sounded impatient, rather than proud. 'You can see my paintings in the British Museum. In Buckingham Palace.' He waved an arm, taking in his surroundings. 'I am a Professor Emeritus here at the Slade.' He gestured back towards the studio. 'People beg to sit for me.'

She just shook her head again.

Yuri began to pace. He took quick looks at Kitty, viewing her from different angles. Then he stopped, suddenly, as if an idea had come to him.

'Are you an artist, Kitty?'

'No. I'm not.' She answered him firmly. But then she pictured her stacks of sketchbooks, every page covered front and back with drawings. And the dozens of paintings she'd taken down from the wall of her bedroom before she left. Her denial was an affront to all the hours she'd spent on them, working secretly in the shearing shed. All the tears that had fallen, smudging the pencil lines, the grubby tracks left by the rubber, the holes torn through cheap paper. She met the man's gaze. 'A bit.'

His expression lightened. 'I will make you an offer. Come and sit for me. I will teach you.'

Kitty's lips parted. She saw herself wearing a smock, a palette in her hand. She pictured herself squeezing tubes of paint, mixing colours. In the classroom along the corridor, she'd seen one of the students holding up his brush in front of his eyes. He seemed to be using it to measure the proportions of the model. There was so much Kitty could learn. So much she could be taught. Yearning broke inside her, invading her body. But when she thought about the man's request, reality took over. He wanted her to come to his home, outside London. They might be there alone; Kitty didn't have a friend to take with her. What kind of girl would even consider such an offer? 'I'm sorry,' she said. 'It's not possible.'

He turned his head from side to side as though to prevent her words from reaching him. 'Please. I have to.' His hands were clasped together, the knuckles white.

Kitty looked at him in confusion. He sounded almost desperate. She glanced back towards the studio. There were people in there he could paint. He could probably choose a model or a student from anywhere in the art school. It was impossible that a farm girl from Australia, who lived in a cheap room and ate pies and mashed potato for tea, could have anything special to offer him.

'Why me?'

'Why you?' Yuri was quiet for a long moment, his hand resting thoughtfully over his mouth. He seemed to be trying to choose the right words. 'Because . . . you are perfect for the painting I want to do.'

'But why?'

'You look like a Russian girl.'

Kitty frowned at him in surprise. She had no idea what a Russian girl might be like. 'I'm Australian,' she protested.

'Lift your face, turn it to the left,' Yuri instructed.

Kitty responded obediently.

'Ah, yes. You are perfect for her.' He sounded pleased, but there was an odd look in his eyes – one of sadness, perhaps, or regret.

Kitty took a step back, eyeing him uneasily. 'Who? Who am I perfect for?'

'No one real,' Yuri said quickly. 'A real Russian girl would be easy to find. What I want is someone who looks like the *idea* of a Russian girl.' He fixed her with a gaze that was almost fierce. 'What I want is you.'

A sudden rustling sound coming from the shrubs nearby pulled Kitty back to the present. She stared around her, instantly alert. She was puzzled: she'd made no noise or movement that might have caused some creature to slither or scamper away. Moments passed, with everything remaining quiet and still. Eventually she relaxed, turning back to the view. She watched a large bird, like an oversized crow with a patch of white on its chest, swoop down to land in one of the baobabs. Its stark black shape joined with that of the tree. The branches looked so stunted – out of proportion with the vast trunk. They were more like roots than limbs, Kitty thought, as if the whole tree had been planted upside down.

From behind her there was the snap of a breaking twig. She spun around. The leaves of a bush were moving as though a breeze had stirred them – but the air was still.

Kitty scanned her surroundings. Between two tall shrubs she glimpsed a piece of ochre cloth, a dark head, an arm. She caught the whites of a pair of eyes. Then she saw the figure of a man holding a spear – standing so still he was almost completely camouflaged. Near him, Kitty now saw, was an old woman bent over like a wind-blown tree. Not far away stood a child.

Kitty got slowly to her feet. She'd been lost in her thoughts, she realised, and not heard their quiet approach. The young man stepped forward. As if at his signal, the bushes became alive with movement. Men, women and children, young and old – even a couple of dogs – emerged. Before long, Kitty was completely encir-cled. Suddenly, she felt far from the shelter of her garden. It came to her that no one knew where she was.

She swallowed nervously. '*Hamjambo,*' she called out. Greetings to you all.

Smiles lit up the faces. The greeting was repeated again and again, travelling through the crowd, being checked over and approved.

'*Hatujambo, Mama.*' It was the old woman who spoke.

'*Shikamu.*' Kitty's next greeting was the one required when addressing someone older or more important. I kiss your feet.

'*Marahaba,*' came the reply. Only a few times.

There were more murmurs of approval. Kitty began to relax. She looked at the figures standing around her. They were draped in traditional plain-dyed cloths, men and women alike revealing bare chests, bare breasts. She saw pierced ears, the lobes so enlarged that they hung in loops to the shoulders. There were elaborate hairstyles, male and female. Strings of beads. Skin daubed with red mud, paint and ash. The wide grins revealed strong white teeth – though all of the men, she noticed, had one front tooth missing and a single round scar burned in the middle of their foreheads. She guessed these were ritual markings of the tribe Theo had mentioned – the Wagogo.

The people gathered closer. Kitty stiffened as hands reached out to touch her shirt, her arms, her hair. She smelled cow dung and wood smoke, along with the taint of urine and sweat. Their closeness added to the heat of the sun. Kitty wiped her brow with her hand.

A young woman thrust a child towards her. Kitty recoiled instinctively. The little boy's eyes were gluey with pus, his mouth crusted with sores. His head wobbled weakly on a swollen neck. The mother smiled as if all were well. Kitty peered into the crowd. She saw, now, that many of the children were malnourished. Janet had taught her the telltale signs: frizzy hair leached of its colour, dry scaly skin, protruding stomachs. She even saw a teenaged boy whose forehead scar, though clearly once healed up, had broken down at the edges into a raw sore. Some of the adults were in poor health as well – a few appeared seriously ill. One man had nodules of flesh all over his face and half of his nose had been eaten away. Another held his head at an angle, his neck distorted by a large lump.

Kitty swallowed on a wave of nausea. Her skin began to crawl. Faced by the mother's complacent manner, she felt almost angry.

'*Mtoto wako ni mgonjwa*,' she said to the young woman. Your child is sick. 'Why do you not take him to the hospital?'

Hospital. The word was passed around, meeting blank looks.

She tried another word. '*Dactari?*' Doctor.

Now they understood. The mother pointed at a leather pouch tied around her child's neck. Kitty recognised a witchdoctor's charm; Janet had told her about them, too. According to the missionary, the methods the witchdoctors used – whether they involved superstition or native medicines – ranged from useless to life threatening.

The man holding the spear, whom Kitty had seen first, stepped up close to the child and his mother. He spoke in simple Swahili. 'I have told her. She must take the boy to the Mission.'

'Is there a doctor at the Mission?' Kitty asked.

'There is no doctor. But the white lady, Sister Barbara, she has good medicine.'

Kitty shook her head. 'This child needs to see a proper doctor.' She thought of the hospital she'd seen on the tour of Londoni that had been arranged for her by Theo. Lisa had guided her proudly through the facilities provided by the OFC – cinema, pharmacy, veterinary clinic, library. The hospital was in a big, new concrete-block building. It consisted of two wards, an operating theatre and an outpatients clinic. At the time of Kitty's visit there had been a child in one ward, recovering from having his tonsils removed. A man with a bad cough was the only patient in the other. Neatly made beds stretched out, empty, to either side of him. In Outpatients, a fair-haired man in dirty work clothes was having a gash in his arm stitched up. The place was anything but busy.

Kitty felt the gaze of the young man. She wondered if he knew about the hospital. She guessed people like these would not be welcome there. There could be a clinic for African workers down on the Units – but since Kitty didn't know if there was, or if these people would be treated there, she said nothing. She was relieved when a teenaged girl drew everyone's attention by lifting up a strand of Kitty's hair.

'*Maradadi*,' she said admiringly, as she let it fall. Smart. Beautiful.

'Thank you.' Kitty imagined what they'd have thought if she hadn't had most of her hair cut off. The soft thick strands were so utterly unlike their own tight curls. She smiled at the girl. 'What is your name?'

Before she could reply, the old woman called out – her voice was cracked with age, but Kitty grasped her meaning: Do not tell your name to this white lady!

For a second, Kitty was offended – she was just being friendly. But then she remembered Janet mentioning that many Africans believed a name held power over its owner. Exchanging names required trust.

'I am sorry,' she said to the old woman. She wanted to acknowledge that she'd been wrong to ask such a question, but the Swahili was beyond her.

The woman seemed to understand. She bowed her head, accepting the apology. Unwilling to risk making another mistake, Kitty remained quiet. She just watched the people while they, in turn, watched her. Seeing more evidence of ill health – and even hunger – she wished she had a solution to offer. Whatever help the people were able to get from the local missionaries, it was not enough. Janet had been quite right. The need, here in Africa, was so great.

Soon the Wagogo started chatting among themselves, occasionally directing a comment to the foreigner in their midst. Kitty began to make cautious replies. Time passed unnoticed, but then she realised she should head home before Theo arrived for lunch. She pointed back the way she'd come. 'I must return to my house.'

She set off in the direction of Millionaire Row. Without hesitation, the people joined her. A child sidled up and took one of her hands; another followed suit. At first, Kitty was distracted by the fear that they had skin infections or infestations of lice that would spread to her. But the little hands felt so small in her hers, the children's gestures so trusting, that soon she did not want to let them go. A song began and grew as it gathered voices. The young man strode ahead, kicking sharp stones out of Kitty's path with his bare feet.

As she walked, Kitty found her eyes drawn to the women – the older ones with withered breasts draping their bony chests; the mothers suckling babies, nipples oozing milk; and the young girls with perfect little mounds that barely moved as they walked along. They were all completely unselfconscious about their bodies. They might have been models posing in a studio without walls – subjects of a painter like Yuri, whose only interest lay in stripping back the layers, seeking the truth of flesh laid over bone.

The people accompanied Kitty until the garden hedge came into view. Then they dropped away – moving as quickly and silently as they had when they'd made their first appearance – leaving her to carry on alone.

*

'You wouldn't believe it, Kitty.' Theo pulled a starched white napkin from its ring and laid it over his lap. 'Down at the Units today I saw a foreman ask some Africans to move a load of wheelbarrows that had just been delivered. They had to be put away in the store.' He gave a dry laugh. 'The men picked them up and carried them on their heads! You've never seen anything more absurd.'

Kitty smiled as she smoothed her own napkin over her knees. 'Could I come to the Units with you one day?' she asked. 'I'd love to see what's happening down there.'

'There's not much to see – for all the work that's been put in. I suppose I could arrange it some time. Just a quick look.'

'I don't mind waiting there while you do your work.'

Theo shook his head. 'That's not the issue. It's just not the place for you to be. If you knew the types we've got down there, you'd agree. Those Irish bulldozer drivers – they set off for the day with a bottle of brandy in each pocket. That's breakfast and lunch. We have to send them to Nairobi to get dried out every six weeks. If they weren't so good at their jobs, we wouldn't put up with them for a minute.'

Kitty watched Theo cut a slice of his schnitzel. There was a separate weekly roster for lunch menus, she had discovered, and today was crumbed steak. She let him swallow his mouthful before speaking again. 'Could I visit the Tractor Workshops, then? Lisa said they were here in Londoni, but she didn't include them in the tour.'

'Why on earth would you want to go there?'

'Remember how I met those engineers on the plane? They told me they were going to be teaching the Africans about engines. I've been thinking – I might be able to help.' Kitty tried to slow down her words. She didn't want to betray the fact that she'd spent quite some time considering the idea after her encounter with the Wagogo. She'd decided she simply had to find something useful to do with her time. 'You see, none of them know a word of Swahili.'

'Out of the question.' Theo sounded shocked. 'They're a rough lot as well. It's a man's world out there.'

'But there are women working in Londoni. I've seen them.'

'Of course there are – secretaries, nurses, hairdressers and what-have-you. But they're single women who have come out here to make a contribution. And it's no picnic for them, I can tell you. We've got them accommodated in rondavels. You've probably seen them – mud huts with canvas tops?'

Kitty nodded. The tiny round buildings were interspersed with the tents in the area around Head Office.

'We've had incidents where intruders have tried to climb over the walls at night. The OFC has actually issued machetes to the ladies so they can defend themselves.'

Kitty tried not to look shocked. She pressed on. 'Are there no married women working here, then?' It seemed surprising. During the war, all kinds of women had joined the workforce in England: age, marital status and social standing were no barrier. Kitty herself had volunteered in a factory for a while, painting camouflage designs on aircraft. Most of the women had given up working when the servicemen were de-mobbed – some returning rather reluctantly to their domestic duties. But here in Kongara there was a shortage of people and an oversupply of work. Everyone was busy and stretched.

'There are a few married women,' Theo conceded. 'They're staff wives with no children.'

'Like me.'

Theo sighed. 'No, not like you. You are married to the Manager of Administration. It would be absolutely inappropriate for my wife to have a job – let alone one that involved hanging around at the workshops. I can't believe you don't see that.'

Kitty cut her slice of schnitzel into small pieces, her knife scraping harshly on Cynthia's bone china.

'So how was your day?' Theo asked.

Kitty didn't answer straight away. When she'd returned from her walk she'd felt guilty about how easily she'd slipped back into her artist's mindset – looking at the landscape and then remembering how she came to meet Yuri. She'd decided to keep her adventure to herself. But after the things Theo had just said, she felt a surge of rebellion. 'I went for a walk. By myself.'

'Where to?'

'Behind Londoni, up towards the mountains.'

'How did you get out there?'

Kitty pointed in the direction of the back garden.

Theo frowned in disbelief. 'You mean you just walked off into the bush?'

'I'm used to being in the bush.'

'This is not Australia! There are wild animals out there.'

'I didn't see any,' Kitty said. 'But I met some local people. There was quite a large group of them. They seemed to be just wandering around. Like me.'

Theo put down his knife and fork. 'That was a dangerous and foolhardy thing to do, Kitty. Some of these bush Africans have had virtually no contact with civilisation. Who knows what they could have done.'

'They were friendly, actually.'

'Promise me you won't do anything like that again!' Theo said.

'Then what can I do?' Kitty looked down at her hands, gripping the edge of the table on either side of the rose-patterned plate. She didn't need to remind him that he'd made her give up the one pastime she loved, and that she'd always been able to do.

'Go to the Club, go shopping. Do what the others do. Surely it's not too much to ask?'

Kitty said nothing.

'Soon we'll have to begin entertaining. It's expected, you know. That will keep you busy.' Theo caught Kitty's eye, smiling while chewing.

She took a sip of water, then found it hard to swallow. She had a bleak vision of the days stretching ahead, battling Eustace and Gabriel at home and being wary of her every step in the world outside.

Theo ate a couple of mouthfuls, then put down his knife and fork again. 'Kitty, you may not think your role here is important, but in its own way it's as vital as mine. Your job is to set an example to the other wives. Kongara is a small world, where everyone has his place. If one part functions badly, the whole project will suffer.' He looked intently at her. 'You believe in what we're doing here – don't you?'

Kitty gave a shamefaced smile. He sounded so kind and reasonable. She remembered how the man on the plane had talked about the war on hunger. 'Yes. Yes, of course I do.'

Theo settled back in his chair. 'Good girl.'

FIVE

Late-morning sun pierced the haze of the mosquito nets. They hung down, draping the bed, as if it were still night-time. Kitty lay on her back, her arm shielding her eyes. Her skirt was twisted uncomfortably around her legs, and she thought of getting up and changing back into her nightie. Instead, she just rolled over. It seemed to take all the effort she could muster.

She pictured her new red Hillman parked out in the driveway, gathering a thick layer of dust. It had been at least two weeks since Theo had brought the car home, presenting the keys to his wife with great ceremony.

'Your very own car.'

Kitty had thrown her arms around him in excitement. 'Oh, thank you. Thank you so much!'

They'd stood together by the car, arm in arm, remarking on the shape, the colour, the shine. Kitty thought it resembled a mini version of Diana's Daimler, but Theo insisted it was completely different. It wasn't brand-new like the Land Rover but the man who'd had it shipped from England had looked after it well. The car had been transported from Dar es Salaam by rail, and since then it had only ever been driven around Londoni.

Kitty opened the driver's door. The hinges were rear-mounted, swinging the opposite way to any other car she'd been in. Taking her place behind the wheel, she switched on the ignition. There was no anxious waiting while the engine turned over without sparking – it kicked into life almost instantly. Kitty grinned up at Theo as she revved the motor.

'Don't go driving too fast, will you,' he warned. 'With roads like we have here, you have to take it slowly.'

Kitty didn't bother telling him that she'd never driven on a sealed surface in her life; in fact, she'd spent more time driving around in paddocks than on roads of any kind. She'd never had a licence, but she was a skilled driver. She could manoeuvre a laden truck, her rear view obscured. She could back a horsebox or trailer into a tight spot, first try. Here in Londoni, apparently, all it took to pass a driving test was to steer down the main street without hitting anything.

'Look at this.' Theo showed Kitty how the front windscreen could be wound out to let in the breeze. 'And if the motor for the wipers ever breaks down, you can do this.' He turned a knob on the dashboard and the wipers jerked their way over the dry windscreen.

'It's hard to imagine needing wipers out here at all,' Kitty commented.

'Just you wait until the rainy season,' Theo said. 'They say the whole place changes overnight.'

Kitty tried shifting gear into reverse, then checked all the lights. Everything worked perfectly. Even though she hadn't driven while in England, she felt immediately at home behind the wheel.

Too soon it was time to lock it up and go inside; Theo had had a long day, and wanted his sundowner. Kitty hung the key ring from her finger as she strolled towards the verandah. The keys jangled cheerfully.

Theo paused near the French windows, turning back to her. 'You'll have to be careful with the front doors mounted that way. If one comes open while you're driving, it'll be flung right back with great force.'

'Don't worry. I'll be careful.' Kitty was touched by the concern on his face, his desire to keep her safe. It was a taste of the old attentive Theo coming back.

'Of course,' he added, 'there'll be no trips to the Tractor Workshops or the outskirts of Londoni. And it goes without saying, the rest of Kongara – including the Units – is out of bounds. In fact, there should be no need for you to drive anywhere but to and from the town centre.'

Kitty faltered mid-step, but said nothing. She knew she shouldn't be surprised. They'd already discussed that there were parts of Londoni where it was unwise – or unsuitable – for her to go. She told herself she should be grateful for what she would be able to do. Having her own car meant she could choose what time she went to the Club or the shops and when she returned home. She wouldn't have to feel beholden to Diana or Alice for giving her lifts. Nor wouldn't she have to negotiate her way through any more loaded conversations or uncomfortable silences while trapped in a neighbour's car. But as she followed Theo inside, her overriding feelings were of disappointment and frustration – something wonderful had been dangled in front of her, then abruptly snatched away.

In the days that followed, she'd made the trip to the town centre most mornings. She'd driven slowly to extend the journey. Once, she'd even done several laps of the roundabout, all the while wondering about its generous scale: the lane was wide and the circle large, suggesting it had been designed to carry lots of traffic. There was a big sign in the middle bearing the words GIVE WAY. Kitty doubted if two vehicles had ever yet encountered one another there.

She'd driven past signs marking the road to the Units, the railway, and Dar es Salaam. She'd even stopped by one that said Tractor Workshops – but only for a few moments. Everywhere she drove in her eye-catching red car, she was aware of being watched. She suspected that if Theo ever wanted to, he could get a report on her every move.

Kitty turned over again, burying her face in the pillow. She felt frustrated and confused. Theo might be making a fresh start here in Londoni – looking to the future of this promising British territory, opening his mind to new ideas – but his change of approach clearly did not apply to his expectations of his wife. Theo had made it plain that she was to conform completely to the protocols of Londoni society. He wanted her to be another Diana.

Kitty thought back to the early period of their relationship, before they were married, while Theo was still at university. After the day when he'd first taken her up in his plane he'd begun flying home every weekend and making excuses to come to the Garden House. He appeared to enjoy the chaos of the studio, not minding when he picked up paint spots on his clothes. He said he preferred the casual meals Kitty and Yuri shared in the kitchen to the formal dinners in his own home. He loved Kitty's long hair, the way it

hung free around her shoulders. When she wore cast-offs from
Yuri's life models – a red silk jacket, a velvet beret, a man's paisley
scarf – he complimented her on her unusual dress sense. Kitty
had been swept away by Theo's admiration. He was so unlike any
man she'd ever met. He knew so much. He talked about music,
theatre, books as if they were his friends. Every item of clothing
he wore, every possession he produced – from his wallet to his
diary, even his shoehorn – was so finely made. And as for his face,
his body – he reminded her of a statue of a Greek god, straight
out of the British Museum. She loved and desired him with every
part of her being. But all along, she'd found it hard to believe he
really wanted to be with her. Theo Hamilton of Hamilton Hall.
A scholar from Oxford. He could have chosen from any number
of girls whose background and accomplishments were more in
keeping with his.

One day she'd asked him, openly and simply. 'Why do you like *me*?'

He'd smiled, tracing the curve of her chin with his finger.
'Because you're different to anyone I know.'

Theo's mother certainly thought Kitty was different. She took
every opportunity to point out how 'Australian' her son's girlfriend
was. How unlike 'us'. Louisa may have thought this would turn
Theo off Kitty – bring him to his senses – but she'd been wrong. In
fact, Theo seemed to take pleasure in his mother's dismay. When
he introduced Kitty to friends of the family, he took care to say she
was an artist, as well as the daughter of an Australian sheep farmer.
A girl from the outback. There was a note of pride in his voice, a
protective look in his eyes. Kitty had the feeling that, if necessary,
he'd defend her from criticism with his last breath.

All that had changed. The shift had begun during the war, as Theo's views of the world altered, and continued into peacetime. Then there had been the scandal, which had rocked Theo and his family to the core. He'd been drawn even further back into the Hamilton fold. And Kitty had been responsible for that. So how could she complain?

Kitty sighed. She bunched the pillow into a ball, then pushed it away and lay flat on her back. The air was close and hot. The mosquito nets, draped around her, might have been the walls of a prison.

Hearing a knock at the bedroom door, Kitty lifted her arm, keeping her eyes closed against the sun.

'Yes?'

'Memsahib?' It was Gabriel. 'Do you wish anything?'

'*Kwenda mbali*,' Kitty said rudely. Go away. She'd already told him there was no need to prepare lunch today. Theo wasn't coming home – he had to take some visiting executives from London to the Club for a meal – and she was not hungry.

She listened to Gabriel's footsteps receding, then let out a deep sigh. Opening her eyes, she gazed dully around the room, taking in Theo's dressing gown hanging on a coathanger. Her own, dropped on the floor. There was the pot plant she'd bought from the stall at the Club. A label hung from the main stem; the name of the plant, scrawled impatiently by Diana, was barely legible. Elsewhere in the house were another half-dozen pot plants. Kitty had bought up all the ones that had been left over at the end of the afternoon. She wanted to support the effort to raise funds for the missionaries. Gabriel had rolled his eyes at her, aware that it would be his job to water them. He could not understand why anyone would bother to look after a plant that produced no food.

Suddenly Kitty sat up, staring at the pot plant with new eyes. She remembered what the young Mgogo man had said about Sister Barbara helping the sick. She knew the Mission was not far away – Audrey had made several trips there in her car to collect all the plants.

Kitty threw back the sheet and jumped out of bed. As she rummaged in the tallboy for her bush clothes, she tried to imagine what Sister Barbara would be like. The missionary hadn't been there at the stall – no doubt she was too busy. Kitty pictured someone like Janet, with her thick-rimmed glasses and no-nonsense manner.

Pulling on the skirt, Kitty glanced at her reflection in the mirror. Her hair was tousled and she had no make-up on. She wasn't even very clean. But that didn't matter – a mission was not the kind of place where people were concerned with showing off their looks. She thought back over the first-aid and basic nursing training Janet had given her, as an adjunct to the Swahili classes.

'In Africa,' she'd said, 'everyone is a nurse and sometimes a doctor as well.'

She'd shown Kitty how to put on a bandage, clean a cut, treat a burn, and taught her other useful skills. And Kitty knew how to work hard – she'd grown up helping out in the shearing sheds, where time was short and the days were long and no one ever complained.

Dressed and ready to go, she paused by the bedroom door. A knot of misgiving formed inside her when she thought of how Theo might view the plan she had in mind. But surely he could not object? Helping a charity was not the same as having a job.

Louisa herself approved of supporting worthy causes. It was a duty, she had often said, to be carried out by those who held positions of privilege.

Even so, Kitty listened out for Gabriel before creeping down the hall, carrying her boots in her hand. Outside the front door, there was no cover – the gardener or the guard could be anywhere. She flew down the steps in her socks, the key poised in her hand. Swinging back the door, she jumped into the car. She put on her boots, and then – sitting low in her seat – she switched on the ignition and drove sedately away.

As soon as she'd left Millionaire Row, Kitty began looking out for someone she could ask for directions. She slowed the car as she approached a group of women walking along the side of the road. They were a colourful sight, several of them wrapped in shop-bought *kitenge* cloths with brightly printed designs. They had babies slung on their backs, the little dark heads bobbing as they walked.

'*Samahani!*' she called to them. Excuse me!

They ran off into some nearby bushes. Kitty sighed, feeling oddly rejected. The next person she saw was an old man sitting in the skimpy shade of a *manyara* bush. Beside him was a woven cage containing chickens. She called across to him.

'*Iko wapi misheni? Na taka kwenda kule.*' Where is the Mission? I want to go there.

The man jumped to his feet, picking up his cage before running over to the car. '*Naenda, sasa hivi!*' he announced. I will go with you, right now!

'No, no, I will not trouble you. I just want you to —'

Ignoring her protestations, he opened the back door, obviously familiar with operating the handle. He shoved his cage along the seat, then climbed in after it. Kitty stared at him helplessly. She felt sure his presence in her car was a breach of protocol, but he didn't look inclined to remove himself. He sat back with a grin on his face, already enjoying the experience of being in a car.

'Well, thank you,' she said. 'Is it very far?'

He shook his head. 'It is near.'

'Let us go, then.' Kitty forced a smile. She would be glad when they got out of Londoni – hopefully unseen – and made it to the Mission.

As she drove off, she glanced at him in her rear-vision mirror. He wore a black suit coat, stained and frayed, along with an ochre-red loincloth. His skinny chest was bare. Beside the mark of the Wagogo in the middle of his forehead was a second scar left by an old burn. The expression on his face was open and friendly, with no hint of the cynicism or resentment – or plain animosity – Kitty sometimes saw in her house staff.

They had almost reached the first bungalows of the Toolsheds when the man suddenly leaned forward, jabbing the air with a knobbly finger. 'This way.'

There was a turn-off to the right. Kitty guided the car onto a narrow road bordered by sparse bush and grass. Before long, she came upon a fenced enclosure set back from the verge. It was packed with heavy machinery. The giant vehicles were like a herd of animals crushed in a holding pen with no space to spare. Kitty slowed down, looking more closely. There must have been twenty of them, all the same. Each had a single wide roller in front and two narrower ones at the rear. Kitty frowned, puzzled. She'd seen vehicles like this before, both in England and Australia, flattening out the surface of tarmac roads. But in Kongara, all the roads were made of gravel and earth. There was no possible use for them here. She eyed the tall grass that poked up between the rollers and the chassis, and the creepers that entwined the engines. The vehicles had just been moved here out of sight, she realised, and left to gather dust.

She drove on, keen to leave the makeshift depot behind. With Theo in charge of Administration, she liked to think of Kongara as being a place that was run smoothly and efficiently. Yet a whole fleet of useless machinery had been sent all the way from England, unloaded at the port of Dar es Salaam, then hauled inland by rail to Kongara. It made no sense. Kitty was reminded of Diana's report that enough cases of Angostura bitters had recently been delivered to the Kongara Club to flavour the cocktails of every Englishman in the whole of Tanganyika for fifty years. Meanwhile – according to Pippa – there were long lists of vital equipment and supplies that the OFC had not yet been able to provide. Kitty told herself that mistakes were inevitable in a venture of this scale. What mattered was the outcome of the work. And going by Theo's latest reports, the labourers were at last beginning to make more headway with the landclearing. As long as progress was kept up, they'd soon be back on schedule. Kitty wondered if – when that happened – Theo would spend less time talking about the Scheme. What would they discuss instead? Neither would risk topics that might lead back to the world they'd left behind. Art, novels, poetry – life in general – would all be off limits. They'd have to resort to chatting about recent events. The picnic in the hills that had been organised by the Club – an elaborate venture with a marquee and silver ice buckets. The play put on at the school. The incident at the pool, where an *ayah* had slapped a child. Or they could go over who had said what to whom after church on Sunday . . . Kitty frowned at the thought. She'd probably prefer to hear about Theo's work problems – even though she found that very frustrating. When she'd joined her husband in Londoni, she'd hoped that each evening they would go over the events of his day together. He would air any worries and concerns he might have and she'd help him find solutions. She'd grown up on a farm, after all, and knew more than he did about agriculture. But already it had become obvious that Theo wasn't interested in seeking advice or input from his wife. He wanted to unload his numerous problems but not in enough detail for it to serve any real purpose. Kitty's role was to murmur sympathies, or offer words of encouragement – and that was all.

Just a short distance further along the road, the old man directed Kitty to take another turn to the right. She let the car idle as she peered doubtfully along a track that was narrow and rough. She was about to ask if he was quite sure of the directions, when she saw a small wooden sign almost hidden by a clump of dry grass. The red-painted lettering had faded almost to nothing, but she could still make out the word *MISSION* and the shape of a cross.

Turning onto the track, Kitty tried to picture the kind of place she was about to encounter. She remembered the photograph she'd seen of Janet's mission headquarters: the long, low building with thick whitewashed walls. There were no flowers growing around the doorway, no curtains in the windows. The concrete verandah was clean and bare. It was the perfect setting for a life that was simple and selfless, where only serious things mattered.

As she drove on, Kitty thought about the time she'd spent with Janet. She had been introduced to the retired missionary by the vicar of the village church, after it became general knowledge that Theo and his disgraced wife were moving to the colonies. Janet was one of the few people in the congregation who showed no interest in who Kitty was, or how she'd found her way into the Hamilton family. There was no sign she was even aware of the trouble Kitty had caused. Janet was concerned only that the young woman should be equipped for her new life in Africa. She had explained that she'd worked in neighbouring Kenya, but that the two countries had much in common.

Kitty had accepted an invitation to afternoon tea. She had no intention of becoming friends with the elderly lady; she simply wanted to glean some practical information. When Theo had accepted his position on the Groundnut Scheme, Kitty had never even heard of Tanganyika. She'd had to consult an atlas to locate the country. The OFC had sent some information – population figures; maximum and minimum temperatures in the capital, Dar es Salaam; a list of items to pack. But Kitty was keen to meet someone who'd actually lived in Africa.

Janet had ushered Kitty into a poky sitting room containing dated furniture. Heavy olive curtains hung at the dusty windows and a dull carpet covered the floor, but the atmosphere was lifted by bright African cloths covering the backs of the armchairs. There was a collection of artefacts as well. Kitty took a seat beside a large cow-skin drum. Not far away was a squat three-legged stool that must have been carved from a single piece of tree trunk.

While Janet went to the kitchen to boil the kettle, Kitty crossed to the far wall to study a hand-drawn map of East Africa that was mounted there. The countries were named in capital letters – KENYA, UGANDA, CONGO, TANGANYIKA. They were all blank, apart from Kenya, which had been shaded in pink pencil and marked with cities, towns and villages. Lengths of blue wool, held by drawing pins, linked place names with photos stuck onto the borders of the map. Most of the pictures were close-ups of men with clergymen's collars, but there were several women and a few African men as well. Kitty searched their faces for clues that they were leading adventurous lives. But they looked no more interesting than the folk in the village church.

Moving to a sideboard, Kitty picked up a small model of a native grass hut. The words *Anglican Missionary Society* were painted on the roof. Nearby was a slot for coins. She rattled the loose change inside. The model was surprisingly light. Kitty saw that it was made from *papier mâché*. Yuri had shown her how to produce a sculpture using nothing more than torn newspaper, flour and water. The method didn't allow the fine modelling that could be achieved with clay and plaster and wax, but it was cheap, and the finished work was easy to move around.

'And if you don't like your creation, my dear,' Yuri had said, 'it makes a good fire.'

Kitty stared down at the little hut balanced in her hand. The memory of Yuri brought a stab of pain to her heart. Tangled emotions rose inside her – grief, anger and guilt. But most of all, a deep sense of loss.

The door swung open and Janet entered. Kitty returned to her seat. After setting down a tray bearing a huge enamel teapot and some plain white cups and saucers, Janet pulled up a chair and sat in front of her guest. She removed her thick glasses, revealing a gaze that was direct and intense.

'Now, Mrs Hamilton . . .' She leaned close to Kitty. 'It's quite simple, really. You need to know how to look after yourself. And how to help others.' She counted off her fingers. 'One. You must learn to speak Swahili – it's widely used in East Africa. If you need to know a tribal language too, you can pick that up when you get there. Two. You want to have some basic nursing skills. And three —' She stopped as Kitty raised her hands, warding off the words.

'But I'm not going to be a missionary,' Kitty said firmly. 'I'll just be living there.'

'My dear,' Janet said kindly, 'when you get to Africa, you'll see. It doesn't matter who you are or why you came. There will be work for you to do.'

By the time they'd finished their second cups of tea it had been agreed that Kitty would return to the house each morning to take lessons in Swahili and bush nursing. In return, Kitty would make a donation to the missionary society. Janet gave Kitty her own well-worn copy of *Teach Yourself Swahili* to study in between times. The language was quite easy to learn, Janet claimed: the spelling was phonetic and the grammar consistent. Kitty decided she wouldn't tell her parents-in-law what she was doing. The whole subject of Tanganyika was too fraught with tension. Even though Theo was due to leave in under a month, no one referred to the move unless absolutely necessary. She didn't plan to tell Theo, either. It was going to be her secret. She imagined how amazed and impressed he was going to be when she arrived in Kongara already on the way to being fluent in Swahili! Luckily, her absences from the Hall would not attract any interest – either from him or his parents – since she'd already developed a habit of taking long solitary walks on the estate each morning after breakfast.

A sharp corner made Kitty slow down once more, bringing her attention back to her driving. She leaned forward over the steering wheel to get a good view of the terrain ahead. Easing the car over a deep rut, she managed to prevent the bumper bar ploughing into the ground. Now moving on at walking pace, she scanned the bush to each side of her. She saw an abandoned mud hut – the walls crumbling, the roof gone – but no other sign that anyone lived around here. She called over her shoulder to the old man, while pointing in the direction they were headed.

'Safi sana?' The direct translation of the words was 'very clean', but she knew they could also be used to mean 'very correct' or 'definitely right'.

'Ndiyo.' He nodded vigorously. 'Na Swahili yako safi sana!' He smiled at her, showing bare grey gums. 'Safi sana sana!'

Kitty smiled back, touched by the compliment. She could see in the old man's face that he really meant what he'd said – her Swahili was very, very correct! But then she wrinkled her nose, picking up the smell of fresh chicken droppings, instantly familiar to her from years of collecting eggs on the farm. She hoped she'd get the chance to wipe down the seats before the green stain sank in.

The track wound up a steep rise. Kitty drove almost at walking pace so that she could take her eyes from the road. She realised they were now in the foothills.

'*Hapa! Hapa!*' Here! Here! The man leaned over the front seat, pointing towards the brow of the next hill.

A white cross came into view, mounted on a tall spire roofed with clay tiles. As the car crept closer, the top of a bell-tower became visible, then the gabled roof of a church. The whitewashed building stood out starkly against the vivid blue sky. Kitty stared in surprise – it didn't look like a humble mission chapel.

Moments later, another large white building was revealed. Kitty brought the car to a halt as she took in an imposing façade, two storeys high, with a row of arched openings at ground level. In front of the two buildings was a wide forecourt paved with pale stone. The middle portion was shaded by the biggest baobab tree Kitty had yet seen in Tanganyika. Nearby were garden beds filled with flowering trees and shrubs; she glimpsed plots of neatly sown vegetables as well. The bright reds and purples of the bougainvillea, set against the white walls with the sky behind, made a striking image – it reminded Kitty of photographs she'd seen at Hamilton Hall of the family travelling on the Continent. Leaving aside the African tree, the scene in front of her could have been a little piece of Italy or Spain. There was an air of tranquillity about it. The place seemed deserted. The only movement was made by a flock of pigeons scouring the cracks in the stone pavement under a long trestle table set up outside the church.

Kitty steered the car into the shade of a jacaranda tree and climbed out. As she straightened her skirt, she noticed the air was cooler up here; there was even a slight breeze. The old man climbed out too, removing his chicken cage and placing it near the trunk of the tree. Motioning for Kitty to follow him, he led the way past the church, and on towards the other building. He aimed for an archway near one end, where a thin yellow curtain hung over an open doorway.

'*Hodi!*' he called out. Someone is here!

Though there was no response, he pushed past the curtain and disappeared inside. Kitty followed him, blinking in the sudden gloom. She took in a large room lined with sofas and armchairs, all made in the same simple style, with dark timber frames and cushions for the seats and backs. Some were draped in coloured blankets assembled from crocheted squares, just like the ones Kitty's great-aunt used to make. On the walls were several photographs and prints of old paintings.

'Look at them carefully,' Kitty's companion instructed. He ushered her proudly towards the pictures, as if showing off rare and valuable artworks. She identified the handsome face of Jesus as a young man from her Sunday school classes – except here, he had a wide yellow halo and his chest was mysteriously transparent: golden light streamed from his red heart, which was encircled by a crown of thorns. The next image was a black-and-white photograph splotched with age. It showed a frail figure with a pale shrunken face, snowy beard and long black robes.

Into the quiet came a slow, shuffling footstep. A stooped old man – almost identical to the one in the photograph – entered the room. He exchanged friendly greetings in Swahili with the African; clearly they knew one another. Then he turned to Kitty, speaking in a language she didn't recognise. Seeing her blank reaction, he switched back to Swahili.

'Welcome, daughter. I am Father Paulo. How can we help you?' He had a strong accent and Kitty struggled to understand even these simple words.

'*Mimi nataka* Sister Barbara.'

He raised a pair of white bushy eyebrows. His face was deeply lined, and there was a tremble in his voice. Thinking he might well be deaf, Kitty repeated herself more loudly.

Father Paulo looked confused. Then he muttered to the African, who nodded and hurried outside.

'*Momento.*' The priest gave her a benign smile. He gestured for Kitty to take a seat, then settled himself into a chair, folding his hands in his lap.

Neither of them spoke, but there was nothing awkward about the lack of words. From outside came the contented sound of pigeons cooing and the rhythmic swish of someone sweeping.

Very soon, footsteps were heard on the flagstones. Kitty stood up just as the curtain flew aside. A man strode in, black robes swirling around his legs, sandals slapping the floor. With a conscious effort to contain the energy in his steps, he came to a standstill in front of Kitty.

'Good morning. I am Father Remi.' He spoke English with only a light foreign accent. Kitty guessed he must be middle-aged; his short curly hair was grey at the temples and his olive skin faintly lined. But vitality flashed in his dark eyes, giving him a boyish air. He held out his hand, not waiting for Kitty to offer first.

'I'm Mrs Hamilton.' As they shook hands, the man's callused palm reminded Kitty of her father's work-toughened skin. She saw a cloth badge on his robe. Embroidered in white on a black background was the outline of a heart, with letters and symbols inside it and a cross growing out of the top. The emblem was sewn roughly over the place where Father Remi's own heart would be.

'You have met Father Paulo. He speaks only Italian and Swahili. And a bit of French.' He said nothing more. Although he'd clearly been in a rush when he came in, he now gave Kitty his full attention. She got the feeling he was waiting for her to explain why she was here.

'I'm looking for Sister Barbara.'

'Sister Barbara?' He appeared puzzled for a few seconds. 'Ah, you mean the *nursing* sister.'

Kitty's lips parted, but she didn't speak. It was beginning to make sense to her now – why the buildings looked wrong, and why these two robed men both called themselves 'Father'.

Father Remi turned to the African. 'Why did you come here?'

The man shrugged and spread his hands. 'This white woman asked me to guide her to the Mission. Here is the Mission.'

As they talked, Kitty's gaze settled on a wooden cross mounted over the doorway. It bore the naked body of Christ, arms and feet nailed in place, head sagging forward. The image was distantly familiar to her. She'd once explored the grounds of the other church in Wattle Creek – the one at the far end of the main street. Among the elaborate gravestones she'd seen several of these effigies. But it had been the statues of angels that had captured her imagination. In the Anglican churchyard there were just plain headstones or bare stone crosses. She'd planned to return and make sketches of the statues, but someone had seen her there and she'd had to promise her parents not to go back again. The place might have been part of a foreign country, the way they'd spoken about it.

'This is the Catholic Mission.' Father Remi confirmed her suspicions. He swung his arm in the direction the car had been headed before they reached the last turn-off. 'You are looking for the Anglicans.' He ran his eyes over Kitty's well-worn bush clothes. 'Are you a new missionary there? Another nurse?'

Kitty laughed, shaking her head. 'No, I'm just . . . one of the wives from Londoni. I thought I might be able to help Sister Barbara. She came to the Club, you see . . .' Her voice petered out. It seemed a ridiculous presumption, suddenly, that she could help real missionaries with their work. She thought of the pot-plant stall, with the tasteful cloth covering the trestle table, and the cheerfully decorated tin that held the cash. The ladies had taken turns to sell the plants, with someone always on duty to guard their handbags that were stacked in a line on a second table. By the time the last plant was gone, everyone had been happily exhausted and ready for a gin and tonic. This was the kind of charity work that English wives undertook.

Father Remi addressed the African. 'Do you know where the Anglicans can be found?'

The man gave an equivocal response. 'This Mission, right here in this place, is a very good Mission,' he protested. 'Why should she wish for another?'

His next words were drowned out by the clanging of a bell. It echoed through the walls, loud and insistent, from the direction of the church tower. Moments later, as if in response, the busy sound of metal clattering against metal started up somewhere close by.

'I regret, Mrs Hamilton, I cannot invite you to stay for a refreshment.' Father Remi was already crossing to the doorway. He backed out past the curtain, still talking to Kitty. 'It was a pleasure to meet you.' He lifted his hand in a gesture that might have been a blessing, or just an ordinary wave.

The bell stopped ringing. In the sudden quiet, Kitty heard the sound of a vehicle labouring up the hill, grinding through its gears. As she crossed to the window, a truck came into view. The open back was crammed with African men all dressed alike in crude shirts and trousers made from off-white canvas. Dotted among them were native guards – they looked the same as the ones outside Head Office that Theo referred to as *askaris*. Each of them was neatly attired in a belted jacket and red fez; they carried batons, and rifles with bayonets mounted on the barrels. When the truck came to a standstill, Kitty managed to read the writing on the door of the cabin: *His Majesty's Prison Services*. Above the words was an emblem – the gentle head of a giraffe, with black spots on yellow, set in a circle of white.

The old priest stood up, addressing Kitty in Swahili that she couldn't understand. From his hand movements she realised he wanted her to move. But rather than directing her towards the doorway through which Father Remi had just gone, he pointed to the internal door by which he'd entered the room himself. Kitty guessed he was suggesting another exit. Through the window she could see the prisoners climbing down from the rear of the truck. If she were to walk out into the yard, she would attract a lot of interest, to say the least.

'Thank you,' she said. The African – who clearly intended to hang onto his role as guide – followed her into the corridor, the old priest coming behind.

Kitty entered a dining room with a single long table in the middle. A vase of orange hibiscus caught her eye; floating on the air was an odd, yeasty smell that she could not place. She was about to head on towards the door at the far end, but Father Paulo pulled out a chair, motioning for her to sit.

'You must have some water first,' he said in Swahili. He went over to a sideboard, where there was a jug covered with a circle of net weighted by coloured beads. With a shaking hand, he poured water into three glasses, and carried them to the table, one by one. Kitty's tumbler was well-worn, the glass scoured; she wondered if the water had been filtered and boiled. But after only a moment's hesitation she took a few big gulps – she hadn't realised how thirsty she was. Sipping the remains of the water more slowly, she glanced around the room. There was a painting of a monk surrounded by animals hanging near the head of the table, and there were more framed photographs of priests, including one with dark skin. She tried to make sense of a strange black-and-white image of a face – bearded, with closed eyes. It was hazy, like the memory of a dream.

'That is our Shroud of Turin,' Father Paulo said. 'The face of Christ after his death.'

Kitty listened politely. 'Very interesting.' She would be glad to move on to Sister Barbara's mission, where she felt sure there would not be so much focus on death.

As she set the glass on the table, she noticed the unusual smell again. She sniffed the air, trying to identify it.

'We are making wine.' Father Paulo drew her attention to a glass-fronted cabinet filled with rows of cut-crystal goblets and wine bottles with no labels. 'Would you like to try some?'

'No, thank you. I should go.' Kitty finished her drink and stood up.

Father Paulo pointed towards the door at the end of the room, but he remained at the table, resting back in his chair. Kitty smiled her farewell, and headed towards it, her guide at her heels.

As she stepped through the door she was met by the smell of cooked food – several big pots were bubbling on a blackened range. The air was hot and steamy. A young African man – tall and thin, wearing nothing but a white apron and a pair of shorts – strode between the sink, the stove and a bench. He wiped his face with a cloth hanging over his bare shoulder. Catching sight of Kitty, he stopped in surprise. Her companion said something that she did not catch. The cook nodded. Then, without warning, he thrust a ladle into her hand – an enamel cup mounted on a curved stick. Barely breaking his stride, he picked up one of the pots, using tea towels for protection against the hot handles, and led the way out of the kitchen.

Kitty stopped on the threshold, the ladle clasped in her hand. Half-hidden by the curtain that screened the entrance, she scanned the scene outside. The cook was marching towards the trestle table outside the church. One end of it was now piled with tin cups and bowls. Two more trucks had appeared and guards were unloading prisoners. The earlier arrivals were already seated cross-legged in rows on the paved forecourt. Altogether, there must have been nearly a hundred men. Kitty could see numbers stencilled with black paint onto their shirts – positioned over their hearts, just like Father Remi's badge. A subdued chatter rose from their ranks. Kitty eyed her car, parked only a short distance away. She could just walk past the table, put down the ladle and keep going. No one would blame her. Some of the men were rolling their eyes and shaking their heads as if they were insane. Others had blank, wooden stares. A man sitting not far from where she stood had an old scar, deep and wide, that ran the length of his leg. Kitty could only imagine what kinds of lives these prisoners had led, what crimes they had committed.

She took a deep breath and stepped out into the sunshine.

Awareness of the white woman's presence travelled the crowd like a wave, leaving quiet in its path. Kitty glimpsed Father Remi bending over a man with a dirty bandage on his leg. The next moment, the priest was walking towards her. When he was close, he gave her a questioning look – his gaze moving from her face to the ladle in her hand and back. Then he nodded to himself, before leading her towards the far end of the table.

'You can stand here. I'll be right next to you.'

Kitty opened her mouth to explain that she was leaving, but Father Remi turned on his heel, hurrying away. People called out to him as he passed – prisoners and *askaris* alike all seemed to want his attention.

Kitty found herself next to a steaming pot of vegetable stew. Her loyal guide stood at her elbow.

'My name is Tesfa,' he announced solemnly. Kitty smiled, understanding that he'd made a decision he could trust her.

'I am Kitty.'

'Kitty, you must do this work carefully,' Tesfa advised. He pointed at the ladle. 'Fill this to the top, one time only. Every man must eat. You must not run out.'

'Did you tell the cook I wanted to help?' Kitty asked him.

'In truth, I did,' he admitted gravely, but offered no explanation as to why.

The cook reappeared, this time bearing a pot full of thick, whitish porridge. After putting it down next to the stew, he handed Kitty an apron. An African woman in a long robe – similar to the ones worn by the two priests, but pale blue – came behind him. She carried a bar of red soap, a towel and a bowl of water.

Kitty held her hands under a thin stream of water, rubbing them clean. Pink-stained foam covered her skin, smelling of lye and disinfectant. Her head was bent, her hair falling forward, screening her face. But she could feel the gaze of the watching men. The air was dense with their scrutiny. As she dried her hands, she glanced over the faces, trying not to let her eyes settle. The whole forecourt was now packed with prisoners. Most of them were in the prime of life, with toned muscles bulging from their slender limbs. A few were older, and Kitty saw some who looked like teenagers. The men's faces were shiny brown with sweat, but their arms and legs were speckled with red dust. Several of the prisoners were moving along the lines, pouring water for others to wash their hands. The *askaris* stood to attention, keeping watch over the scene. One of them tapped the end of his baton against the palm of his hand.

Father Remi came to stand beside Kitty. After acknowledging her with a quick smile, he turned to face the crowd. Everyone became quiet and still. The priest made the sign of the cross over his chest, just like Paddy had done in the plane before each meal and at take-off and landing. Bowing his head, he spoke in a language

Kitty guessed was Italian, though she couldn't think why he'd be addressing a gathering of Africans in his mother tongue. The foreign sounds gave his speech mystery and weight, but she assumed the priest was just saying grace – the same as her father did each evening, reeling off predictable phrases that stemmed the energy of the room, until the final word, 'Amen', unleashed a clatter of knives and forks.

When he finished speaking, Father Remi reached for a utensil made of wood with a paddle-shape at one end.

'Now, let us begin.' He plunged the paddle into the stiff porridge as the first prisoner moved up to the table.

For the next hour, Kitty barely looked up from her work. The stew was made with kidney beans, tomato, onion and sweet potato. Fortunately, there were no large chunks of food to share out; every scoop was the same as the one before. As Kitty relaxed into the rhythm of dipping and pouring, she began glancing up at each man as he came to stand in front of her. At first, the prisoners were set apart from one another only by age or build. But as time passed, she began to see how very different the faces were. One obviously belonged to a comedian, another to someone timid. She detected, in turn, wisdom, anger, resignation, even playfulness. Many of the men bore the marks of the Wagogo – the scar in the middle of the forehead, the missing front tooth – but others were obviously from different tribes. Almost without exception, the men thanked her for their food.

'*Asante. Asante sana. Asante sana.*'

The sibilant sounds overlaid the shuffle of feet and the clinking of tin as they picked up their bowls and cups.

When the first pot was empty, the cook appeared with another. Kitty used the back of her hand to wipe the sweat from her forehead.

'Are you tired?' Father Remi asked. 'You can stop. Others can help.' He waved his ladle, taking in the nearby prisoners, the woman in blue – a nun, Kitty guessed – and some other Africans dressed in standard ochre cloths who had joined the throng.

'No, I'm fine.' Kitty began ladling more energetically, hiding her dismay that she could be so easily replaced. She understood she was not indispensible – how could she be, when she'd only turned up by mistake? Yet she felt strangely territorial about her role at the stew pot. Apart from anything else, she realised that for the last hour or so, she'd not had time to think about herself even for a moment. She could feel the change in her mind and body – thoughts and emotions pushing out, rather than turning in on themselves. Her legs were tired, hunger gnawed her stomach and her throat was dry, yet energy flowed through her. She felt light and alert, and free from herself. Part of her wished she would never have to leave.

SIX

Kitty sat in a chair on the verandah, legs crossed at the ankles, a crisp cotton skirt covering her knees. She gazed out at the view of Londoni. In contrast to the place where she'd just been, it looked even more lifeless and barren than usual. As she ran her fingers thoughtfully over the string of pearls that draped her neck, images from the day cycled through her head. She saw the kitchen gardens, densely packed with vegetables and herbs. The bright patches of flowers that had been planted alongside the crops, as though colour mattered just as much as food. Airy chicken sheds. A pen with two fat pigs. A pond dotted with ducks.

'Why is everything so green?' Kitty had asked Father Remi as he'd led her on a tour of the Mission. Just being in the foothills didn't explain such verdant growth.

'There is a permanent spring on that hillside.' He pointed up behind him. 'We pipe it down here. We have all the water we want.'

Tesfa walked with them, along with two small children who giggled shyly whenever Kitty even glanced at them. Father Remi was relaxed now that the prisoners had left and the hard work of the day was behind him. He paused to pat a kitten resting in the sun, and to pick a sprig of thyme, rubbing it between his fingers to release the pungent oil.

Kitty bowed her head, walking beneath a frangipani tree laden with cream and yellow flowers. She drew the strong perfume into her lungs, wanting to drive out the smell of blood overlaid with anti-septic that still lingered with her. Before the *askaris* had returned the prisoners to the trucks, a number of men had left the main groups, gathering by one of the arched doorways. Father Remi called them into a large room where he unlocked a metal cabinet containing labelled chemist's bottles, boxes of tablets, rolls of bandages and other medical items. With the help of the old African nun, who'd been introduced as Sister Clara, he'd begun treating cuts and sores, exam-ining eyes and using a thermometer to check peoples' temperatures.

When Kitty offered to help, Father Remi handed her some Dettol, a plain jar containing some kind of ointment, and a roll of cotton wool. He showed her where to fill a bowl of water. Then he beckoned over the man with a dirty bandage on his leg who Kitty had noticed earlier. 'Just remove the bandage and clean the wound. Before you do the dressing, dab on a bit of the ointment. I make it myself – it works well. Ask me if you need help.'

The prisoner sat down on a chair and Kitty knelt in front of him. A sour smell rose from the bandage as she unwound it. The last section was stuck to the wound beneath and she had to soften the dried blood with warm water before she could lift the gauze away. She was conscious of Father Remi glancing in her direction as she laid bare an ulcer the size of a large coin.

Kitty studied the sore. A thick scab covered most of it, but pus leaked at the edges. She frowned, remembering what Janet had taught. *A wound must heal from the inside out. A scab can hide a deepening infection . . .*

Kitty picked up a pair of tweezers from an enamel kidney dish and poked at the scab. She looked up at the prisoner. '*Samahani.*' Please excuse me.

'*Si neno,*' the prisoner responded. It is nothing.

He didn't even wince as she began to peel off the scab, which made Kitty wonder what level of pain or discomfort the man had become accustomed to – while in prison, or before. Finally, she pulled the scab free, tearing the skin fibres underneath. Raw flesh was exposed, pale pink against the man's black skin. Dark fluid oozed out. Kitty swallowed on a surge of nausea.

'*Vizuri,*' she reassured the prisoner. Good.

As he nodded, obviously trusting her completely, Kitty was aware that Father Remi was watching her. She turned to the task of washing out the gaping hole.

When the sore had been cleaned and disinfected, she used a cottonwool ball to smear on the musky-smelling ointment before putting on a new bandage. Kitty wondered how long the white dressing would stay clean, and how long it would be before the pus soaked through again.

'Do you have scissors?' she asked Father Remi.

He brought her a pair, then stayed to watch as she cut the end of the bandage in two so she could wind one strip back around to meet the other, where it could be tied securely.

'You said you were just a wife,' he commented. 'I think you are a nurse!'

Kitty shook her head. 'I only know a bit about it.'

'And I've heard you speak Swahili . . .'

'Only a little,' Kitty said modestly.

'Sister Barbara will be very pleased to meet you.'

There was clear regret in his voice. Kitty bent her head to hide the pleasure she felt. He wanted her! She wished she could say, right then, that she'd be just as keen to return here to help, whenever she could. But she kept quiet, letting Father Remi's comment hang in the air. She liked him – the way he exuded energy combined with thoughtfulness. And she sensed a gentle spirit in the old priest, Father Paulo. Sister Clara was kind and helpful, as were the other people she'd met at the Mission. Tesfa, as well. Kitty had only been here a couple of hours, yet she was at ease with them all. But they were Catholics. Everyone Kitty and Theo mixed with – at the Club, or the tennis courts, around Head Office or at the two supper parties they'd attended in homes on Millionaire Row – were Protestants. They all appeared, each Sunday morning, at St Michael's Anglican Church. They filed into the pews according to status. Richard and Diana sat at the front, along with any OFC executives who were visiting from London. Behind them sat Theo and Kitty, sharing a row with Alice and her husband, Nicholas. The medical officers, unit managers and other middle-level staff, along with their families, fell in behind – and so on.

The Catholic church was on the far side of Londoni towards the Tractor Workshops. In contrast to St Michael's Anglican, which was a striking stone building set on a rise overlooking the whole settlement, the place where the Catholics met was a converted military shed – much like the one used for the Kongara Club, only smaller. Kitty wasn't sure who went to it. No doubt

Paddy did. And presumably the other engineers who'd been on the plane; Kitty had watched out for them week after week, but none had shown up at St Michael's. In fact, there must be many hundreds of people living in the Toolsheds and in the various tents and rondavels of Londoni who had never attended the Anglican church. And apparently, there was a second, bigger Catholic church out at the Units; the Irish contractors, along with a large cohort of Italians, were its main patrons. It occurred to Kitty that there must be many more Catholics involved in the Scheme than Protestants. Yet their existence was barely mentioned by anyone she knew. That was how it was, here in Kongara – the senior staff and middle management were all English and Protestant. They kept to themselves. Catholics occupied the lower ranks. Kitty didn't need Theo to tell her that it would be no more suitable for his wife to spend time at this mission than for her to teach Swahili at the Tractor Workshops.

As Kitty finished tying the bandage, the prisoner stood up, making way for the next patient.

'When will this man be treated again?' Kitty asked Father Remi. 'A wound like this needs daily care.'

'He will return tomorrow. Do not worry. I will make sure he is looked after.'

'How often do they come?'

'Monday to Saturday. They work as labourers on the farm next door.' Father Remi searched for something in the medicine cabinet as he spoke. 'It is too far for them to return to the prison to eat. Anyway, they get better food here. And, as you see, we can help them in other ways.'

Kitty removed a simple sticking plaster from a man's hand, revealing a recent cut. As she dabbed it with antiseptic, she responded to Father Remi. 'Surely the farmer should be responsible for their food – if they're working for him?' There was an indignant tone in her voice. She could just imagine the kind of person who was prepared make use of prison labour – profiting from the efforts of powerless men, some in poor health, and teenage boys who should be in school.

'Bwana Taylor pays for the food, and he pays us to prepare it. We use the money to fund the work of our Mission. The arrangement suits everyone.'

'Did you say Taylor?' Kitty recognised the name of the man in the ramshackle vehicle she and James had met on the road – the same individual Theo had described as a 'naysayer': the white Tanganyikan who had tried to sabotage the whole Scheme, just to protect his own interests.

Father Remi nodded. 'Do you know him?' He began applying ointment to a man's infected eyes.

Kitty shook her head vehemently. 'Not at all.'

The conversation had ended there – but Taylor's name had come up again, later on, when they were on a tour of the gardens. Father Remi had led Kitty and Tesfa to the far boundary of the Mission. There they'd looked out over a whole hillside of vineyards, with others stretching behind.

'This is where the prisoners come to work,' he explained.

The grapes were set out in rows as neat and straight as the rows of tents in Londoni. But where Kongara was a grubby patchwork of grey and white, broken up by pale gravel roads, the nearest hillside was patterned with dabs of bright green – Winsor Green, with a touch of Naples Yellow – set off by the red soil below. The plants were healthy, promising a good crop. Looking further, though, Kitty could see other vines that were just grey sticks.

'Why are some so healthy, and others dead?'

'The ones that look dead have been harvested and pruned,' Father Remi explained. 'The others haven't even flowered yet. We get three crops a year, just by controlling the water. It makes good sense to spread out the harvest.'

Kitty gazed over the vineyards. It was a farmer's dream: to have heat and water all year round. To be in charge of the seasons. With a spike of regret, she wished she could describe this place to her father. She could write it in a letter, but unless something happened to heal the rift between them – which didn't seem likely after all these years – she would never hear his response.

'Father Paulo brought the original cuttings back from a visit to Italy to see his sister,' added Father Remi. 'We began making wine for communion – and for the table, of course. That was twenty years ago.'

'You've been here all that time?'

'I was twenty-seven when I came out from Italy.'

Kitty stared at him. 'How often do you go home?'

'I don't take leave any more. I have no family to visit since my mother died. Neither has Father Paulo. So both of us stay here.' He scanned the landscape as he spoke. 'This is our home now.'

He turned his attention to gathering vegetables, making up a basket for Kitty to take home. He put in some fat tomatoes and several heads of sweetcorn still wrapped in their husks. He pulled up a couple of beetroot and some carrots, shaking the red soil from the roots. From a spindly tree he plucked a large pawpaw, lifting it to his nose and breathing its ripe smell. Finally, he added a bunch of herbs. Kitty identified sprigs of parsley and mint, thyme and sage.

They were about to leave the gardens – it was time for Kitty to return to Londoni – when Father Remi stopped suddenly. He bent over a large plant with clover-like leaves. It grew a foot high and twice as wide.

'Do you know what this is?' he asked Kitty.

From they way he spoke, she knew it must have some special significance. 'Is it a peanut?' she guessed. 'I've never seen one before.'

He ran his fingers through the stems, ruffling the leaves. 'It is an amazing plant.'

Kitty smiled politely. It looked rather ordinary to her – especially considering this species of plant bore the weight of so many hopes and expectations. 'It's very advanced,' she commented. 'Down at the Units they're still ploughing.'

Father Remi nodded. 'They have to wait for the rains. You could never irrigate fields of that size.' He squatted down beside the peanut plant. 'When it is fully grown,' he continued, 'yellow flowers appear. Each one lasts only a day, but more keep coming – this goes on for about a month. The plant can fertilise itself, but the bees play their part as well. After fertilisation has taken place, the petals fade. What is left is the ovary.' Father Remi studied the peanut as he talked. Kitty was grateful his face was hidden. The words he used, delivered in his melodic Italian accent, had an air of intimacy as if he were unveiling something deeply private.

'The ovary grows into a pod with a hard shell. It holds inside itself the beginnings of two or three seeds. It has a sharp end, which grows pointing down to the ground. At the right time, the flower stalk bends over and the pod is forced into the earth.'

He pushed the foliage aside, showing the bare soil beneath, where the seedpod would be planted. Kitty felt a blush spreading over her cheeks. It was not to do with Father Remi's presence. There was nothing suggestive in his manner towards her. His old-fashioned robe, the embroidered badge on his chest, and just the fact of him being a priest, marked him out as being someone set apart from ordinary men. Yet his words conjured a vision of sensuality that spread from the single plant at their feet to embrace a whole land pulsing with life. The fragrance of the garden flowers, the touch of the sun on Kitty's shoulders, even the birdsong coming from the trees – they were all a part of it. The air itself seemed to whisper of growth, fertility, even the act of sex . . . Kitty's thoughts drifted to the white bedroom back on Millionaire Row. Theo's body moving over hers. The moan of pleasure escaping his lips. Her breasts tingling from the touch of his tongue . . .

The images were from a night about a week before. The memory had been obscured by the disappointment and frustration surrounding the car, but now it all came back to her, fresh and potent. Theo had returned from work early, kissing Kitty on the lips and presenting her with a box of chocolates. The cardboard lid was dented and the chocolates inside had a whitish look, suggesting they'd melted at least once on their journey all the way from Switzerland to Kongara. But the thoughtful gesture had brought tears to Kitty's eyes. All evening, Theo had made an effort to be bright. He'd enquired about the details of his wife's day, instead of talking only about his own. He'd complimented her on her outfit. Kitty had responded like a wilted plant under a shower of spring rain. So often, in the time since she'd arrived, Theo had been tired by the end of the day, his mood flat. When they went to bed he'd kiss her briefly, then roll over to sleep. Some nights, after being remote and preoccupied all evening, he would suddenly want to have sex with her. When this happened Kitty found it hard to respond in the way that she knew she should. But now, when Theo led her to their bedroom, her body was ready, longing for his.

With foil wrappers scattered around them and smeared chocolate on the sheets, they'd made love more than once, moving between tenderness and passion. Kitty was reminded of the carefree days before they were married. Back then, they'd escape together from Hamilton Hall, sometimes before a dinner party was even fully over; or they'd leave Yuri to paint alone in the studio. They'd lie on the cool flagstone floor of the bathing pavilion, moonlight gleaming on their naked skin, the night air enfolding them, velvety and secret. Here in Londoni – in their own bedroom in their own home – their lovemaking had been even more perfect. Their bodies had become like one creature, their union complete.

'The peanuts continue growing underground for three to five months.' Father Remi's voice summoned Kitty's attention. She nodded to show that she was listening. 'Then they are ready to be harvested. You just pull up the plant – and there they are.' As he finished, he looked up at her. He gave her a smile tinged with pride as though he were in some way responsible for the miracle he'd described.

Kitty smiled back. She felt touched by his enthusiasm – but even more, she was inspired by the memory his words had evoked. Thinking of how kind and loving Theo had been that night gave Kitty hope. She should forget her complaints about her life and be grateful for what she had. If she could only remain positive, and be warm, kind and happy, everything would be all right. There would be more gifts, more romantic evenings, more love . . .

The sound of Theo's Land Rover broke into Kitty's reflection. Jumping to her feet, she hurried to the open French windows, then called out to Gabriel that the bwana was home.

Returning to her chair, she prepared to greet Theo. She fought off a feeling of guilt – reminding herself it had not been her intention to go to the Catholic Mission. It was just a simple mistake. Not even worth mentioning. If anyone had already reported seeing her car, she'd have to give an explanation to Theo – but she hoped he would never need to know where she had been. On her way home, she'd stopped near the roundabout to have the car-washing boys remove the thick red dirt the Hillman had picked up from the tracks. The car now wore only the fine white coating of dust that came from the formed gravel roads of Londoni. When she'd dropped Tesfa off at the *manyara* tree she'd given him the basket of vegetables and fruit, realising it was too risky for her to keep the priest's produce. It had taken her some time to convince Tesfa to accept it – he was offended on Father Remi's behalf and bemused by Kitty's rudeness. She wished she'd been able to explain that taking the food into her own kitchen would arouse questions she did not want to answer; it was not possible to buy produce of this quality in the little shops – called *dukas* – that served the town. As they had transferred the goods from Father Remi's basket to a string bag from the car boot, Tesfa had discovered a bone-handled penknife – the one Father Remi had used to harvest the herbs. The basket was now safely concealed in the boot, and the knife in the glove box. A faint stain of chicken droppings on the back seat of the car was the only evidence of the day's venture.

Theo flung the door of the Land Rover shut behind him and hurried up the steps without a backwards glance. He gave Kitty a brief kiss. 'God, I need a drink. What a day!'

Kitty trailed inside after him. Theo fidgeted by the drinks trolley while Gabriel made a gin and tonic, then began preparing the whisky soda.

'You wouldn't believe it.' Theo loosened his tie and undid his collar – a gesture he normally despised. 'The things I have to deal with . . . A load of fertiliser finally arrived – long overdue. It gets sent to the Units to be used on some new acreage. The blokes spreading the stuff had never seen fertiliser before.' Theo's voice rose; he paced impatiently, not bothering to look at Kitty as he addressed her. 'It turns out they put cement into the ground. The sacks got mixed up at the railway depot and no one knew the difference. So that's going to be just great when the rains come!'

Kitty held her glass against her lips, suppressing a smile. She understood Theo's frustration, but there was a comical side to the story.

Theo grabbed his drink from Gabriel and took a long gulp. 'The ground is hard enough as it is. It's almost impossible to plough.

So much for the sandy soil that was meant to be here. It's half bloody clay!'

Kitty lowered her glass, taken aback by Theo's outburst. There was nothing funny about the issues he was describing now. She was reminded uncomfortably of the road-rolling machines she'd seen, fenced off and left to the weeds.

'It would help,' Theo continued bitterly, 'if the OFC had employed a few farmers among the soldiers and sailors. Most of the people I'm dealing with haven't a clue what they're doing!' Theo broke off suddenly. He turned to Gabriel, pointing in the direction of the kitchen. 'Leave us!' Gabriel stood still for a moment, stung by the curt tone. Theo took a step towards him. 'Get out!' he shouted. 'Go on.'

As Gabriel scuttled away, Kitty stared at Theo in surprise. She understood he was angry with himself for criticising the OFC in front of an African servant – even expressing such disloyalty to his wife was unwise. But she was still shocked by his behaviour; shouting at house staff would be unimaginable at Hamilton Hall.

As Theo poured himself another whisky, she walked over to the window, turning her back tactfully, allowing him the chance to recover his composure. She heard him settle in his armchair, banging his glass down on the side table.

'I do apologise,' he said eventually. 'Inexcusable of me.'

Kitty made no response for a few seconds. She thought he should call Gabriel back and say sorry to him. While it was true that the houseboy's manner towards her bordered on insolence at times, he'd done nothing to deserve the treatment he'd just received. But as she was deciding what to say, she remembered the resolution she'd made in the garden at the Mission. Her thoughts turned to a magazine article Pippa had read out a few days before while they were all sunbathing at the pool.

'"How to be a Perfect Wife".' She'd announced the title in a serious tone. Everyone had turned their heads to listen – even Diana. '"It goes without saying that she looks and smells delightful. But this is not enough. The Perfect Wife is always available to offer comfort and reassurance. She never criticises, and avoids offering advice. Her home is a sanctuary for her husband, who has been hard at work all day . . ."'

Kitty walked back over to Theo. Standing behind his chair, she rested her hands on his shoulders. She bent to kiss his head. 'Poor Theo,' she murmured. 'I'm sure things will be better tomorrow.'

She felt the muscles of his shoulders soften; then his hands came up to cover hers. He tightened his grip, like a man afraid of falling. Kitty returned the pressure. She felt strong, bending over him like this – giving him the support he needed. This was her job, she reminded herself. It was the reason why she was here. To stand at Theo's side and be his wife.

SEVEN

Kitty stood at the bar, watching Alfred and another waiter hovering over the coffee grinder. The percolator had finally arrived from London and the patrons of the Club were keen to taste some freshly ground beans. The pair had already tried switching on the grinder – they'd recoiled from the loud, sudden noise it had made, then looked on, astonished, as the vibrations caused the machine to jiggle along the bar as though it had a life of its own.

Not far from where Kitty stood were two men lounging at the counter. They'd greeted Kitty but not introduced themselves. From their heavy suits and perspiring faces she guessed they were visitors from London.

'He's a clever old fox.' The taller of the two ate peanuts from a bowl as he spoke. 'You have to hand it to him.'

'What's he done now?'

Kitty could hear the men clearly. She wondered if she should move tactfully away. Of course, she should not be standing here at all – she should be at the ladies' table behind the Japanese screen, waiting for the staff to serve her. But she wanted the chance to escape the group for a while, and coming out to enquire why her coffee had not appeared was her excuse. The mood among the women was tense this morning. For almost a week, Diana had been ill in bed with malaria. At first, her absence had given rise to a sense of relaxation; in spite of Alice's attempts to step into Diana's role as the senior memsahib, there was a feeling that no one was in charge. Eliza ordered a gin and tonic before noon and drank it while working on her crocheted squares. One morning, Audrey had joined her children and their *ayah* at the other end of the room. Not only that, she'd turned up in a pair of trousers. Pippa and Evelyn had swapped gossip freely. They'd even dared to question whether Diana really had malaria, since everyone in Kongara took chloroquine tablets each Sunday as routinely as they attended church. They hadn't been prepared, though, to say what other ailment might have kept her at home for so long. This initial stage, with its sense of freedom and excitement, had not lasted long, however; now, the atmosphere had become dull, with irritable squabbles breaking out.

'One of the bulldozer drivers pushed over a baobab down on Unit Three,' the tall man continued. 'You know – those odd-looking trees with a wide trunk?'

'I've seen them. Ugly things.'

'A skull fell out.'

Someone started playing the piano, the noise blurring the men's words. Kitty kept her eyes fixed on the counter but edged closer, wanting to hear what came next.

'It was a disaster. Apparently, these baobabs are often hollow, and the natives use them as burial places – especially where someone has died in unpleasant circumstances.' He spread his hands. 'The African workers point-blank refused to allow the bulldozing to continue. They said the spirit of an ancestor had been disturbed. So old Stratton was called down to decide what to do.' He paused, letting his companion absorb his words. 'He went to see the local chief. He explained to the old fellow that it was a good thing the grave had been opened, because now that the spirit of the Unknown One had been disturbed, they could make use of his wisdom. Brilliant move!' The man broke off, overcome with amusement.

'Keep going.'

'So now, when Stratton has his meetings with the Africans – he holds council up on the hill behind Unit Headquarters – he brings the skull along too. He sits it on a chair beside him and it whispers wisdom in his ears. The Africans will agree to anything the Unknown One says!'

The shorter man wiped his brow with a handkerchief. He shook his head. 'God, what a place! One knows they're primitive, but still . . .'

When Kitty looked up from the counter, she realised the two waiters had been listening to the interchange as well. Their faces were impassive, but when Kitty met Alfred's gaze she saw anger smouldering there. The Englishmen ignored their presence completely; the tall one spoke again.

'You know, one of the chaps went out to a village to round up some workers. Must have been quite remote because he had to stay overnight.' He shuddered at the thought. 'The chief paraded half a dozen virgins in front of him. They thought he might like to take one into his hut. He declined, of course. Ghastly idea.'

Alfred grabbed the coffee grinder and moved it over to the bar, the electrical cord being just long enough to reach. When it was beside the two Englishmen he turned it on. As the harsh noise jarred the quiet, they stared in astonishment. The tall one seemed about to command the African to move the offending object away. But he, too, must have glimpsed something in the waiter's expression. The white man turned on his heel and walked off, his companion following behind.

Kitty met Alfred's gaze again. She knew she should show disapproval of his insubordination. But when she recalled the outrage and surprise on the men's faces, a smile began tugging at the corners of her mouth. Alfred smiled back at her. But the exchange of humour faded quickly; they both became solemn. Alfred's act of defiance was so small, and the disrespect for his countrymen shown by the Englishmen so deep. Kitty wanted to make some kind of apology on behalf of her race. Alfred watched her face, as though he was waiting to hear what she would say.

'My coffee,' she murmured finally. 'I was wondering when it might come.'

'Very soon, Memsahib,' was the reply. 'Please return to your chair. I will serve you.'

When Kitty reached the ladies' table she found that Alice had retired to the powder room. Pippa was talking about a party she'd been to, at the far end of Millionaire Row.

'It was a really strange party.' Her voice was lowered to a whisper, causing her listeners to lean forward in their chairs.

Evelyn raised her eyebrows. 'Why? What that happened?'

'At the end of the evening all the men put their car keys in a bowl. It was a kind of game. Apparently they'd played it before. The wives take turns to be blindfolded and pick out a set of keys. Then they leave with the owner of the keys.' Pippa broke off, scanning her audience. 'They spend the night with them.'

'You mean they . . .?'

Pippa nodded.

There was a stunned silence. Kitty struggled to take in what was being said. She'd once overheard talk in the shearing sheds at Seven Gums of a man who was playing cards offering a night with his wife to clear a gambling debt. But it was another thing to picture an event such as Pippa described taking place in a home on Millionaire Row – a house just like Kitty's, right down to the pink towels in the bathroom.

'So – did you?' Evelyn glanced guiltily in the direction of the powder room as she spoke.

'Of course not,' Pippa replied. 'We went home. But everyone else stayed. The Carruthers, the Bennets, the Wilsons . . .'

There was a shocked quiet. Kitty knew the couples named – she and Theo had had dinner with the Wilsons. Mrs Wilson was overweight, her face brightly made-up as if to distract attention from her body. Kitty couldn't help wondering which of the husbands she'd spent the night with.

'Did Gerald want you to?' Evelyn breathed the question.

A flush spread over Pippa's cheeks. 'No. No, he didn't at all.' The words tumbled from her mouth. 'And even if he had, I wouldn't have done it. It's disgusting, wives being handed around like that . . .' There was a defensive tone in her voice – Kitty suspected she regretted having shared the story of the key party.

Evelyn shook her head wonderingly. 'Why do they agree?'

Eliza smiled. 'Perhaps they want to.' She gave a mischievous giggle. 'They might be bored with their own men. They might —'

'It's no laughing matter,' Audrey broke in. She spoke loudly, deliberately. 'Some might find adultery acceptable – personally, I don't know what kind of woman would sleep with someone else's husband.'

The air was suddenly taut. Audrey was staring straight at Sally, who sat opposite her. Sally's head was bent, but her short dark hair offered no shield for her face – her lips were pressed together, her eyes fixed on the floor.

'Why should one woman set about destroying another woman's life?' Audrey was now addressing Sally directly, her face flushed, the pink tone clashing with her frizzy orange hair.

Sally gripped the arms of her chair with white-knuckled hands. Kitty watched on, wide-eyed. Was it possible that Sally was involved with Audrey's husband? The Senior Medical Officer; father of Dickie and Fiona . . . Kitty studied Sally, taking in her thin hunched shoulders. Of all the women who met together at the Kongara Club, Kitty knew her the least. Sally was married to the Chief Veterinary Surgeon, Alan Carr, and had what Theo would call a 'regional accent'. She made only intermittent visits to the Club, and when she was there she rarely spoke, never swam, and always returned home for lunch.

Suddenly, Sally jumped to her feet, stumbling away from the table. She bumped one of the Japanese screens, rattling the bamboo as she disappeared from view.

'Oh dear.' Evelyn bit her lip.

Audrey sniffed, unrepentant. 'Well, it's no secret. Poor Cynthia.'

'At least she's a widow, not a divorcee.' Pippa shuddered. 'Imagine if her husband had left her – run off with Sally!'

Kitty examined the faces of the women at the table. She realised how little she knew of them. She'd been in Tanganyika for over two months now, and had spent hours and hours in their company, yet she had no idea what might really be going on in their lives. It sounded like Sally had been having an affair not with Audrey's husband, but with Cynthia's – Major Wainwright! Was that why Sally seemed so subdued? Was she grieving the loss of her lover, mourning his terrible death? Kitty wondered if Theo was as ignorant as she. This wasn't the kind of thing she'd ask him about, though. She wouldn't want to risk sounding naïve or – even worse – to expose herself as a gossip.

An uneasy quiet continued until Alice returned from the powder room. She took out her notebook, preparing to deliver a report on the last meeting, which had been about the publication of their newsletter, 'The Nutshell'. As she talked, a sense of calm seemed to spread out around her. The women drank in her words as if – like children – they were relieved to have someone take charge again.

The heat was stifling in the gloomy interior of the Arab *duka*. Kitty wandered along the narrow aisles that ran between the loaded shelves, stepping around sacks and avoiding the sharp corners of tin trunks. All the items that would be stocked in a typical English shop were on offer – washing powder, shaving cream, toothbrushes, shoe polish and suchlike. But dotted here and there among the merchandise were more exotic items like bangles, silk prayer carpets, bottles of rosewater and pomegranate syrup.

Kitty was not looking for anything in particular – she just didn't want to go home yet; she'd have over an hour to kill before lunch, and then there was the whole afternoon stretching ahead of her. She thought back to a time, before she became Theo's wife, when the days were too short for all that she wanted to do. In the Garden House studio she used to work late into the night, often with Yuri at her side. Hours were like minutes, whether lost in quiet pleasure or filled with fierce excitement. Kitty closed her eyes, remembering the feeling of smoothing paint onto linen, gently stroking the taut surface with her brush. Or making long, fluid lines that evoked the grace and skill of a dancer . . .

She cut off the memory – those days were finished. She focused on a display of tins and bottles, reading the dusty labels. But her thoughts soon wandered again. She pictured what would be happening at the Mission. The trucks would be arriving, the *askaris* supervising the unloading of prisoners. The kitchen would be a hive of activity, pots bubbling on the stove.

But that was not her world either.

She picked up a sunhat with a wide floppy brim, then put it back down. She was aware of Ahmed watching her from his place at the counter, an arsenal of rifles hanging on the wall behind him. He was a striking figure with hooded eyes, a hawk nose and skin like finely tanned leather. His loose black turban always seemed ready to fall, but never did. He wore a curved silver dagger tucked into the sash tied over his long tunic. Every time Kitty had been in here she'd found him smoking a pipe that looked like a tall candlestick with a hose attached to it, set up on the counter. Today was no exception. He drew in smoke through a container of water, making long gurgling sounds that drifted across to where she stood. She breathed the aromatic smoke along with the smell of spices, leather and soap.

Kitty scanned the shadows, letting her eye be caught by the glint of gold embroidery, the shine of coloured glass. She came across a decorative brass object with a series of holes in its base. She had no idea what it was.

'Mrs Hamilton.' Kitty looked around to see Ahmed beckoning her towards the counter. 'I have something special. Only for you.'

As she approached, he brought a bolt of silk cloth from behind the counter.

It was a deep, glowing orange. He unrolled some of the cloth, letting it rest in luxurious folds on the counter. 'It is very fine.'

Kitty felt the cloth between her thumb and fingers. It had the soft weight and clingy touch of pure silk.

'This would make a very beautiful dress for you. Maybe you want a blouse?'

Kitty smiled absently at him. An image was being conjured in her mind – but it was neither a dress nor a blouse. She saw instead the outlines of a pair of harem trousers, and the sculptured contours of a lampshade skirt.

Ahmed brought a huge pair of scissors from behind the counter. 'How much do you want?'

Kitty held up her hand. 'I'll think about it.' Ignoring his sigh of exasperation, she walked back over to the rows of shelves, pretending to be interested in a collection of china animals. As she gazed at a dog wearing a frilly skirt, balancing a ball on its nose, she could still feel the bolt of orange cloth shimmering behind her.

In her mind she saw Yuri holding up the skirt, then the trousers – lifting them to the light in turn, before laying them out on the chaise longue. He added a fitted bodice, then a couple of scarves. Along with the orange tones, there was purple and green and flashes of gold. Behind the smell of mothballs lay a rich perfume that reminded Kitty of her grandmother's bottle of French scent.

'The colours were chosen by artists,' Yuri told her, as he stroked the silk with hands freshly washed but still stained with paint. 'For the performance of the ballet *Scheherazade*.'

Kitty just nodded. She knew nothing about ballet beyond what she'd learned from one of her friends who'd had a few lessons; the girl had shown Kitty how to hold her head high, keep her shoulders down, and raise her arms in an elegant arc.

'It was completely new. Before Bakst designed for the *Ballets Russes*, the dancers' costumes were pale pink, lilac, mint green. He used strong colours and put them together – blue with purple, red with yellow, green with orange.' Yuri picked up the skirt. 'Of course, these clothes were not made for the stage. Look at the stitches, the finish of the seams. They were made by Anna Chernova, a couturier from Moscow.' He showed Kitty a hand-signed label sewn onto the waistband of the skirt, bearing the maker's name. 'She was one of the first to be inspired by the *Ballets Russes* – long before Coco Chanel. The Tsarina Alexandra, the last Empress of Russia, wore her dresses.'

Yuri's voice faded. He lifted the bundle of silk, burying his face in its folds. Kitty watched in silence, aware that he was lost in his memories – exotic memories she would not even try to guess at: visions of famous people, places, events. She couldn't get used to the idea that he was here, with her. Prince Yurievitch and Kitty Miller from Wattle Creek.

She didn't ask Yuri how he came to have these clothes. At the time, she'd not been living with him for very long – it was before Theo had flown into her life in his little red aeroplane. In those early days she preferred to collect information where she could, rather than seek it directly and risk exposing her limitless ignorance. She didn't want to do anything that might jeopardise her right to remain in the Garden House. Men liked their privacy, she knew. Her father was secretive about even quite minor matters, as though information were treasure to be stored up. If he talked about his plans concerning the farm or a trip to town, or told a story about growing up at Seven Gums, it only happened when – and if – he decided it should. Kitty had learned at a young age that it was unwise to pry.

Yuri handed the silk skirt to Kitty, re-entering the present as seamlessly as he had left it behind. He passed over the other garments and ushered her towards the screen to get changed. Hidden from view, she pulled off her own clothes, plain and cheap, not even bothering to hang them on the hook. She could hear the wind whining at the shutters. Winter had set in – but it was warm in the Garden House. Yuri had a whole bank of electric heaters that he plugged in whenever he had a model sitting for him. Kitty bent to pick up a handkerchief that lay on the floor. Lacy-edged, it had the letter *L* embroidered in one corner. It must have been dropped there by Lucinda. The woman hadn't been here for weeks, but her portrait dominated the studio. Kitty tried to avoid seeing it. There was something unnerving about the way Lucinda's long, willowy body was stretched over the chaise longue, looking taut, even though she was resting comfortably. Then, there was the awkward angle of her head. But mainly, it was the expression in her dark eyes. She appeared tortured, haunted – and cold, in spite of the rosy tones of the paint. Yuri was not satisfied with the image. He never was.

'Making a painting is like trying to capture a dream,' he'd told Kitty. 'It grows and changes, right under your eyes. Your hands are not your own. You can never master the process. Yet you cannot give up.' There had been a desperate tone in his voice as if he – like Lucinda's body – was traumatised by the process. 'In the end, you just have to let it go. You have made a small step – perhaps you are closer to that dream, or that nightmare, than you have been before. That is the best you can hope for.'

Yuri's dealer, Jean-Jacques, was coming any day now, to take the portrait away to be exhibited in London, or perhaps Paris. Kitty would be glad when it was gone. Yuri would be relieved too, she knew. He seemed to find his own paintings painful to encounter. Except the ones of her. These pictures were never given to Jean-Jacques; they were all here in the studio, stacked against the wall and covered in a calico dust sheet. Kitty had been staying in the Garden House for three months now. The stack was growing wider, deeper – at least fifteen paintings, standing back to back. Kitty found it strange to think of her face repeated there, each version quite different, and yet the same. It was rare for Yuri to paint a model more than once. When he'd explored the mystery of one body, he liked to move on to another. But with Kitty, he wanted to persevere until he'd captured that look he'd first seen. That Russian girl.

Yuri had no qualms about scraping the paint from a canvas, destroying days of work. His models had to keep returning until he was satisfied – enough – with what he'd achieved. They didn't mind, even though they were not being paid for their time – Yuri chose faces and bodies that interested him, rather than relying on professionals offering their services. Lucinda was an art student who felt honoured to model for Yuri and was keen to learn from the process as well. A young man who sometimes posed, Edward, was also from the Slade. Amelia arrived in a sports car, a long silk scarf fluttering out behind her; she was an heiress, wealthy and single. Yuri had made a sculpture of her. In the moulded form she looked bulkier than she did in real life, the features coarse, but she was not offended. Another of the models Kitty had met was the wife of a well-known playwright. All of them undressed without any embarrassment and let Yuri arrange their bodies – placing their hands, arms, legs wherever he wanted them to be; adjusting their hair so that it lay, just so, against their skin. Amelia didn't even bother to put on a gown when she took a break; she wandered around the studio, sipping a cup of tea, her heavy breasts swaying with each step she took. Yuri's housekeeper stayed out of the studio when the models were there, setting down the tea tray outside the door – but that was due to her feelings, not theirs.

When Kitty had spent enough time making sketches of Boris, the skeleton mounted on a stand in the hallway, or Claudius, the Roman statue borrowed from Hamilton Hall, Yuri invited her to set up an easel beside him and make use of his models. Kitty had found it excruciating at first – not only having to display her drawing skills to the cool gaze of the models, but overcoming her awkwardness about their exposed bodies. She had barely been able to bring herself to draw Edward. There were no cotton underpants worn in Yuri's studio, like there were at the Slade; the young man posed completely naked, his legs sprawled apart. Kitty didn't even want to try to capture, with her piece of charcoal, the way his penis flopped across his thigh. But Yuri had insisted she try. The ill-founded rules of society did not apply in the studio, he explained. There was nothing shameful – or even very personal – about the naked body. It conveyed the essence of the human being. He had spoken with a deep passion, borne out by the way he dedicated himself to his work. Painting the nude was the highest challenge, he explained, the greatest achievement. The whole history of art was evidence of this – from cave paintings right up to the work of the modern masters. So were the furnishings of England's finest homes. In Hamilton Hall, naked bodies were to be seen in numerous paintings, drawings and etchings. There must have been a dozen nude statues as well, ranging from the little cherubs on Louisa's writing desk to Venus standing in the middle of the lily pond, to the man wearing nothing but a laurel wreath, who graced the front hall.

Yuri's models always lingered at the end of their sessions to share a glass of wine and some bread and cheese. However, they were never invited to stay overnight – the students were driven to the train station in Yuri's Morris; the other two departed in their own cars. Kitty could tell they wanted to be condescending to her but were unsure of her status. Though Yuri introduced her as a friend, they could see she was also his pupil and his house guest. Kitty didn't know if they were aware that she too modelled for him – whether any of them had lifted up the dust sheet and discovered her portraits. If they had, she wondered what they thought of the fact that he'd painted her over and over again. And that she was not naked, as they were, but instead wore precious garments that they'd never even seen.

Finally, one day, Amelia had asked if Kitty was related to the prince in some distant way, as if that might explain her presence at the Garden House. Kitty had told her how she'd met Yuri by chance, and been invited to come and live there. She could see that her story sounded no more convincing to Amelia than it did to Kitty herself. She still felt that Yuri must have made a mistake. He'd seen something – or someone – in her that wasn't really there. And when he realised his error, he would surely send her away.

The thought of that happening made her feel cold inside. She wanted desperately to stay here with Yuri. True to his promise, he'd given her lessons in drawing, painting, anatomy, sculpture, and even the history of art. And he'd been impressed by her progress, going so far as to say that she had natural talent. If she worked hard, she could become an accomplished artist. His belief in her seemed to make her hands deft, her eye discerning, her focus clear. It all felt like a dream come true.

But it was not just the teaching that she treasured, or even the thrill of working alongside a famous artist. Throughout her childhood she'd had to fight for attention. Her brothers always seemed to come first. They were younger, noisier. Perhaps they were more interesting. After all, a farming family had more use for sons than a daughter. Here in the Garden House, Kitty had Yuri to herself. Where her art was concerned, he was a tough master, giving praise only where it was warranted. But in all other matters he would go out of his way to offer her encouragement. When Kitty experimented with how she dressed or did her hair, he never made her feel self-conscious. Rather, he would compliment her on her taste. Kitty felt her confidence growing. She began to believe that one day she might even have her own special style, like the red-haired girl she'd first seen in the British Museum.

When Yuri looked at her, Kitty felt beautiful. There was more admiration in his eyes than she'd seen expressed by any of the boys in Wattle Creek – even the Irish shearer who had courted her over two seasons, before failing to show up at Seven Gums for a third. Yuri didn't flirt with her, though, or make her feel uncomfortable. Of course, he was far too old for her. But the fact was, he never flirted with anyone. Kitty saw how women tried to seduce him – the life-drawing models, female friends who visited, and even one of the ladies from the village. Then there was Lady Hamilton. The first time Yuri had introduced Kitty to her – simply announcing that the young artist was now living with him, and making no attempt at seeking approval for what was technically an extra tenant – it was obvious that the mistress of the Big House was attracted to him. But he was as impervious to her charms as he was to the others. It was part of his allure, Kitty suspected – the way he held himself back from them all.

There was a veil of mystery over other parts of his life as well. Kitty had assumed, at first, that all his income came from selling paintings. He always managed to find money when needed, though it sometimes took him a week or so to get hold of it. But one day, he'd told Kitty he had another source of wealth. When he'd escaped from Russia during the revolution, because the Bolsheviks were murdering anyone they accused of supporting the Tsar, he'd taken with him a suitcase full of heirlooms. There were ornaments encrusted with diamonds, valuable jewellery, rare watches, figurines of solid gold. Since arriving in England he'd been sacrificing the family history to pay his bills, selling off treasures, piece by piece, that he'd admired since childhood. But he didn't mind, as long as it meant he was free to continue working. Kitty had no idea whether he still had plenty of heirlooms left to sell, or if he might soon run out. He appeared to follow no budget, and have no plan for the future. Kitty wondered if his life here in this small rented cottage was a perverse reaction to the loss of his old world – one of such extraordinary privilege that she couldn't begin to picture it, even with Yuri's reminiscences. His accounts of balls at the Imperial palace and parties at country estates made what Kitty had seen of the Hamiltons' lifestyle seem lacklustre and unimaginative. Yet now, Yuri made do with unwanted furnishings scrounged from the outhouses of the Hall – armchairs with exposed springs; a cupboard with a missing hinge and a drooping door; the dining table with a wobbly leg. At the same time, he employed a housekeeper and drank fine wine. There was something mad and careless about it all. In some ways, he lived like the successful, well-established artist he was. In others, he behaved like a person doing penance for a dark and haunting crime.

Kitty emerged from behind the screen, the costume in place but gaping open at the back. Without speaking, she crossed to Yuri and turned around. She felt his fingers moving up her spine as he fastened the long line of buttons. She held out her arms like a child being dressed. Yuri adjusted the bodice and then draped the scarf over her shoulders. Glancing down, she saw how the skirt flared out at her knee, mimicking the shape of a lampshade. Beyond that, the loose legs of the harem trousers fell in soft folds, billowing out from the bands that encircled her ankles. Yuri gathered up her hair, pinning it on top of her head. She remembered the dreamy feeling of having her hair done by her mother. Often, Kitty's mother was in a hurry, dragging the brush through knots and tangles, and binding the strands roughly into a plait. But when she was slower, gentler, those moments were some of the most intimate her daughter remembered sharing with her. Now, Yuri's touch – gentle as a butterfly – carried Kitty back, a bittersweet echo of what she had lost.

When she was fully dressed – with a long strand of shiny beads around her neck, a turban decorated with an egret feather covering her hair – Yuri studied her. As he swept her with his intent gaze, she let her own eyes play over his face. She traced the lines of his wrinkles, fanning out from the corners of his eyes. She took in the unruly grey hair, long and straight, that he frequently combed back with his fingers. His lips were thin, yet gave no hint of meanness. The bottom one was often pushed up, suggesting the look of a determined child. She tried to work out how the separate elements combined to form the generous expression that she associated with him. But perhaps it was just that she saw in his face a reflection of all the kindness she had experienced.

When Yuri finally nodded his approval – having smoothed out the skirt and tucked a loose strand of hair behind her ear – Kitty went to sit on the chaise longue. She clasped her hands in her lap. She was ready for Yuri to tell her what pose he wanted.

'Don't move,' he said. 'I want to paint you just like that – waiting for something. Waiting for life.'

The look of deep concentration that she knew so well came over his face. He devoted all his energy to his painting, working like a man enslaved. He was a perfectionist – he had to be, or he could never have painted the way he did. But Kitty sensed there was more at stake for him than this: something dark and painful underpinned his desire to capture her face – her self – on canvas. She often had the feeling that when he saw Kitty, he was thinking of someone else. A lover, wife or daughter, perhaps – a woman he'd loved and lost, whose story he was keeping to himself. Once, he'd even addressed Kitty by the wrong name.

Katya.

Yuri had let the mistake go uncorrected, as if to avoid drawing attention to it – after all, the words were almost the same. But Kitty had stored the name away, like a clue.

Katya was the one, she felt sure, to whom Yuri's heart still belonged.

Sometimes, as Kitty sat in front of Yuri's easel, his eyes searching her face, her body, she felt uneasy. Maybe she should not be letting him use her to evoke the memory of someone else. Maybe he should not be asking it of her. But then she reminded herself that this was an artist's studio. There were no rules. Nothing was wrong. Everything was right.

Kitty settled into her pose. She formed a picture of herself as if from afar and fixed it in her head – that way, when she had to stop for a break, she could return to exactly the same position. But she didn't need to interrupt Yuri very often. She had learned how to soften each set of muscles in turn, tensing others so that she held herself still. Now, as he began to work, she relaxed, letting the sound of the brush dabbing paint onto the canvas fill her head. She let go of all her concerns – the nagging regret she felt about the silence from her family, and the fear of what she would do the day Yuri finally told her she had to move on. She felt so safe and content, sitting here. She wished that time could be held as still as her body trapped in its pose. That nothing would ever change.

Kitty drove away from the strip of *dukas*, keeping her eyes on the road, wary of encountering without warning a chicken or a goat or even an unattended child. From the corner of her eye she could see – resting on the passenger's seat – a bundle wrapped in newspaper and tied with string. She pictured the orange silk hidden inside. She hadn't been able to resist buying it. Perhaps, some time in the future, she would have it made up into a dress, or even a pair of trousers, if she were brave enough. But not yet. It would remind her too much of Yuri. Worse, it could remind Theo of the Russian painter as well.

Theo had seen the *Scheherazade* series of paintings. After he had started visiting the Garden House – when he and Kitty were in love and wanted to share every moment they could – Yuri decided to show them to him. He had told Kitty he wanted to make it clear to Theo there was nothing scandalous about the pictures. That way, Theo could defend her reputation to his family, if questions were ever asked. Kitty had agreed. She was well aware of how she was viewed in the village. Everyone knew she was living alone with the

Russian painter. It helped that Yuri was a man almost old enough to be her father, and that he was famous – a prince. But still, when Kitty met people in the post office or the shop, she could feel disapproval running alongside their curiosity. Sometimes she sensed they were undressing her in their minds, making her one of Yuri's nude models, or maybe even his lover. It worried Kitty that the Admiral and Lady Hamilton would inevitably be suspicious of her too. Yuri had pointed out that the Hamiltons were more educated than the village folk, their world view more expansive. They were art collectors, museum patrons. Nevertheless, showing Theo the paintings seemed a sensible precaution. He'd be able to see how demure Kitty looked, in spite of her exotic costume, like a classical ballet dancer caught offstage. He'd know there was nothing sexual in the way Yuri displayed her – she looked only defenceless and innocent, a simple vessel waiting to be filled by the passion of the choreographer.

Yuri chose an evening when they'd all just enjoyed a roast leg of lamb left by the housekeeper. They'd eaten at the kitchen table, after Yuri had removed the dehydrated corpse of a rat he'd found somewhere and kept for Kitty to draw. Even though Kitty had sponged clean the place where it had lain, Theo had chosen a seat at the opposite end of the table. Now he lounged there, his chin propped on his hand, his collar unbuttoned. Kitty noticed he'd wiped the last of the gravy from his plate with a hunk of torn bread. She had never seen him so informal and relaxed.

'I have something to show you.' Yuri beckoned Theo to follow him to the studio. Kitty trailed behind them, apprehensive. She'd never told Theo she posed for Yuri – she didn't know if he suspected, if he'd heard rumours. She'd explained her relationship with the prince as being simply that of teacher and student. To support this, she'd shown Theo some of her artwork: drawings, paintings and sketches. His praise had been so extravagant she knew it was meaningless – yet it made her love him even more.

She let the men go ahead of her down the corridor. Their footsteps were hollow thuds on the worn carpet. As he entered the room, Theo stopped short, his back stiffening visibly. As Kitty came in behind him she saw why. Yuri had set out all the paintings. They were propped up against easels, cupboards, walls. Kitty stared around the room, meeting her own gaze in face after face. The theatrical clothes made her body not hers – but her hands, her hair, her eyes were unmistakable. She'd seen the images one by one, as they were completed. But now, set out together like this, she felt dwarfed by their impact.

She watched Theo's expression, her breath trapped in her chest. Yuri didn't say anything. He smoked quietly, eyeing Theo as if the young man, too, could be the subject of a picture.

For a long time, Theo made no comment. Then he nodded, reaching a decision.

'Impressive. They're very good.' He clapped Yuri on the shoulder. Kitty smiled, relief flowing through her. 'Of course,' Theo continued, his manner mock-gallant, 'you haven't done her justice!'

'"Beauty is in the eye of the beholder",' Yuri responded. 'Isn't that one of your English sayings? You and I, we cannot see with the same eyes.'

The two men prowled the room, moving from one painting to another. Kitty could feel tension brewing between them – as if

some kind of contest were being played out. There was a thread
of antagonism beneath the careful courtesy, the light banter. On
various occasions, Kitty had heard each of the men speak negatively
of the other. Yuri thought Theo distracted Kitty from her art. Theo
believed Yuri held too much influence over his girlfriend. In this
moment, it seemed, the animosity was rising to the surface. She
began to wish that the paintings had remained in their corner, hidden beneath the cloth.

But in the end, showing Theo the pictures had proved to be
the right move. After a servant from the Big House happened to
see Kitty through the window of the studio, posing for Yuri in one
of the *Ballets Russes* outfits, Theo had been able to step straight in
as planned, deflecting any criticism. The Admiral, it turned out,
was completely unperturbed. Of course a lady could appear in
a painting – Hamilton Hall was stacked with family portraits by
famous painters. Louisa's reaction had been harder to pin down.
Kitty detected an undercurrent of hostility, which only made sense
later when Yuri explained he'd declined to paint Lady Hamilton's
picture. Whatever her private feelings, Louisa publicly endorsed
the Admiral's support for Kitty continuing to sit for Yuri. It helped
a lot that Yuri had assured everyone the works were not for sale.
Back then, it seemed, nothing of great importance was at risk in
the whole situation. Not surprisingly, Louisa and the Admiral had
insisted on viewing the portraits – but the biggest issue that arose
from their visit to the studio was the discovery that Yuri had damaged the walls. If he didn't have a rag at hand, he would wipe the
excess paint from his brushes on the nearest surface. Louisa had
been shocked to see that a whole area of the wall nearest his easel

was coated in a crust of paint marks, many layers deep. Every colour of the palette was there. The rough, hasty dabs captured in shape and texture the impatience of the artist in the grip of his quest. To Kitty, it was a work of art in itself. But the Hamiltons saw only a ruined wall. Yuri promised to have the studio repainted when he ceased to be a tenant in the Garden House. In the midst of the upset, the portraits of Kitty were all but forgotten.

Kitty drove slowly towards a huge shed with rows of heavy machinery lined up outside. Here, at last, was the Kongara Tractor Workshop. Kitty eyed the place with interest, trying to ignore a nagging feeling of guilt. She knew she shouldn't be here. The decision to flout Theo's boundaries was linked, somehow, with her having given in to the desire to own the orange silk – as though two failings were no worse than one. It was like dieting; once you'd fallen for that slice of cake, you might as well forget about watching what you ate for the rest of the day.

She saw a couple of Africans using a welder, holding up crude masks to protect their eyes. There were two swarthy Europeans sitting on an old fuel drum, smoking cigarettes. A group of fair-skinned men were standing around an engine laid out in bits on a tarpaulin. Kitty searched their faces, but found no one she knew. She was about to drive on – feeling half sorry she'd failed to find her friends, and half relieved that she could now leave, innocent of any serious crime – but then she heard the sound of voices chanting. She followed it towards its source, near a second shed. There she brought the car to a standstill, letting the motor idle.

A tall man with sandy hair was standing in front of a crowd of Africans seated on wooden benches. He held up a piece of metal – some engine part that Kitty didn't recognise.

'What is this?' he called out in English.

His students yelled back in unison. 'Cranki shafti.'

Kitty laughed to herself. They always had to add that vowel! She watched the teacher enviously. As if he could feel her gaze, the man looked across. The next moment he was striding towards her, offering a friendly grin.

'Can I help you, ma'am?' Resting his arm on the roof of her car, he bent to her level. 'Are you looking for someone?' He had the same soft accent as the Irishmen Kitty had met on the plane.

'Yes, I am – Paddy O'Halloran.' As she said the name, Kitty felt a wave of longing, remembering how at ease she'd felt with him, how encouraging and uncritical he had been. 'Do you know him?'

'Oh, aye – I know old Paddy! He's working in Dar es Salaam.'

Kitty frowned. Perhaps there was another man with the same name as Paddy. It might be common in Ireland, like John Smith in Australia. 'He was definitely meant to be stationed here. There was a group of them who arrived from England together – engineers and mechanics.'

'They were transferred, that lot. No point in fixing the tractors here. They're all shite. Pardon me, but there's no other word I can use.'

Kitty was surprised. 'What's wrong with them?' She scanned the ones she could see: the paintwork was bright and new; there was plenty of tread on the tyres. They looked a lot better than the one her father made do with at Seven Gums. She wondered if the men were overly fussy with their tractors, like the women were with their furnishings.

'They're all ex-army. It turned out the last lot had spent the war sitting on a beach in the Philippines. The dear old OFC bought them sight unseen, shipped them straight here. We made one good tractor out of every ten.' He shook his head. 'They were that rusty under their fancy paintwork you could make holes in the metal with your finger. So now they're working on the tractors when they come off the ships. When they find something worth having, they send it out here. Makes sense.' He gave a smile. 'Well, a bit more sense!'

Kitty forced herself to smile in return, hiding a sense of loss that she knew was out of proportion to the tenuous link she had with her travel companions. 'Well, thank you.' She couldn't resist asking, 'How are you going with your class?'

He smiled again, shrugging his shoulders. 'Shite.'

Kitty gave him a sympathetic grimace, then lifted her hand in a quick wave. 'Must get going. Thanks!' As she drove off, she saw the man in her rear-vision mirror, watching her with curious eyes – probably wondering who she was and why she'd been asking for Paddy. She considered going back to explain their connection – to make sure she hadn't given rise to gossip that might circle back to Head Office. But she kept driving. She could make things worse, drawing attention to herself. And she didn't want to risk speaking to the man again – she couldn't trust herself not to beg him to find a way for her to take over his job.

*

Kitty leaned back in her chair as Gabriel placed a bowl of soup in front of her. She knew one should not adjust one's posture to accommodate the movements of staff, but the action was instinctive. She picked up her spoon straight away. She knew Theo didn't have long for lunch and could not begin eating before she did.

At the first sip, she stiffened. The soup was spicy, with even a hint of chilli. What had Eustace been thinking! Kitty didn't mind the taste, or the faint burning on her tongue – Yuri had introduced her to eating foreign food. But the dish didn't fit with the boarding school meals that Theo enjoyed. It certainly wasn't part of the usual lunch menu. She watched nervously as he leaned over the soup dish, breathing in the steam.

'Mulligatawny!' Theo exclaimed. 'My father's favourite.'

'How nice.' Kitty tried not to look taken aback – after all, she was meant to know what her own cook was planning to serve. At the same time she felt a rush of frustration. No matter how much she tried to find patterns and work out the rules, there was always an exception lurking, waiting to catch her out.

'You know the story of it?' Theo didn't wait for her to answer; he was so used to assuming her ignorance. 'It was invented in the days of the Imperial Raj when we were running India. The local cooks didn't understand the whole idea of serving soup before the main course. They didn't even know what soup was. So the British officers told them how to prepare it – using stock, meat and so forth. Of course, the Indians can't cook anything without adding spices. So this was the result.'

'Fascinating,' Kitty said. She heard the false tone in her voice – she got tired sometimes of being shown to be ill-informed – but there was no sign that Theo had picked it up.

He devoured the soup, along with some bread, then waved away the next course. 'Got to go, I'm afraid.' He nodded at Kitty – the kiss was only for the mornings. Moments later, she heard the Land Rover starting up, then the crunch of gravel as he drove off.

When she left the table, she made a mental note to ask Eustace to write down the odd name of that soup. She went into the sitting room and sat down. From the kitchen came the distant sound of dishes and pots clattering in the sink. Kitty almost wished she could go and join in, just for something to do. She managed a wry smile. Perhaps she should take up smoking. Or learn some kind of handcraft. Crochet. Weaving. Anything that could not possibly be construed as art . . .

Still at a loss, she wandered into the bedroom, where she pulled out Ahmed's package. She wanted to see how the cloth looked draped over her body, the colour set against her skin. Surely there was nothing wrong with doing that? As she opened the bundle, the smell of sandalwood rose up. At first she thought it was just the aroma of Ahmed's shop, trapped in there, but then she saw a small oblong shape – a bar of soap. She'd forgotten: on impulse, she had bought it for Diana. The idea had come to her while she was loitering in the *duka* trying to make up her mind about the piece of orange silk. Kitty was amazed at herself now for even considering such a gesture. Going next door with a 'get well' gift could be seen as impertinent, almost invasive. On the other hand, Kitty remembered how Diana had come to the airstrip to meet her in Theo's place, and how she'd showed Kitty over her new home and introduced her to the Kongara Club. In her own way, Diana had been quite kind to Kitty – even if she had only been doing her duty.

Kitty weighed the soap in her hand. Maybe the other women were already commenting on the fact that Kitty had not visited Diana, when she lived right next door. It might be safest just to pop round and hand it over. She wouldn't need to stay.

In case her nerve failed her, Kitty set off straight away. As she tiptoed over the gravel, protecting her heels, she wondered whether she should have wrapped up her gift. Or would that seem pretentious when it was just a bar of soap? She made herself knock as soon as she reached the front door; if she delayed, she knew she might leave.

Footsteps approached. Then the door swung open. Kitty stepped back in surprise. Instead of a houseboy, she found herself facing Diana's husband. It was early afternoon – much too late for Richard to have come home for lunch. For a brief unguarded moment, he looked strained, almost haggard, then a courteous smile transformed his face.

'Kitty! How kind of you to call.' Kitty opened her mouth to explain why she was here, when he launched on. 'I can't invite you in, I'm afraid. Diana's not up to having visitors.' He had a strangely authoritative presence, considering he was quite short for a man and slightly built.

'Yes, of course. I understand.' Kitty handed him the bar of soap – wishing now that it had been wrapped. 'I imagine it takes some time to recover from malaria. I trust she's improving, bit by bit?'

Richard hesitated. In that instant, Kitty heard a low wailing sound coming from the direction of the master bedroom. Richard gave her a wooden stare, then gathered himself. 'She's certainly on the mend. I'll tell her you called. She'll be touched. Charmed.'

He pushed the door shut. Kitty remained there for a short time, replaying in her mind the mournful cries she'd just heard. She hadn't imagined it. There was no thud of departing footsteps on the other side of the door – she thought Richard might still be standing there, waiting to hear her leave.

She walked back along the driveway. It was clear to her that Diana was in distress, and that Richard didn't want Kitty to know. It made her feel uneasy. She considered returning, demanding to see Diana. But that would be impossibly rude – Theo would be horrified. She reminded herself that Diana was theatrical, hysterical. That day when the Daimler had almost hit the little girl, she'd completely overreacted. Then, there was the bottle of pink pills Kitty had seen. For someone like Diana, suffering from bad blood – and possibly bad nerves as well – a bout of malaria might be hard to bear.

By the time she reached her own front door, her concerns had faded. Poor Richard was probably worn out by Diana's fuss. No wonder he'd behaved oddly – he was worried about her. His English manners meant he didn't want to talk about his wife's illness, but the very fact that he was there, at home, was proof that he cared. Kitty imagined him hurrying to the bedroom to wipe Diana's brow, stroke her hair. As General Manager he was even busier than Theo – everyone wanted to make demands on his time – but his wife came first.

Kitty paused, her fingers resting on the door handle. What would happen if she became ill? Would Theo spend time at home looking after her? If she was honest, it didn't seem likely. Since the day he'd brought her the box of chocolates there had been occasional moments of affection: a lingering hug, a pat on the bottom as she passed, a compliment delivered with a smile. Once he'd come home with a bunch of flowers he'd bought from a charity stall at the Club. Another time he'd given her a slice of a cake that had been shared around at Head Office in honour of a birthday. Kitty could see Theo was making an effort. But she still felt as if the main act of his life was played out at Head Office; all else was just an afterthought.

She looked over to the house next door. A dull pain formed inside her. She couldn't avoid thinking that the reason Richard was there, and not at his desk, was quite simple: he loved Diana more than Theo loved her. But was it fair to compare one marriage with another? There were so many factors at play. Maybe Richard and Diana had enjoyed an untroubled life together, notwithstanding her health problems. Richard had fought in the war, but he may not have suffered like Theo had. Even if he had, the experience didn't affect everyone to the same degree. And anyway, perhaps it was nothing to do with Richard – and everything to do with his wife. In spite of her odd ways, Diana always looked perfect. She was funny and interesting. And of course, she was the daughter of an English gentleman. She knew how to behave, even if she didn't always do it. She could make the right choice when she wanted to, without even having to think.

Kitty remembered the disastrous picnic she'd arranged last weekend. It was a simple affair with just her and Theo and one small basket of provisions. Kitty had prepared the main part of the meal herself. Ignoring the disapproval of her cook and houseboy, she'd baked her mother's specialty, egg and bacon pie. When it was cooling on the kitchen bench the evocative smell made Kitty want to cry with longing for her home. The place from which she'd yearned to escape now seemed a haven of simplicity and familiarity. To complete the packed lunch she'd found some bananas and a bottle of lemonade. She'd chosen a place up behind Londoni, near the water tower. There was a good view over the plains and she knew Theo would be reassured by the presence of the African caretaker who strolled around in his khakis, a rifle over one shoulder and a bow and quiver hanging from the other. Finding a private spot, Kitty had produced the old travelling blanket – the one they'd used in England, with Theo's great-grandfather's initials embroidered in the corner. Looking at it spread over the ground, Kitty could almost imagine the little red plane parked nearby. But her optimism about the occasion had been short-lived. They'd had to move soon after setting up, when Theo noticed a trail of safari ants approaching. The new location turned out to be littered with spiky seed pods that stuck in their clothes. The pie, sweating inside a cake tin, had looked unappetising. Kitty realised she should have brought the folding chairs. She should have asked Eustace to prepare whatever Cynthia would have ordered for a packed lunch. She should have gone to the proper picnic site set up by the OFC. Maybe she should even have invited another couple to help create a festive mood. Now, thinking back, Kitty shook her head with frustration. How had she got it so wrong?

She'd just have to try harder, she told herself. It wasn't fair to blame Theo for her own shortcomings. Instead, she should be thinking about what she could do to make him want to spend more time with her. She didn't need one of Pippa's magazines to know that a happy husband hurries home eagerly at the end of each day.

Kitty knew Theo was more than satisfied with his meals; no change was needed there. But perhaps the bunch of flowers he bought her was a hint about interior decorating? When he said she should spend her days doing what the other women did – going to the hairdresser or the tailor, even playing tennis – could this be his way of suggesting her presentation was below par? Maybe she'd put on some weight. Her old accent was creeping back. Her face was too tanned.

She was making mistakes she could not afford, and it was time to stop.

As she stepped inside, she lifted her head, sucking in her belly and straightening her back. She imagined a string pulling up from the top of her head, giving her perfect posture as she walked along the hall.

EIGHT

Theo used his bread and butter knife to tap a straight line around the top of his boiled egg before slicing it neatly off. Kitty eyed him from across the table as she toyed with her own egg; its shell, where she'd cut it, was a ragged mess. He was wearing a crisp white shirt and the trousers that belonged with one of his best suits – too dark for the climate, but very smart. It had been ages since she'd seen him dressed in his khaki field clothes; these days, he had to spend all his time at Head Office. The rains were due to start soon and ploughing was behind schedule. Down on the Units, the contractors and native labourers were working into the night, but the abrasive soils kept on breaking the ploughshares. The people at Head Office, along with a steady flow of visiting executives from London, were holding urgent meetings to try to solve the problem.

'Who's arriving today?' Kitty asked. 'Someone important?'

Theo sighed. 'The DC has requested a meeting. As if we haven't got enough on our plates already.'

'The District Commissioner?' Kitty queried. She wanted Theo to know she remembered the initials – that she took in all the things he said to her.

Theo nodded. 'He has to dig his oar in now and again, or he feels left out. The Colonial Office finds it hard to accept that the Scheme is run by the British Ministry of Food and not by the Government of Tanganyika.'

'It does seem odd,' Kitty commented.

Theo waved his hand dismissively. 'The Colonial Service is just too slow, too . . . old. The Ministry of Food is new. Fast-moving, efficient, a place for fresh ideas.'

Kitty hid the surprise she felt as she listened to her husband. She still couldn't get used to hearing him express forward-thinking views like this. His experiences in the war had prompted him to turn so firmly to the past, adopting the belief that whatever was old was best. Old families, old homes, old books and paintings . . . She looked at his left hand resting on the table. On his little finger he wore a gold signet ring. The Hamilton coat of arms engraved there – the lion, the leaf, the book – was an ever-present symbol of the power of history and tradition. When she'd met Theo, he'd not been wearing the ring. He'd taken it off as a gesture of rebellion against the principle of inherited privilege. In the kitchen of the Garden House there had been long, late-night discussions – arguments, really – between Theo and Yuri, as the older man tried to defend the imperial court and the cause of the White Russians. In those days, Theo talked passionately about justice and equality. But the war, it seemed, had brought everything into question. There had been the terrible disaster when he'd crashed his Lancaster and been the only survivor. And that was only the beginning. He'd watched all but a few of his friends die, one after another. Over the course of the war over half of Britain's airmen were killed. He'd seen so many last letters written, last meals eaten, last cigarettes stubbed out . . . Theo's mates died fighting to protect the British way of life, which was deeply grounded in tradition. They fought for their king – and there could be no more powerful statement of inherited privilege than royalty. By the time the war was over, the signet ring had reappeared.

With the coming of peacetime, Theo's newfound commitment to his heritage had found an outlet in the task of reinstalling the family treasures at the Hall, so that Louisa and the Admiral could move back in. The main building had been requisitioned by the army not long after the war began. Kitty had been there the day the order was delivered. She and Theo were already married, and lived in some rented rooms near the airfield. Kitty had returned to visit her new relatives – but mainly to see Yuri. He was still adding paintings to the series of images of Kitty, working from sketches now that she was no longer there to sit for him. An ordinary black car had driven up to the front of the Hall. A man in uniform saluted the Admiral before handing over a typed document. When the old man finished reading it, the paper was nailed to the front door. Louisa had stood in front of it, wide-eyed with dismay as she mouthed the words written there: *RAF Requisition Order of Premises. Emergency Powers (Defence) Act 1939.* When the shock wore off, and the Admiral declared that the family must do its duty with a good will, the Hall was stripped of its fine furniture, the art collection, the wall hangings and carpets. Everything was stored in the gate-keeper's lodge. The Admiral, his wife and a staff of three took over the Garden House. It was all very sudden; there had been no time even for Yuri to repaint the brush-marked walls in the studio. Kitty sometimes wondered what different path her life might have taken if the house had not been requisitioned. If Yuri had not been forced to move into the cottage at the edge of the village – that small and secret place, cut off from the outside world . . .

The Big House was handed back to the Hamiltons soon after the war was over. When the last military vehicle had driven away, Theo had swung into action. As he supervised the unpacking of boxes and the moving of furniture, he had been determined to recreate the family home exactly as he'd known it. Small details mattered – every ornament or piece of framed embroidery had to be returned to its rightful place. He even commissioned a stone-mason to repair the marble fireplaces that had been damaged by soldiers poking at burning logs as they tried to stay warm. Kitty had assisted Theo where she could – there was little else for her to do, now that she was a resident at Hamilton Hall. Her role as a volunteer for the war effort was over; she was a country gentle-man's wife. Sometimes she wandered into the Garden House – the rooms now echoey, empty – searching for signs that Yuri had once lived and worked there. But the Hamiltons' occupancy had all but erased any record of those years. There was just the odd smear of oil paint, overlooked by the decorators. Dents in the floorboards made by the legs of the easel. The scratch on the kitchen window where Yuri had shown Kitty how real diamonds can score a line in glass. Once she'd found a desiccated rat – not in the Garden House, but in the stables. It reminded her of the one Yuri had given her to draw, and of how pleased he'd been with the result. She could almost hear his voice, feel his congratulatory touch on her shoulder . . . Theo had come upon her crouched over the dead creature, her body racked with sobs. He'd been kind at first, but then frustrated at such extreme emotion being expended on a dead rodent, when there were enough real reasons for tears.

Kitty avoided going to the village. She knew that, like an addict drawn to their poison, she'd find herself walking to the far end, past the mill, to stand outside the little cottage where Yuri had lived – breathing its sooty creosote smell, staring at the windows, tracing the patterns of brown stains on the backs of closed curtains. There was no point in torturing herself, she knew. No act of penance could turn back time. And even if it were possible, what different choices would she have made?

Restoring Hamilton Hall had filled Theo's days, causing him to rise early and work until dusk – but there had been something desperate about his commitment. When the project was over, he'd sunk into listless apathy. Now, the Groundnut Scheme was demanding a similar level of dedication from him. Kitty's relief at seeing Theo so relaxed and engaged when she'd first arrived was giving way to a sense of unease. Was Theo simply doing a difficult job, fighting the war on hunger? Or was the Scheme his new obsession? She hoped the fact that he was now talking of the need to turn from the old and embrace the new was a good sign. That it meant he was becoming free again. He was returning to the view of the world that had been part of the man she'd fallen in love with. But she had a creeping fear that the shift was too sudden and too great.

Theo poured milk into his teacup, then tilted the pot to pour.

'So, why does the District Commissioner want to see you?' Kitty asked.

'This time,' Theo explained, 'they're making a fuss about conditions in the Native Labour Camps. It's true – there is some unrest. The water is rather brackish down there. They say the food rations are inadequate. But the big issue seems to be that the Africans thought they'd be able to bring all their wives and children here. That's completely impractical. We've still got lots of European contractors waiting for proper housing so their families can come out here. The Africans will just have to wait.'

Kitty wondered whether to betray that she knew some of them had brought their wives to Kongara anyway. Pippa had scandalised the women at the Club with talk of a filthy slum that had grown up on the other side of town, out past the workshops. Wives of the native labourers lived there, alongside a growing population of African prostitutes.

'I saw one,' Pippa said. 'She was outside the police station. She looked ghastly – red lipstick and blue eye shadow. It just doesn't go with black skin!'

There had been silence while her words sank in. The image was hard to picture.

Kitty decided not to comment on what Theo had said. Obviously, he knew the slum was there. If she let on that she did too, he could well use its presence as proof that he was right in instructing his wife to keep to the central part of Londoni.

'Have you met the DC before?' Kitty asked. She eyed the butter, waiting for Theo to notice and pass it across.

'A few times. He's a reasonable enough fellow. Been here a long time. Very experienced. But there's a cloud hanging over him. He was mixed up in some shady business a couple of years ago, involving a local white farmer. It was that dreadful chap Taylor. You saw him one day – remember?'

Kitty gave a brief nod, giving up on the butter and pretending instead to be focused on her egg. She had an irrational fear that whatever Theo was about to tell her might end up exposing the fact that she'd driven out of town to the Catholic Mission – that she'd seen Taylor's vineyards and spent time feeding his labourers, tending their wounds.

'Taylor was to go to prison – for what crime, I've no idea. It's all rather hush-hush. But the point is, the District Commissioner allowed him to serve his sentence in some kind of private jail, instead of sending him to Dar es Salaam.' He glanced up at Kitty, giving a short laugh. 'You know what they call a prison here? *Hoteli ya mfalme*. The hotel of the king.'

Kitty gave a thin smile. Theo looked pleased with his Swahili phrase, but the words were barely recognisable – mispronounced, and distorted by his strong English accent.

'Of course, it would be appalling for a white man to be locked up in an African jail,' Theo added. 'But still, in a colonial setting especially, justice should be seen to be done. There's no doubt the DC went out on a limb for Taylor.' Theo frowned thoughtfully. 'It just makes one wonder if there's some connection between the two. Knowing what we do of Taylor – that doesn't reflect well on the DC.'

Kitty sipped her tea, hoping there was no sign on her face of her keen interest in Theo's story. What crime had Taylor committed? How long had he been locked up for – and where? She couldn't decide if the fact that the man had been jailed himself – albeit in a private cell – made it better or worse that he now fed off prison labour.

Theo picked up Cynthia's salt pot, using the tiny china spoon to create a little pile of white on the side of his plate next to the wedge of butter he'd removed from the block in the dish. He chose a triangle of toast from the rack.

Kitty dug further into her egg. Then her hand froze as she saw a bloody red blob in the yolk. The beginnings of an embryo. She wasn't offended by the sight in the way Theo would be; she'd grown up on a farm where roosters mixed freely with the hens. Most of the eggs were fertile, but you couldn't tell as long as they were eaten soon enough after being laid. Kitty's mother sometimes used eggs of questionable freshness, especially when the hens eased off laying, and the odd spot of blood didn't bother anyone. But there was no need for this to happen in Londoni – villagers were always eager to sell their eggs. Eustace should be checking every egg he intended to use by making sure it wouldn't float in a bowl of water. Kitty told herself she must remember to instruct him to be much more careful in future. She knew she should put her egg aside quickly, before Theo discovered this evidence of bad housekeeping. But instead, she just sat there, staring into the yolk, her gaze snared by the red stain. It reminded her that her period was due. Her third one since she'd arrived. She nursed a hope that she might be pregnant, but it was only faint.

As the pressure of work had intensified, Theo had had a desk installed in the spare bedroom and he'd spent long hours in there during the evenings, writing reports, checking the typescripts, reading documents from London. Late at night, after he'd finally finished, he'd linger in the sitting room, winding down with a whisky or two. Often, he then slept in the spare room with his desk, even though Kitty had never complained of being disturbed. Around the middle of this last month, he'd spent five nights in a row in there – the crucial dates on Kitty's calendar. Several times, she had almost gone in and told him, straight out, that they had to make love. Right now, tonight; and again the next night, whether they felt like it or not. It was the right time. But men didn't want to know about periods and ovulation – Pippa's magazine had warned about the likelihood of acute embarrassment, the loss of romance. A perilous path for a wife to take. Adopting a different approach, Kitty had tried to seduce Theo away from his deskwork, hovering at his shoulder in her silky nightgown, her thigh pressing against his arm. Alongside thoughts of conceiving a baby, she was still clinging to the hope that the night of lovemaking they'd had, after sharing the box of chocolates, might be repeated. She'd bent over, letting her breasts spill towards him. But he'd just looked up at her in a distracted way before returning to his paperwork.

Theo left the table to get ready for work. Kitty sat alone, her breakfast abandoned. The day stretched ahead of her, barren and unappealing. She buried her face in her hands, a dark weight pressing in around her. Perhaps she would go back to bed, as she'd done on so many other mornings. Perhaps she would stay there all day, pretending to be ill . . .

'I won't be home for lunch today.' Theo's voice reached her through the open door, cutting off her thoughts. 'I'll see you later on.'

Kitty lifted her head as sudden anger sparked inside her. Her husband didn't even offer reasons for staying at work any more. Nor did he give estimates of what time he might reappear. He was probably glad that telephones had yet to be installed in the houses on Millionaire Row (one more example, according to Pippa, of the inability of the OFC to prioritise in any sensible way). It meant Theo didn't have to think of calling his wife to notify her of delays. It was as if she'd become almost invisible to him, a speck at the edge of his horizon. Did he never wonder whether or not she was happy here in Kongara? Did he even care? Why was it always up to Kitty to listen to him, and offer comfort? She was trying so hard to be a good wife. Couldn't she at least expect some effort on his side? She heard the sound of his footsteps again, moving towards the front door. With a shock, she realised he was about to leave without kissing her goodbye. Anger evaporated, replaced by a spike of panic. But then the steps became louder. Kitty looked up as Theo entered the room. He flashed her a smile, his teeth white against his tanned skin. The navy jacket he now wore, set off by his white shirt, combined to highlight the fairness of his hair. He was breathtakingly handsome. Kitty's anger melted like snow in the sun. When he leaned over her chair to kiss her cheek, she breathed in the smell of toothpaste and citrus aftershave, grateful to be close to him.

'I love you,' she said. She spoke again more strongly, overriding the pleading note in her voice. 'I love you.'

Theo gave her a nonplussed look, then ruffled her hair. 'Me too. Have a lovely day, darling.' He tapped her on the shoulder and strode away.

Kitty squinted in the sudden brightness as she walked outside. Nearing her car, freshly dusted by the gardener, she remembered she'd forgotten her swimming bag. But she kept on walking. She'd only just managed to force herself to get dressed and put on her make-up. If she went back to her room, she might stay there.

Inside the car she opened the glove box, feeling for her sunglasses. Her hand closed around an object she didn't recognise until she pulled it out. Father Remi's penknife – the one Tesfa had found while emptying the basket of produce. She'd forgotten she'd put it in there. She ran her fingers over the bone casing, the warm smoothness reminding her of the tortoiseshell on Katya's powder compact. The penknife was old and well used, the handle crazed with cracks. She opened the blade and tested the edge on her thumb, angling it sideways so she wouldn't cut herself. It was sharp and straight.

Kitty brushed away some dried earth that had fallen from the blade onto her dress. It left a pink blush on the white spots that dotted the background of red. The sight reminded her of standing in Father Remi's gardens, looking down at the rich red soil, the ground almost covered with greenery even though it was still the dry season. Set above the dusty plains with all the bare plantations, the place was like a vision. A land of milk and honey. But that was only part of the picture, she told herself. There were the prisoners as well, each with their own tragic story, no doubt. And the *askaris* armed with batons and rifles. Kitty's thoughts turned to the man with the ulcer on his leg. Was it still festering beneath the surface, or had the antiseptic won out? She hoped Father Remi had found time to change the dressing each day.

She weighed the knife in her hand. A good knife, she knew, was a precious possession. Her father wore his in a pouch attached to his belt. He never removed it, even for church. It didn't take long for her to reach a decision. Now that she'd found Father Remi's knife, she would have to return it. It was the only thing to do. She wouldn't stay, she promised herself. She'd come straight back. She'd have lunch at the Club. She'd even sit with Alice.

As Kitty drove into the Mission yard, she was surprised to see the prison trucks already parked there. Their open backs were empty – the prisoners were sitting in rows on the forecourt. She glanced at her watch. It was later than she'd thought.

Emerging from her car, Kitty retrieved Father Remi's basket from the boot. Then she hovered by the vehicle, wiping off her lipstick with the back of her hand. She wished now that she'd gone back inside the house before driving off, to wash her face. She should also have changed into Janet's sensible clothes. The red-and-white spotted dress was too eye-catching; the cloth clung too closely to her figure.

She could not see Father Remi among the prisoners. Nor was he standing by the serving table. Instead, Sister Clara and two younger nuns were waiting ready by the pots. Kitty felt suddenly reluctant to parade herself in front of the crowd. For a second, she thought of Louisa. Which points of etiquette would she recommend to a lady faced with greeting a hundred or so male prisoners? Glancing about her, Kitty saw a path leading down the side of the church. If she could make her way around the back, she could get to the other building. Father Remi might well be in there. If not, she could wait in the reception room for someone to appear, then ask for him to be called.

Kitty's high-heeled sandals were as unsuitable as her dress and make-up. As she wobbled over the paving stones, she didn't dare look back to see if her presence had been noticed. She felt sure the sound of her car arriving, the banging of the door and the boot, would have attracted at least some attention. Reaching the church, she turned down the side path, slipping gratefully out of sight.

The path was made of soft bare earth. The heels of her sandals sank in at each step. Before long, Kitty crouched to take them off, adding them to the basket. She strode on, foot-sure and comfortable. As she went, her gaze travelled up the high stone wall to where pigeons stalked the edges of the tiled roof, making cut-out shapes of grey against the blue. She was almost at the corner when she felt something tugging at the back of her dress. With a lurch of fear, she spun around. A small monkey peered up at her, its hand clutching her hem. Kitty stiffened, trying to pull away. The animal stood only a little taller than the level of her knee, but she remembered Janet's warning about the danger of catching rabies from the bite of a monkey or dog. She was relieved when her dress was let go. But then the monkey reached up and grabbed her hand instead. The grip was firm; the little fingers folded around her own. For a moment, Kitty just stared at it. Something about the wispy fur made her think the animal was quite young.

She bent to look at the pale, hairless face. The big dark eyes were so shiny they might have been swimming with tears.

'Hello there.'

The monkey was clearly tame – someone's pet. She wondered if it was meant to be wandering around on its own. An impatient chattering sound broke from the thin-lipped mouth. Kitty glimpsed teeth, a pink tongue. Then the monkey began dragging her forwards.

As she followed it along the path, a memory stirred in Kitty's head. She felt she'd seen this animal before. Then it came to her. It was the creature she'd first thought was a naked child, crouched on the bonnet of that ramshackle shed-on-wheels.

Taylor.

The hand tugged her on, around the corner. She almost walked into a metal pipe, poised in the air at chest height. A man stood with his back to her some distance away, holding the pipe in the middle, balancing the unwieldy load on his shoulder. Kitty could see he was trying to manoeuvre one end towards a hole in the side of a water tank. As she watched, the end close to her began to tilt. Without thinking, she pulled her hand free of the monkey's grasp, put down the basket, and rushed forward to steady the pipe.

'*Asante!*' the man called back. '*Shika tu.*' Hold it still.

Kitty didn't reply, but did as she was instructed.

'*Inua tu!*' Lift it up!

As soon as she'd complied, another stream of Swahili was flung in her direction. This time it was too fast for her to translate, but she could see what was needed. She walked her end to the left, holding it aloft.

The man struggled to ease the pipe into the hole, which was in an awkward spot near the top of the tank. Kitty made it easier for him by adjusting the height of her end. She was a farmer's daughter; it didn't occur to her not to help out in a situation like this. At the same time, though, she watched the man through narrowed eyes. It was Taylor, she felt certain. The presence of the monkey was not the only clue.

She recognised the unruly, sun-streaked hair from the glimpse she'd had of him on the road. She studied him while he worked. He had the build of a shearer: strong but agile. His bush shirt had the sleeves torn off above the elbow, revealing forearms bulked with muscle.

'*Imekwisha.*' It is finished.

He turned around, rubbing his hands on the seat of his dirty trousers. He stared at Kitty in open shock – looking away, then back, as though to check that the woman in the red and white dress was really standing there.

Then he strode towards her, relieving Kitty of her load by resting her end of the pipe on the branch of a tree. 'I'm so sorry, I thought you were Tesfa. He was here, just before.'

With a single bound, the monkey leapt up onto his shoulder. The man's hand rose to steady the animal. 'This is Gili.'

'We've met,' Kitty said.

'I hope he hasn't caused any trouble.'

Kitty shook her head.

'I'm Taylor.' He moved his right hand, but then let it drop. Kitty could see he wasn't sure if they should shake hands or not. She felt a flicker of satisfaction. He had no manners. He knew less than she did.

'I'm Mrs Theodore Hamilton.' Kitty kept her arms by her side. She didn't need Louisa to advise her that Taylor was precisely the kind of man a lady would choose not to greet with a handshake.

Taylor's eyes travelled over her, moving from head to toe. Kitty stared back at him. He was probably no older than Theo, but he had the weathered skin of a man who worked outside. There was stubble on his chin. A smear of mud on his forehead. She found his gaze unnerving, piercing and inscrutable at the same time. His voice was disconcerting as well. He had no accent at all – as if he came from nowhere, or everywhere.

'I don't mean to be rude,' he said finally, 'but – apart from having bare feet – you look like you should be down at the Kongara Club having tea.'

His words were so apt, Kitty had to smile. 'I should,' she agreed. She glanced at her watch. 'In fact, right now I am meant to be at a meeting of the planning committee for the Christmas Ball.'

He raised his eyebrows. 'Christmas is ages away.'

'There's a lot to arrange – apparently the Ball is the social highlight of the year. Today they're discussing music and dancing. Maybe it's best I'm not there – I can't do a single one of the dances. I don't even know the steps.'

'Well, that's no good. You'll be thrown out of the Ball.'

Kitty smiled again. It was relief to have the issue of the dancing made into a joke. And the way he teased her brought up memories of Paddy – his straightforward, easy ways. But then Kitty reminded herself who Taylor was. She took a step back, picking up her basket. She wasn't sure how they'd come to be chatting like this; the shared task with the pipe and the antics of the monkey must have created a false sense of connection. She held out the penknife. 'I just came to return this to Father Remi.'

'There it is!' Taylor looked pleased as he took it from her, slipping it into his shirt pocket. 'He said he lost it. But all the time it was you.'

Kitty felt herself blushing as she walked on. Taylor came behind her. They reached an open doorway leading into the rear of the church.

'He should be in here,' Taylor said. 'Thanks for your help, by the way.' He nodded towards the water pipe. 'I'll be glad when I get the other end of that pipe back in place.'

'Why don't you get your prisoners to do it?' Kitty decided it was time to let Taylor know she was well aware of the kind of business he ran.

'Well, I could have. I only just noticed it had been removed. The Fathers are very busy. They overlook these practical things sometimes. I like to check over all their buildings before the rains come.'

'That's kind of you.' Kitty's tone was tart. It wasn't much of a gesture on his part, considering the Mission had the job of feeding and caring for his workers.

Taylor looked puzzled. Kitty wished she hadn't spoken. The last thing she wanted was to begin a conversation about this man's morals. She was about to make an excuse to walk off when Gili suddenly leapt down from Taylor's shoulder, launching himself into her arms.

She staggered backwards, dropping the basket, as she grasped the animal's body, her fingers disappearing into fine soft fur. Two long arms wound themselves around her neck. A faint smell rose to her nostrils, reminding her of times, years ago, when she'd lain in the sun with the farm dogs, burying her face in their thick coats.

She realised Taylor was staring at her, open-mouthed. 'Gili is usually afraid of strangers. He was tortured by the people who captured him. He still has the scars.'

'That's terrible. Poor creature.' Kitty wrapped her arms over the monkey's back, lodging him securely against her chest. She felt oddly gratified as though she'd done something to deserve Gili's trust. She found she liked the feeling of the animal clinging onto her, the tickle of fur against her neck. She rested her cheek on his downy head.

'He's so . . .' She hunted for the word that would describe the quaint miniature nose, mouth and ears; his comic antics; but also the intelligence that burned in his wide-open eyes. 'Like a real baby.'

'Much less trouble, from what I've been told.' Taylor grinned. His eyes crinkled at the corners, showing he smiled a lot.

The drone of male voices coming from the other side of the church suddenly rose to a new level. Kitty guessed the meal was about to be served. The stone forecourt crowded with prisoners seemed a world away from where she stood, with this man she didn't know and a monkey in her arms. Pigeons, cooing in the belltower, were louder, more present. So was the hidden choir of insects humming in the midday sun.

'I spoke to you in Swahili back there,' Taylor commented. 'You understood.'

'I only speak a little.' Kitty felt half proud and half embarrassed. She knew she'd made good progress with the language but felt – at the same time – as if she'd been caught out doing something unseemly or pretentious.

'Why would someone like you learn Swahili?' Taylor sounded genuinely interested.

'Well, I thought it might be useful. I didn't know what it would be like here. I thought I might be able to . . . do something.' Kitty felt a wave of emotion rise up as she spoke. She was aware of all the frustration she'd suppressed; all the words she'd bitten back – each and every one of them was still there, just waiting to burst out. 'I have to go.'

'I'll take you to the Father, then,' Taylor said.

'No, it's all right. I don't need to see him. If you could just give him that . . .' She gestured towards the basket, lying on its side where she'd dropped it. Her sandals were on the ground nearby.

Taylor went to pick them up. In his work-roughened hands, the thin straps and high heels looked delicate and impractical. 'You seem quite at home in bare feet.'

Kitty lowered her gaze. He could see right through her, she felt sure. He'd probably detected her accent was fake, her manners a thin veneer. She didn't really belong in the Kongara Club. Someone like Alice would never have taken off her shoes, or joined in with a man's outdoor work. Taylor could tell Kitty was an outsider, like he was. An imposter. But even as these thoughts came to her she knew she couldn't afford to accept that picture of herself. She had to belong in the world she now shared with Theo.

She lifted her head, flicking back her hair in the way she'd seen Diana do. She adopted the dismissive, critical gaze she saw so often in Londoni. 'They should make some proper paths in this place. Out of concrete.'

Kitty peeled the monkey from her body, handing him over to Taylor, taking her shoes in return. The exchange had a domestic feel to it – as though it were something they'd done often before, and would again.

'Next time you come, use the shortcut,' Taylor suggested. 'It's much quicker. And once the rains start, the main road will be flooded. The track cuts straight across the hill. Joins onto the other end of that top road. The one with all the big houses. Do you know where I mean?'

Kitty nodded, but said nothing. She didn't want to reveal that she lived there, in Millionaire Row – the best address in Tanganyika. It might cause Taylor to think less of her. She viewed herself with astonishment. Why would she care what someone like Taylor thought?

The man smiled at her again. Kitty realised what was so striking about his eyes: the irises were blue-green around the pupil but gold at the edges. She felt drawn to them, like a moth to light.

'Thank you, but I won't be coming back.'

The line between Taylor's brows deepened for just a second. But then a mask came over his features. 'Goodbye, then.' His voice was neutral.

'Goodbye.'

Kitty walked away, still barefoot, the sandals swinging from her hand. She imagined she could feel Taylor's eyes – his strange intense gaze – following her. She fought an impulse to turn around.

She headed back along the side of the church with a reluctant step. She wanted to stay here – to help serve lunch. To work in the clinic. To see the two Fathers again. Tesfa, as well. She wanted to play with Gili.

She could keep her distance from Taylor.

But she forced herself to keep on, quickening her pace. She'd made mistakes before – not understood where she was headed. But this time it was going to be different. She could see the danger.

She knew to fly away.

NINE

Kitty leaned forwards over the steering wheel, peering at the petrol gauge. The red needle was hovering dangerously close to empty. She was glad Theo was not here to see how careless she'd been; he insisted his driver keep the Land Rover tank at least half full at all times. She let the car coast downhill, then drove evenly and slowly, watching the red needle all the way to the petrol pump outside Ahmed's *duka*.

She left the car while it was being filled. Several times before, she'd had to ask Ahmed's assistant not to smoke while operating the pump, and each time he'd made an elaborate protest about it. Crossing the road, she noticed the Daimler parked under a tree. James stood beside it, idly wiping away dust with a rag. She wondered if that meant Diana was up and about at last, supervising the shopping. If so, she'd probably be back at the Club tomorrow. Kitty shuddered at the thought of the scenes that would play out as everyone resumed their place in the old order. At the same time, though, she hoped to hear that Diana had indeed recovered. She was still haunted by the pitiful sounds she'd heard coming from the bedroom on her visit next door.

Diana's houseboy and cook were selecting fruit from the row of baskets outside the greengrocer. Kitty looked around, but saw no sign of their mistress. She strolled over to James. When he saw her, he jumped to attention. 'Good afternoon, Memsahib.'

'Hello, James. Is Diana here?'

'No, Memsahib. She is not shopping. She remains in her bed.' He shook his head. 'It is very bad.'

Kitty was puzzled. 'I thought malaria was quite simple to treat.'

He made no response for a moment, then glanced around him as if afraid of being overheard. 'She does not have malaria. She suffers from something else.'

Kitty thought of the pink pills she'd seen on the floor of the car. 'I've heard she has a problem with her blood. Something that affects her nerves.'

James shook his head again. 'It is in her heart.'

'Her heart?' Kitty's eyes widened. Kongara was no place for someone with a heart complaint. The hospital looked impressive, but like many of the services here it operated in an erratic manner. Sometimes the facility seemed overstaffed; other times it was hard to get an appointment at the clinic. Rumour had it that while vital medical supplies often ran short, the storerooms were crammed with unnecessary items. And there wasn't even a proper ambulance – the doctor just came in his jeep. The nearest real hospital was in Dar es Salaam. Kitty could see her concern mirrored in James's eyes. She realised his solicitous manner was not just the result of good training. He cared about Diana.

'I do not know the name in English,' James continued, 'but we call it *hali ya kutokua na furaha*.'

Kitty identified the word 'joy' straight away. Janet had used it a lot. The verb was more complicated. And it was in the negative. She pieced the translation together. 'The state of being without joy.' A chill came over her as she grasped the true meaning of Diana's cry – it was the wail of a person lost in deep despair.

'She is very ill,' James said. He spread his hands, the pink palms upwards. 'Her sisters should come to her aid. They should not leave her alone.' There was a sharp note of outrage in his voice.

Kitty looked at him in confusion. Surely he must know that if Diana had any sisters, they would be far away in England? Then she understood – he was referring to Diana's friends: the ladies she met with each day at the Club. Kitty tried to think which one of them Diana seemed closest to. In Kongara, nobody had known anybody for very long, but considering Diana spent so much free time with the other wives, some real bond between her and at least one of them must surely have grown.

Kitty searched her memory for signs of the kind of intimacy she'd shared with her oldest friend, Ruth Herbert. They'd met in Grade One at Wattle Creek School, and had been firm friends right up until Ruth had left the district to find work. Kitty thought of the infectious laughter they'd shared, the spontaneous hugs, the way they used to finish one another's sentences. She couldn't associate anything like this with Diana. The wife of the Managing Director was clever and funny and beautiful; she could be kind, too. But she was so unpredictable. That was the problem. You never knew what she was going to say or do – you never knew who she would be. People always sought Diana's approval, but at the same time they kept a wary distance from her. As a result, Kitty now saw, Diana was quite isolated – perhaps even lonely. Kitty was glad she'd at least made the effort to take her neighbour a little gift.

'Has no one else been to see her?' she asked James.

'Only you. And you did not speak to her.' Anger flared in his eyes. 'Mr Armstrong wouldn't let me see her. He sent me away.'

James's face became impassive. 'I have just taken him back to Head Office after a lunch appointment at the Club. Now he sits at his desk. There are many papers for him to read. And people are waiting to see him. I believe he very will busy for the rest of the day.'

Kitty tapped at the front door. With the house staff out shopping, there was no one to answer it. She didn't want to risk waking Diana by pounding on the door. She listened for footsteps, but the house remained silent.

James had given her his key. The residents of Millionaire Row had been instructed to keep their homes locked at all times, since a spate of burglaries had been carried out in the area of the Toolsheds. Crime was on the increase in Kongara, and the response of the OFC had so far been unsatisfactory. A new Chief Inspector had been sent over from Scotland Yard, but people referred jokingly to his inadequate station as Scotland Inch. After an outcry, the OFC had promised that an additional contingent of *askaris* – tried and true, from the King's African Rifles regiment – would soon be brought from Dar es Salaam. Meanwhile, there was a general sense of unease about security. Alice blamed the problem on the shanty dwellers. She'd given her views over lunch at the Club, and proposed a solution.

'We have plenty of bulldozers.' She'd poked the air with one finger to underline her words. 'We should just bring a few up from the Units and clear that slum. Push over all the huts. It could be gone in a morning.'

'Where would the people go?' Kitty asked. 'All those women and children?'

Alice gave her a pitying look, as if she were slow-witted. 'Back to where they belong.'

'What about the prostitutes?' Pippa queried. 'All those men – and no one for them to have sex with. That could make things even more dangerous!' She shuddered. 'For us, I mean.'

'Don't be disgusting,' Alice had retorted.

Luckily, Eliza had arrived just then, causing a distraction with a striking new hairdo – a pile of curls forming a pyramid on top of her head.

Kitty pushed open the front door and crept inside. 'Diana?' she called softly. 'It's me, Kitty.'

Slipping off her sandals in order to move quietly, she crept down the hall to the main bedroom.

The door was open a few inches. Through the crack Kitty could see Diana on the bed, stretched out on top of the sheets. Her blue silk negligee was rucked up, baring her legs to the thighs. She lay with her arms flung out carelessly, like a child abandoned to sleep. Her red hair flopped over the pillow, her face resting to one side. Kitty pushed the door open a little further. She had never seen Diana without make-up before. The woman was, if possible, even more beautiful. Her porcelain skin and even features made her resemble a statue of an angel. Her lips, parted, were a perfect bow.

The only flaw in the picture was a line of saliva running from the corner of her mouth. Kitty drew away, embarrassed. Diana would hate anyone to see her in this state – bare-faced, dribbling. Kitty peering into her bedroom was an unforgivable invasion of privacy.

She was about to close the door when something else caught her eye – on the floor near the bed was a pill bottle. It lay on its side, the top missing. Kitty recognised the label: Aspro. Beside it was another open bottle of a different shape. Kitty could see that this one was empty. Looking back to the bed, she saw another container. It was plain brown glass, with a chemist's label.

For a long moment, Kitty just stood there – as though gripped in the deep stillness that emanated from the figure on the bed. Then she launched into the room, jumping onto the bed, crouching by Diana. There was not only saliva at the corner of the woman's mouth – there was a crust of dried vomit as well.

'Diana!' She grasped both shoulders and shook hard. 'Diana – can you hear me?' There was no response; not even the flutter of an eyelid.

Kitty pressed her ear against Diana's chest, listening for a heart- beat. She could hear nothing behind the sound of her own panicked breath. Grabbing Diana's wrist, she made herself calm down, feel for a pulse.

'Thank God,' she murmured as she picked up a faint but regular beat. She put her cheek to Diana's mouth, but couldn't feel any movement of air. Diana's chest, her breasts – clothed in silk, a white ribbon at the neckline – were as still as the rest of her. On the bedside table Kitty noticed a small hand mirror. She reached for it, knocking over another empty pill bottle, and held it over Diana's mouth and nose. She waited for a few seconds, gazing down at the silver oval engraved with the initials *DA*. Diana Armstrong. It was hard to fit the name – and all that it meant – with this helpless, inert figure.

A slight mist clouded the mirror. Kitty closed her eyes with relief – Janet had taught her how to do mouth-to-mouth but she wasn't at all confident she could have carried it out properly. She stared at Diana. The woman was breathing, her heart was beating, but she was deeply unconscious.

Through the window, Kitty could see her car parked outside. Prompted by James she'd come straight here, not even pausing to deposit the Hillman in her own driveway. The fastest way to get Diana to the hospital would be to drive her there herself. But Kitty didn't think she'd be able to carry her. She remembered how hard it was to move a sheep that had died in the paddock – even after it had been sheared, the farmer grabbing one last fleece. It wasn't just the weight: a limp body was hard to manage. She'd have to call Eustace and Gabriel.

She ran into the hallway, but then she faltered. What if Diana were not really in danger? Kitty didn't want to be the one who exposed her – in the state she was in – to the men's mockery and derision.

She went into the sitting room, hunting around helplessly, her thoughts racing. She knew there were no telephones in the houses, but still found herself searching for the squat black shape. Then the drinks trolley seemed to rise into her vision, catching her eye. It was made of stainless steel; she and Theo had one the same. Theo joked that the OFC had ordered them specially reinforced to withstand a heavy load of liquor. Kitty swept the bottles to the floor. Something broke, scattering glass. The ice bucket rolled away with a clatter.

In the bedroom, she managed to pull Diana off the mattress, manoeuvring her so that she ended up resting belly down over the trolley, arms and legs hanging. She scooped the empty medicine containers into her pocket. Then she steered the trolley out through the kitchen door, where there was only one step down onto the concrete path. When she reached the gravel Kitty had to bend over, arms outstretched, and push with all her strength. She saw that Diana's hands were being dragged in the gravel, but didn't stop. Reaching the car, she wrenched open the rear side door, then she lined up the trolley and forced it to tip. As Diana fell onto the seat, her head bumped against the side of the car before coming to rest at an uncomfortable angle. Her knuckles were grazed – raw and bleeding.

Seconds later, Kitty was pumping the accelerator. The wheels spun on the gravel as she sped away.

There were no vehicles parked outside the hospital. The blinds were lowered, the doors closed. Apart from a cleaner sweeping the verandah, there was no sign of life.

Kitty jumped from the car, leaving the door open. She ran to an entrance marked *Admissions* and burst inside. It was quiet, the air dim and still.

'Hello?' she called out as she raced into one of the wards. The beds were all made up – sheets and blankets folded tightly over the mattresses – but there were no patients. The next ward was the same. She turned down a corridor.

'Is anyone there?'

A man appeared in a doorway – a short, bulky figure in a white coat. 'Whatever's going on?'

'I've got someone in my car, outside,' Kitty panted. 'She needs help.'

The man just stared at her. Kitty knew she looked a sight: there was monkey fur on her dress; her bare feet were dirty. She pushed back her hair. 'Come with me. Please – it's an emergency!'

'Dr Meadows should be out there somewhere. And Nurse Edwards . . .'

'Aren't you a doctor?'

'I'm a thoracic surgeon.'

Kitty grasped his arm. 'There's no one else around.'

'I don't do hands-on medicine,' the surgeon protested as he followed her back along the hallway. 'I just came in to check some X-rays.'

Without breaking her stride, Kitty pulled the medicine bottles from her pocket. 'I think she's taken all these. She's unconscious.'

The surgeon jerked to a stop, picking out the one that bore a chemist's label.

'What is it?' Kitty demanded. 'Is it dangerous?'

He gave no answer, but broke into a run.

'Hold her head,' the surgeon instructed Kitty. He was rubbing liquid paraffin over the end of a long rubber tube. 'I'm going to insert this into the oesophagus. I'm Frank, by the way.'

'Kitty Hamilton.'

Frank looked up, the tube poised between Diana's lips. 'Wife of the Admin Manager?'

'That's right.'

'I'll have to watch my language.'

Kitty didn't reply. She wondered what he'd think if he knew how much time she'd spent in a shearing shed where every second word was an expletive. For his part, Frank seemed a mild-mannered person; well brought up.

'Hold her nose shut, would you, please?' he asked Kitty. He pushed the end of the tube into Diana's mouth. He frowned anxiously. 'I haven't done anything like this for years.'

As he forced the tube further and further in, Kitty flinched. He was rough, almost clumsy, as though Diana were an object, not a person. Kitty had to remind herself he was trying to save the woman's life. He was clearly very worried about Diana's condition. He kept stopping to check her pulse. A fine sweat had broken over his brow.

'The key thing is,' he said, 'you have to make sure you're getting into the stomach, not the lungs.' He motioned for Kitty to pick up a bowl he'd filled with water. He lowered the free end of the tube into it. After watching for half a minute, he nodded, satisfied. 'No bubbles. That means we're in the right place.' He gestured towards the bench, where he'd placed a large funnel. 'Get me that.'

He fitted the tube over its end. Next, he emptied a jug of water into the mouth of the funnel. Kitty swallowed on a wave of nausea as the liquid gurgled down the tube.

'So who's your friend, then?'

Kitty didn't answer straight away. She felt a fraud, accepting his use of the term 'friend'. 'She is Mrs Armstrong.'

Frank froze, the jug tilted, ready to pour. 'The General Manager's wife? Bloody hell. Now I'm even more nervous.' He pointed to the bench again. 'Bucket. Thanks. Hold it below the level of the patient. The force of gravity will suck out the contents of the stomach.'

As Kitty followed his instructions, a memory came to her – she was a little kid, watching from behind a tree trunk as a couple of half-drunk shearers used a length of garden hose to steal petrol from their overseer's car.

Water began to trickle from the end of the tube.

'Looks pretty clear,' Frank commented. But then a blob of white sludge fell into the bucket, along with a few flecks of blood. 'Here it comes.' The man's face, as he watched the bucket, showed a mixture of concern and annoyance. 'I can't believe I'm doing this. Where the hell is Meadows?' He turned towards the door as if he could will the duty doctor to appear. 'I suppose he thought since there are no inpatients at the moment, he could nick off for a bit.' He snorted. 'I bet he's at the Club. And Sister Edwards has probably gone hunting for him. That's one thing about Kongara – you can always be tracked down.' A fleeting smile crossed his face. 'She'll give him a piece of her mind.'

The surgeon repeated the process, pouring in another jug of water. This time, when Kitty lowered the bucket to create suction, liquid spewed from Diana's mouth as well as the tube. Kitty looked at Frank in alarm.

'It's all right,' he said. 'That's a good sign.'

He filled and emptied the jug seven or eight more times; Kitty lost count. He kept on taking Diana's pulse, and pushing back her eyelids to check her pupils.

Finally, the water that was running into the bucket turned clear. While Frank was preparing to pour in a last jugful, Diana's hand fluttered up, grabbing at the tube.

Frank shot Kitty a look of triumph. 'She's coming round.' He began pulling the tubing back up. Diana coughed and moaned.

Kitty let out a ragged breath. As relief ran through her, she began to tremble. She realised how tense she'd been. 'She's going to be all right?'

'Well, I hope so.' Frank wiped his face on his forearm. 'There could be organ damage – that's the trouble with phenacetin. Sometimes the liver can't recover.'

Kitty stared at him. 'You mean she could still die?'

'Let's not fear the worst,' Frank said hastily. 'It's lucky you found her when you did – and managed to get her here so quickly.' He looked directly into Kitty's eyes. 'Do you know why she tried to do this?'

Kitty shook her head. Only James's words came to her. *The state of being without joy.* That diagnosis could be applied to several people in Kitty's life: her Auntie Madge; her own mother, at times; Louisa, too. And Theo, when he'd returned from the war. But what had driven Diana to the point of trying to kill herself, Kitty had no idea.

A faint moan came from Diana. Kitty bent over her, stroking her hair. It was stringy with oil; there were snarls and tangles. Along with the smells of vomit and disinfectant, she picked up the odour of stale sweat. She saw that the blue negligee was stained with spilled food. Kitty felt a surge of anger that Diana had been allowed to get into such a state. It seemed Richard was not the attentive husband she'd thought he was. The house staff had neglected their mistress as well. Unless, perhaps, Diana had simply refused to wash, or change her clothes.

'We need to get her husband here as soon as possible,' Frank said. 'You'll have to drive to Head Office.'

Kitty left Diana's side reluctantly. As she headed for the door, Frank called after her. 'When you've spoken to Mr Armstrong, get someone to find Meadows and tell him to get himself down here. War hero or not, he bloody well deserves to be sacked.'

His voice broke off as footsteps were heard in the hallway. Seconds later, Richard strode in.

'What's happened? What the hell's going on?' He sounded like a schoolteacher demanding an explanation for unruly behaviour. He stood by the table, staring at Diana. His eyes travelled over her body, then moved down to the bucket.

'Your wife has taken an overdose,' Frank said. 'But we've washed out her stomach. I think she'll be all right.'

Richard just frowned. Looking past him, Kitty glimpsed James hovering in the hallway. When he'd returned from the shops, he must have seen the trolley on its side in the driveway, then discovered Diana was missing and driven back to tell Richard. Kitty acknowledged him with a nod. On the driver's face were all the emotions missing from Richard's: concern, confusion, relief.

Richard swung towards Kitty. 'What are you doing here?'

Kitty took a step back. 'I found her – in the bedroom. I brought her here.'

'She may well have saved your wife's life.' There was a steely note in Frank's voice. Kitty could see he was as taken aback by Richard's manner as she was.

'Oh, she never takes enough to kill herself.'

A shocked silence filled the room. Water dripped into a sink somewhere. The electric light buzzed. Frank opened his mouth to say something, but then appeared to think better of it.

Suddenly, Richard seemed to get a grip on himself. Moving to Frank's side, he clapped him on the shoulder. 'Thank you, old chap. Looks like you've got things under control.' He patted a piece of the blue negligee, draped over the edge of the table. 'Poor Diana. She gets overemotional about things.' He spread his hands. 'One feels so helpless.'

Diana mumbled something, her fingers making little butterfly movements. Kitty was about to step towards her, but was daunted by Richard's presence. She felt like an intruder now – her involvement no longer wanted.

'I suppose I should probably go.' She addressed Frank, avoiding Richard. 'Shall I call in at the Club and look for the doctor?'

'No!' Richard wheeled round. The look on his face was – at last – one of urgency, almost fear. 'I need to talk to you first.' He turned back to Frank. 'If you'd excuse us. It won't take long.' Without a glance at the figure laid out on the table, he led Kitty from the room.

'It goes without saying, Kitty – your help is very much appreciated.' Richard paced the waiting room as he spoke. Kitty stood near the door, which had been closed firmly behind her. She was taller than Richard, yet she felt childlike and small under his gaze. He seemed to be waiting for her to say something. She struggled to quell the outrage she felt over the way he'd reacted when he first saw Diana.

'I'm just glad I called in,' she said. 'It doesn't bear thinking about – what could have happened. There were so many empty bottles . . .'

Richard came to stand in front of Kitty. She could smell his aftershave – something spicy and sweet. 'Kitty, I cannot stress enough how important it is that this incident be kept private.'

'I won't say anything.' Kitty spoke firmly. She didn't like the thought of other Londoni people – especially the women at the Club – finding out what had happened, any more than he did. Having helped rescue Diana, she now felt a strange protectiveness towards her.

'It's for Diana's sake, of course. But I'm thinking of the Scheme as well. It's hardly reassuring to the rank and file, to have something like this connected with senior management. I can't afford to let it get out.'

As Kitty took in his words, it dawned on her that the second issue could be the one that concerned him most. That the Scheme mattered more than Diana. 'I understand,' she said, forcing her tone to remain neutral.

'I appreciate that, Kitty. I really do.' He took a packet of cigarettes from his pocket and offered her one.

'I don't smoke, thank you.'

'Sensible girl.' He bent over a flaring match, drawing on the cigarette until the tobacco glowed red. 'I blame myself – I should have stepped in earlier.' He blew out a stream of smoke. 'It's very clear. She needs to go home.'

Kitty frowned at him in confusion – of course, Diana would go home, as soon as she was well. Then she understood. 'Home' was England.

'It was a mistake bringing her here in the first place,' Richard continued. 'I thought the change might help. Fresh start and all that. But I just have to face the facts. It hasn't worked.'

'What about you – your job?' Kitty asked.

Richard gave her a puzzled look. 'What do you mean?' Then his face cleared. 'Well, obviously, I'll stay here. I couldn't possibly abandon my post – just walk out on the Scheme. But she'll be well looked after, don't you worry.'

'Who by?' Kitty asked. Again, James's words came back to her. 'Does she have a sister in England?'

'No. She has a brother in Cornwall. But what she needs is professional help. She'll have the best available, you can be sure of that.'

Kitty nodded. His plan made sense; clearly Diana needed to see a psychiatrist. And if she was so unhappy here in Kongara, she'd no doubt be glad to leave – even if it meant being separated from her husband, at least for a while.

'I'll send her to Nairobi first. There's a flight she could catch on Friday.'

The hasty nature of his plan made Kitty feel uneasy. 'But she could recover here,' she protested. 'Where her friends can visit.'

'What friends?' Richard's expression was suddenly raw – pained. Then he was remote and cool again. He shook his head. 'There will be no visitors. I must make sure you understand, Kitty. We're talking about suicide here. It's a shocking thing. It's against the law. It simply mustn't get out.' There was an almost panicky edge to his voice. 'Frank will maintain professional silence. Meadows and the nurse won't be in a hurry to expose the fact that they weren't here when they should've been. James is a loyal servant – he won't talk. That just leaves you, Kitty. You must not tell anyone what happened today. You must not even tell Theo.'

Kitty's lips parted. She didn't want to start keeping secrets from Theo again; it had bothered her enough, not telling him about her visits to the Mission.

'Theo would understand,' Richard said. 'A gentleman knows the value of privacy.'

He was right, Kitty knew: Theo would indeed understand, if he were aware of the circumstances. After all, he'd had his turn of being embroiled in a public scandal.

'I'll make sure he's kept back at Head Office,' Richard said. 'You go home, get changed, have a stiff drink. And think up a story about how you've filled your day.' He gave her a searching look. 'Don't let me down.' He drew on his cigarette, before saying the words again. 'I mean it. Don't let me down.'

There was a threatening tone in his voice, all the more potent for being delivered in his refined accent. Kitty wondered, suddenly, what it was like for Theo, working under Richard. Was this why Theo put in such long hours? Was he afraid of the consequences if he let his boss down?

Richard waited for Kitty to nod, then flashed her a smile. He had prominent eyeteeth that drew attention when he opened his mouth. They made him look slightly dangerous – and attractive, in a visceral way. Kitty could see how he'd managed to capture such a beautiful wife. She smiled back, as if he'd won her over completely.

'I want to thank you, on Diana's behalf,' Richard said. 'When she's up to hearing about it, I'll be sure to tell her how you came to the rescue. I expect she'll send you a card.'

'But I want to see her, before you take her away.'

'I think not . . .' He shook his head. 'No.'

Kitty couldn't bring herself to nod her head again, or murmur agreement. After all she'd been through today with Diana, she just had to see her again. Richard was waiting for her to respond. She knew she should accept his authority – as the General Manager, as Diana's husband, as a man – but there was something about standing here in her bare feet, the concrete cool and firm beneath her, that made her feel strong. She remembered how she'd forced the trolley over the gravel, how she'd found Frank and convinced him to take her seriously. She lifted her chin, drawing herself up to her full height. 'I want to say goodbye to Diana. I think you owe me the chance to do that.' She kept on looking at Richard, refusing to blink.

'She'll be in a private room,' he said curtly. 'I'll tell Edwards to let you in.'

TEN

Kitty turned down the narrow street that ran along the side of the hill, in the no-man's land that lay between Millionaire Row and the rest of Londoni. The OFC had planned to build an enclave of smaller houses here, for employees who deserved better accommodation than the Toolsheds but didn't qualify for one of the executive homes. They'd only completed the first few dwellings before time and money had been diverted elsewhere.

Kitty drove past the three identical cottages that were known as the Triplets. They were barely larger than the ones that had earned the name 'Toolsheds', but they had solid brick walls and tiled roofs. The same gardener clearly cared for the three front gardens: they had identical plantings of *manyara* and bougainvillea, and each had a patch of geraniums to the left of the front door.

There were a couple of empty blocks next – perhaps the plan had been to have two sets of triplets, or maybe some twins. Then the tiny place called the Shoebox came into view. Kitty slowed to walking pace. The front door of the cottage was open. An African man carrying a tin of paint was just about to step inside. Another man was washing windows.

Kitty wondered which employee of the OFC had been evicted to make way for the new occupant. The evening before, Theo had announced that he and Kitty were going to get a new almost-neighbour. He had arrived home late, as Richard had promised, having been detained in a meeting. But he'd been in a surprisingly good mood. Though it was well after dark, he'd suggested sun-downers on the verandah. Kitty had listened quietly while he told her about the latest problem he was tackling. She presumed the fact that he sounded so bright meant he had a solution in mind. Evidently, the issue was to do with the local bees.

'No one else has been attacked, have they?' Kitty asked. The fate of Cynthia's husband still haunted her. If she glimpsed even a single bee, she kept her distance.

'No, thank God. It's the opposite problem. It turns out they're terribly lazy.'

He'd gone on to explain that the pollination rates during the previous season had been alarmingly low. It was one of the rea-sons – possibly the main reason – why the harvest had been so disappointing. It was just fortunate that the Minister of Food had been able to convince Parliament back home that the initial year of the project should be discounted, making this current year the 'first' harvest. His excuses were valid. No one had expected there to be so many setbacks with clearing and ploughing. And no one had expected the rains to come so late, and then fall with such ferocity that the plantations were all but washed away. But this season it simply had to be different. The targets must be met.

'So what can you do about the bees?' Kitty interrupted. After the tension of the afternoon she felt on edge, and not in the mood to listen to a whole litany of the Scheme's problems and misfortunes.

'Ah, well – good question.' Theo sounded almost smug. 'We are going to bring in some European bees. We'll establish a series of colonies down on the Units.'

Kitty just looked at him. She wasn't about to mention that in Australia serious problems had been caused by deliberately introducing foreign species. Rabbits – intended as food – had bred in plague proportions, stripping the pastures of grass. Thistles, brought in to remind people of England, had taken over whole tracts of the landscape. And these were only two examples.

'Of course, we need an expert to oversee the program. So I got on the telephone and spoke to an old friend of mine who used to be mixed up with bees. I was at Eton with her brothers.' His eyes warmed at the memory. 'I used to visit their estate and there she'd be, dressed from head to toe in a mad outfit, smoking the bees from her hives, collecting honey – the whole bit. Splendid sight. Anyway, it turns out she's still dabbling with beekeeping. I asked her for a recommendation. And she said . . .' He paused, giving Kitty a triumphant look. 'She said she'd love to be involved herself. I spoke to the people in London, and it's all sorted out. She's coming to Kongara!'

Kitty forced a smile. From his eager speech, a few words stood out. Eton. Their estate. Splendid. 'What's her name?'

'Lady Welmingham. Charlotte. She's going to come as soon as she can, but it'll be a month at least before she can get organised. She'll be staying in the Shoebox. I've already got the Housing Committee onto redecorating it. You know what it's like getting anything done around here. Obviously, the place is much too small for her – no room for staff quarters. I hope you don't mind, but I said we'd have her up here for the evening meal. You'll like her, Kitty. I know you will.'

Kitty swallowed. She remembered meeting another of Theo's friends who boasted the title of Lady. She was a daunting figure who wore the latest fashions, spoke four languages and played both the piano and the violin. Louisa had invited her to stay at the Hall in a blatant bid to tempt her son away from his Australian girlfriend. No doubt Lady Welmingham would be just as daunting. And that aside, Kitty didn't want to share her evenings with anyone but Theo. But, as always, she felt at a disadvantage. She had no right to refuse Theo anything, any more.

'Of course she can eat with us.' Kitty tried to sound bright. Perhaps the presence of the visitor would mean Theo would start returning home on time.

Coming to a standstill right in front of the Shoebox, Kitty glanced over the narrow façade. The whole place was probably smaller than Lady Charlotte's sitting room back in England. Kitty just hoped she would not be too comfortable here. That she would set up her hives – or whatever she had to do – and hurry home.

Movement on the doorstep of the cottage caught her eye. The man with the paint tin was coming back outside. There was a worried expression on his face. Perhaps he thought this woman was the new tenant, arriving early. Kitty gave him a reassuring wave, and drove off.

*

The door bore a wooden plaque with the words *Private Ward* printed in gold capitals. Sister Edwards unlocked it, keys jangling from a large bunch in her hand, then peered cautiously inside.

'She's sleeping. Would you like to come back later?'

Kitty shook her head. 'I'll just sit with her for a while.'

'I shall be right outside,' Edwards said. 'I don't want to lock you in with her, but she must be kept secure.'

Kitty looked at the nurse in dismay; it dawned on her that this was Diana's new place in the world – she was officially mad. She'd proven she was a risk to herself. Maybe she was a risk to other people, too.

As the door closed behind her, Kitty approached the bed. Diana lay on her back, covered to the chest with a sheet. Her hands rested at her sides, the chipped polish on her fingernails making strident splashes of scarlet against the white linen. Her grazed knuckles bore the yellow stain of iodine. Her eyelids were puffy and veined with pink; her cheeks were colourless. In place of the silk negligee she wore a simple calico nightdress that obviously belonged to the hospital. Her hair had been washed and scraped back from her face, pinned down flat. Kitty looked at her in dismay. She pictured Sister Edwards at work, turning Diana into the textbook image of a patient – or inmate.

'Diana? It's me, Kitty.'

There was no response. The fan creaked steadily as it stirred the hot air. Kitty felt sweat break out over her body. The rains were due, the humidity rising. Clouds kept appearing over the mountains. They hovered there, tantalising – but nothing came of them. The air seemed thick with waiting.

Kitty reached out to the hand closest to her, stroking it gently. She hoped Diana could tell, somehow, that she was here – that not all of Diana's 'sisters' had left her alone.

The eyelids fluttered, then opened. 'I'm not asleep,' came a whisper. In the shadowy room, Diana's eyes, overly large in her face, were more green than grey.

Kitty pulled back her hand, suddenly unsure how she was going to be received. Did Diana even know she'd been the one who had found her and brought her here?

'Don't go away.' The voice was low, urgent; the eyes were wide with fear. 'Stay with me. Please.'

'Shhh, shhh. It's all right. You'll feel better soon. Richard's going to find the best doctors for you.'

Diana shook her head. 'I can't go back to England. They'll lock me up.'

Kitty took a breath. She felt out of her depth. Then she heard footsteps in the hallway. As the door opened, Diana closed her eyes, feigning sleep again.

'Just checking all's well,' said Edwards. 'I have to go and admit a patient. But I won't be far away. Call me if she wakes up.'

'Of course.' Kitty managed a serene smile.

As soon as the nurse's footsteps receded, Diana half sat up; she leaned towards Kitty. 'You have to help me. There's no one else.' She spoke firmly now, like the old Diana: in charge of herself and everyone around her.

'I don't know how to help you,' Kitty said. 'I don't know what's wrong with you.'

'What's wrong with me . . .' Diana repeated the words as though trying them on for size. Beneath the blank canvas of her face, Kitty could see thoughts struggling for form. She sank back onto the pillow. 'I killed my child.'

The words penetrated Kitty like an arrow, striking to the core. She gasped in horror. 'What do you mean?'

'I was running late to collect him from school. I'd stayed out shopping too long. Tried on one dress too many. When I got there, I parked on the wrong side of the road.' Diana spoke in a monotone, sounding like someone delivering lines they'd spoken – or said in their head – many times. 'Phillip always waited for me under the oak tree, right near the school entrance. But when I didn't show up, he decided to catch the bus. I saw him standing in the queue with the older children. He was looking worried. I always picked him up. I was always on time. The bus pulled into the kerb. I wanted to stop him getting on. So I . . .' Her voice faltered, and she took a ragged breath before going on. 'I called out to him. He looked up and saw me. His face lit up. He waved. And he ran straight across the road towards me. I shouted at him to stop, but he kept coming. It was like a nightmare – everything happening slowly, but fast at the same time. The car couldn't see him because of the bus . . .' There was a short silence. Diana stared at the ceiling, tears running from the corners of her eyes, back over her temples. 'He was thrown in the air like a toy. His head hit the road. I'll never forget the sound it made. I ran to him. There was so much blood. His eyes were closing. I picked him up. I tried to hang onto him. I begged him not to die. The ambulance men lifted him onto the stretcher. They were gentle, as if my little boy were still alive. But then they covered his face because he didn't need to breathe.' She began to sob, her shoulders shaking.

Tears ran down Kitty's face. There were no words for her to say.

Diana cried quietly. 'He was only five years old! My precious baby. My little boy.' After a while, Diana gathered herself, rising onto her elbow. 'I could not forgive myself. I never will. I know Richard blames me, too. The grief drove us both mad. Everywhere we went – at home, in the village – we saw Phillip, we thought of him. People kept away from us. They didn't know what to say. Who could blame them? The war was over; people didn't want to hear about more tragedy.'

Kitty nodded. She'd picked up the same attitude when Yuri was found dead – as if there was only space for so much pain in the world and it had all been used up.

'That's why we came to Kongara. We decided we wouldn't tell anyone about Phillip – we wouldn't even say that we'd ever had a child.' She gave a rueful half-smile. 'At first, I thought it might work. I tried. I tried so hard. I thought if I acted like I was coming through it – surviving – it would become true. But underneath, I was falling apart.'

Kitty remembered Janet's words. *A wound must heal from the inside out.* She wished the old missionary were here, now, to offer her advice.

'You don't know what it's like, Kitty. I see myself in the mirror each morning – and I remember. I know I didn't deserve to be a mother. I didn't deserve him.'

Kitty looked down at her hands, twisted together in her lap. She was reminded of how she'd felt when Yuri finally told her about Katya – struggling to grasp another person's agony, so awful it was beyond imagining.

'I tried to kill myself before, once in England and once here. But this time I nearly succeeded. Richard said if you hadn't come, I'd be dead.'

Kitty chewed at her lip. Diana's face was unreadable. Was she blaming her for saving her life? She had never doubted that Diana had taken the tablets of her own free will. Yet it hadn't occurred to her not to interfere. A desperate person isn't in their right mind. Surely anyone would have done what she did? But even as Kitty justified her interference, she knew there had been something more at stake for her. She'd recognised it last night while sitting on the sofa, waiting for Theo, with all the images of the day tumbling through her head. It had come to her that in rescuing Diana she'd been trying to make up for not being able to save Yuri.

On the evening of his death she had been at an RAF dance with Theo – she'd worked it out later on, when she was told the date. She'd been laughing and chatting, wearing her best dress, while Yuri put the last touches to his painting – the last touches to his life. If only she'd been at the cottage. She could have stepped in, to rob the man of his death. To catch him as he dropped, to cut the rope, lower him to the floor and hold him in her arms . . .

'I'm glad you saved me,' Diana said. 'I want to live.'

Kitty stared at her. Was that how it was? In the face of death, the will to survive bites back? Would that have been true of Yuri as well?

'Something happened, Kitty – in the bedroom. I could see you helping me, getting my body off the bed. I was above you – us – looking down. And there was someone else there, watching.'

Kitty shook her head. 'No, there wasn't.'

Diana smiled, a light entering her eyes. 'Yes, there was – standing in the corner. A little boy.' Tears flowed again, but the smile lingered. 'It was Phillip. He told me it was not my time to die. Not with words, but with his eyes. I just knew what he meant.' She gazed into the corner of the room, as if to find him there. The look in her eyes was warm, proud, fond. It was not an expression Kitty had ever seen on Diana's face before – but she knew it well from watching other women. Mothers.

'I told Richard that I saw Phillip, but he said it was just the drugs. And my crazy mind.'

Kitty kept her demeanour neutral. She thought Richard was probably right, but didn't want to say so.

'He doesn't believe I can change,' Diana continued. 'That's why he's sending me away.'

Without warning, the door opened. A young African woman in a white uniform hovered on the threshold.

'It's all right,' Kitty said. 'You can come in.'

She lowered her eyes politely. 'I am not allowed. Nurse Edwards sent me to tell you it is time for you to go.' She chanted her message like a schoolgirl.

'I will. In a minute,' Kitty said.

The African glanced uncertainly along the hallway. 'I am here to lock the door.'

'*Dada yangu ananihitaji*,' Kitty pleaded. My sister has need of me. '*Naomba msaada yako.*' I beg you to show kindness.

The woman looked torn for a few seconds, then turned away.

When she was gone, Kitty leaned towards Diana. 'What do you want me to do?'

'Talk to Richard. Make him give me another chance.'

Kitty took a breath. Speaking to Richard was the last thing she wanted to do. For Diana's sake, she would – of course – but she had no idea what to say to him. She couldn't imagine a new and different version of Diana – calm, steady, predictable. Would she take over Alice's job, writing notes and keeping a check on the time? Would she pick up tennis and have lessons to polish her serve? Learn to knit? If Kitty couldn't picture Diana's changed life, how could she convince Richard to believe in it too?

'You'll do it, won't you?' Diana begged. Sudden fear flashed in her eyes. 'Please. Before it's too late. There's no one else to help me.' Her hand rose from the bed, reaching out for Kitty.

'I'll do my best.' Kitty tried to sound more confident than she felt. She stood up, turning to the door.

Diana called after her. 'He loves me.'

Kitty couldn't tell from her tone whether the words expressed a hope or a belief.

She turned back with a smile. 'Of course he does.'

ELEVEN

Kitty and Richard stood next to one another at the window of his spacious tent. From outside came the busy sounds of Head Office – vehicles coming and going, urgent voices calling instructions, the whistle-calls of *askaris* on parade. Neither of them spoke. They just gazed towards the mountains. Clouds still loitered there above the pointed peaks, looking heavy with rain, but keeping their distance from Kongara. Everyone seemed to have fallen under their spell. It was as if by constantly watching the sky, people believed that the clouds could be willed to move closer and unload their precious cargo. Kitty wasn't sure if by keeping their eyes trained on the sky she and Richard were simply following the status quo, or if they were avoiding meeting one another's eyes.

Kitty had prepared what she would say about Diana while she drove over from the hospital. She wanted to subtly remind Richard that she had some power in the situation: she knew her silence was important to him. At the same time, she planned to appeal to his sense of decency. She hoped other emotions would play their part as well – if it were true, as Diana had said, that Richard did love his wife after all.

Somewhere during the short journey a proposal had come to her. When she'd eventually persuaded the fierce secretary to admit her to the inner part of the tent where Richard was working at his desk, she'd explained she had something important to discuss. As soon as he'd sent all his staff outside, beyond earshot, she'd launched into her speech.

Now she was finished. Her last words still hung in the air, halting and awkward. She struggled to look calm and resolute, even though her stomach was knotted with tension.

'So you think Diana will be cured,' Richard said finally, 'if she spends her time helping feed a gang of African prisoners?'

It sounded ridiculous, put like that. Kitty tried to think how she could convey the way she'd felt when she was at the Mission – the relief of having a focus that lifted her out of herself.

'Does Theo know you've been going there?' Richard asked.

'I only went twice. And no. I didn't tell him.'

Richard glanced sideways at Kitty. 'So we've all got secrets. Small ones and big ones.'

Kitty stared at the clouds. Was he simply referring to her visits to the Mission behind Theo's back? Or did he know something about her past life?

Richard cleared his throat. 'Did Diana tell you about our child, Phillip?'

'Yes, she did,' Kitty said. 'I'm so sorry.' The words sounded trite and useless.

Richard covered his face with his hand. For a time, he was silent. 'Did she tell you she saw him? She had some kind of vision?'

'Yes.' Kitty offered nothing more. She didn't want to tell him she no longer believed in ghosts. Or angels, for that matter. She'd left her childhood superstitions behind long ago, adopting Yuri's views instead. The end is the end. Death is final. He was very clear on that – even though the truth was that he'd tried to cheat death by making Katya live on through Kitty. And it had worked, in a way. When he'd taken his own life, onlookers saw it as a gesture of despair. But Kitty knew he'd acted out of a sense of completion. The job had been done. He'd laid down his tools, and left . . .

'She is so much better this morning. Calm. Almost happy. I just don't know what to think. My rational mind says send her home. But my heart says . . .' There was a catch in his voice. He seemed very different from the man Kitty had seen the day before. Here in his office were all the trappings of authority – a huge mahogany desk with turned legs and claw feet, his own telephone, piles of papers, a heavy glass ashtray engraved with the emblem of the OFC. There were even framed documents mounted on the canvas walls. Dressed in a smart linen jacket, shirt and tie, Richard was very much the big boss. Yet in this moment he was torn between hope and fear, like any ordinary man. It occurred to Kitty that perhaps Diana's conviction that she'd seen their dead child had in turn changed her husband, whether he shared her belief or not.

'The thing is, Kitty, I can't risk anything else happening. I just can't. I was angry with her yesterday, I admit it – but I do care about her very deeply.' He broke off, letting Kitty absorb his statement.

Kitty nodded. She understood he'd come as close as he was able to professing that he loved his wife. His behaviour in the midst of the crisis had been driven by panic, frustration. Now his concern shone through.

'She was diagnosed with neuropsychosis, back in England,' Richard continued. 'It's like shell shock – much the same as soldiers get. I thought that coming out here, having a complete change, might help her recover. But now, I don't know if she'll ever get better.' He gazed out beyond the hovering clouds, as if looking back in time. 'If you could have known her as she used to be . . . Diana was the life of the party. Funny. Impulsive. Always making up a new plan, then changing her mind. She carried everyone along with her. She was a bit crazy, but that's what people loved about her. She's still the same person, except everything's gone out of balance. There's something desperate about her. She's like a person held together by string, terrified of falling apart.' His voice cracked. 'It's hard to watch.' Kitty wanted to reach out and touch him, to offer comfort. But when she lifted her hand he stiffened and stepped away. 'Believe me, if I thought there was something that could be done for her, here in Kongara, I'd seize on it. However, I've got reservations, to say the very least, about your suggestion.'

Kitty stared down at the floor. She had doubts about her proposal as well. But if it could be made to succeed, Diana would escape being sent away to a lunatic asylum, and Kitty would finally have a real purpose to her days. If she could not be an artist, then at least she could be useful. When she spoke, she tried to sound confident. 'I believe it could help her. We can only try.'

'But really – why would this work at the Mission make any difference to how she felt? You say you'd be serving food to prisoners, doing lots of cooking and washing up. It just sounds like hard labour to me. Diana would hate it!'

'It is hard work,' Kitty agreed. 'But that means there's no time to think about yourself. And your own problems feel small compared to theirs. You can put your worries aside – be free . . .' She let her words trail off, acutely aware that she was speaking personally.

Richard gave her a searching look, as if he understood that her own needs were involved as well as Diana's. But then he frowned again. He began pacing, his eyes still fixed on the window. Eventually he came to a standstill, facing Kitty. 'I'll give you a month. If there's any sign she's going backwards, the deal is off straight away. Meanwhile, I will inform Theo of the arrangement.' He rubbed his hands over his face. 'I must say it would all be much easier if they weren't Italians. We were fighting them not long ago. They were the enemy. Of course, we've got plenty of them working on the Units, but the idea of my wife being involved with an Italian Mission is rather – well, odd.' He looked questioningly at Kitty. 'You couldn't swap? Go to the Anglican place?'

Kitty shook her head; images of the time she'd spent helping with the meal and the clinic ran through her head. She pictured the oasis of greenery – the abundant gardens. 'It's the right place,' she said firmly. 'The Fathers are very nice.' She felt guilty about not mentioning Bwana Taylor. After all, he was an enemy of a more immediate and serious kind: he'd tried to sabotage the Scheme. And he'd been in trouble with the law. But he was not a part of the Mission. Just because Kitty had seen him when she went to return the knife didn't mean he often hung around there.

'All right, leave it with me,' Richard continued. 'Don't say anything to Theo yourself. He thinks Diana's in hospital with a complication of her malaria.' He moved quickly to logistics and planning: cars, drivers, road maps and safety. He sounded strong and clear again – the General Manager of the Scheme, back in control.

When Theo returned home that evening, he asked Kitty to take a seat in the dining room. Between meals, the bare table dominated the space, its gleaming surface a river of black. It was a location that invited serious conversations, the breaking of big news.

'I don't know how to tell you this.'

Kitty tried to read Theo's face. Had Richard spoken to him already? Or had there been some fresh disaster down on the Units?

'I've had the most extraordinary request from Richard. It seems Diana has taken it into her head to be involved in some kind of charity work. At the Catholic Mission, of all places.' He looked at Kitty in bemusement. 'I didn't even know there was one. Anyway, I'm afraid he's asked you to join in as well. Keep an eye on her. She's been ill, as you know. Richard doesn't want her to overdo things.'

Kitty considered how to respond without giving away what she knew. She opened her mouth cautiously, but before she had the chance to form a word, Theo waved his hand to cut her off. 'I don't know any more than that. You'll have to talk to Diana.' He frowned. 'It's a bit much to ask. It'll disrupt your time at the Club – just as you're settling in there so well. But I'm afraid I had to agree. No choice.'

Kitty felt torn between excitement about what had been negotiated – it was what she wanted, more than anything – and a feeling of dismay that Theo had been so clear about where his loyalties lay. What if she had been horrified by the proposal? Would there still have been no choice? She kept her tone neutral. 'It's all right. I don't mind.'

Theo's face relaxed. 'Well, that's good. Apparently, you're to go to the Mission tomorrow to make arrangements. I don't see why you should have to rush out there on a Sunday, but that's Richard for you – everything has to happen immediately, preferably yesterday, and no questions asked.' He smiled ruefully. 'Are you sure you don't mind? It will help me, if you help Diana.'

Kitty smiled back. 'I'm quite happy to do what I can. Really I am.'

Theo stood up, gesturing towards the sitting room. 'Let's drink to that.'

The next morning, as Theo dressed for church, Kitty tried not to look impatient. She felt like a child being let off school. Leaving aside the lure of the Mission, she was escaping the weekly ritual of church.

Every single Sunday since she'd arrived, she and Theo had filed into St Michael's – a brand-new stone building set on a low hill overlooking Kongara. Churchgoing was much like an extension of visiting the Club: the right clothes had to be worn; the right people greeted or ignored; the correct expression of polite interest adopted. During the services, Theo sang and prayed with conviction. When he'd been fighting in the war he'd told Kitty he no longer believed in God. How could he, with all the horror that was being allowed to continue? Kitty hadn't been sure if it was God he could not forgive, though, or himself: one night he'd broken down, telling her how many ordinary German people – mothers, fathers, children – he had

bombed into extinction. There were thousands. But after victory
had been achieved, Theo seemed to have rediscovered meaning
in the religion of his upbringing, in much the same way that he'd
embraced a belief in the traditions of British society, and in the
country itself.

Luckily for Kitty, she knew how to flip her way back and forth in
the *Book of Common Prayer*, and when to stand and when to sit or
kneel. The family had always gone to church in Wattle Creek, the
four boys positioned between Kitty and her mother so they could
make sure the brothers didn't fidget too much. Apart from this task,
Kitty would use the time to daydream. She'd stare unseeing at the
altar with its simple wooden cross and the one stained-glass window
with the picture of Jesus the Shepherd, which was appropriate for a
farming town, though no one in Wattle Creek carried a crook around
in case they needed to rescue a young sheep. She imagined the life
she was going to have in the future, in some faraway place. When
Gloria visited the family, the old woman attended church too – but
she didn't say the Creed or take communion. As Kitty squeezed past
her along the pew to take her turn at the altar, Gloria's bony knees
seemed to nudge at her legs, sending a secret message of rebellion.
When Kitty escaped from the world of Seven Gums, church was
one of the things that she had planned on leaving behind.

Yet in the village church of St Luke in the Fields, a stone's
throw from Hamilton Hall, Kitty had found herself mouthing the
same old lines from the same prayer book. To fill the hour, she
would look around her at memorial plaques made of wood, brass
and stone. She counted the number of times the name Hamilton
appeared. On the honour board at the Wattle Creek church, her

own surname showed up once: a distant relative had been killed in the Great War. But in St Luke's, Theo's name (her name, now) could be seen everywhere. It was attached to various bequests made over the generations – the pulpit, the choir stalls, even the light in the gateway arch had been generously provided by the family from the Big House. But other than these points, nothing was very different. The vicar talked in the same singsong voice. Dust made the same spiral dances in the glass-stained sunlight. The wine had the same thin metallic taste. Kitty would eye her watch, torn between wanting the service to end and not wanting to face what awaited her outside in the churchyard. The intense scrutiny had been hard enough to take at the beginning when she was simply a new source of interest in the village. At the end, when she was in disgrace, it had been a torture.

Now, standing in the bedroom on Millionaire Row, the weight of all the boredom and anxiety she associated with churchgoing seemed to gather around Kitty, stifling her breath. She forced herself not to fidget while Theo tied his shoes, combed his hair, folded his handkerchief. When he finally drove off in his Land Rover, leaving her alone, she almost skipped outside to her own car.

The shortcut to the Mission was narrow, but the natural rock of the hillside provided a firm surface without ditches or corrugations. It was less dusty up here so Kitty wound the windows down, welcoming the touch of moving air against her skin. She glanced towards the mountains as she drove. The clouds hung there, looking tantalisingly dark – but no closer to Kongara.

Though she was approaching the Mission from another angle, the bell-tower was still the first sign that she was drawing near. It rose up ahead, tall and confident. Then the steep roof of the church came into view. She reached a sprawling village that bordered the edge of the compound – a collection of the long, low Wagogo houses made from mud, interspersed with enclosures for pigs and goats patched together from sticks and thornbush. As Kitty passed by, children ran out, shouting with excitement and chasing after the car. She waved at their parents working in their *shambas*. She was surprised to see they were planting seeds. They must be expecting the rains to finally begin. It was a risky plan, – an act of faith. If the rain didn't fall, the seed would dry up in the earth and be wasted.

The track terminated at the north end of the compound, near the main mission building with its row of arches. The place was peaceful without the trucks, guards and prisoners. Kitty tried to picture what Sunday would be like, back at His Majesty's Prison – the Hotel of the King. After six long days working hard on Taylor's land, the prisoners were no doubt glad to be left alone in their cells.

As Kitty climbed out of her car she heard singing coming from the church. The sounds that reached her bore no resemblance to the hymns and organ music she associated with Sundays. The singing was layered with harmonies and backed by drums. There were other instruments as well: what sounded like a whistle, and a deep-throated horn.

She walked over to a doorway in the side of the church, positioning herself at an angle so that she could peer inside without attracting attention to herself.

250

A line of women stood in front of the congregation, singing and dancing. They wore brightly patterned *kitenges* wrapped around their bodies, along with necklaces and armbands; some had scarves on their heads, wound into turbans. One had a baby tied to her back. They jiggled their shoulders as they pounded on drums lodged between their knees. An old woman broke from the line, leaping out in front to dance alone. Her skinny body was graceful, belying her age – she moved like a young girl trying to attract a lover. The other dancers took turns to dance around her, egging her on, using their tongues to make a high-pitched cry of celebration. Kitty watched, rather shocked, before edging forward cautiously to view the rest of the congregation.

The church was packed with people of all ages – every one of them swayed or shimmied in time with the drumbeat. She saw the nuns in their blue habits joining in. And there, sitting near the back, as if they'd just come in for a look, were Father Remi and Father Paulo. Kitty wondered if the service had ended; what she was witnessing was more like a party – the audience taking over after curtain call. As though in answer to her question, the old woman returned to the chorus line. Then all the dancers began moving down the aisle towards the big doors at the rear of the church. The rest of the congregation left their places on the rows of long wooden stools, joining the exodus. The two Fathers also rose to their feet, heading for the doorway, where they shook hands and swapped smiles with the people as they left.

Eventually, it became still and quiet in the church. Kitty stepped into the gloomy interior. The peace and stillness now seemed as powerful as the display of sound and movement had been. Light streamed through windows of coloured glass, making patterns on the terrazzo floor. Kitty walked towards the altar, her flat-soled boots making barely a sound. As she passed a hanging incense burner, she picked up a sweet smoky perfume.

She paused beside a lectern holding an open Bible. The text, she noticed, was neither in English nor Swahili. Reading a few phrases, she was reminded of the old documents that hung on the walls at Hamilton Hall. The Admiral had told her the family mottos and historical declarations were in Latin. He'd pointed out that a good grasp of the ancient language was the mark of an educated person (not someone who'd been to Wattle Creek School) and explained that it was the original language of the church. As Kitty scanned the elaborately printed text, it came to her that Father Remi had been speaking in Latin – and not Italian, as she'd assumed – when he said grace in front of the prisoners. She wondered if anyone besides the Fathers was able to understand what was being said.

She moved on, coming to a halt at a table covered in yellow cloth edged with white satin. There were candlesticks set out on it, and a marble stand bearing the image of an old priest who resembled Father Paulo – similar to the one Kitty had seen in the reception room, where she'd first met the two Fathers. At either end of the altar were odd flower arrangements consisting only of greenery. Closer inspection showed they were pot plants – the same succulents in little woven baskets that Sister Barbara had prepared for the stall at the Club. On one of them, Kitty glimpsed the corner of a label bearing a scrap of Diana's illegible writing.

Behind the altar was a large statue of Christ nailed to a wooden cross. The figure was naked but for a loincloth and a crown of thorns;

the head was tilted towards one shoulder, the eyes closed. Blood oozed from the sites of the nails that pierced both of his palms as well as his crossed feet. Kitty turned away, wondering how it was that people became accustomed to such a macabre image. She found herself facing another statue: a tall, slender, beautiful woman holding a baby in her arms. She wore her blue gown with elegance, and her hair – though made from plaster – looked soft and lustrous. The baby was well fed, clean and happy. They made an attractive pair. They even had matching necklaces: long strands of local beads hung around their necks. Pippa's magazine could have included an image of this woman in the column about the perfect wife and mother.

The statue was just a cheap mass-produced cast, Kitty could tell – but the original work in wax or clay had been sculpted with skill by an artist who'd served their time in anatomy class, or else had a natural eye for the proportions of the human figure. The limbs and fingers were a bit long, and the baby was more like a small person than an infant – but that had probably been done on purpose to heighten the sense of elegance in the mother Mary, and to mark out the baby Jesus from others of his kind. The faces were finely modelled, with symmetrical features. The paintwork was restrained – a muted blush on their cheeks, faded tones on the rosy lips, china-blue eyes, yellow-gold hair. As she took in all the details, Kitty shook her head – the statue was ridiculously out of place here. What did those robust women, with their strong features and dark skin, who'd been dancing in here moments ago make of creatures like these – so fair and delicate and foreign?

Yet the steady eyes of the mother held Kitty's gaze. An odd sense of comfort and calm emanated from her, somehow made all the more potent by the delicacy of her form. Kitty found herself thinking of the young Mgogo with the sick child she'd seen that day when she'd walked out past the rear boundary of her garden. She pictured her own mother, holding little Derek, the baby of the Miller family, on her hip. She even pictured Diana – a vision of beauty as perfect as Mary – with Phillip held safe and sound in her arms. Then, with a stab of pain, Kitty thought of the spare bedroom in her house, crowded with Theo's desk, his papers, his clothes, his single bed – making a mockery of her own dream of becoming a mother.

There was a long cushion on the floor at Mary's feet, placed there to allow people to kneel in front of the statue and pray. Deep hollows, where knees had pressed into it over time, suggested many worshippers came here. Kitty stood looking down at it. She wished she believed in some power like this that could help her. Even if it was just a fantasy, it would be a comfort to bow down and pour out your soul . . .

'She is our Blessed Mother Mary.'

Kitty turned to see Tesfa standing behind her. He still wore his black suit jacket, but he'd exchanged his ochre loincloth for one with white and tan woven stripes. Kitty felt underdressed in Janet's working clothes; even here at the Mission, she managed to look wrong.

'*Umekuja.*' You have come. He smiled broadly. '*Karibu sana.*' You are very welcome.

'*Asante.*' Kitty smiled back, pleased to see the old man. He seemed almost like a friend now.

Tesfa gestured to the statue. 'She is very old. She lived in the small church, before this big place was made.'

He began showing Kitty around the church, pointing out the side chapel with the second altar, the steps to the crypt. By the baptismal font he mimed pouring water over a baby's head. He stopped by a tall cupboard with a white curtain instead of a door, set against the wall. There was a hole in one side of the box at head height, filled in with wooden lattice.

'This is the place for telling your sins.' Tesfa drew back the curtain, revealing a plain, empty space. 'The Father stands in here, behind this cloth. He cannot see you. You cannot see him.' He shook his head wonderingly. 'He becomes not a man.' He faced Kitty, his gaze intent. What he said next contained words that could not be directly translated. Janet had spent some time over one of them in her lessons. *Uchawi.* It was often used in connection with the work of a witchdoctor or tribal chief – someone who was believed to have supernatural powers. It could be negative or positive, according to the context. The closest English word was too limited, but it was all we had: 'magic'. The adjective Tesfa put with it Kitty knew well. This word, too, had a range of meanings. Strong, hot, dangerous, effective.

Kitty repeated Tesfa's words as she stared into the dusty box. *Uchawi kali sana.*

The slap-slap of sandals – footsteps approaching – made Kitty turn around. Father Remi strode towards her. 'Mrs Hamilton! Welcome back.' He looked into her face, his own expression poised between pleasure and concern. 'Is there some way we can help you?'

His voice echoed in the lofty space. As Kitty's eyes met his, she felt a surge of pain rising up – a tide of tangled emotions that caught her by surprise. She thought of the baby she longed for. And the huge hole she felt inside since she'd had to give up being an artist. But above all, she thought of her marriage. Theo had changed so much. She could blame the war or his family background – but she knew the real fault lay with her. She'd betrayed him. He couldn't trust her. She could not trust herself . . . Tears pricked her eyes. She wanted, suddenly, to stand at the latticed window, close to the hidden place where strong magic could be worked – and tell the priest everything she'd promised Theo to keep secret. She sensed Father Remi was a good, wise man. He would know how she could redeem herself. But she had not come here on her own account. She took a breath, managing a smile.

'I do hope you can, Father Remi,' Kitty said. 'My friend is very ill.'

The steps to the cellar had once been whitewashed, along with the walls, but the edges had worn through to the stone. Father Remi climbed down ahead of Kitty, one hand gripping a wooden railing. The walls were thick, the roof low. The sour, yeasty smell Kitty had noticed that first day when she'd entered the dining room was now quite powerful. They passed through a room stacked with empty bottles. Huge wooden barrels lurked in the shadows.

'We'll find some wine first,' Father Remi said. He was gathering provisions for a special lunch to celebrate the old priest's eighty-fifth birthday. Kitty had reluctantly declined an invitation to stay and share in the feast – Theo would be expecting her back; it was the first Sunday of the month and they'd be having a curry lunch at the Club. But she'd followed Father Remi to the cellar, keen to extend her visit a little longer.

She'd already spoken to Father Remi about Diana, telling him the whole story. When she'd proposed that Diana join her in helping regularly with the work at the Mission, he nodded his head straight away.

'Acts of Mercy work both ways, healing the giver as well as the receiver.'

'Acts of Mercy.' Kitty had echoed him. The words sounded like an incantation – part of the strong, sharp, dangerous magic Tesfa had described.

'There is a list.' He'd counted on his fingers. 'Feed the hungry, give drink to the thirsty, clothe the naked, harbour the harbourless, visit the sick, ransom the captive, and bury the dead.'

Though the list was short, Kitty knew the tasks were huge – especially here in Africa. Janet would have approved of Father Remi, Kitty thought, even if he was a Catholic.

Father Remi looked back over his shoulder. 'Watch your step, Kitty. The floors are uneven. This end of the building is much older than the rest – it was part of the original mission built by the Germans. They were Benedictines.'

'Did they come a long time ago?' Kitty asked. The place felt ancient, as if it could have been here since Roman times.

'Not really – they arrived in the early 1900s. There was a competition between the Protestants and the Catholics to transform the Wagogo. They were a powerful tribe back then, with lots of cattle. The Germans decided to make Kongara a regional centre. I don't mean the part they call Londoni. I mean Old Kongara. It's further on, past the turn-off.' He pointed in the opposite direction to the Groundnut Scheme settlement. 'They built a fort there – that's where the prisoners are billeted. Around the same time, this Mission was made much bigger. The chapel was replaced with a proper church. The building with the arches was added onto the old mission house. It was going to be a seminary where priests could come to study from all around. But when the Germans were defeated in the Great War they lost their territories in East Africa. Everyone forgot about Kongara.'

He broke off as they entered a larger room dominated by a bulky piece of machinery. It had what resembled a giant corkscrew set in the top. 'That's our grape press. We don't use it much any more. We're building a proper winery at Taylor's farm.' After bending to move a bucket out of the way, he led Kitty into another small room. 'The Passionists took over the Mission in 1920. Three priests were sent here by Rome to run a famine relief camp – Father Paulo was one of them. That was the time of the worst famine anyone can remember. The people call it *Mtunya* – the Scramble. It began during the Great War. The Germans and the British in turn made the Wagogo provide grain, meat and young men for their armies. Then there was a bad drought and they lost what little food they still had. They have never recovered their power.'

Listening to his long speech, Kitty was struck by how fluent his English was. With his earnest tone he sounded like a teacher imparting vital knowledge. She tried to take in all that he was saying. She'd been under the impression that the Groundnut Scheme had been established in 'the middle of nowhere'. The way Father Remi spoke made it sound as though Kongara had long been at the centre of a wide stage.

'Do the Wagogo like having the Scheme here?' she asked.

The Father waved his hand in an equivocal gesture. 'It provides work for the young men so they can stay in the area. But it's upset the balance of life here. Food has become much more expensive because of the high demand. We're seeing undernourished children in the villages, adults too – and there hasn't been a drought for years. We're even beginning to hand out food again.' He came to a standstill near a big window that overlooked the plains. In the distance, dust clouds rose from the Units. There was a worried look on the priest's face. 'New people are moving into the area because of the jobs. That's a problem, too. What's going to happen afterwards – when the Scheme closes down and the British pull out?'

'Oh, it's not going to close down,' Kitty said confidently. 'It's a long-term venture.' She found herself parroting Theo. 'It will run indefinitely. There could even be expansion into other crops. And they're going to hand it all over to the Africans, just as soon as Tanganyika becomes independent.'

Father Remi eyed her in silence for a few seconds, then he turned from the window, signalling a change of topic. 'You know, some of the prisoners who have been released now live on Taylor's land. While they were serving their time they learned how to build, how to farm, and now they work for him as free men.'

Kitty frowned. 'You sound like you have some respect for Taylor and his schemes.'

Father Remi smiled. 'Yes, indeed.'

'You don't find his interest in the prisoners suspicious? I mean, is he really trying to help them, or just feathering his own nest?'

Father Remi looked at Kitty squarely. 'Let me tell you a story about Taylor. He was once a prisoner himself.' Kitty was about to say she already knew that, when the Father continued. 'During the war he spent two years locked up in an underground jail in Abyssinia. It was a small space with no windows. Dark. Ridden with vermin. When he was let out he couldn't walk, couldn't see; he was very weak. In time he recovered physically. But he had a fear of being in a closed space. They gave it a name – claustrophobia. When he returned here, he stayed outside as much as possible, under the open sky. If he entered a room, the door had to be left open. He was like that for a long time.'

Kitty stared at the priest in surprise. When she thought back over her encounter with Taylor on her last visit, she recalled no sign that he had ever been traumatised. He seemed relaxed, at ease with himself and the world. But then, he had been outside. She thought about him being imprisoned – apparently quite recently – on the orders of the District Commissioner. 'You'd think, after that experience, he'd make sure he didn't get locked up again.' As the words left her lips, she regretted her tart tone; it reminded her of Louisa.

'Come with me. I want to show you something.'

The Father picked up a bottle of wine from a rack in the corner, then opened a door into another narrow corridor. 'This was a secret part of the building. The Germans wanted a place where they could hide, during the Great War, if the British invaded.'

'The British would never attack priests!' Kitty exclaimed. Theo had instructed her in the rules of war; civilians should not be targeted.

'It was not that the priests feared being killed,' Father Remi said. 'They were busy, like we are, and didn't want to be locked up in an internment camp for the rest of the war.'

Father Remi unlocked a narrow door and tried to push it open. The wood stuck in its frame and he had to shove his shoulder against it.

A small rectangular room was revealed, containing a single bed and a wooden side table. There was a sink in the corner with a bucket underneath it. The white plaster walls were bare but for a simple crucifix. High up, there was one little window with no curtains. It was above eye height, but let in a shaft of sunlight. A patch of blue sky could be seen.

As Kitty stepped inside, she noticed a line of marks drawn in lead pencil on the wall near the door. It was a tally – each set of four vertical marks was finished off with one that was horizontal. Kitty counted by fives. Fifty-eight.

Walking further in, she faltered. The far wall was covered in drawings. There was a baobab tree with twisted branches and a fluted trunk, a candle with a wind-bent flame, some pieces of fruit with their contours carefully shaded to show form and bulk. But most of the images were of a monkey. The animal was shown in many poses – sleeping, eating, rolling on its back. Some were full portraits, others disembodied details: a hand, a tail, the curved spine. At one end, the drawings were quite crude. But by the time the artist had worked their way along to the other, the results had dramatically improved. The later sketches captured the cheekiness of the face, the movement of the agile limbs, the sharp little teeth, tufts of baby hair. There was no doubting who it was.

Kitty turned back to Father Remi. 'Gili.'

The man crossed to stand by her. 'Taylor was locked up in here. I was his jailer. It was a terrible time for him. He only survived by drawing and walking around this small space. And because of Gili, of course. I would sit outside and listen to his footsteps. They were only faint – his feet were always bare. Feeling the ground beneath him was the only thing that kept his mind in his body, he used to say. We could not let him out, or he would have been transferred to the prison in Dar es Salaam. Being a European, he'd have been kept on his own. At least here he was among friends. We never left him. There was always someone outside this door – me or Father Paulo, Tesfa or one of the nuns. We sang to him when he could not sleep, and when he was afraid. You can imagine what it was like for him to be locked up again, after what he had been through.'

Kitty stared at the drawings as she took in what Father Remi was saying. When he fell quiet, she turned to face him. 'Whatever did he do? What was his crime?'

Father Remi leaned against the wall. He turned the bottle over in his hands as he talked, picking at the remains of an old label. 'It happened nearly two years ago. Taylor had already begun working with the prisoners. There was an Mgogo called Ndemu who'd been convicted of killing a man with a spear. The man had challenged Ndemu to a duel. They were both in love with the same woman. Because the death was the result of a duel, Ndemu was not convicted of murder and sentenced to death, but he was to serve five years in jail. Ndemu had known Taylor since they were boys.' Father Remi looked up at Kitty. 'Taylor was born here, you know. His parents farmed the land next door to us – where he is now. He grew up with the Wagogo. Ndemu was one of his peer group. At their initiation into manhood, they made promises to stand beside one another like brothers, whatever life might bring. When Taylor heard of Ndemu's conviction he arranged for him to be brought to the fort in Old Kongara so he'd be nearby. Ndemu could work with the other prisoners on Taylor's land. They'd see one another.

'When he arrived, Ndemu was ill. Taylor got the Prison Medical Officer to examine him, but there was nothing physically wrong. We sent good food to him from our kitchens. But he just got weaker and weaker. Everyone could see that he was dying. Ndemu was convinced he was under a curse. You see, after the duel, he'd run away, leaving his spear stuck in his victim's chest. He believed the man's relatives were using the spear to cast a spell on him. The only way for him to escape the death curse was to retrieve the spear from them. And to break the spell, he had to do it himself.'

Kitty frowned, taken aback by the matter-of-fact tone of Father Remi's voice; there was no suggestion that he found talking about spells and curses even slightly unusual.

'Taylor went to the District Commissioner and asked for Ndemu to be released temporarily, but he was refused. The authorities believed the man would not return. Taylor then offered to take his brother's place in prison, as a kind of hostage. The DC knew about Taylor's claustrophobia. At that very meeting, Taylor had insisted on standing near the open door. Maybe the DC wanted to see if Taylor would really do such a thing for his African friend. Maybe he admired Taylor's loyalty. I don't know. But he agreed to the proposal. Ndemu would be released to go in search of his spear. Taylor would be locked up until the man returned. I asked the DC to allow him to be imprisoned here, in this room, so that we could support him. I gave my word that he would remain under lock and key until the DC gave permission for him to be released.' Father Remi pointed to the window. 'We had to put bars up there. We removed them as soon as the whole thing was over. I will never forget the look on Taylor's face as he walked in here. He was sweating, trembling . . . I could hardly bring myself to close the door. I turned the lock as quietly as I could. It was terrible for us all.' Father Remi nodded towards the marks on the wall near the door. 'It took just over eight weeks for Ndemu to return. The man was cured of his curse. And so was Taylor.'

'He doesn't have his fear any more?'

When Father Remi responded, his voice was soft with distress. 'It was a trial by fire. The fear burned itself out, in the end. So yes, he's cured. But it was a harsh miracle.' As if the memory was too painful to dwell on, he straightened up, holding out the bottle. Ruby red glinted through the glass. 'This is from our sangiovese vines. Made in 1938. They say you can taste cherry, earth, cedar.' He shrugged, smiling. 'I'm not sure about that. But I think Father Paulo will enjoy it.'

'It should be good,' Kitty agreed. She knew from the Admiral's lectures at the dining table that red wine improved over time. Ten years sounded impressive.

'Now, the food cellar.'

They headed back towards the room with the big window. Next to it was a wide, light gallery that ran along the rear of the arched building. A whole bank of French windows opened onto a stone patio. The land beyond rose quite steeply, leading the eye up towards the mountains. Kitty wondered if perhaps the clouds had moved a fraction closer.

Father Remi went to a cupboard that had ventilation holes in the side – oddly reminiscent of the confessional, but much smaller. He unhooked a large leg of dried meat. 'Prosciutto.' He stroked the wrinkly, salt-dusted flesh almost lovingly. 'Aged for eleven months.' He indicated a shelf holding three large wheels of cheese. 'Could you bring one of those?'

Kitty felt the solid, damp weight of the cheese as she lifted it down. The smell of rind and mould rose up to her as she cradled it against her body. 'Did you make these too?'

'We try not to buy anything. We've got pigs, ducks, geese, a few cows for milk, chickens for eggs and meat. You saw the garden.' He grinned at her. 'We are Italian peasants. We make everything we need. And we waste nothing.'

They climbed back up the stairs, emerging from a trapdoor in a corner of the reception room. A rich aroma of roast meat greeted them. Through the open door to the dining room, Kitty could see the long table spread with a white cloth at one end. There was a vase of mixed garden flowers in the centre. Wine glasses towered over solid-looking white plates. There was a pepper grinder three times the size of the one at Hamilton Hall, and salt in a shaker, not a little bowl. Kitty knew these days how to assess a table setting – noting what was correct, wrong or unacceptably odd. But as she scanned the laid-out cutlery, she noticed only one thing: the number of places that had been set. Three.

'Taylor always comes for a feast day,' Father Remi answered her unspoken question. 'He'll bring a bottle of his verdicchio. His winery is only young. But he claims his *vino bianco* has a nutty flavour with a hint of honey.' He raised his eyebrows in mock scepticism.

'Maybe.' Then he became still, his head tilted, listening. There was the sound of a vehicle engine outside. 'That will be him.'

Only seconds later, Gili bounded into the room. He ignored Father Remi completely, running straight to Kitty, jumping into her arms.

Father Remi watched in amazement. 'He is afraid of strangers.'

Kitty rested her cheek on the firm little head. 'We've met before.'

Taylor walked in then, faltering mid-step as he caught sight of Kitty. He was wearing an ironed shirt, open at the collar. The stubble was gone from his face, his hair had been combed, though a few rebel strands had already fallen over his brow. He held a bottle of wine in one hand, a loaf of bread in the other.

For a long moment, the two just stared at one another. Kitty was aware of the monkey, eyeing his master from her arms. She felt oddly guilty, as if she'd deliberately courted the animal's favour.

'So you did come back,' Taylor commented.

'I took the shortcut. Thank you.'

'I'll get Father Paulo.' The priest left the room, heading into the kitchen.

Taylor looked past Kitty's shoulder towards the table. She could see him counting the places set there, just as she'd done before.

'I'm just going,' she said.

'Oh. That's a pity. Father Paulo is an excellent cook.'

In spite of herself, Kitty searched his face. Was he disappointed, as well, that he was not going to share her company? She hoped her own feelings didn't show too clearly on her face. She'd like nothing more, right now, than the chance to sit down and enjoy

the food and wine – not to mention the easy conversation she felt
sure would soon be flowing.

'Come and see this,' Taylor said, 'before you go.'

Kitty followed him outside, Gili still nestling in her arms. His
fur, tickling her neck, smelled of warm bread.

Taylor crossed the stone forecourt, coming to a halt under the
giant baobab.

'Look.'

He pointed at the bare, gnarled branches of the tree. At first
Kitty could see nothing unusual. But then she noticed buds swelling
on the ends of the twigs. From the colour emerging from the tips,
she thought they must contain white petals, not leaves.

'It means rain is coming,' Taylor stated. 'The tree can tell. Soon,
the flowers will come out. They're big, the size of saucers, with
white, waxy petals. They open in the evening and live for one night
only.' There was pride in his voice, as if he were somehow responsible for the spectacle he was describing. 'The white petals reflect
the moonlight, so that fruit bats and bush babies can find them
easily. They come to sip the nectar and feed off the pollen. In that
one night, fertilisation must take place. By midmorning the next
day, the flowers are bruised and brown and finished.'

He gazed up at the tree as he spoke. Kitty recognised, from
the look in his eyes and the tone in his voice, the love a person
feels for the plants and animals, the land, where they were born.
She'd felt that sense of deep belonging herself once – for the land
around the farm, in their forgotten corner of New South Wales.
She'd taken pleasure in finding the first signs of the seasons changing. She'd loved observing the unexpected transformation of the

wattle trees as their leaves lost their baby shape – like little green paddles – moving on to the feathery fronds of adulthood. She'd relished the presence of the pointy-nosed bilby and the duck-billed platypus – animals straight from a storyteller's imagination, at home in her own backyard.

She carried Gili across to Taylor. The monkey tightened his grip around her neck for a moment, resisting being handed over. But when Taylor put out his arms, Gili moved obediently into them.

'Goodbye, then.' Kitty addressed them both, her eyes moving from man to monkey and back. She pictured Taylor in his white-washed cell, drawing images of Gili. The company of the playful creature must have made all the difference to him as he endured the terrible punishment he'd taken upon himself. She'd misjudged him so badly – she almost wanted to say sorry.

Taylor lifted his free hand in a farewell salute.

As Kitty walked away she imagined him still standing there, looking up into the branches of the strange African tree. She wished she could have stayed longer, just to bask in his affection for this place that he called home. The way he'd spoken, the details he knew about the flowering, had made her aware of the deep hollow that lay inside her, where her own love of a landscape had once been. As she'd grown older, she'd turned against the bush she had loved. The farm had become a prison. She'd escaped to England – the land of museums, grand houses and neat green fields. There had been much to admire and discover. And, of course, there was Theo. But deep down she'd known she would never really belong there. Perhaps that was one of the reasons why she had been so close to Yuri – he was an outsider too.

She climbed into the car, swinging the door shut with a bang that sent a flock of chickens running for the bushes. She was struck by the thought that she didn't belong in Londoni, either. It was, after all, a little piece of England transplanted to Tanganyika. She was lost. She remembered the word Father Remi had used. 'Harbourless'. That was her state. She didn't belong anywhere any more.

But that was not quite true, Kitty quickly reminded herself. She belonged with Theo. They'd be together until death parted them. That was what they had promised in their hasty marriage ceremony, held in a church they'd never entered before, and witnessed by an RAF mate of Theo's who'd been killed on his next mission. Taylor was not the only one who knew how to stick to a promise. It was something Kitty had been taught from childhood. A promise must stand. For better, for worse. Harbour or harbourless. She had made her choice.

Kitty looked up at the mountains as if she could draw reassurance from their solid, timeless presence. Instead she felt a wave of despondency. She needed more than just Theo in her life. He was simply too busy to pay attention to her. Perhaps things would be different once the teething problems of the Scheme were solved. Perhaps, given time, the love they'd once shared might bloom again. But for now, she was deeply lonely. She thought again of the Blessed Mary, holding her child. A baby could make all the difference.

The vision of becoming a mother brought up anxiety, though, as well as joyful anticipation. Theo's frequent absence from her bed was not Kitty's only concern. Really, there had been plenty of chances for her to fall pregnant. They'd been married seven years, after all. It was true that most of that time had been overshadowed by the war, with constant separations and emotional stress. And the years that had followed had brought their own trials. But even so, they'd been together long enough. They should both see a doctor to find out what was wrong. Kitty tried to remember which kind of surgeon Frank had said he was. It didn't matter – clearly, there were specialists attached to Kongara Hospital. She would simply have to talk to Theo about it, no matter what Pippa's magazine advised.

As she bumped along the shortcut track, she felt a sense of relief mixed with trepidation. She was not looking forward to confronting Theo – the idea of pushing him, insisting, arguing back, made her stomach twist in a knot. But it had to be done. She breathed out slowly. Now that she'd made her decision, she knew she had to act. She must do it soon. Before the rain came, filling the trenches and blocking the roads – sweeping aside everything in its path.

TWELVE

The hum of casual conversation drifted above Kitty's head as she knelt by the prisoner's side. Carefully unwinding the dressings from his ulcerated leg, she could see that the wound had almost healed – the gauze came away freely and was only lightly marked with stains.

'*Vizuri sana,*' she said as the bandage fell away. Against the black skin, it was not easy to see any pink tinge that would signal lingering inflammation – but there was no sign of puffiness and no weeping around the scab. She pushed at the area gently, looking questioningly up at the prisoner.

He smiled. '*Hakuna maumivu.*' There is no pain.

Kitty smiled back at him. She knew nothing of his story – where he came from, what crime he'd committed. She didn't even know his name. But she felt a bond with him. An ulcer such as he'd had could easily have led to overwhelming infection. He could have lost his leg, or even died. They'd shared a perilous journey together.

'*Bahati nzuri,*' she said simply. I wish you well.

'*Na wewe pia, dada yangu.*' And the same to you, my sister.

He walked away with no sign of a limp. As the next patient came to take his place in the chair, Kitty looked across the room to where

Diana was sitting at a desk. On one side of her was Father Paulo, and on the other, a prisoner called Chalula, who knew English but could not write. A grey-haired prisoner sat in front of the three. He was dictating a letter, Chalula was translating the words into English, and Diana – under Father Paulo's critical eye – was writing them down on a notepad. Kitty thought she must be tired; she'd only been out of hospital three days and they'd been here since ten o'clock this morning, helping prepare and serve the meal. Diana had taken everything in her stride: the Mission, the prisoners, the chaos of all those bodies lining up to be fed – and now this work as well. She'd been so grateful that Kitty had managed to convince Richard to let her stay in Kongara that complaints or queries seemed far from her mind.

Now, as Diana wrote, there was a frown of concentration on her face. She made slow, deliberate strokes with her pen, shaping the letters carefully. While Kitty was watching, Father Paulo leaned over, holding a magnifying glass to her work, then pointing out some error with a shaky forefinger. Diana nodded, accepting his correction. She was like a student on her best behaviour. Her hair was pinned back, her face bare of make-up. On Kitty's suggestion she'd come dressed in some of Richard's field clothes. Her innate sense of style managed to make even these man's clothes look glamorous. But all her focus was on the task at hand. She was deep in thought, the tip of her tongue resting in the corner of her mouth.

Kitty's next patient had itchy spots around his wrists. He knew the cause, and so did she. He had an infestation of a mite that burrowed into the skin. It was not a straightforward case of scabies, though – where he'd been scratching there were small infected sores. Janet's notes said this indicated an underlying health problem: the man's immune system was weak. Kitty wrote a note for the guards to take back to the Prison Medical Officer, requesting the man be properly examined. Kitty didn't know if this would happen or not – the local PMO didn't spend anywhere near enough time at the prison in Old Kongara. He was content to let the Catholic missionaries do his job.

Kitty gave the prisoner a bar of anti-parasitic soap and instructed him to wash his whole body with it, leaving the lather to dry on his skin. When the man left, she went to scrub her hands in the sink, using lots of soap and disinfectant. She felt itchy herself at the thought of insects living under a person's skin.

There was a moment's break while a guard tried to decide who should be seen next. As she sat waiting, Kitty's thoughts turned back to the previous evening. Her hands clenched in her lap as images returned to her, sharp and painful.

She'd waited, tense and anxious, for Theo to come home. She'd decided this was the night she would raise her concerns about why she had not yet fallen pregnant. Her speech had been prepared. The words were carefully chosen to be clear without being pushy. But when Theo had finally shown up, an hour late, it had not been long before she realised he'd been drinking. His speech was slurred and he'd stumbled as he climbed the stairs to the verandah. He'd gone straight to the drinks trolley, brushing Gabriel aside and pouring his own double whisky.

The servant had met Kitty's gaze. In his eyes was a blend of contempt and fear – a boss who was drunk was both pitiful and dangerous. She'd signalled for Gabriel to return to the kitchen.

Theo had emptied his glass, then he began making a gin and tonic for his wife. Kitty had watched in silence. Back in England, she had seen Theo drunk plenty of times – in the war, the pilots drank together to take the edge off their fear, or to erase for a few hours the memory of their lost friends. No one blamed them for an instant. Yuri had sometimes drunk too much vodka as well – by the end of a long evening he'd sometimes be a bit inebriated. But it was another matter for Theo to be coming home from work drunk like this. The first time it had happened, Kitty had been shocked. Then, when the situation was repeated, she'd been angry and upset. She'd waited all day for her husband's company and then the man who'd turned up was a stranger she did not like. Last night, she'd felt a sense of despair. How could she even be thinking of having a baby with a man in the house who drank?

Theo had held out Kitty's glass, having poured a double gin. When he was drunk he always wanted her to drink too, as if that made his state more acceptable. When she'd declined, Theo slammed her glass back down on the trolley, causing the drink to splash over his hand. But he'd barely noticed.

Kitty had left him there in the sitting room – another whisky already in hand – and gone to bed. She was hungry, but could not face watching Gabriel serve a meal to Theo when he was in this state. She'd seen it before. Theo would fumble and spill things and pretend all the while that he was sober – a glass was just so slippery, or a jug was in the wrong spot, too close to his elbow. And, of course, Gabriel was always at fault.

She'd lain awake, listening to the sound of her husband talking to his servant. She just hoped that when he was finished with his binge, he would not come and sleep in her bed. When she'd finally heard the door to the spare room bang shut, she'd breathed out with relief. But she had still not been able to sleep. She'd spent hours just looking at the ceiling, tracing the tiny cracks that had already appeared there. Eventually, tears had welled up, overflowing and running back over her temples onto the pillow.

Once these first tears had escaped it had been impossible to stem the flow. Kitty had cried for what felt like hours. This morning, she'd had to use witch-hazel to soothe her red, puffy eyes. It must have worked, since no one had made any comment, but she still had a slight headache. While she waited for her patient to appear, she pressed her hands over her eyelids, then massaged her temples. It was not lost on her that she'd brought Diana here today to forget about her problems and now Kitty needed the same treatment herself. Standing up, she stretched her legs and scanned the room, letting the reality of her surroundings – this new setting, this new day – take over.

Nothing could be further removed from last night's scene than this. The mood of the place was calm, busy, purposeful. Father Remi was rifling through his medicine cupboard. The prisoners still waiting to be seen were polite and patient. The guards were relaxed. One of the nuns was singing as she did some washing up.

Kitty looked over to the writing desk. The old prisoner had gone now and in his place sat one of the youngest prisoners Kitty had come across. He was barely more than a child. He was talking to Father Paulo in Swahili, but all the while staring at the white woman holding the pen. After some time, Chalula relayed the translation.

'But this is terrible!' Diana's voice rang out. 'It's a clear case of mistaken identity. Something must be done.'

'We can send a petition to the District Commissioner,' Chalula suggested.

'But this boy should not be here,' Diana said. 'He's innocent. For heaven's sake, he's just a child.'

The figure in front of her bowed his head. After a few moments, his shoulders began to shake. Chalula repeated the phrases that came from him in bursts. Kitty couldn't hear them, but the effect on Diana was clear. She leaned forward, grasping the boy's arm.

'Don't worry. I'm going to help you. I will deliver this letter personally. If the DC won't intervene, I will go to Dar es Salaam myself and see his superior.'

There was a steady murmur while Chalula gave his translation. As the meaning of Diana's words became clear, the teenager lifted his head. On his face, Kitty saw a look of longing and fear – then hope breaking through.

'If I have to,' Diana stated, 'I will take this case up with the Colonial Office in London.'

'*Londoni?*' Chalula queried.

'No – I mean the *real* London, in England. The home of the King.'

'Ah!' Chalula sounded impressed as he passed the words on.

Kitty watched Diana's face. Her eyes were lit with passion and concern. Her own heartbreak was being overlaid with another woman's nightmare: somewhere, there was a mother whose son – little more than a child – had been dragged from his village, falsely convicted and locked away with criminals. Fate had struck an innocent victim. But this time there was something Diana could do about it.

Kitty smiled at the thought of Diana on a mission. She'd be a formidable force, making use of her status as Richard's wife, perhaps dropping names of men she'd entertained in her home. (Mr Strachey, the Minister of Food, had reportedly been her guest.) With beauty and charm in Diana's arsenal as well, Kitty anticipated the DC would find himself making all kinds of promises.

Diana lifted her head, pausing in her work. Meeting Kitty's gaze, she gave a faint nod. Kitty felt a rush of relief – she sensed Diana was feeling the same way she had, on the day she'd first come here. The plan Kitty had convinced Richard to try was already working.

The next patient sat down in the chair. As they exchanged greetings, Kitty wiped her brow with the back of her hand. Then she looked around her, picking up an odd feeling in the air. A rising tension, a building of energy. She could see she was not the only one aware of it. People were shifting restlessly. The men closest to the doorway and the windows turned to peer outside.

A current of excitement travelled the room, gathering momentum. Everyone began moving outside – slowly, at first, then with growing urgency. When Kitty's patient stood up and walked away, she followed right behind him.

As soon as she stepped outside she could smell it, feel it.

Rain!

The first big drops fell, throwing up dust as they hit the ground. The gaps between the splashes grew shorter until they joined together in a downpour. Prisoners, guards, nuns, the two Fathers – everyone stood out in the open, lifting their faces to the sky. Kitty joined them. Within moments she was soaked, warm water pounding her skin. Instinctively she spread her arms, opening her whole body to the rain. All around her, people were dancing, singing, shouting with joy.

The intensity of the deluge increased until it was almost frightening. It drummed loudly on the rooftops, and beat a tattoo on a collection of old fuel drums stacked near the edge of the forecourt. It bounced off the trestle table outside the church.

The sense of relief was tangible, the rain literally washing away fears of drought and famine. The people up here in the hills had the spring water to rely on, but the prisoners and guards came from further afield. They were thinking of their home villages, where dry *shambas* were being watered, creeks fed, waterholes refilled. Kitty saw a guard hugging a prisoner with delight. Father Paulo clung to the arm of Tesfa, the pair of old men shuffling their feet together. Chalula and Diana stood near the edge of the crowd. Diana tipped back her face, opening her mouth to drink straight from the clouds above.

Theo came home from work early. He jumped from the Land Rover as soon as it stopped, and bounded up the verandah steps, scooping Kitty into his arms. Luckily, she'd already bathed and changed from her work clothes.

'Planting has begun!' He sounded like a child let out of school. 'It's happening!'

Kitty smiled back at him. She tried to imagine the scene that would have played out at Head Office when the first raindrops fell.

She doubted they'd have gone outside to dance. Had they opened champagne? Sent telegrams to London? Had the men kissed their secretaries?

Kitty and Theo stood on the verandah looking down towards the Units. The rain had stopped for the moment, leaving the landscape fresh and clean. You could see the lines of specially adapted tractors already at work on the plantations, spreading the seed nuts. Kitty pictured the excitement of the workers greeting the rains. Down in the labour camps and the contractors' quarters, the Irish, Italians and Greeks, as well as the natives, would all be celebrating in their own ways. The clubs and bars would be full. At the lower end of Londoni, Ahmed and the other Arabs would be doing the same. So would the Asians, like Mr Singh the greengrocer. In the shanties, the workers' wives would no doubt be dancing. Kitty wondered about the prostitutes. Would they take time off to mark the occasion? Or was this going to be their busiest night in months?

'I'm hungry,' Theo declared. 'Let's go straight to the dining room.'

'I'll let Eustace know.' As she followed Theo inside, Kitty wondered if skipping the sundowners was a sign that he knew he'd gone too far last night. Or perhaps, now that the tension of waiting for the rains had eased, he'd decided to pull himself up, step back in line.

As they took their places, Theo rubbed his hands together. 'Monday. Just what I feel like!' He unfolded his napkin, smoothing it over his knees. Then he jerked up his head as if suddenly remembering something. 'How did it go today – at that Mission place? Did you have to stay for ages? Was it too awful?'

'No, it was fine,' Kitty said. 'We helped in the kitchens first. We made huge pots of *ugali* – that's a kind of porridge made from corn meal. Then we helped with serving it out.'

'Well, that's good. Did Diana behave herself?' Before Kitty had time to answer, he turned away from her. 'And here comes Gabriel.' He beamed at the houseboy as he set down the dishes. 'Good man.'

Kitty hid her disappointment at Theo's obvious lack of any real interest in how she'd spent her day. At least he was happy and relaxed for once. And it was an important night.

She waited for Gabriel to retreat. 'I want to talk to you, Theo,' she said. 'It's something serious.'

He held up his hands in mock horror. 'What have I done?'

Kitty took a breath, then launched into her speech – telling him how she wanted a baby, that she knew he did too, and how it should have happened by now.

'Just give it time,' Theo responded. He took another serving of corned beef, spooning on the white sauce.

Reaching across the table, Kitty put her hand on his arm. She felt like a little girl demanding attention from a grown-up. 'Theo, we've been married for nearly seven years. I know we've been apart a lot. And . . . you've been very busy and tired lately.' Theo threw her a sharp look, but she pushed on. 'But I think there must be something wrong. I want to see a doctor. And if there's nothing the matter with me, I want you to see one too.'

There – she'd said it. She caught her breath, shocked at her own temerity.

Theo just stared at her. Then he gave a little shake of his head as if to make sure he was awake.

'Let me see if I understand. You want to discuss this . . . issue . . . with a doctor?'

Kitty nodded. 'There are specialists at the hospital. You can ask for an appointment.'

Theo stood up. 'Out of the question, Kitty. I'm amazed you've even suggested it. Can you imagine what it would be like for me if it became known that we were having problems in that department?'

'I'm sure the doctor would be discreet.'

'There are no secrets in Kongara; you should know that. I'm sorry, Kitty. The answer is no.'

Kitty bent her head. Her hair had grown a little and the locks screened her face. But there was nothing to hide her tears when they fell – single drops splashing the tablecloth.

Theo moved to stand beside her, putting his arm around her shoulders. 'Kitty, darling, don't be upset. I tell you what – if nothing happens by the time the harvest is in, we'll go to Nairobi. How does that sound?'

He smiled down at her, pleased with his plan. Kitty was glad that at least some compromise was being offered, but she was still frustrated that there seemed to be no limits to Theo's preoccupation with what other people thought of him. She had to remind herself that this was partly – or even largely – her own fault. She'd humiliated him so deeply and so publicly that he was now over-sensitive. She felt, once again, that she had no right to push him.

She made herself smile back. 'Thank you.'

There was silence then. Theo sat down again, studying his half-empty plate with its smears of mashed potato, and the little pile of unused salt resting near the rim. His face had fallen back into lines of worry and dismay. The light-hearted mood had been completely destroyed. And nothing had been achieved – Kitty wasn't sure Theo was genuinely serious about going to Nairobi. She regretted having even opened her mouth. Trying to think of a way to change the subject, she seized the first thought that came to mind.

'Did you know the baobab tree can predict when the rain is coming?'

Theo looked at her with incomprehension. 'Who told you that nonsense?'

Kitty's lips parted as she hunted for a reply, then she shook her head. 'Just someone at the Mission. It's probably not even true.'

She watched Gabriel take away the first-course plates and then serve the Bakewell tart. As Theo bent his head over his slice, she stared past him towards the windows that opened onto the yard. All she could see there were the stubby branches of a harshly pruned frangipani tree. There were no baobabs in the gardens of Millionaire Row – the trees were much too primitive and strange; too African. But that didn't stop Kitty picturing a towering tree trunk, its wrinkled bark folded into deep vertical flutes. A cluster of massive roots, gripping the earth. She let the image grow clearer, carrying her away from her pain and disappointment – back to the Mission, where the giant baobab kept company with the church and the bell-tower. She wondered exactly when the white petals had begun to unfurl, ahead of today's rain. Another image came to her then – a man standing beneath the branches, face upturned, his features painted silver in the moonlight. He was watching the slow emergence of the flowers. Beside him, a monkey capered about, casting mad leaping shadows over the ground.

In the weeks that followed, everyone got used to working around the rain. There was no pattern to the sudden downpours that could be relied upon. They came when they felt like it – then the sun would show its face for a while, drying up some of the puddles, before another storm broke.

Diana and Kitty went to the Mission each Monday, Wednesday and Friday. Kitty drove there in her Hillman, needing all her driving skills to negotiate the mud and to steer along the track when rain fell so heavily that she could barely see. Diana always rode in the back – not because she wanted to be chauffeured, but because she didn't like sitting next to someone at the wheel. She had yet to overcome her fear of driving.

The prisoners now took their meals inside the church, the only building large enough to shelter them. They sat in rows on the long benches. Dressed in their plain canvas clothing they were like some strange order of monks who wore stencilled numbers in place of embroidered badges. Awed by the setting, they spoke less than they did outside. As Kitty helped serve out the food, she felt as if she were taking part in a sacred task – there was the sense of a sacrament being performed.

Sometimes the duties carried out by the two women changed – they might spend time in the kitchen or the laundry. If it was not raining, they might do some gardening. But Kitty always worked in the clinic after lunch, and while she did that, Diana sat devotedly at her writing desk. She had already made some progress. Her letter about the young prisoner had been delivered in person to the DC and an appeal process was underway. Now she met with the boy to pen letters home to his parents. She didn't know much Swahili yet, but with spelling advice from Father Paulo she was able to take down dictation.

Taylor rarely appeared at the Mission. Like everyone else, he was busy making use of the rain. When his path crossed with Kitty's, the two swapped light comments about the gardens, Gili, the clinic, the vineyards. But sometimes, as their eyes met, a potent energy flared between them. Kitty found it hard to turn away, and when she did, she still saw the man's face, the look in his eyes. She sensed danger in their friendship – as she had from the time of their first encounter, fixing the water pipe. She knew she should keep her distance. Yet whenever she was at the Mission she couldn't help watching out for him. When she got the chance, she tried to find out more about him – casually, so as not to betray too much inter-est. She asked Father Paulo what his first name was, and learned that since the death of his much-admired father he'd only ever been called by the name they both shared. His mother had been highly respected too, by the priests as well as the Africans. Kitty discovered Taylor had been to school in Nairobi and later studied overseas. Tesfa let drop that he was a skilled chess player and a reader of many books . . .

Gili was always the harbinger of Taylor's arrival. He came straight to find Kitty. He liked to sit at her feet when she was work-ing in the clinic, playing with the ends of bandages she unrolled. When she was serving food he insisted on sitting on the table beside the cooking pots. If someone he trusted was close by, he was quite confident, even cheeky. Once, there was an upset when he stole a handful of *ugali* from one of the plates. When the prisoner expressed his outrage, Gili jumped onto the man's shoulder and wiped the porridge in his hair. Kitty looked on in dismay. Now she knew how her mother had felt when the boys got up to mischief in public. It was only later, when Kitty was in the midst of placing a thermometer under someone's tongue, that a smile came to her lips.

On the days when Kitty and Diana stayed away from the Mission, they went along to the Club. This was part of the arrangement that had been brokered between their husbands. Dr Meadows and Sister Edwards had maintained a judicious silence about Diana's admission to the hospital, and it was accepted by all that it had been due to an attack of blackwater fever, a complication of malaria. The ladies were led to believe that the scare of being seriously ill had produced a rather extreme desire (typical of Diana; she never did anything by halves) to help others. As a result, Kitty and Diana had taken up charity work at the Catholic Mission. It was definitely odd, but no one was in a position to question what Mr Armstrong had sanctioned. Alice, in particular, seemed unsure whether to be jealous of Kitty, who'd been coerced into joining the mad scheme, or to be glad she had not been seized upon by Diana as a companion herself.

The women sipped coffee, swapped magazine articles and developed plans for social events, just as they had always done. The Christmas Ball was discussed. How many carols would the school choir sing? Should the children wear uniforms or party clothes? Someone had to be found to play Father Christmas, Alice pointed out, and the suit sent from London the previous year had still not been located. All the while, Kitty was aware that Diana was constantly being scrutinised. Clearly, everyone – from Alice and Evelyn to Pippa and Eliza – was struck by how much she'd changed. Diana no longer gorged herself on large quantities of sweet treats before disappearing to the powder room. She was even-tempered and more able to focus on Alice's meeting agendas. When she signed her name for Richard's account at the Club, she wrote neatly and carefully. Most bizarrely, she was seen at one of the tables by the pool, practising calligraphy with an old-fashioned pen and ink. Kitty thought onlookers probably concluded that Diana had been tamed by her illness – that she'd become more ordinary, more like everyone else. But Kitty knew the truth was quite different: Diana's lively spirit and quick wit were still there. But her real life was now being played out on another stage.

As far as the Scheme was concerned, the relief at the coming of rain was short-lived. Where the ground had been as hard as concrete beforehand, it was now like a big soft pudding. The tractors sank to their axles. The tracked vehicles that were sent to their rescue became bogged as well. And in the tent settlement in the heart of Kongara, the drainage trenches were full to the brim and threatening to spill over. In the midst of all this, there was a race to get the rest of the seed nuts into the ground. These first rains of the season never lasted long. The big rains would come later, and would sustain the established plants until harvest time. But only if they were there . . .

The problems were so daunting that Theo no longer even complained about them to Kitty. He came home silent and gloomy, reporting only the quantity of peanuts that had been planted to date – there must have been some kind of chart at Head Office. When the first frantic stage of sowing was over, his attention turned to the number of seedlings that had sprouted. From the figures, Kitty could see that the situation was disastrous.

The only bright topic of conversation, where Theo was concerned, was the propsect of working with Lady Charlotte Welmingham. Unfortunately it seemed she wouldn't be able to make it to Kongara quite as quickly as Theo had hoped. But she was still committed to coming. He clung to the date of her anticipated appearance as if it held some magical power to solve all his woes. Kitty was torn between feeling jealous that another woman was of such importance to him, and longing for anything to happen that might lift Theo's spirits. She tried asking Theo leading questions about the honey expert, trying to gather clues as to what kind of person she was. Since he remained vague – not saying she was beautiful, slender, witty or a good sport – Kitty comforted herself with the thought that she might be overweight, or unattractive. Big-boned, perhaps. Horsey-looking, with prominent teeth. Or with the snouty, pointed features of a hound. As it was clear Theo was going to be spending lots of time with the apiarist, Kitty could only hope that this unat-tractive picture would turn out to be true.

THIRTEEN

The Daimler pulled out of the Mission compound, turning onto the shortcut track that wound through the village. The rains were now over and the surface was firm and dry, but James still drove cautiously between the mud huts. He'd brought the two women to work this morning after Kitty's Hillman failed to start. Kitty had been surprised at his eagerness to help out, considering it would mean driving the precious car on the shortcut track. When they got to the Mission he'd surprised her again: instead of remaining with the Daimler as a driver normally would, he'd asked Tesfa to show him around. As Kitty carried out her tasks she had glimpsed the pair, now and then – Tesfa giving long lectures on every point of interest and James drinking it all in. It had dawned on her eventually why the man was so intrigued. He'd been watching Diana set off for the Mission for nearly six weeks now. (Richard had agreed his wife could continue going there after the trial period ended.) No doubt James had heard rumours of what she did with her time. Now he wanted to see it for himself – this place that had rescued his mistress from the state of being without joy, and brought her back to life.

With the day's work behind them, they were heading home. Diana filled Kitty in on the progress of her latest campaigns. She had two more special cases among the prisoners. She was trying to get a man released on parole for good behaviour – he was one of Taylor's most hardworking labourers. She was also investigating the case of a prisoner convicted of murder five years ago. Doctors agreed the young Mgogo had had a severe reaction to a prescribed anti-malaria medicine. In a drug-induced psychosis, he'd killed his beloved wife. Regardless of His Majesty's Justice system, he would pay for the crime (of which he had no recollection) for the rest of his days. Diana believed that to add incarceration to his torment was cruel and unjust. It was her intention to have him set free.

As they passed the village square, a gang of children ran out to the car as usual. Diana no longer flinched at the sight of them, but Kitty saw her meet James's gaze in the rear-vision mirror. Today, a young boy ran right up to the Daimler, calling out for it to stop. When James slowed to a walking pace, a girl came up beside the boy. She was carrying an object that Kitty didn't recognise at first. But as it was held out towards her, she saw the shape of a monkey made with clay. The sculpture – a little under a foot tall – showed an animal caught in the midst of making a jump, all his energy poised in his feet.

'Oh, look at that!' Diana leaned past Kitty to get a closer view. 'It's so lifelike!'

The two children, along with several others, pressed up against Kitty's window. As she wound it down, they held out the sculpture.

'Who made it?' Diana asked.

The children pointed excitedly at Kitty, not needing to speak English to guess the question.

Kitty nodded, keeping her eyes on the monkey as the girl waved it around. A few days earlier she'd come across the children playing around the edges of a newly formed creek. The red earth had turned into rich thick clay and they were using it to make models of cows. Kitty had hesitated, but then sat down to join in. This was not art, after all – it was nursery play for children with no school. All of the cows that had been made were roughly the same: a simple, stylised shape. Kitty couldn't help wanting to broaden the scope of the children's work. She'd gathered a large ball of clay, kneading it until it became smooth and malleable. Soon, she'd found the image of Gili forming in her hands.

'*Peleka nyumbani*,' the boy called through the car window to Kitty. Take it home with you.

They thrust the figure towards her. The clay was hard and dry. Someone must have placed it beside a cooking fire to bake; one side was slightly blackened.

'*Asante*.' Kitty thanked them, touched that such care had been taken of the object she had made. The sculpture was surprisingly good, considering she'd never sketched Gili. As she turned it over in her hands, it occurred to Kitty that she may have been influenced by Taylor's mural on the walls of his old cell. Something about the works had stayed with her. She knew what it was: every one of the lines that made up the images was the result of the man's intimate knowledge and love of his pet.

She thanked the children again, then James drove on towards Londoni. The monkey rested on her lap, a small solid weight.

'I didn't know you were an artist,' Diana said.

'Oh, I was just playing.'

'You're talented,' Diana insisted. 'And clearly very skilled. You must have been to art school.'

Kitty looked at her but said nothing. She wished she could tell the truth – especially since Diana had confided in her. But how could she explain why her being an artist had to be a secret? In the end she just shook her head – after all, she hadn't been to art school; she'd learned from her own private teacher. As Kitty gazed out of the window she could feel Diana watching her with curious eyes. Clearly, Diana suspected Kitty was hiding something – but she was too polite to push for an honest answer.

James insisted on driving Kitty right to her verandah steps, even though she said she could easily walk across from the house next door. She stood still, holding her monkey sculpture until the car had rolled away out of sight.

She went straight to the back garden, bending over to search for a secluded nook. After some time, she chose a spot near the base of a bougainvillea bush. The tangled branches had grown in a curve, forming a natural grotto edged with purple flowers. The vibrant tone of the petals seemed to match the playful spirit of the monkey. Kitty checked there was no one watching before bending down and pushing the statue into place. Stepping back, brushing rosy clay dust from her hands, she smiled at the sight of it there. Then she headed inside to get changed.

As soon as she stepped into the hallway she knew something was afoot. A bunch of flowers had been crammed into a vase and set on the side table. The aroma of roasting meat came from the kitchen – which was correct, for Friday, except that it smelled like beef or lamb, definitely not chicken.

Gabriel scooted past the end of the hall on his way to the sitting room. Kitty followed him. Could it be a surprise, she wondered, prepared for her by Theo? Perhaps he wanted to make up to her for being so distant and irritable. Or he regretted having been so unbending in the conversation about the baby . . .

'What's happening, Gabriel?'

The houseboy put down the ice bucket he'd been carrying and proceeded to check the levels in the bottles of spirits. 'You are expecting a visitor, Memsahib. Someone very important. The bwana sent a message.'

Kitty looked at him in confusion. Had she been told about this and forgotten? Who could it be? So far, she'd not had to host an evening with someone important from London – that was Diana's role. But with the Managing Director's wife having been ill so recently, perhaps Theo's home had temporarily replaced Number One as the address to hold a company dinner.

'Who is our guest? What is his name?'

Gabriel gave her a triumphant grin, clearly enjoying being in possession of knowledge his mistress did not have. 'She is a lady.'

Kitty stared at him. A lady.

Charlotte.

Dismay mixed with panic descended on Kitty. She'd gone from dreading Lady Welmingham's arrival to managing to put it from her mind. She'd certainly never expected the woman would just suddenly appear. Why hadn't Kitty been told she was in Kongara?

She gathered herself, putting on a smile. 'How nice.' Then she scanned the houseboy critically. 'Make sure you change your tunic. It doesn't look quite clean.'

Gabriel bowed his head. 'Yes, Memsahib.'

The tunic was spotless, they both knew that – but that was not the point.

The candlelight added a golden tone to Lady Charlotte's long red hair. Her locks trailed over her shoulders, contrasting with the green velvet of her dress. Even Kitty could see that the woman was perfectly turned out – her pearls and her full-length gown, offset by her loose hairstyle, struck the right note of low-key formality.

Kitty studied the Englishwoman as she chatted to Theo. Charlotte paused often to smoke, a long tapered cigarette holder balanced between her manicured fingers. She had eaten tiny portions of the meal, before sending gracious compliments to the kitchen. Gabriel kept fawning over her, using every bit of his domestic training to the limit.

'Do you remember Billy Alston?' Charlotte was asking Theo. 'He was a year ahead of you boys.'

Theo groaned. 'How could I forget him!'

'He was killed in the war.'

Theo's face stiffened with shock, but when he spoke his tone was calm. 'Poor old Bills.' Kitty was reminded of the matter-of-fact way he used to inform her of the regular deaths in his squadron.

'Yes. Awful.' Charlotte flicked ash into a tray at her side.

Kitty thought of asking the woman what she'd spent her time doing during the war – hoping to hear she'd just stayed at home, doing her embroidery and collecting honey from her hives. But Kitty suspected Charlotte might well explain that she'd worked night and day as a volunteer nurse – perhaps in her own family mansion, which had been willingly handed over to become a hospital for wounded soldiers. She could just see Lady Charlotte in a nurse's uniform, looking wonderful, being wonderful . . .

The pair talked and talked. Kitty couldn't remember when she'd last seen Theo so enlivened and loquacious. Now and then, Charlotte threw a morsel of conversation to her hostess – she knew her manners. But soon the talk drifted back to people, events and places Kitty knew nothing about. Occasionally, to underline her words, Charlotte touched Theo's forearm. The two seemed familiar – easy and comfortable in one another's company. They had the same confidence, the same accent, the same small mannerisms and turns of phrase. They could have been born to be together.

As she watched on, Kitty wondered whether Theo had discussed with Charlotte the need to keep secret the scandal surrounding his wife. Charlotte couldn't have missed hearing about it – she moved in the same circles as the Hamiltons. She would have read the newspapers, heard the gossip in the London clubs. Theo would have had the chance to talk to her this afternoon – evidently they'd already spent hours together at Head Office. On the other hand, Kitty realised, he might well have raised it much earlier, during the telephone calls to England to plan her trip out here. If he had, Charlotte would have agreed, undoubtedly, to remain quiet on the subject while she was in Tanganyika. She was, after all, what Louisa would dub 'one of us'.

As the evening wore on, Theo and Charlotte moved from reminiscing to talking about life in Londoni. At last, Kitty had the chance to contribute: she made some helpful comments and Charlotte responded warmly. But then the conversation turned to the serious topic of the Scheme. Tonight, instead of just unloading his frustrations and anxieties about work, Theo made an effort to explain the issues properly in a way he'd never once done with his wife. He even left room for his guest to comment and ask questions. It was not surprising, Kitty told herself, since Charlotte had come here to work alongside Theo and the other men. But still, she felt hurt and left out.

'Good Lord, is that the time?' Charlotte finally exclaimed. 'I must get back to the Shoebox.' She gave a playful grimace that conveyed the accommodation was so far below her usual standards that it was comic – however, she was going to be a good sport about it.

They swapped farewells. Kitty addressed her guest as Lady Welmingham. She knew – from Theo's advice, years ago – that she could only drop the formal title if invited to do so. And that gesture had not been made.

Theo insisted on accompanying Charlotte home, even though she offered to make do with the driver as an escort. As he shepherded her from the room, his hand hovered at the small of her back. In his other hand, Kitty noticed, he carried the woman's scarf: a gossamer length of honey gold, surely chosen to match the apiarist's calling. Charlotte swayed a little as she walked – perhaps due to all the wine she'd drunk, or it could have been the high tapering heels of her golden slippers. The movement of her hips caused ripples in the shimmering velvet of her long skirt.

Kitty stood on the verandah watching the red tail-lights of the Land Rover diminish, then disappear. She didn't want to go back inside, where cigarette smoke hovered in the air, along with the expensive-smelling musky scent that wafted from Charlotte's hair and clothes. Instead, she walked down the stairs, then on round the side of the house. Warm light flowed from the windows, giving the house the look of a real home – a place where children slept in their beds, under coverlets patterned with trains or fairies. Kitty turned her back on it, looking into the darkened garden. Her feet carried her over to the bougainvillea bush. Crouching down, she peered in at the little statue, caught in the light that shone from the open kitchen door.

There he was. Gili. Kitty remembered the pleasure of moulding the contours of his body, the triumph of seeing his wild spirit captured in clay. The act had made her feel alive – a fresh energy springing up from deep inside her.

She felt none of that now. She felt nothing.

Gazing down at the statue, she saw how the monkey was the shape of a little child. Small and vulnerable. He had no hope of surviving when the next rains came – the clay had been dried, not properly fired. Even in the shelter of his flowery arbour, the downpour would find him. He would be slowly worn away. By harvest time, he'd be no more than a shapeless lump, the magic all gone.

FOURTEEN

It was peaceful in the church, the sun angling in through the high windows, the sound of pigeons cooing in the bell-tower. Father Remi and Kitty were at work polishing the pews, bringing a shine to the timber. Now and then they came upon dried droppings left behind by chickens that had been brought along to church for the Sunday offering. Or they found spots of dried-up porridge that had fallen from prisoners' plates, back when the rains had driven them inside.

Kitty moved her rag with a steady rhythm, back and forth. She hoped she looked convincingly calm, steady. She glanced at Father Remi working on the next bench. He appeared relaxed, lost in his task, barely aware of Kitty's presence – quite possibly at prayer, or reciting Latin texts to himself.

Kitty turned towards the Blessed Mary, taking in her serene face – wishing she could be like her. No doubt the Holy Mother was pure and clean, all through her plaster body to her white heart – whereas inside Kitty was a churning morass of dark emotions so overwhelming she could hardly breathe. At the centre was anger, jealousy. At the shrivelled edges, loss and disappointment.

And wrapped around it all, like a wreath of thorns, was a layer of hard, black guilt.

She didn't know why her feelings had boiled up like this, now. Perhaps it was to do with Charlotte's constant presence in her home. Kitty hardly had a moment alone with Theo these days. It had only been a few weeks since Charlotte arrived, but already it felt like months. Last night, after Theo had left to escort her to the Shoebox as usual, Kitty had deliberately dropped one of Cynthia's Royal Doulton dinner plates onto the floor. Then she'd smashed a cup, followed by a saucer. She'd laughed at the sight of the splintered shards. But while she was cleaning up the evidence – hastily, in the unlikely event that Theo came straight back – she'd broken down in tears. Perhaps she'd just become too tired of trying to manage it all. The secrets, the lies, the rules. The things that could not be said. It had all been going on for so long . . .

Now, as she polished the church pew, her hand slowed. She gripped the cleaning rag and pushed, but it didn't seem to want to move any more.

There was a creak of floorboards as Father Remi suddenly stood up. 'Let's pick some fruit.'

Kitty looked at him in surprise, then nodded. She would be glad to get out into the fresh air – and perhaps a different task would help take her away from herself.

She followed her companion outside. He led the way towards the shed where the baskets were stored, but instead of going in to get one, he kept on walking. When they reached the bench under the peppercorn tree, he sat down.

'Aren't we picking fruit?' Kitty asked.

'No.' He said nothing more. He just waited, his gaze fixed into the distance.

Kitty understood he'd created the space for a conversation; now it was up to her to fill it up, if that was her choice.

She felt the words gathering inside her, joining forces, adding to their strength and number. 'I need to speak to you,' she said. 'As a priest. Can we do it out here?'

Father Remi waved an arm across the landscape. The rains had made the bush surrounding the irrigated vineyards and garden plots turn green. The whole scene was bursting with new life. 'To me, there is no better place,' he said.

Kitty was quiet for a time, her thoughts travelling back. Five years felt like nothing, the memories were so clear. Faces, voices, smells – all returned to her. She drew in a deep breath. Then she was ready to begin.

The morning sun shone through the windows of the Garden House, throwing a pool of golden light onto the dining table. Kitty fidgeted with her napkin, picking at the lace edges, as she waited for Louisa and the Admiral to finish their breakfast. When Louisa finally rose to her feet, Kitty immediately followed suit.

'I'm going to visit Yuri,' she said. 'I don't expect I'll be back for lunch.'

She could see her parents-in-law trying to think up some task for her to carry out: they seemed to take pleasure in keeping her busy when she came to visit, even though they still had several servants at their beck and call. Kitty hurried to the door before Louisa or the Admiral had a chance to speak. She made her farewells, and was gone.

She was glad to escape. In the generous spaces of the Big House, Theo's parents were dominating enough; cooped up with them in the Garden House, surrounded by too much over-sized furniture, Kitty felt stifled. And though they were quick to express displeasure if she didn't spend enough time with them, on the rare weekends when she was able to make the long trip from Skellingthorpe, they showed no real interest in her life. They never enquired about any news she might have; they were not even all that keen to hear about how Theo was coping in the air force. They spent all their time either complaining about their cramped quarters, or pointing out how proud they were that Hamilton Hall was involved in the war effort. It was all Kitty could do during her visits to sit and nod and smile for the requisite periods of time.

As Kitty was about to set off across the walled garden, Mrs Ellis – the cook who'd served the Hamiltons for decades – called her back to the kitchen door.

'Are you off to see His Highness?' she asked.

Kitty smiled at her. 'How did you guess?' No answer was needed; Mrs Ellis knew she was always keen to get away and visit Yuri.

'I have a little something for him.' Mrs Ellis ducked back into the kitchen, then reappeared with a basket in her hand. A rich buttery smell rose up as she handed it to Kitty. On a plate carefully lodged in the bottom was a golden cake spotted with cherries and dusted with icing sugar.

'He'll be delighted,' Kitty said.

Mrs Ellis's face lit up. She used to consider it a privilege to make cakes for 'our prince' when he lived in the Garden House, and now that he'd moved to the village she liked to send him treats when she could. Somehow she managed to save up the necessary ingredients from the Hamilton family rations.

Waving goodbye to the cook, Kitty turned her back on the Garden House. She picked a path between the vegetable plots, heading towards the rear of the property. She wanted to avoid the Hall, with its powerful military presence. The vast edifice of the place was even more daunting with lines of army trucks and jeeps parked outside than it had been when the family was in residence.

Kitty walked quickly, the basket swinging on her arm. It still seemed to take a long time to reach the village. When Yuri's cottage finally came into view, she felt a wave of anticipation. She had hours free to spend with her old friend.

She knocked at the front door with its bold red paint that matched the hue of the pillar boxes so closely it might have been put there by employees of His Majesty's Royal Mail service. It took Yuri several minutes to respond. She imagined him sighing with annoyance as he put down his brush. He would not be expecting anyone, and he hated being interrupted.

As he flung open the door, his expression was hostile. He was still putting on a shirt, pushing the ends into his trousers.

'Kitty!'

She barely had time to put down her basket before he pulled her into his arms.

They stood there locked together for a long, quiet moment. Kitty rested her head against Yuri's shoulder. There was something so tender in the way he held her. It was nothing like the touch of a lover – more like what Kitty imagined the embrace of a soft-hearted father could be. (Not her own father, whose most affectionate gesture had been to ruffle his daughter's hair.)

'Come in, come in.' Yuri almost danced ahead of her. He got rid of the shirt, leaving just his old trousers, the familiar rag stained with turpentine and pigment hanging from the waistband. 'I hope I haven't put paint on your dress.' He turned back, smiling. 'No, I hope I have. You look too smart. You look like your mother-in-law.'

'I do not!' Kitty protested. She'd dressed carefully for her trip, choosing a cotton frock with a small floral print. It was summery and light; it made her feel fresh and carefree.

'I was joking. You look lovely – you always do.'

They fell into their old comfortable ways immediately. It was as if they were back living together in their tiny family of two. Kitty still found it strange to see Yuri in this new setting – it was only her third visit. In the room he was using as a studio, he'd covered the floor and all the furniture with calico dust cloths. It gave the space a timeless, dreamlike quality.

On the easel was a canvas that had been scraped back – a failed painting, about to be born again. She wondered what – who – Yuri was going to paint next. She envied him the sense of adventure that a new canvas offered. In the flat in Skellingthorpe, she sketched sometimes – that was all. The space was too small for a studio, and with her volunteer work she didn't have much spare time. But more than that, art seemed a frivolous occupation, when she was constantly in the company of pilots who were risking their lives on a daily basis.

Around England, many art schools were closed. The Slade had been bombed, the grand old buildings destroyed, the noble statues smashed – there had been a photograph of the devastation in *The Times*. Many artists, like Kitty, had become involved in the war effort. But others, like Yuri, kept on working. There were still exhibitions, reviews. People still bought and sold art. It was part of the strangeness of wartime. Picasso was holed up in Paris, under German occupation – but he never stopped painting, expressing his response to the horror of war. Yuri admired his old friend for this, but in his own work he steered well away from the whole subject. He was still focused only on his private battle to conquer the human form. Kitty wondered if his experiences during the Russian Revolution – the Red Terror – meant he had to hide from this new war. He could face no more.

'Are you hungry?' Yuri asked.

They both just laughed. When Kitty stayed with the Hamiltons, she was always hungry. At Louisa's dining table she tried to eat ladylike portions. And the effort required to hold her cutlery correctly, to pick things up in the right order and in exactly the right way – tilting the soup dish away from your body, not towards it – spoiled her enjoyment of food.

'Let's have a picnic in the garden,' Yuri suggested, heading for the kitchen. When they opened the fridge, Kitty recognised some of his old housekeeper's specialties: Cornish pasties (meat chopped, never minced) and spicy herrings in aspic. Like Mrs Ellis, she'd remained loyal to him – coming now to this little cottage even though it was a huge step down from the prince's previous abode in the grounds of the Big House.

'You can't get good cheese any more,' Yuri commented. He held a bottle of red wine between his knees, flexing his muscles as he fought to remove a stubborn cork. Kitty noticed how fit and strong he still looked. He was only in his sixties – but plenty of Theo's more senior colleagues at the RAF base were old and unhealthy at that age. 'I'm running out of wine, too,' Yuri added. But he didn't seem to care. He hummed as he piled the food onto a paint-stained tray.

When they spread the picnic blanket on the overgrown lawn, they had to stamp down the grass with their bare feet before it would lie flat. Then they set out the food, gloating over each item. Mrs Ellis's cake was placed centrestage; the pasties, herrings and some salad were arranged to each side. The pair ate in easy silence. They didn't need to swap details of what they'd been doing. The world of everyday life – of being at war – felt far away and irrelevant.

After they'd both eaten they carried their glasses inside, still sipping the rich red wine. In the studio, a more sombre mood set in. Yuri told Kitty he was unable to get canvas or paints, even on the black market. He would be working on old bits of board and using house paint if the war didn't end soon. Then he talked about the purge of museums in Germany. Hitler hated modern art, he explained. The Führer believed the artists who were involved in the new movements couldn't see colours or forms as they truly were in nature – therefore they were racially inferior. Hitler was, of course, an aspiring artist who'd been rejected by the Vienna Academy of Fine Arts. Kitty listened with some puzzlement – Yuri had been over all this before, and he wasn't a person who liked to repeat himself. There was a distant look on his face, as if he was just using the conversation as a distraction.

Suddenly, he broke off. 'Kitty, I want to show you something.' Conflicting emotions scudded over his face: anticipation and pleasure, backed by pain. He disappeared briefly, returning with a leather carpetbag in his hand. He carried it against his body like something precious. Sitting down on an old couch, he motioned for Kitty to join him. Placing it by his feet, he pulled open the top.

'These are her things. They were sent to me, just a week ago. After all these years.'

Tension and excitement twisted in Kitty's stomach. She knew whose possessions they were. 'This is Katya's bag?'

'She had it with her when she died.' A spasm crossed Yuri's face, then he composed himself. 'Someone who was on the train must have kept it all these years. Then it passed into other hands – I don't know the whole story. There is a community of Russian émigrés in Paris and in London. We know one another's families. Someone made the connection with me and sent it to my agent.'

Reaching into the bag, he took out a small object made of silver, about the size of a cigarette case. He clicked a catch and it opened out into two picture frames joined together by hinges. He passed it to Kitty.

She stared in silence at an image that could have been Kitty herself – the hair, the eyes, the mouth. Katya was elegant, though. Sophisticated. Her hair was piled on top of her head, showing off a diamond-encrusted coronet. Earrings hung from her ears, making her neck appear long and graceful. She looked like a princess. Of course, she was a princess . . .

It took a while for Kitty to drag her attention to the other photograph. A young man gazed out at her, his eyes bright, a smile touching his lips. Yuri was pretending to be solemn for the camera, but he was clearly a joker, someone who laughed a lot.

'You were a beautiful couple. You both look so happy.'

. Next, Yuri brought out a round amber-coloured disc. A powder compact made of tortoiseshell. He stroked it lovingly, tracing the gold outlines of the initials engraved in the top.

'I brought this back for her from a trip to Paris. I had her initials engraved. There are three – a Russian wife has her father's name as well as her husband's.' He held it out for Kitty to examine. The decorative letters on the surface of the translucent shell cast a shadow inside onto the palette of powder. 'I gave her lots of presents. They were mostly jewellery from the family collections, very valuable. Priceless, in fact. But this – this was something I chose specially for her. She treasured it.' He handed it to Kitty. 'It is yours. I think she would be glad for you to have it.'

Kitty pressed her lips together, tears stinging her eyes. 'Thank you. I'll treasure it too.'

She turned it over in her hands, admiring the smoky orange and brown streaks in the shell. Then she opened it up, revealing a mirror set in the lid. She could see a portion of her face reflected there: one eye, the bridge of her nose. If she moved the compact around, she could gather a complete picture of her face. It was strange to think that the faces of two women – decades apart, worlds apart – had both been captured in this way. Katya, the original. Kitty, her stand-in.

Yuri took some clothes from the carpetbag: delicate, lacy items. Gloves, a scarf. A white silk nightgown. Stockings. He trailed the lengths of cloth between his fingers. 'Some things are missing.

She must have carried more than this . . .' He was still for a moment – then he closed his hands into fists, crushing the garments. His lips twisted with pain.

Kitty felt young and useless, her life an empty page compared to his. But she reached out her hand, covering one of his. She held him, until his grip softened. She leaned towards him. 'Yuri.' She sensed she was calling him back from far away. 'Tell me now. What happened to Katya?'

She knew what she was asking – she was pushing Yuri to enter the dark pit he'd stepped around for all the years he'd known her. Just occasionally, he'd talked about Katya – mentioning a favourite food of hers, or a piece of music. Then there were the exotic clothes Kitty had worn for the portraits. She guessed they belonged to Yuri's wife but had never directly asked. There had been a big blank space, an unspeakable silence, surrounding Katya's fate.

Yuri rested his hands on the silk nightdress. Though they were stained with paint, the skin dry from being constantly cleaned with turpentine, Kitty imagined them as they once would have been, smoothing this same length of silk over the body of his lover.

'We were artists, both of us.' His voice was low but steady. There was a remote look in his eyes, as if their clear blue reflected the sky of a distant land. 'We didn't care about wealth or society – but we were born into it. Our families had country estates, palaces in St Petersburg. We were both related to the imperial family, through different lines. But we lived in a much simpler way than our friends and relatives did. We spent time with other artists. We painted and drew and visited exhibitions. Everything was . . . wonderful.' Yuri's English was completely fluent after all his years of living in

Britain, yet as he spoke about the past Kitty noticed his Russian accent becoming more pronounced. 'Of course, we saw the warning signs. A revolution was coming. Katya and I, we believed in change. Count Tolstoy was a family friend – we admired his novels, his ideas about society.' He broke off, shaking his head. 'But we never imagined what would happen. We did not see the danger. Then we heard the Tsar had been shot, with all his family – little Alexei, and the four girls. We knew them; we used to play with them on holidays at the summer palaces. All over Russia, the Bolsheviks were murdering what they called counter-revolutionists. Aristocrats like us were class enemies of the people.' He broke off. 'I've told you about this – the Red Terror.'

Kitty nodded. She seemed to have learned more from Yuri about the history of the world – recent and long past – than she'd picked up during all her years at Wattle Creek School.

'My studio was burned by a mob of soldiers,' Yuri continued. 'Painting was declared a decadent occupation. I lost every painting I'd done. All my pictures of Katya.'

'You painted her.' It was a statement, not a question – of course he had. Kitty felt a flicker of jealousy as she saw Yuri's love for his wife burning in his eyes.

'That was how I learned about the body of a woman, by painting and by making love with my Katya. Now, when I paint, a body is no more than a physical presence. Each one is a new challenge – a conquest of colour and form – a battle that must be won. With Katya, it was different. I was trying to see past flesh and bone, to her soul.' He gave Kitty a small smile. 'I painted her quite badly. I was young. I did not have the skill I have now.

'We decided we had to escape from Russia. Lots of our friends were already living in Paris. And we had a special reason to want to be in a safe place.' A warmth entered Yuri's voice. 'Katya was three months pregnant. We were so excited.

'We decided to travel separately to attract less attention. I left by train. I had one suitcase. It was much heavier than it looked. I refused help from porters and carried it myself. Among my clothes and shoes were family heirlooms. Diamond jewellery, gold statues – things we would be able to sell. All the White Russians did this when they left. We did not expect to return. Along with my suitcase, I took painting equipment – an easel, my paints. I pretended I was going to Paris for an exhibition.

'My plan went smoothly. In Paris, I waited for Katya. The arrangement was for her to go by train to the Crimea to join the Dowager Empress Marie at her summer palace in Yalta. Other relatives of ours were already there. They were going to sail to England on a ship sent by the King. He had promised to rescue Marie. She was the sister of his wife, otherwise I don't think he would have been so concerned.

'I received news that the HMS *Marlborough* had arrived at Yalta and taken on board all the members of the imperial family who were there, along with many more White Russians fleeing from the Bolsheviks. I was so relieved. I knew Katya was safe. But then, when the ship reached the next port and all the passengers disembarked, I heard nothing from her. I sent cables. I made inquiries. Still I heard nothing. I assumed she was on another ship, heading for England. I just waited in Paris, hoping for news. It was . . . terrible. I was helpless.

'At last, I heard that the Dowager Empress was due to arrive on a ship docking in Portsmouth. I travelled to England so I would be there when it arrived. The Queen of England was there to greet her sister. There were lots of White Russians waiting to be reunited with their friends and family. It took hours for the ship to dock, for the passengers to disembark. There were animals on board – pets. That surprised me.'

Kitty sensed Yuri was slowing the telling of the story, adding details, because he was afraid of what he had to say next.

'You could see that this was a ship of refugees. They tried to be dignified, but they had hardly any luggage. What they had was heavy, like mine. They, too, did not want to make use of the porters. I waited at the gangplank. I stood there until the last person walked down and went away. I couldn't move. I felt that if I stayed there, she might still appear – but that the moment I walked away, everything would be finished.

'Then I felt someone tugging my coat sleeve. My heart leapt as I turned round. But it was not my Katya standing there. It was a woman I'd never seen before.

'"Prince Yurievitch?" She recognised me. "I am Alexandra Baronova."

'I grabbed her arm. "I am looking for my wife. Do you know where she is?"

'She just stared at me. I wanted to take hold of her shoulders and shake out some words. Eventually she just nodded. Tears fell from her eyes. My whole body went cold; I began to shake.

'Someone was calling her. She was waving them away. Now she was sobbing. "I can't bear to tell you."

'I clung onto the railings of the gangway. She took a breath, gathering her strength. When she talked, she looked past me. She could not watch my face.

'They had been on the same train to the Crimea. They didn't know one another personally, but she recognised Katya, just like she'd recognised me. Everyone knew us – we were always at the ballet, the theatre, the salons. Alexandra had shared a carriage with her. They were both dressed in their oldest, plainest gowns – like all the other refugees on the train. They did not want to be identified as representatives of the overthrown class – that was another way the Bolsheviks spoke of us. The carriages were packed with Red Army soldiers. One of them noticed Katya. He'd come from her family estate in Siberia. At first, Katya tried to deny who she was. But the man said that he'd worked for her father. That he'd been starved and beaten by the tyrant, which was not true.

'They taunted her for some time, Alexandra told me. They touched her body, they pushed her around. The other passengers were too afraid to intervene. They were either Bolsheviks or they pretended to be, for the sake of their own safety. You could not blame them.

'Then the train stopped. They were in a forest. It was winter – the ground was covered in snow. The men made Katya get off the train. Alexandra stood at the window – she could see and hear everything.'

Yuri's voice was hoarse with pain, but he pushed himself on.

'They asked her for her jewels. The story had been spread around that when the imperial family were executed, the princesses did not die from the first shots that were fired. They were protected by the layers of diamonds and gold sewn into their clothes. Katya said she had no diamonds. It was true. We thought she'd be safer with nothing.'

Yuri covered his eyes with his hand – as if he wanted to hide from the horror of his story.

'The soldiers began jabbing their bayonets at her, ripping her skirt, her shirt, until the garments fell to the ground. They searched for diamonds in the snow. Alexandra told me that Katya just stood there, half naked. She was strong and graceful; she did not try to run or plead for rescue. The soldiers became angry. There was not one diamond. All they were able to take from her was her wedding ring.

'They tore off the last of her clothes. She wore only her boots. I know those boots. Black, with buttons at the side. They were made to measure for her by a bootmaker in Moscow.'

Yuri's voice slowed. Each word seemed wrenched from his heart. 'The soldier who had known her since she was a child pierced her belly with his bayonet. Then he stabbed her in the heart. She fell back onto the snow, blood pouring from her wounds. She must have died almost instantly. She would barely have had time to think of the life of our baby being ended. To send a thought to me, as she left . . .

'Only now did Alexandra look at me. Her face was wet with tears, her lips swollen. "Then the men climbed back on board and the train pulled away. That is all I can say."'

Yuri sat with his head bowed. A clock chimed somewhere in the cottage. Outside, a cat meowed.

Kitty felt frozen by horror. No words of comfort were possible. She could picture the two of them sitting here, unmoving, for hours. She was surprised when Yuri began to speak again.

'I could not bear to return to Paris, except to collect my possessions. We'd had so many good times there – and there were lots of other artists, émigrés, whom we'd known together. I moved to England. I knew what Katya would have wanted me to do – marry again, have children, be happy . . . But I decided, instead, to devote myself to my art. That's what I've done ever since. For twenty-four years and three months. I have learned so much. I think she would have been proud of me.'

There was a pause, a heartbeat – then he spoke again.

'My only wish . . . would be to paint her once more, with the skill that I have now.'

His voice was barely audible. It was almost a whisper to himself.

'Paint her now.' Kitty's words matched his with their softness. She said them again. 'Paint me.'

She crossed to the old chaise longue where she'd lain so many times – draped in Katya's exotic clothes, or wearing her own. She unbuttoned the front of her dress, shrugging it from her shoulders. It fell to the floor with a sigh. She saw its echo in Yuri's eyes. The vision of a skirt, landing on snow.

She took off her petticoat, undid her bra, pulled down her underpants. That was all she was wearing, in this summer weather. She was bare.

Sunshine slanted in, painting her skin gold. Her hair draped her shoulders, a dark mantle.

'How shall I lie?' she asked.

Yuri stared at her. In his face she saw a deep hunger flaring like fire exposed to oxygen. Kitty waited for him to come over and arrange her position. But he shook his head. 'No. Stand.'

Moving to the easel, he swept the canvas aside. In its place, he put a drawing board with a wad of papers clipped on at the top and sides. He picked up a pencil, testing the end with his thumb. All the while, he never shifted his eyes from the woman in front of him. 'Look straight at me.'

He drew quickly, covering sheet after sheet, working like a man possessed – as if time were short, the task huge, and the importance of its execution immeasurable. Muscles flickered and clenched in his arms, shoulders, chest. These were the studies, Kitty knew. The painting would come later: a long, solitary task, done after she was gone. They no longer had the luxury of Kitty having days to spend sitting for a painting.

The sound of pencil scratching paper filled the air. Whenever Yuri glanced up from his drawing, his eyes went straight to Kitty's. The warmth of the sun matched the warmth in his gaze. There was something sharper, more probing, in his eyes as well. Kitty understood that this was no conquest to be fought over form and colour. She was now one with Katya. And he was looking into her soul.

Tears began to slip down the man's cheeks. He wiped them away, leaving a grey trail of carbon. The tears kept falling; he kept on drawing. Kitty held her head up, chin lifted, arms raised just a little – suggesting the beginnings of a gesture that would never be made. She didn't waver, though her own eyes blurred with tears.

To hold herself still, she had to lose herself in the pose. She had little sense of the minutes passing – perhaps they made up an hour, maybe much longer.

Finally Yuri put down his pencil. Then, as though the last energy in his body had been used up, he fell to his knees, burying his face in his hands. Kitty ran to his side. She was no longer his model – no longer his lost wife. She was just herself.

She pulled his head against her breasts, wrapping her arms around his bare shoulders – skin meeting skin, sweat and tears blending. She wanted him to feel her love for him, her gratitude for all that he'd given her – as a girl with no home, as an artist, as a friend.

She held him while he sobbed. Now he was the child, and she had strength to give. His grief wore out into a deep quiet. Finally, he drew away. He seemed changed, somehow. His expression reminded Kitty of someone – it took her a moment to make the connection. Then she remembered the image of him in the silver frame. He looked younger, unburdened. As if, from now on, he would find it easier to laugh.

For the next four months, Kitty was unable to leave Skellingthorpe. Theo was nearly at the end of his reserves of fortitude and bravery. Like a child kept up too late, he was irritable and argumentative. His features were haggard. When he managed to get leave, he wanted to spend every moment with his wife. And even if he was unable to be with her, it made a difference to him to know she was nearby.

Kitty thought often of Yuri, wishing she could see him, after that last time they'd been together. She sent him two letters and a postcard depicting a scene in Wales with a striking sky that looked painted, not photographed. It didn't worry her that she received no reply; Yuri rarely picked up a pen if he could be painting instead. When the landlady called her to the telephone one morning, she thought first of Theo, then of his parents. But the man on the line introduced himself as a Mr Underwood, a solicitor. After confirming Kitty's identity, he spoke bluntly.

'It is my sad duty to inform you that Prince Yurievitch is dead. He took his own life.'

A cloak of ice fell over Kitty. She clutched the receiver to her ear with rigid hands. Underwood allowed her a few moments to absorb his news. Then he went on. It had happened a week ago, he explained. The gentleman had already been buried – without a ceremony, in a council cemetery – in accordance with his last wishes. He had specifically asked that his friend Kitty Hamilton not be contacted until afterwards. The instructions had been laid out in a letter he'd sent to Underwood's office, posted on the evening of the last day of his life.

When she heard this, Kitty gasped. A spike of outrage pierced the numbness of shock and disbelief. She understood that Yuri would not have wanted a funeral – with the inevitable talk of things he did not believe in – but surely she could have been at his burial . . . Hadn't she earned the right to be there to say goodbye?

The memories that rose up brought a thrust of pain so sharp and deep it took her breath away. When they'd last been together, everything had been so wonderful – so raw and so rich. Had he known then – as he'd kissed her goodbye at the garden gate – that they would never see one another again? Just when they'd finally reached out to one another more deeply than ever before?

The call continued. Mr Underwood proposed that Kitty meet him at the cottage as soon as possible. There were things to sort out that required her presence. Meanwhile, he advised discretion. His client had dismissed his housekeeper weeks ago and the police had agreed to keep the matter quiet. It was lucky the cottage was tucked away on its own. As far as the solicitor was aware, no one in the village knew what had happened.

'I'd like it to remain that way,' Underwood stressed, 'until you and I have met.'

Kitty heard herself agree, even while she struggled to take in the meaning of what she'd been told. In moments, it seemed, they'd planned to meet the very next day. Then Mr Underwood was expressing his condolences, apologising for his haste. And he was gone.

Ignoring the curious gaze of the landlady, Kitty walked back to her room. Stumbling blindly past the table and chairs, she collapsed on the bed. Theo was at the base, preparing for a mission. Kitty thought of trying to contact him by telephone, but she couldn't risk upsetting his concentration. Instead, she just lay on her bed, stunned into stillness and silence.

As reality sank in, questions crowded her head. One kept rising to the surface. Why now? After all that Yuri had survived! Kitty was not shocked that he'd ended his life this way – it fitted with who Yuri was, to choose for himself when to finish his journey. But after sharing Katya's story that day – just a few months ago – he'd seemed so relieved, like a man set free.

Kitty turned on her side, curling in on herself, wanting to become small again. Too small to be seen. Too small to be hurt so deeply.

The next day, she left a note for Theo in case his bombing raid was cancelled and he got the chance to come home. She caught the train and then the bus, finally reaching the village near Hamilton Hall.

When she stepped down in the little square with its ancient water pump and horse trough, she headed straight towards the cottage where Yuri had lived. She feared that if she let herself falter – if she lingered along the way – she would not be strong enough to face going there at all.

There was no sign of Mr Underwood. Entering the garden, Kitty moved mechanically to sit down on the bench and wait. She stared at the windows with their lowered blinds, dusty glass. Then she looked towards the back garden, where she and Yuri had had their last picnic. It was hard to picture how it had been back then, in the middle of summer – the air warm, the flowers in full bloom.

Now autumn had turned to winter. The trees were bare, the ground black and dank with rotting leaves. Though the sun was high in the sky, frost still lingered in the shadows beneath the hydrangea bushes. Kitty could feel the cold seeping in through her overcoat from the damp wood of the garden bench. She checked her watch. Mr Underwood was only a few minutes late, yet she felt she'd been sitting there for ages. She was impatient for him to arrive – but afraid, at the same time, of having to face the emptiness inside the cottage. She eyed the red front door with its slot for receiving mail. It was hard to believe that if she knocked, there would be no Yuri to answer.

There would be no Yuri. There would be no Yuri any more.

The thought circled in her head, unable to settle. The grief and shock was still too fresh.

There was a whining creak as the garden gate swung open. Kitty turned to see a portly figure in a grey suit, briefcase in hand. She stood up, collecting her handbag and umbrella. Mr Underwood acknowledged her with a nod as he walked down the path. There was a businesslike spring in his step. Kitty wondered how often he found himself in a situation like this – dealing with emotion, propriety and legality all at once.

As he introduced himself to Kitty, she saw him checking her face for signs of distress. No doubt he was relieved to find no trace of tears.

'Are you ready to go inside?' Mr Underwood gave her a stern look, like a schoolmaster signalling to a student that he was expecting to see appropriate behaviour.

The closed-in air bore the familiar smell of turpentine. The solicitor led the way down the hall.

'I came as soon as I opened the letter.' He spoke over his shoulder. 'I met the police here and explained what I knew.' He paused, clearing his throat. 'I don't know if the fact that this . . . act . . . was not done on impulse makes it better or worse.'

As they entered the kitchen, there was a rustling sound behind the wainscot – mice, already. Underwood put the keys down on the table, a casual gesture as if he were the new tenant here. Kitty scanned the room. Since Yuri had arranged that Underwood would bring her here, she felt sure there would be a letter for her – a last communication. Not on the kitchen table, where the police and other strangers would find it – somewhere only she might think to look. She checked the tea caddy; the box for odds and ends of string; she even peered inside the plastic anatomist's skull that rested on the mantelpiece. But she found nothing.

Underwood was keen to take her to the room Yuri had used as a studio. When he finally had her attention, he ushered her along the hall – but then he paused on the threshold, blocking Kitty's path. He turned to face her. 'Nothing has been moved in here,' he said, 'except for . . . the deceased.' He glanced behind him at an exposed beam in the ceiling. A wrought-iron hook had been hammered into the timber. The rope had been cut down.

'His will leaves everything to you,' Underwood stated. 'But there's not much, I'm afraid. Just what's in this cottage – old furniture, clothes.'

Kitty wondered vaguely where Yuri's supply of diamonds was hidden. Or perhaps his wealth had finally dried up. She didn't care. She'd inherited money before, and while she'd reaped great benefit from it – not least, the chance to meet her husband – she'd left a trail of anger and brokenness behind her in Wattle Creek.

'And there's the painting,' added Underwood.

Kitty pushed past the man, striding into the studio. Where the chaise longue had been was a huge rectangle shape, draped with calico and propped against the wall.

'That's how I found it,' Underwood said. 'I have not lifted the cloth. My client made his wishes very clear. You were to be the first one to see it.' There was a note of impatience in his voice, blended with tolerance. Clearly, he felt Yuri had been unduly demanding with his instructions, but as a solicitor, Underwood knew how to fulfil his duty. 'There seems to be some great importance attached to it. That's why I wanted to keep the whole affair under wraps, so to speak, until you came.'

Kitty pulled the cloth away. As it fell around her feet, she stepped back, reeling under the power of the image that was unveiled.

A young woman, naked, standing in the forest. Snow at her feet, black leafless trees in the background. Soldiers were all around her – grinning teeth forming white slashes in grim dark faces. Bayonets at the ready. Sharp angles, glinting.

The woman looked calm, strong, yet heartbreakingly vulnerable.

'Oh my God.' Underwood gasped. 'It's you.' He turned to Kitty, lips moving as he tried to form words.

Kitty nodded, keeping her eyes on the painting. It was an extraordinary work. Yuri had poured all his pain and love into it. He'd used every skill he had mastered. There was a dreamlike beauty to the image, but it was backed by a mood of menace and terror. You had no doubt this innocent young woman was about to be killed.

Kitty stared at the slight roundness of the bare belly – only noticeable if you knew to look. Its meaning tore at her heart.

Lowering her gaze – retreating from the impact of the scene – Kitty began to examine how the painting had been made. The huge piece consisted of six smaller canvases joined together. She walked around the back. The name of each of them was scrawled there. *Girl in Harem Trousers. Girl Waiting. Girl Sleeping.* Yuri had painted over all these images he'd made of Kitty, combining the canvases into one. Returning to the front of the picture, she studied the materials and technique. Different kinds of paint had been used: some was thick and lumpy – found, perhaps, in the garden shed. Large sections had been worked in oils, but the black of the forest could have been made with creosote, or some kind of tar. It was still tacky to the touch.

Underwood moved to stand between Kitty and the painting. His eyes remained wide with shock. 'If you were my client,' he said firmly, 'my advice to you would be to burn this picture right now.' He gestured towards the fireplace.

Kitty looked at the man in mute outrage. Then she shook her head. 'This is the best painting of Yuri's life!'

The man ignored her. 'Look, I know who you are — I've done my research. If anyone sees this, they will think that the future Lady Hamilton posed in the nude. It won't matter how much you deny it, no one will believe you.'

'I did pose in the nude.' As Kitty said these words she knew that even if she talked for hours she would never be able to make the solicitor understand why she had done such a thing – what it had meant to Yuri and to her.

Underwood worked to bring his features under control. 'Make no mistake, the Hamiltons are not some bohemian family who would find such behaviour acceptable. They are respectable people. They are related to the King.'

Kitty said nothing. Underwood moved further along the painting, to the part where the soldiers stood, shoulder to shoulder in a ring. He jabbed his finger towards them. 'It may be lost on you, Mrs Hamilton, but while most of these soldiers appear to be Russians, not all of them are.' His voice rose. 'Look at the other uniforms. That's a Nazi airman. That's a British infantryman.'

Kitty studied the painting. The solicitor was right. In the gloomy light that surrounded the men – a dark fug that might have risen from their souls – the uniforms appeared nondescript. But when you looked more closely, there were insignias, badges, caps and hats with particular designs.

'This is a pacifist statement,' spluttered Underwood.

'I think Yuri *was* a pacifist,' Kitty said. 'He didn't support the war.'

'Well, that may be. But you, Mrs Hamilton, are not. You are the wife of a pilot in the King's Air Force.' He began pacing. 'I understand Yurievitch was your friend; you would feel bad about destroying his last painting. I'm no artist but it's very . . . powerful. Realistic. Perhaps it is a great work. But you must hide it away. I can arrange it for you. This painting must never see the light of day.'

Kitty chewed at her lip. She couldn't contradict Underwood's words. But this was not just Yuri's farewell to her – the one he'd chosen in place of her being at his burial. It was his last message to the world he'd left behind. And it was his tribute to Katya. The painting had to be exhibited. And soon. It was a work meant to be seen now – to point out that innocent people suffer at the hands of all who engage in war.

'At least think about it,' Underwood urged. 'Think about your husband and his family. Think about your place in this village – this country.'

'Thank you for your concern,' Kitty said. 'I understand all that you've said.'

Underwood looked at her in silence, waiting for a verdict.

'I'll have the painting removed,' she stated. 'It will be gone by the end of tomorrow.'

She saw him weighing her words, looking for some clue as to whether it was bound for a vault or a gallery. The truth was, she didn't know herself.

He gave her an encouraging smile. 'Sensible girl,' he said firmly. 'I shall leave you the keys.'

*

The war stretched on for two more years, almost three. Then, at long last, the Allied victory was declared and the dawning of peace was celebrated throughout the country. Kitty and Theo were soon reinstalled at Hamilton Hall, along with his parents, and life settled into a predictable routine. One spring morning the family met in the drawing room to share tea and scones, as they did each day except Sunday, at eleven o'clock sharp.

The clink of teacup on saucer added another layer to the rhythms of the three ticking clocks that were back in their time-honoured places on the sideboard and the mantelpiece. Kitty gripped her cup, the small mismatched noises grating on her nerves. She moved her gaze from the Admiral perusing his morning paper to Theo, who was reading one of the books from the Hall library – a thick, leather-bound tome with gold writing on its spine. Louisa's grey head was bent over a piece of embroidery. Blackwork, she called it; the patterns she sewed in dark thread stood out starkly against a cream background. The result reminded Kitty of something a spider might create. Her own embroidery – a practice sampler – lay in her lap. She noticed the cloth was puckered here and there where she'd drawn the thread too tight.

'Isn't this nice?' Louisa said, looking up. Her tone was bright and cheerful. 'Everything back as it should be, at last. You'd never know the place was full of strangers just a few months ago.'

Kitty smiled politely, and so did the two men – even though everyone knew Louisa's remark was optimistic rather than true. All the rooms had been refurnished – the heirloom antiques stood in their rightful places, paintings had been rehung, statues had been unveiled and the fine china returned to the servery. But the presence of the soldiers who had been billeted here for so many years lingered in the myriad dents in the timberwork, indelible scuff-marks on the floors, and graffiti scratched into the plaster walls.

'At least the garden's looking better,' Theo said. 'The new chap's getting the hang of things.'

'I miss old Freddie,' said the Admiral.

Louisa sniffed. Kitty knew she felt betrayed by the head gardener, who'd departed along with the soldiers. His was just one of many defections that the mistress of Hamilton Hall had had to accept. During the war, she'd lost more than half her old staff. Many had enlisted – which Louisa felt bound to applaud – and some of them had been killed or injured. Others, like Freddie, had taken up new opportunities that came their way, either during the war or with the coming of peace. Louisa had not found it easy to rebuild her household. She now had to make do with fewer servants, and the ones she did have displayed a changed attitude to their superiors. The blending of classes during the war – with people sharing quarters, sharing work – had permanently eroded the boundaries. The egalitarian era that Theo had once espoused to his university friends seemed set to dawn. The Admiral lamented that accents had lost their clarity – that you could no longer tell where a chap came from. He was referring to people of the working classes, of course. His peers spoke the King's English and still all sounded exactly the same.

Kitty suppressed a sigh as she picked up her needle. She missed her old life in Skellingthorpe, even though she knew she was looking back on the era with rosy eyes. There had been some terrible times, yet there had been an edge of excitement in those years that made every moment – an unexpected shared meal, a snatched kiss, each new morning spent together as husband and wife – feel special. The threat of danger and death made life sparkle. It was wonderful now to feel they were both safe – not to have to fear the arrival of a devastating telegram. But there was an odd sense of being in limbo, caught between the end of something and the beginning of what might come next. It wasn't just Kitty who felt this way, or the Hamiltons; the mood of the whole country was grey, uncertain.

Kitty glanced up at Theo. He looked tired. He was still plagued by a recurring nightmare that had begun after the crashlanding that killed his crew. If anything, the dreams had become more frequent since the war ended – now, they sometimes happened several nights in a row. He would scream out in his sleep, yelling the name of his copilot, Bobby, who'd been burned to death in front of him. The nightmare held Theo in a deep grip. It took Kitty a long time to wake him up – and when she did, he couldn't talk about what he'd seen. The horror of those nights seemed to suck the life from his days. There was a haunted look in his eyes, a tremor in his hands. While he was still flying regular missions, the RAF doctor had diagnosed Theo's condition as 'combat fatigue'. He had been de-mobbed soon after V-Day. The air force was glad to see him go: worn out physically and mentally, he'd been barely capable of doing simple deskwork by then. Like a child let out of boarding school, he'd been eager to go back home.

Though Kitty had dreamed of being able to live in the Garden House, alone with Theo, she hadn't even raised the possibility. She knew it was Theo's place to reside in the Hall. And this was where he wanted to be – their new bedroom was his grandmother's old room; their parlour his old schoolroom. She could see he felt safe in these places layered with childhood memories. And with what he'd suffered, she couldn't wish to deny him that comfort.

Shifting her gaze, Kitty observed Louisa's figure – motionless but for the steady movement of her hand plying the needle. Her skirt and jacket, though freshly pressed, were well worn. She showed off the patches and darns like badges of honour – proof that she knew how to be thrifty. Lady Hamilton was determined to set a positive example in the village, just as much as she was intent on restoring the old patterns of life at the Hall. The daily rituals made Kitty feel stifled. She dared not think of how she would adapt to the existence she could see stretching ahead of her. She imagined her own mother looking on, shaking her head, lips pursed. What had Kitty expected – the Miller girl from Wattle Creek marrying an Englishman from a class way above hers? Kitty used the end of her needle to count threads, locating the correct spot to start the next row of cross-stitches. What *had* she expected? She'd never even asked that question. She was in love – nothing else mattered. And no one had spent much time thinking about the future during the war. How could they, with lives ending every day? Theo's proposal to Kitty had been desperate rather than romantic. He wanted to marry her before he was killed. He'd won extra leave in a lottery and arrived home unexpectedly. It was only a year into the war, and she was still living with Yuri in the Garden House. She'd been peeling potatoes, a scarf tied over her hair.

'You look like a peasant,' Theo had said. Then he'd taken her in his arms, pressing her face against the soft bulk of his flying jacket. When he'd spoken, his voice was muffled. 'Marry me, Kitty. Please.'

She'd pulled away, taken by surprise.

'We have to get married. I need you near me. You have to move to Skellingthorpe.' Then he'd broken down, sobbing. He'd told her that he'd lost two men in his last mission. Good friends. In the one before, he'd lost another. They were doing night raids into Germany and the toll was catastrophic. 'I want to die as your husband.'

Kitty had taken off her scarf, using it to wipe away his tears. When Theo looked into her eyes, she searched for a glimmer of that brightness she loved so much. But it was lost beneath fear, deep and black.

'You have paint on your skirt, Kitty.' Louisa's sharp tone made Kitty jump to attention. Following the older woman's gaze, she saw a blob of oil paint near the hem of her plaid skirt.

'Prussian Blue,' Kitty said. 'I'll scrape it off.'

Louisa gave a faint shake of her head, as if Kitty were talking in a foreign language, before returning to her blackwork. Kitty stabbed her needle into her own piece of cloth. After they'd all finished their tea, she'd be able to escape. Only another quarter of an hour to go – then she could be at her easel.

The privilege of having a studio in the Garden House was Kitty's reward for behaving as she should. In a brief conversation with her daughter-in-law, Louisa had made the terms and conditions quite clear; the way she'd spoken, she might have been an old hand at keeping a daughter-in-law in her place. Kitty was not to spend too much time in her studio. She was not to have visitors (a ruling which Kitty understood was intended to preclude her from having life-drawing models). And it went without saying that she was not to mark the walls or floor with paint. This last injunction was the closest Louisa came to acknowledging that the place had ever been used as a studio before. Yuri's name was not mentioned any more at Hamilton Hall. He'd committed suicide, which was, frankly, unforgivable – especially when so many brave fellows were sacrificing their lives to serve their country. And then, there had been that trouble in Paris over one of his paintings. The Admiral had read about it in *The Times*. Kitty had been there, in the drawing room, when he'd reported on the article.

'Outrageous! If I'd known he was a pacifist, I'd never have let him darken our doors.'

Kitty had stared at the floor, scarcely able to breathe. But the Admiral had said nothing more. He'd turned the page, shaking out the papers as though to rid himself of his link with this traitor. She'd closed her eyes in relief. Yuri's dealer, Jean-Jacques, had been right. Paris was a long way away. And the world was still preoccupied with war.

The day after her meeting with the solicitor, Kitty had returned to the cottage. She'd paced the dingy rooms, agonising over what to do next. She wished she'd never seen the painting. She wished she hadn't posed for it. She seriously considered taking the solicitor's advice and burning the canvas in the back garden. The alternative – allowing the work to be displayed – was unthinkable. Her reputation would be destroyed. Not only that, she'd be hurting the whole Hamilton family. And most of all, Theo. After everything he'd been through . . . But her steps kept returning to the painting. When she stood before it, falling under its power, she regretted nothing. She felt proud to have been Katya. Her soul swelled with love and admiration for Yuri as a man, as a painter and, more than anything, as a husband.

She'd felt sick as she dialled the dealer's telephone number. She'd done it quickly, before her nerve failed.

When he'd received the painting, Jean-Jacques had written straight back to Kitty, sending his letter, as arranged, care of a post office that was two villages away from Hamilton Hall. He'd said – as Kitty had known he would – that it was a work of great importance. The best painting Yuri had ever done. Jean-Jacques had recognised Kitty in the picture – he'd met her years before at the Garden House and he'd seen Yuri's portraits of her. He assured her he understood the delicacy of the situation. He promised to wait for the right time and place to exhibit the work.

In August of the following year, Paris was liberated from German occupation. Not long afterwards the Salon d'Automne reopened, with Picasso being one of the first influential artists to exhibit there. Jean-Jacques decided this was the ideal venue for Yuri's last painting to be exposed to the world. The Salon was prestigious. It was known for showing work that was brave and new. And it was far from London.

Yuri's painting had caused a sensation, Jean-Jacques reported to Kitty. He gave her more information than had been written up in *The Times*. Apparently, the British Foreign Secretary had tried to have the work removed from display. It was totally unacceptable, he claimed, to see Nazis, Russian rebels and Englishmen grouped together, with the suggestion that all were guilty of war crimes. The slur on the King's armed forces was too much to bear. The Salon refused to cooperate, and the furore only added to the public's interest in the exhibition.

But no one made a link between Kitty and the contentious painting. The smaller portraits Yuri had made of Kitty had never been displayed; there was no reason for anyone to think of her. And anyway, a French art critic identified the figure in the work as the artist's wife, who'd been tragically killed years before. After the exhibition, Jean-Jacques had sold the painting to a collector from America. The agent had turned down other offers, but decided this man would be a suitable owner. He was a renowned recluse, who kept his collection to himself.

It was the perfect outcome. Yuri's picture had been seen; it had made its point – and now it would be hidden away on a secluded ranch on the other side of the Atlantic.

Jean-Jacques informed Kitty that the collector had paid a high price for the work, and that – after his commission – it all belonged to her. Kitty had asked him to send some funds anonymously to her family at Wattle Creek: enough for a tractor, a truck and much more besides. She presumed they guessed the money was from her, though they must have wondered how she had come by so much wealth. She'd been tempted to ask Jean-Jacques to write to them with an explanation. But then it would look as if she hoped to buy their forgiveness. To even try would be taken as an insult. She made do with picturing her father enjoying a tractor that started without being towed, a truck that ran smoothly. Sometimes she played games with herself, choosing what the boys might have been given as presents. Perhaps her mother had bought something for herself. It was bittersweet, imagining all these things she would never see. But at least she could comfort herself with the thought that she'd given back what she had taken from them all those years ago – and added more besides.

Now, as Kitty sat with her head bent over her sampler, plying her needle dutifully, she turned her thoughts to what she would paint on the newly stretched canvas that awaited her in the studio. Without Yuri to guide her, she found it hard to decide on a subject. As she tossed up between a still life and a self-portrait, she heard Louisa rise to her feet and begin gathering cups and saucers, ready to pour more tea. The delicate rattle of fine china punctuated each day, regular and familiar. Kitty didn't have to look up to know exactly how Louisa would tilt the teapot, then move the strainer from one cup to another, each with its little tideline of milk. Today, the ritual was interrupted by the sound of heavy footsteps in the hallway.

'That new butler moves about like an elephant,' Louisa complained.

The door opened – too wide and too fast. The servant marched in.

'Something for you, madam.' He refused to wear white gloves, but managed to lower his eyes courteously as he held out a polished salver, upon which rested a large cream envelope.

It would be an invitation, Kitty knew. As soon as a semblance of order had been established, Lord and Lady Hamilton had begun sending out invitations on notepaper embossed with the family crest, summoning their friends to balls, soirees or weekend hunting parties. They duly received invitations in return. The sending and receiving, the packing and unpacking, created a sense that things were going back to how they had once been.

Louisa held up the envelope, looking puzzled. 'No crest.' She accepted the letter-knife from the butler, then sliced open the top. *'The Trustees of the Victoria and Albert Museum request the pleasure of the company of . . .'* Her face came alive with pleasure. 'We're invited to an art exhibition. A celebration of peace. How lovely. Things really are going back to normal.'

Kitty gripped her sewing, scrunching the cloth. Her heart pounded with instant panic.

'Do we usually attend such events?' The Admiral sounded irritable and confused. The events of recent years had aged him considerably, and he now felt the need to check things with his wife.

'Yes, of course we do. We're patrons of the V&A. They always invite us.' Louisa looked up. 'We'll make a day of it. Have lunch at the Savoy. The whole family.'

Kitty bowed her head, hiding her face in her long hair. She told herself an invitation to an exhibition didn't mean anything. As Louisa had just said, the Hamiltons were patrons of the museum. It was nothing to do with Yuri. But still, cold fear snaked inside her. Was disaster finally going to strike? Just when she'd begun to think she might be spared?

As Louisa handed round the invitation, Kitty stood up. 'I don't feel well.'

Louisa frowned over her glasses. 'What do you mean, you "don't feel well"? Are you ill or sick?'

The two words had quite separate meanings in this family, but Kitty couldn't think what they were. 'I don't know. Both.'

A light entered Louisa's eyes. 'Could you be pregnant at last?'

Kitty shook her head mutely. She made herself walk calmly from the room. In the hallway, she broke into a half-run. But there was nowhere to go. Nothing to be done. She tried to think how to contact Jean-Jacques to find out if there was any way the painting could have made its way to London – but there was no chance of making a private telephone call from this house, and she had no excuse to make a trip to the village. She would have to think of something . . .

Upstairs, she closed the curtains, as though the gloomy light might offer her some safety. She lay on her bed, stiff-limbed like a wooden doll. She ran through the facts in her mind. Yuri's work was well regarded in London. A group exhibition could easily include one of his works – but it would be a painting loaned from one of the museums or from a private collector eager for publicity. Katya's picture was in the hands of a recluse in faraway America. She need not be concerned. But still, she felt a sense of foreboding that logic could not banish.

Eventually, there was a knock at the door, and Theo appeared at her side.

'Poor old you. Are you coming down for lunch?' Kitty rolled onto her side, folding herself into a ball. 'Mummy's been on the telephone. It seems the invitation arrived here nearly two weeks ago. The butler only just discovered it.'

Kitty lifted her head. They'd missed the exhibition!

'It's opening tomorrow. Everyone will be there. Possibly even His Majesty.' Theo crossed to the window and opened the curtains, letting in the harsh morning light. 'Buck up, darling. Mummy's already choosing what to wear. Why don't you do the same?'

A diamond necklace hung heavy and cool around Kitty's neck. From the corner of her eye she caught the glitter of the matching brooch, pinned to a cashmere stole. The clasp of the necklace had snarled in her hair, and when she moved it pulled at the roots. She could have torn the hair free, but the pricks of pain distracted her from the tense knot in her stomach.

At her side in the back of the Daimler sat Theo, wearing his best suit. He smelled of Imperial Vetyver, the gentleman's cologne favoured by the Hamilton men. The scent slid beneath the cloying perfume that wafted across from Theo's mother. She too wore diamonds, along with an elegant grey ensemble. The Admiral had put on the dress version of his naval uniform, even though his son had refused to join him in military garb. They were all on their way to London for the grand opening at the V&A.

Kitty's outfit had been chosen the previous afternoon. As soon as she'd emerged from the bedroom, she'd been accosted by Lizzie – Louisa's faithful maid – and summoned to the mistress's dressing room. Kitty had paused outside the door, taking a deep calming breath.

'Go on, then, madam,' Lizzie had urged, waving her inside.

The vast chaise longue with carved lion's feet was draped with frocks and gowns, jackets and hats. The Hamilton jewels had been brought from the safe. Velvet-lined boxes were set out on the dressing table.

'I thought you might like to borrow something.' Louisa smiled encouragingly, but there was an accusing tone in her voice. Kitty should have been an heiress with her own family jewels. She should have been a well-bred young woman with a sense of style and an eye for quality. But Louisa was determined to be gracious – to try to make the best of what she had. Part of Kitty felt almost sorry for her. Theo was her only child, and his choice of wife had robbed her of the chance of gaining a daughter she could like and understand.

Louisa lifted a diamond necklace, holding it up to catch the light. 'This has been in my mother's family for generations.' She held it out to Kitty. 'You should wear it, with the matching earrings.'

'Oh, I couldn't. It's much too . . .' She knew better than to mention the value – that would be vulgar. 'Special.'

'Nonsense.' Louisa was warming to her task. 'I want you to look wonderful. You haven't a decent dress or suit. Neither have I, for that matter. But everyone is in the same boat, thanks to rationing. We've all had our garments recut and retrimmed until we're sick of the sight of them.' She sighed. 'Hopefully things will change soon. But for now,' she gave another smile, 'we must rely upon accessories, mustn't we?'

Kitty noticed Louisa's use of 'we', several times in one speech. It was almost as if the woman felt some affection for her son's wife. Kitty wished she could forget about the painting and enjoy the attention she'd often craved. She tried to put her concerns from her mind, giving herself over to being dressed up by Louisa. This way, she would at least know that she looked right.

Now, sitting in the car, Kitty still carried with her the image she'd seen in the bedroom mirror. She wore a Norman Hartnell dress of red brocade that Louisa had once worn to Buckingham Palace. A dove-grey stole draped her shoulders, its soft tone offsetting the sparkle of diamonds at her throat and ears. She wore black gloves and a wide-brimmed hat, pinned at an angle over hair that Lizzie had piled expertly on top of her head. With the perfect tone of red on her lips – close to Alizarin Crimson, in fact – and plenty of mascara, Kitty was striking; almost beautiful. She looked well groomed and rich, like the wife Theo should have chosen.

When she'd descended the main staircase that morning, he'd gazed proudly up at her. The memory aroused conflicting emotions.

It made Kitty fear, even more, that something was about to happen that would destroy everything. But at the same time it gave her confidence, helping her rise above her obsessive anxiety about the exhibition.

'Don't look so worried, darling,' Theo said. He squeezed her hand. 'You look wonderful.'

'Thank you,' Kitty said. 'So do you.'

The Daimler glided to a halt outside the Savoy. The Hamiltons were to take lunch there – at their usual table – before going on to the museum. Kitty looked up at the façade, with its golden statue of a Roman soldier standing above the entrance. This was where her adventures in London had first begun. She wondered if any of the doormen might recognise her – but, of course, she knew they wouldn't. Thousands of people had come and gone since she was a guest. And today, in her diamond jewellery and Hartnell gown, she bore no resemblance at all to the wide-eyed Australian girl she had been back then. As she stepped from the car, she lifted her head and gave a small, ladylike smile.

It was late afternoon when the Hamiltons arrived at the V&A. Theo walked between his parents, offering them each a steadying arm as they negotiated the steps to the entrance. Kitty trailed after them, her gaze fixed to the ground.

The wide hallway that led from the foyer to the main gallery was crammed with people. Kitty now walked beside Theo, pressing close against him. The smell of cigar smoke mingled with expensive perfumes and hairspray. The men were smart in their suits or uniforms but they were outshone by the women, who all seemed to have made a special effort with their outfits. Many looked grand but dated, like Louisa and Kitty – only a few had managed to acquire fashionable new gowns and striking modern hats. Everyone was pushing forwards. There was an excited murmur. Kitty swallowed on a tense throat. She'd never been to an opening before. Was this eager crowd normal?

As they neared the doors to the gallery, Kitty's step faltered. She saw a familiar figure hovering up ahead – portly, bald-headed, arms flung out in an extravagant gesture.

'There's that fellow who used to come and see the prince.' Theo pointed towards Jean-Jacques.

'Oh, yes,' Kitty said faintly.

'I'd be surprised if they've hung one of his paintings after that fuss in Paris. But I suppose his earlier work is still admired.'

Peering through the crowd, Kitty met Jean-Jacques' gaze. His eyes widened. For an instant, he looked panicked. Then he raised his shoulders in a small shrug.

Kitty caught her breath. His message was clear. The painting was here. How and why it had happened, she didn't know or care. She made herself keep walking. Thank goodness Louisa had dressed her up so much. She was nothing like Yuri's Russian girl. Maybe no one would see the resemblance between Katya and her . . .

By the time they reached the doorway, Jean-Jacques had disappeared. It was immediately apparent that everyone's interest was focused on the far end of the gallery. Kitty stared above the heads of the people gathered around a large painting hung there. She saw the dark purple sky, the roiling clouds, the stark branches of the forest trees.

Her feet kept moving in a steady rhythm, but inside she lurched between thoughts. She could just run away – back outside, down the stairs, into the side streets . . . But what would she say to Theo – that she felt ill again? And maybe it was better for her to be here, so that at least she would know what was being said about the painting.

The next moment, it seemed, she was standing in front of the picture. Louisa and the Admiral were on one side of her, Theo on the other. No words were uttered. But they knew, Kitty could tell.

Everyone knew.

The realisation hit Kitty with a power that crushed out her breath. The way people were looking from her to Katya and back again left no room for doubt: they understood that the painted image and the woman standing in their midst were one and the same. The wife of Admiral Lord Hamilton's son.

A space opened up around Kitty, Theo and his parents, as the other guests shrank away. There was a shocked hush. Further back in the crowd, voices murmured as news of the event unfolding was passed back. At the edge of her vision, Kitty saw Louisa draw herself up, lifting her chin. Theo straightened his shoulders as well, clamping his arm to his side, trapping Kitty's hand against his body. Though the Admiral was clearly confused, he adopted the same posture as his wife.

Kitty wanted to hang her head, but she forced herself to follow their example. She tried to look – as the three other Hamiltons did – as though whatever might happen, whatever might be said and done, it would not impact upon her. A scandal had broken out, but the family would not deign to acknowledge it. Drawing on all the authority of their noble ancestry, they were capable of rising above any crisis.

'We Hamiltons were there when the Magna Carta was signed,' Louisa had once explained. 'We are a very old family.'

'We Hamiltons.' That included Kitty. No matter what transpired, the family would stand by her, she knew. They had no choice. The Admiral liked to boast that no Hamilton marriage had ever been dissolved, whether by annulment or divorce. Regardless of what Kitty had done, they were stuck with her, and she with them.

Kitty dared not look at Theo's face. She could feel fury, disbelief, pain emanating from him. She felt like a child who had inexplicably torn down a sandcastle that had been built with love and care. *But I had to do it*, she reminded herself. *For Yuri. For Katya.*

Suddenly, a man was talking to her – asking her a question.

'Mrs Hamilton, can you confirm that you were the model for this painting?'

Kitty nodded but said nothing. A tremor passed through Theo's body, but his expression did not change.

Within seconds, there were two other men standing in front of her. One had a notebook and pen in his hands.

'What was the nature of your relationship with the late Russian prince?'

'Did you have your husband's permission?'

'How do you feel about the controversy over the picture?'

'Are you a pacifist?'

Kitty just stared past the reporters or critics – or whatever they were. She was being examined, she realised, by dozens of pairs of eyes. Her image was being compared with that of Katya's – and the focus was on her breasts, her hips, her legs. A young man nearby gave her a suggestive smile.

She searched around desperately for Jean-Jacques – but there was no sign of him. Even if there had been, she wasn't sure he would have attempted to intervene. She wasn't sure about anything concerning Yuri's agent right now.

She heard a question being directed to Theo. 'Do you support your wife's view of the war?'

When he refused to answer, the attention shifted to his father.

'I have no idea what you're talking about, old boy,' the Admiral kept saying. Kitty couldn't tell if he was genuinely at a loss – as he sometimes was, these days – or if this was his way of rebuffing the questions.

Finally, Theo stepped forward, holding out one arm like a shield against the journalists. When he spoke, his voice was thin and tight. 'A statement will be issued by our solicitor. That is all.' He nodded at his mother. 'Let's go.'

As one, the family group turned from the painting. At that moment, there was a bright flash. Kitty saw a man holding a large black camera. He met her gaze. He wore a look of excited satisfaction, backed by pity.

In the hallway, the incoming guests had no knowledge of the scene that had just unfolded. They made way for those who were departing – stepping aside, keeping up their easy chatter. For a time, the atmosphere was almost normal. The four made it outside, into the open air. Kitty stumbled, catching her heel on a chipped paving stone. Theo made no move to steady her.

The Daimler was not in sight – the driver had been told to return in an hour's time. Theo left a message for him with a porter, and summoned a cab. When it was barely at a standstill they all climbed inside.

For several minutes there was a stunned quiet. Then Theo wheeled around to Kitty.

'How could you?'

Kitty just looked at him. If she had all the time in the world, she knew she'd never be able to make him understand the choices she had made.

'Have you seen it before?'

She nodded.

'Why didn't you tell us it was in there?' Louisa demanded, her voice sharp as chipped ice. 'You let us come along like lambs to the slaughter . . .'

'I didn't know it would be here. I feared it might. But I wasn't sure.'

At least that answer was simple and true.

A strange, choked laugh came from Theo's throat. 'And you really did strip off and pose for that old man . . . ?'

Kitty flinched from his tone – he made what had taken place between her and Yuri sound dirty. But there was only one answer she could give. 'Yes. I did.'

He swallowed, his Adam's apple rippling his neck. 'You regret it, of course . . . It was a terrible mistake . . .'

Kitty took a breath, but said nothing. She refused to lie to him.

The look Theo gave her then was more frightening than anger would have been. It was one of pure incomprehension, as if he'd just realised his wife was of a completely different species to him.

'I'm truly sorry I've hurt you.' Kitty's words sounded shallow and cheap, but she meant them. Theo didn't deserve this; neither did his parents.

'Stop talking, both of you,' Louisa commanded. 'Let's just get home.'

The way she spoke made 'home' sound like a fortress. As the cab drove on, leaving London behind, Kitty pictured how the great wrought-iron gates at the entrance to Hamilton Hall would creak open to receive them, then clang shut, closing out the world. The scenario would be repeated when they reached the double front doors, with their metal studs and lion-head knockers. Inside the Big House, more doors would be opened and closed, curious servants banished. Lattice screens would be unfolded, thick curtains drawn. Only then, cloistered in this private world, would the family decide Kitty's fate.

She was almost looking forward to being punished – the prolonged anxiety, stretching over years, had been agonising. Now the worst had finally happened. She was prepared to pay whatever price they asked of her; she knew she'd caused irreparable harm to the Hamilton family honour. She'd do whatever it took to restore Theo's faith in her, and eventually win back his love. Yet at the same time, she knew that if events were replayed she would not change the choices she'd made. As the grey streets of London gave way to patches of green, then open countryside, her thoughts kept churning, round and round. She was sorry, but she would do it all again. She regretted hurting Theo but she didn't regret comforting Yuri. She felt she was caught in an impossible maze where she would keep on walking forever. There would be no end, and no hope of escape.

FIFTEEN

Kitty stared ahead at the drooping branches of the peppercorn tree. Clusters of pink seeds, hanging among the feathery leaves, lent their spicy tang to the air. She peered through them at the blue sky. The sun had moved on past noon into its slow descent. She and Father Remi had been sitting together a long time. It must be close to the hour when the bells were rung for afternoon prayers.

With her hands, she wiped tears from her eyes. They felt hot and red – she'd not been able to tell her story in the matter-of-fact way she'd planned. But Father Remi hadn't minded. When she was unable to speak, he just told her to take her time. There was nothing more important that he was planning to do.

She told him everything – honestly, hiding nothing. When she'd finished her account of what happened back in England, she went on to explain how the events still affected her life now. She told him about the agreement she'd made with Theo to give up being an artist – so that no one would link her with her old self, and so that he need not be reminded of what she'd done. She talked about the tension that still persisted between her and her husband. She even expressed her fears about Theo's relationship with Charlotte.

During her long speech, Father Remi had shown little reaction. He was a still, quiet presence beside her.

When she finally reached the end of what she had to say, she felt a huge sense of relief – it had been good to be able to talk openly to someone at last. But at the same time she was now even more mixed up than she had been before. Over the two years that had passed since the terrible day of the exhibition, she'd forgotten how she'd felt when she made her decision to pose as Katya, and then to send the painting to Jean-Jacques. She'd been influenced by the views of others: that what she'd done was dirty, deceitful, irresponsible, even cruel. But now, as she revisited the whole story, feeling the emotions again, she understood the path she'd taken. When she thought of how she'd been treated by Theo and his family, anger welled inside her. Yet during the journey into the past, she'd also relived the distress she'd caused Theo, and felt the pain of the rift that had grown between them. Her hands twisted tensely in her lap, her thoughts and feelings in turmoil.

Glancing sideways, she could see no clue to how Father Remi felt about her, now that he knew everything. His head was bent, his hands clasping his knees. When he eventually looked up, she was surprised to see the hint of tears in his eyes. But his voice, when he spoke, was calm and firm.

'You've made your confession, Kitty. What happens next, in our church, is that the priest declares Absolution, assuring the parishioner of God's grace and forgiveness.' Father Remi's accent grew stronger as he said these words – as if the phrases had their origin long ago, in some distant seminary. 'Then he suggests an act of penance. It might involve reading scripture, saying prayers. Sometimes there are pilgrimages or special offerings.'

Kitty nodded. She didn't mind what kind of penance he prescribed – as long as it helped in some way to draw a line under the past.

'In this case,' Father Remi continued, 'I cannot declare Absolution.'

Kitty stared at him in dismay – then she lowered her gaze to the ground. A beetle scurried by, printing tracks in the sand with its busy feet. Her hands gripped the bench. The priest's manner was gentle, but there was no room for confusion over what he'd just said. She heard him take a breath, ready to continue, and dreaded what was coming next.

'When I think of what you did for your friend Yuri – what it must have meant to him – and the consequences you have suffered. I feel . . .' He broke off; Kitty realised his voice was choked with emotion. He took another breath, and began again. 'What I see is a brave young woman choosing to offer herself up to an act of mercy. I see no sin, Kitty. I see only love.'

Kitty looked up. 'But I let Theo down. I hid things from him. I —'

Father Remi held up his hand. 'Sometimes it's not possible to make a simple choice between right and wrong. Doing good can also cause harm.'

'So what can I do?' Kitty suddenly felt desperate. Her marriage – her life – was a mess. Father Remi's sympathy would not solve her problems.

'It's simple,' Father Remi said. 'Put aside all the things others believe about you, all the things they want from you. Be true to who you really are.' He laid his hand over the badge of his order. 'The heart knows the truth. Search your heart.'

He waved an arm towards the garden, as though it were out there, beyond the confines of talk and deliberation, that she would discover his meaning. Kitty forced a smile, hiding her disappointment. If there was none of Tesfa's dangerous magic to be given out, she'd at least hoped for some practical guidance.

The priest picked up the basket and held it out to her. 'Let's pick that fruit.' He smiled back at her. 'Then I want to show you our grotto.'

A path made of flat stones led between two oleander bushes dotted with magenta flowers. Kitty ducked her head, avoiding the spiked tips of the leaves. Her loaded basket bumped her knee as she followed Father Remi on, matching his brisk pace.

Peering past him, she saw what looked like a child's playhouse, except that it was a solid building made of rendered concrete, with a gabled roof. In the middle of the façade was an arched entrance with no door – clearly, this place Father Remi called a grotto was intended to be available for use at all times. The walls were thick and sturdy, out of keeping with the miniature scale of the structure. They were unpainted, but a line of whitewash had been daubed around the entrance, perhaps intended to draw the eye of a passerby, inviting them in.

Father Remi stood aside, letting Kitty approach the grotto. 'We finished the building over a year ago. It was built to mark a very special miracle that took place here.' He spoke as if the occurrence of ordinary, everyday miracles could be taken for granted, like the arrival of migratory birds after winter, or the coming of night after day. 'A child was healed of blindness. She was six years old and had been unable to see all her life. For many years, her father refused to bring her to us. But then he died from malaria and the mother decided to come. Father Paulo prayed over her and she was healed. She can even read now.'

'She'd been completely blind?' Kitty couldn't help sounding sceptical.

Father Remi nodded. 'She was led everywhere by her older sister. It was the most wonderful of all the miracles we have seen.'

Kitty raised her eyebrows. 'So there have been others?'

He nodded. 'Father Paulo has a gift.'

'You mean he just prays for people and they get healed?'

'It's not that simple. I wish it was. Then we wouldn't have to bother with our clinic. The nuns could give up their nutrition and hygiene teaching. Everyone could be healthy. But a true miracle is the deepest of mysteries. It is something that our minds, trained in logic, simply cannot understand. It's not such a puzzle to the Africans, of course. Their minds are undamaged by rationalism. That's one of the reasons I love working here. There is so much for me to learn.'

He guided Kitty towards the archway. 'The village people decided there should be a grotto built right here, where the child was standing when she was healed. They worry that Father Paulo is old – he will leave this world soon. They hope something of him will remain here. And so do I.' As he spoke, Father Remi looked in the direction of the small graveyard where past inhabitants of the Mission were buried. Kitty felt sad for him. She guessed that when he lost his colleague a replacement priest would be sent.

Someone chosen in faraway Rome – a complete stranger, moved here like a chess piece in a game. She was glad Father Remi would still have his friend on the next-door farm. The thought of Taylor brought a half-smile to her face. The last time she'd seen him, he'd been inexplicably dancing some kind of jig with one of the prison guards. Gili's attempts to mimic the pair had caused widespread amusement among the onlookers. Kitty could still remember the sound of laughter spreading through a crowd of a hundred men. While it lasted, they were bound together – prisoners and guards, serious criminals and petty thieves, the hopeful and despairing, weak and strong.

Putting down her basket, Kitty walked inside. The air was cool and smelled of concrete and stone. As her eyes adjusted to the dim light, she saw a pair of low wooden stools offering a place to kneel before an altar set out from the back wall. The front of the table was draped with a cloth of green and white stripes, faintly tinged with red dust. On the bare wooden top was a stand for candles, along with two matching ceramic vases. But there was no dripped wax marking the timber, and no wilting flowers, not even a single curled petal. Clearly, the grotto was not yet in use.

'As you see,' said Father Remi, 'there is no statue.' He pointed to where a concrete plinth had been erected behind the altar. 'We are still waiting for it to come.'

'You order them from Italy?'

'The ones in the church come from there. However, they are very expensive and we need our money for other things.' He came up beside Kitty, turning to meet her gaze. 'But that isn't the main reason the grotto is not yet finished. We want something different for this place. We'd like a statue of a child – an African child. So of course, we cannot get that from Italy.' He eyed the blank space behind the altar thoughtfully as if he could already see what he envisioned standing there. He turned to Kitty, his face brightening. 'Really, we should have the statue made here, with one of the local children as a model.'

Kitty looked at him without speaking. She couldn't tell if this thought had just occurred to him, or if he was simply feigning a new idea. Regardless, a thread of excitement stirred inside her. She could already feel the clay beneath her fingers. A child's shape forming – big head, willowy arms, rounded belly . . . Her heart beat faster. Then she shook her head. 'I can't do it. I'm not an artist any more.'

'Yes, you are. The children showed me the model you made of Gili. I suspected you were a trained artist. And now, I know your story.' He took Kitty by the shoulders, turning her around to face him square on. 'You can't go on denying this part of yourself. No one has the right to ask you to do that.'

Kitty nodded slowly. She felt excited, daunted. She was afraid of what his words would mean – but she could feel that they were true.

'Sunflowers are the solution,' Theo announced to Kitty. 'They're going to save our bacon.' He was pacing the sitting room, glass in hand. 'They grow like weeds in Australia, apparently. The Ministry of Food has got several schemes being set up over there as we speak.' He broke off to take a swig of whisky, then laughed. 'We're going to try them here – on a big scale, just like the groundnuts. And all because of a parrot!'

Kitty smiled guardedly. She understood his relief that there was hope of rescuing the reputation of the Groundnut Scheme: sunflower seeds could be made into margarine just as easily as peanuts. And the thought of plantations full of big yellow flowers was instantly uplifting. But Kitty was aware of an edge to Theo's voice. His movements were a fraction too quick, his eyes overly bright. She wasn't sure if he'd been drinking before coming home, or if he was not as relaxed as he pretended to be.

'Some fellow from the Ministry of Food was in Queensland,' Theo continued, 'at the home of one of the Australian staff. There was a parrot in a cage. The Australian commented that the bird kept spilling sunflower seeds through the bars. Wherever they landed, they grew!' He laughed again. 'Sounds like an improvement on groundnuts.'

'Are they easier to harvest as well?' Kitty had never heard of farming sunflowers (it certainly wasn't done around Wattle Creek) but that wasn't why she'd asked this. She just wanted to frame a sensible question – the kind Charlotte might have posed. Perhaps now that Theo was talking seriously to a woman about his work, this new approach could be extended to include Kitty too.

'Well, obviously – but you don't need to know about all that.' Theo crossed to the trolley and poured himself another whisky. These days, Gabriel didn't linger after preparing the first round of drinks. When Theo had taken a long gulp, he raised the glass as though to propose a toast. 'I've got some good news for you.'

Kitty kept her small smile on her lips, concealing her unease about what could be coming.

'Your days of slaving at that Catholic place will soon be over! Aren't you pleased?'

Kitty stared at him. 'What do you mean?'

'Richard and Diana are taking home leave at the beginning of January. You won't have to babysit her for much longer.'

Kitty couldn't decide how to react. She already knew Diana and her husband were making a trip back to England. It was a big step for them. Seeing family and friends would bring up fresh grief over their son's death, but they wanted to make this step towards acknowledging their past. Kitty was glad they were going. But it hadn't occurred to her that with Diana away she would lose her reason to be at the Mission.

'I'm to be Acting General Manager,' Theo announced.

'Congratulations,' Kitty said softly.

'When they return,' he went on, 'I see no need for you to take up this charity work again. You've done a great deal to support Diana – but enough is enough.' The way he spoke with such authority, he might already have stepped into Richard's shoes. 'If she wants to keep going there when she comes back, she can do it on her own.'

When she responded, Kitty tried to make her tone light. 'Oh, I'm happy to keep helping out. I've come to rather enjoy it.'

Theo gave her a sharp look, then waved one hand dismissively. 'Well, very soon you won't have time. You will be the senior memsahib of Kongara. This is your chance to make your mark!'

Kitty twisted her glass in her hands. She tried out different words and phrases in her head: reasons why she still had to go to the Mission. But nothing sounded right. In the end, she just opened her mouth and began.

'I want to keep on going there, Theo. I have things to do.'

Theo's eyes widened with surprise. What she'd said was close to open defiance.

'What things, exactly, would those be?' There was a sneer in his voice – but behind it, Kitty sensed rising anxiety. Theo hated anything disorderly, and she was breaking the rules. But she could not give in.

'I've been asked to make a statue.'

'Statue?' Theo froze, his drink poised halfway to his lips.

'It's going to be of a child. An African. I'll work in clay first, then make a plaster cast. Unless I can find a way to work in bronze . . .' She knew she was running on, saying too much. It was not as if there was any chance Theo might be seduced by the details of her project. Eventually, she fell quiet.

Theo said nothing for a while. Then he spoke to Kitty slowly, as though to a child or a foreigner. 'You made a promise to me. You gave up being an artist.'

Kitty licked her lips before taking a breath. 'I shouldn't have made that promise. And you shouldn't have asked me to.' She forced herself to hold Theo's gaze, though every part of her recoiled from the look on his face. 'Theo, when we met, I was an artist. Don't you remember? It was my dream. It was why I came to England – leaving my family behind, using all my grandmother's money. Becoming a real artist meant everything to me.'

'Clearly it means more to you than I do.'

'It's not like that. I'm not choosing between you and art.' Kitty felt sick, her legs shaky. She sensed everything was at stake in this exchange. The outcome would determine the future happiness of her marriage – her whole life.

'Oh, yes you are, Kitty. Because you made a promise. Now you're going to let me down again. You think you can do what you like. Maybe that's how people behave where you come from. Or is it that you just can't stick to anything? You get led astray by whomever's around. That Russian. Now Diana. You can't see what's in front of you.'

Kitty looked helplessly at him. He wasn't even making sense.

'But I must warn you, if you are intent on this flagrant disobedience – thumbing your nose at everything I stand for – you are making a grave mistake, and one that could cost you a great deal.'

Kitty moved towards him, holding out her hands. 'Please, Theo. We don't have to argue like this. Can't we just talk calmly? Listen to each other . . .' Reaching him, she put one hand on his arm.

'Don't touch me,' he said coldly, brushing her away like an insect that might bite. He slammed his empty glass down on the coffee table. 'I'm going out.'

Kitty opened her mouth to tell him to wait, stay. But he was already at the door.

'I won't be back for dinner. And don't expect Charlotte, either.'

Moments later came the sound of the Land Rover engine revving loudly. Then there was the grinding of gears as Theo drove off.

Kitty collapsed into a chair. Her heart was pounding. She covered her face with her hands. She knew Theo would be going straight to the Shoebox, into Charlotte's understanding embrace. Almost certainly, he would not come back until late. He'd be drunk by then. He'd probably stagger to the single room – unless he decided to come and issue more threats to his wife. She watched herself as if from a distance. This situation was a disaster. She should be crying, at least. Instead she just closed her eyes. As the tension of the argument faded, she felt a dull anger take its place. Then she felt deeply exhausted. She curled up in the chair, losing herself in sleep.

The next thing she knew, Gabriel was bending over her, announcing that dinner would soon be served.

'The bwana is returning?' he asked. 'With Lady Charlotte?'

Kitty could see the gleam of interest in his eyes. No doubt he'd overheard everything that had been said. She shook her head wearily. 'No, he's not coming. In fact, why don't you and Eustace eat the dinner? I'm not hungry.'

Surprisingly, a flicker of concern passed over the young man's face. 'The memsahib should eat.'

The meagre words of kindness broke through Kitty's defences. She found she could not speak.

'I have an idea,' Gabriel said, looking pleased with himself. 'I will bring some food to your room. A plate of sandi-wichi.'

'Thank you.' Kitty smiled, her eyes blurred with tears. 'Sandwiches would be perfect.'

SIXTEEN

Kitty leaned her head against the smooth bark of the baobab. Hidden from view behind the wide trunk of the tree, she could hear sounds of activity in the Mission compound. The nuns were singing as they swept the forecourt. Father Remi called out to Amosi, the cook. A dog barked in the distance.

She had driven out here early, leaving Diana to come in the Daimler at the usual time. She just wanted to get away from Millionaire Row. It felt too close to Head Office, to the Shoebox – to anywhere else in Londoni that Charlotte and Theo might be.

He had stayed out most of the night. When Kitty heard him returning – small sounds jolting her wide awake, proving she'd been listening for him in her sleep – the first light of dawn was already creeping around the edges of the curtains. As she expected, he headed straight to the spare room. There was a thud as he stumbled in the hallway; then came the heavy snoring of a person who'd drunk too much.

When Kitty finally slept again, it seemed only moments before she snapped awake. The sounds of breakfast being served came from the dining room. Throwing on her dressing down, she hurried out to see Theo. She knew she looked a mess – her eyes were bleary, her hair unbrushed – but she wanted to talk to him before he left the house again.

Theo was already buttering a slice of toast, a cup of tea at his elbow. He didn't lift his gaze as Kitty walked in. She took a slow breath, trying to remain calm.

'Where were you, all that time?' she asked.

'I don't wish to discuss it.' He kept his head bent over his plate of fried eggs and bacon.

Kitty clenched her teeth in frustration. Of course he didn't – he never wanted to discuss anything. Not their marriage, and certainly not his health. She thought of how she'd pleaded with him over the years, to consult a civilian doctor about his nightmares, and the other symptoms of combat fatigue that hadn't gone away. It was to no avail: he was like a child who believed that by putting his hands over his eyes he could make the world disappear.

'I waited up for you,' she said.

'Well, you shouldn't have bothered.' He cut into his egg, letting the yolk spread.

'You were with her, weren't you?'

Theo gave no response. He just looked down at his plate while he chewed and swallowed. Then he drained his cup of tea and stood up. After slapping down his napkin next to his plate, he strode out of the room. Kitty could hear him brushing his teeth in the bathroom, then walking to the front door.

When he'd driven away, Kitty sat at the table, numb with dismay. The nothingness Theo had left her with was unbearable. She stood up, her steps drawn to the spare room.

The air was tainted with the smell of stale cigarette smoke. Theo's shoes – normally placed side by side under his bed as he was trained to do in boarding school – had been kicked off carelessly and left where they'd landed. From the chair, Kitty picked up his jacket. Lifting it to her nose, she recognised Charlotte's distinctive perfume. As she dropped it back down, she noticed his crumpled shirt on the bed. There were red wine stains down the front. On the collar was a smudge of lipstick – dark, muddy red; nothing like the clear tones Kitty wore. And there was something else: a single red hair, long and curly, clinging to the sleeve. She picked it off, holding it between finger and thumb. It occurred to her that Charlotte's hair was about the same length as her own had been before Theo had forced her to chop it off. Did he enjoy the feel of the long strands draping his skin as they made love? Did he wind Charlotte's hair around his hand, pulling her face towards his?

Maybe they weren't actually lovers, Kitty told herself. Maybe they had just kissed and cuddled. But then, why would they have stopped? There was nothing to hold them back – after all, Lady Welmingham was not married. Therefore Theo was perfectly enti-tled to have an affair with her, and she with him.

Louisa had made sure to explain to her daughter-in-law the rules that governed extramarital affairs between members of Britain's aris-tocracy. The 'little chat' had taken place not long after Kitty and Theo had moved back to Hamilton Hall. Several times before, Louisa had taken Kitty aside like this. The girl was an Australian, with a family about whom very little information had been forthcoming. Louisa could see there was a lot Kitty did not know about how people like the Hamiltons lived. She was always blunt and to the point.

'The first responsibility of a wife is to produce a male heir. Until she's done this, there is absolutely no possibility of her having an affair. For his part, a gentleman will never sleep with a married woman – of his class, obviously – who has not yet had a son. That would be very poor form indeed. So what I'm saying to you, Kitty, is this: no playing around until you have given Theo his heir. Then, you can do as you damn well please.'

Kitty had let out a shocked laugh. Louisa had spoken in the same practical manner she used when discussing topics like floral arrangements or disciplining servants. Kitty had to replay in her mind what Louisa had just said, to make sure she'd understood.

'So Theo is free to have an affair right now, and I'm not?'

'Seems unjust, I know – but yes. The thing is, the paternity of the heir simply cannot be in question.'

Kitty stared at her mother-in-law. Was this how Louisa's marriage had been played out? Had she indulged in affairs? If Yuri had responded to her attempts to flirt with him, would she have taken him as her lover? For his part, the Admiral clearly had an eye for women – especially young ones. Kitty saw it in the way he looked at the girls at church and the female servants. She'd even seen his gaze lingering on her own figure – following the movements of her legs as she crossed one over another, even though she made sure her skirt was pulled well down.

'So have I made myself clear?' Louisa's face was stern; she was deadly serious.

'You don't need to worry,' Kitty said. 'Neither of us will be having affairs with anyone. We love each other.'

Louisa had given her an odd look, then – it could have been pity, envy, or a mixture of both. Then she'd just nodded and walked away.

Kitty shook the long red hair from her fingers and flung the shirt back onto the bed. She strode out of the room, slamming the door behind her. Moments later, she was dressed in her work clothes and heading outside to her car.

Now, standing in the shade of the baobab, the painful events of last night and this morning were more distant. Kitty felt steadier – as if by resting her body against the tree, she'd absorbed some of its strength. Father Remi had told her that this particular baobab – he used the Swahili name, *buyu* – was believed to be up to two thousand years old. She imagined it being here, century after century, while humans came and went, with all their pain and joy, dreams and disappointments.

She tried to think practically about her situation – starting by naming the emotions that churned inside her. She was angry, she was afraid, she was jealous. And she was shocked: it had happened so quickly – Charlotte had barely been here a month! She was also embarrassed. For all she knew, an affair had been going on ever since the apiarist had arrived, and was already the subject of gossip in Londoni. She felt a fleeting irony at the thought that she might be whispered about once more – but this time it was Theo who had caused it. She probed her wounds further, searching for something more heart-rending. But the truth was, she did not feel devastated. Perhaps Theo had hurt her too many times, and let her down too badly. Deep inside, she just felt numb and empty.

So what would happen next? She and Theo would stay together – that went without saying. Charlotte would return to England, eventually, and marry a suitable man. At some stage, Theo would want to have sex with his wife again. After all, he had to father his heir. Maybe they would even make that trip to Nairobi. But there would be no real love or trust between Kitty and her husband any more. They would never be the happy family she'd envisaged. With a shudder of pain Kitty realised she'd failed in her aim to have a better marriage than her mother. In fact, she'd fared worse. Kitty's father was tough and ungiving, but she doubted he was unfaithful. And there was a basic loyalty between her parents. Come drought or bushfire, illness or other disaster, Kitty felt sure they'd stand shoulder to shoulder and take the blows together.

The sound of a large vehicle arriving broke into her thoughts. It came to a halt just the other side of the tree. Kitty frowned – it was too early to be the prison truck. She edged around the trunk to take a look. From her first glimpse of the old-fashioned spoked wheels and the bulbous headlights set close together, she recognised Taylor's ramshackle shed-on-wheels. Gili was sitting there on the bonnet, crouched in his wooden box. When the engine stopped he jumped to the ground. Kitty saw Taylor climb down from the driver's seat.

The pair caught sight of Kitty at the same time. The man was surprised but gave a friendly wave. As Gili bounded over, Kitty wiped her face, hoping she didn't look like she'd been crying. Then she stepped forward, opening her arms.

She held the monkey against her chest, comforted by his embrace.

'Good morning,' Taylor called to her. He'd moved to the rear of the vehicle, where an African man was handing down some boxes of vegetables. There were another half-dozen tribesmen riding on the back tray. Kitty eyed them curiously, peering over Gili's head. Their faces were painted with red ochre; ash whitened their chests and shoulders. They carried spears, bows and leather quivers spiky with arrows, as if dressed for a battle.

Kitty smiled cautiously as she moved nearer to offer the appropriate morning greetings. '*Hamjambo. Habari za asubuhi?*'

The oldest of the men replied for the whole group. He assured Kitty the morning was good, as were their homes, their families, their cattle and their *shambas*.

Kitty forced herself to say that everything was fine with her life also. These greetings were about courtesy, not truth. As she spoke, she studied the Africans more closely. Several wore armbands made of hide and feathers, the adornments drawing attention to their well-toned biceps. Necklaces decorated their broad shoulders. They looked utterly different to the plainly attired tribesmen she'd seen around Londoni – exotic and dangerous.

Taylor approached Kitty, reaching out his hands for Gili. The sleeves of his bush shirt were rolled up to his elbows, leaving his tanned forearms bare. The morning light fell across his face, showing up his strong jaw and broad brow. His eyes met Kitty's and held them for a brief, potent moment. She peeled the monkey's skinny arm from around her neck.

'Where are you taking these men?' She couldn't imagine why Taylor would be involved in tribal fighting. Then it occurred to her that some kind of ceremony might be taking place – when the Minister of Food had made his last visit to Tanganyika, the Kongara Club had arranged a display of tribal dancing with Wagogo dressed up just like this.

'We're going to collect wild honey,' Taylor said. He gestured towards the plains, in the opposite direction to the plantations. 'We have to drive for an hour or so – beyond those hills in the distance. You get to an area of open grassland dotted with thorn trees.' He smiled at her. 'It's beautiful country.'

There was a brief silence. Kitty's mouth seemed to open of its own accord. 'Can I come?' She bit her lip, amazed at herself for being so forthright. Taylor looked taken aback as well. 'It's all right,' Kitty added hastily. 'I shouldn't have asked.' But even as she brushed her request aside, she felt how much she really did want to go. She longed, suddenly, to get away somewhere new, where she could forget about her life. She could sense the mood of anticipation among the men. It reminded her of when she used to set off to muster stock with the farmhands, lunch packed in their saddlebags, a big day ahead. When they found the honey, she told herself, she would stay back, well out of the way of the bees.

'I'd love you to come,' Taylor said, still looking surprised. 'But women aren't usually allowed on an expedition like this. I'll have to see what they say.'

The conversation was quite lengthy. Kitty focused on Gili, while men pointed at her and argued among themselves. Eventually Taylor came back over.

'They have agreed to let you come, because they know you work hard here at the Mission. Also, since you are a European, you don't really count as a woman.' He gave a grin. 'I've had to promise to be responsible for you. To make sure you behave in a suitable manner.'

Kitty laughed. 'I'll be very good.'

She could feel the despair of the morning falling away. She hurried across the forecourt to let the nuns know what she was doing. Yesterday she'd arranged with Father Remi to spend time this morning discussing her setting up a studio out here. He was encouraging her to explore the options even though she hadn't yet committed to making the statue – there was still the issue of Theo's permission. He wanted to show her a spot at the rear of the Mission building that he thought would be ideal. But the plan could be postponed; Kitty knew the Father wouldn't mind.

Taylor was waiting at the passenger side of the vehicle when she returned. 'It will be a rough ride, I'm afraid. Not what you're used to.'

'I'll be fine.' Kitty smiled inwardly at the idea she only belonged in saloon cars and limousines. Without waiting to be assisted, she swung herself easily onto the seat and let Gili curl up on her lap.

Taylor looked at her for a second, then went round to take his place behind the wheel. He leaned to turn on a jury-rigged ignition switch that could have belonged in a kitchen. The engine roared into life, a faulty muffler doing little to subdue its noise. As the vehicle picked up speed, it sounded as if there were dozens of things loose and rattling. Kitty shifted sideways, avoiding a broken spring that dug into her hip.

'Are you all right?' Taylor shouted over the racket.

'Fine, thanks!'

Kitty settled back in her seat. She gazed ahead through a windscreen of sorts that had been mounted on the bonnet. The glass was scarred and dirty but it provided some protection from wind and dust. It was way too noisy for any conversation to be possible.

With no words travelling between the two, the proximity of their bodies seemed heightened. Kitty stole sideways glances, taking in the deep lines around the man's mouth and between his brows. His chin darkened by stubble. The sun-bleached hair on his arms. When she looked ahead again, she was aware that now he was glancing at her. She wondered what he saw. A woman who'd made no effort with her appearance, obviously. Did he also see that she'd hardly slept? She felt the words 'unwanted wife' must be written on her forehead. Humiliation was surely etched on her face. But if he saw any of this, he gave no sign of it. When their eyes chanced to meet, he gave her a warm look. Then he waved a hand, taking in the sky and the land as if to share with her its beauty.

When they'd only been driving a little while – skirting the foot-hills – Taylor pulled up beside a man walking on the road with a young child. As they exchanged greetings in Swahili, Kitty heard a reference to a wife who'd been ill. The woman must have recovered, though, because Taylor and the man were both smiling as they swapped farewells. Before driving on, Taylor pointed in the direction of the hillside nearby. For a moment Kitty couldn't see what he was showing her. Then she picked out the gabled roof and stone facade of a house, almost camouflaged in an outcrop of boulders.

'That's my house,' Taylor said.

Peering more closely Kitty saw it had big windows overlooking the plains and a terrace in front. At one end of the building there was a tower with a fanciful turret. Whoever had designed the place was not only concerned with practicality.

'It was built by my father.' The pride in Taylor's voice was unmistakeable. 'I was born there.'

'It looks like a lovely home,' Kitty said. 'There must be quite a view.'

'Best in the land.' Taylor grinned. When he drove on, Kitty noticed how he let the vehicle pick up speed slowly, so that as they passed the man and his child they did not shower them with dust.

They left the green hills behind, descending to the plains. Amid the red earth, grass, shrubs and small trees were more baobabs than Kitty had yet seen in her time in Tanganyika. While still maintaining a dignified distance from one another, the giant trees were grouped in clusters. As the vehicle trespassed among them, Kitty had the idea that conversations were being suspended – then taken up again when privacy was restored.

The tracks petered out, and Taylor steered cross-country. It took another half-hour to reach the place where the landscape began to change. At first it was subtle – fewer baobabs, larger shrubs, thicker grass. The odd thorn tree appeared, its canopy a perfect curve against the sky. Then there were more of them – and more still. Soon they were in open woodland made up entirely of these graceful trees.

Finally, Taylor brought the vehicle to a halt. Dust settled, coating Kitty's skin, hair and clothes. Gili sneezed, shaking out his fur. Taylor offered a water bottle to Kitty.

'Thirsty?'

She took several big gulps – the water was lukewarm but it soothed her dry throat. She used the bottom of her shirt to wipe the top of the bottle, then handed it back. It seemed an oddly intimate gesture when they knew each other so little. She turned away as Taylor tipped back his head and took a few long swallows.

Behind them, the men jumped down from the vehicle and began to organise their weapons.

'Are they going to hunt?' Kitty asked.

'If they see a gazelle or an eland, they'll go after it,' Taylor said. 'But the spears and arrows are mainly for protection. There are lions out here. Elephant and buffalo as well. Don't worry, though. You're in good hands.'

'I'm not worried.' Kitty glanced around her, hoping for a glimpse of a wild animal. She'd yet to see any of the creatures she'd always associated with Africa. Bowie, the old hunter, had been right – the big game had all fled from Kongara.

'But stay close to me,' Taylor warned.

Kitty looked down at Gili, nestled in her arms. He was being very calm and quiet. She guessed he'd learned how to behave on trips like this.

One of the men walked a little way off from the group. He was strikingly tall and strong, with muscles bunched tightly on his slender limbs. Lifting up his face, he began to whistle.

Taylor spoke in an undertone. 'That's Nuru. He's calling the honey guide. A bird. When it hears him, it will answer – with a special whistle it only uses to communicate with humans.'

'That's amazing.' Following Nuru's gaze, Kitty searched the treetops.

'It's the only bird out of seventeen similar species that does this,' Taylor added.

Nuru whistled again, a clear melodic sound. Then he froze, head tilted to one side, his expression intent. As a reply travelled clearly on the air, he swivelled around, hunting for its source. A grey bird broke from the foliage of a tree up ahead. It flew off, swooping low. Nuru strode after it, followed by everyone else. While their leader watched the honey guide, the other men scanned the undergrowth on all sides, checking for any danger.

The bird flew on, stopping to perch on branches now and then – just until Nuru and the rest of the group caught up – before flapping off again. Kitty watched in amazement; there was no doubt the little bird was actively cooperating in their quest for honey.

Eventually, the honey guide settled on a branch and stayed there.

One of the men said something to Nuru. Kitty picked up a warning note in his voice. She turned to Taylor to see if he would explain what was going on.

'He said, "I hope you paid this honey guide last time".' Taylor's voice was muted. 'If Nuru didn't, the bird will remember. It might bring us to the lion's den.'

Kitty peered nervously into the surrounding bushes, wondering if he were being serious or not. Nuru was joined by another man and together they searched the nearby trees. After several minutes, he gave a triumphant wave.

'*Nimeipata!*' I have found it!

Kitty could see a hole high up the trunk of the tree. A few bees were coming and going from it. She stared in mixed wonder and alarm – the bird really had led Nuru straight to a bee's nest! Taking a cautious step backwards, she clutched Gili to her chest. 'Aren't these bees dangerous?' She tried to sound casual, but she was thinking of Cynthia's husband – picturing his agonised figure covered in stinging insects.

'They smoke the bees before they take the honey. It confuses them. The men will get a few stings, but the swarm won't attack.' Taylor sounded so confident that Kitty felt reassured. She put Gili down, then watched on while Nuru used matches to set fire to a pile of twigs. As a small blaze flared up, another man held something in the flames.

'Looks like they've found some dried elephant dung. It makes good smoke,' Taylor commented.

Now that the source of honey had been located, lighthearted chatter broke out.

'How do you know about the honey guide – the seventeen species?' Kitty asked him.

'Nuru told me. His ancestors have been living here for a long time. They were Dorobo originally – hunter-gatherers. But they joined the Wagogo generations ago when they took up farming.'

Nuru put the piece of smoking dung in his bag and climbed nimbly up the tree trunk. Kitty noticed that the honey guide, sitting in its tree, was watching on keenly. When Nuru reached the hole, he used a strip of hide to make a sling, holding himself in place, leaving his hands free.

As he pushed the dung into the nest, bees began milling around the entrance. Kitty frowned anxiously, but Nuru showed no sign of concern. Soon they formed a cloud around him. Kitty heard him exclaim as he was stung – but he was undeterred. Reaching inside the hole, he pulled out a large chunk of honeycomb, dropping it into his bag. Then he produced another. The onlookers shared smiles of anticipation.

When Nuru finally climbed down, his bag was bulging. The

first thing he did was to take out a hunk of honeycomb and place it on the ground near the tree where the honey guide sat. The bird flew down and began pecking at the comb.

'It has to be one of the best pieces,' Taylor said, 'with larvae in it. That's what the bird expects.'

'And would it really lead people to a lion if it wasn't paid properly?'

'I've heard it has happened,' Taylor confirmed.

Nuru began handing out chunks of honeycomb. Taylor and Kitty sat on a fallen log, after checking for scorpions. Gili squeezed in between them. The tribesmen broke off bits of honeycomb and chewed them up, closing their eyes in pleasure.

Kitty accepted the piece that was given to her. Gili immediately stole one corner and crammed it into his mouth. Honey leaked onto Kitty's fingers as she lifted the honeycomb to her lips. It was crunchy, waxy, with pockets of sweetness. The honey was unlike any she'd tasted before – it was velvety on her tongue and had a flavour that reminded her of clover flowers. She was aware of the Wagogo awaiting her verdict.

'Delicious!' She swallowed, and licked her lips. But then, as she took a second bite, her jaw froze. There was something in the honey – creamy, with an odd taste. Lowering her hand, she examined the chunk of comb. Like the honey guide, she'd been given a piece containing larvae. She stared at the pale, wormlike shapes for a few seconds, then made herself have another bite. She didn't need anyone to tell her the special treat was an honour that had to be gracefully accepted.

Taylor nodded approvingly. 'You don't have to eat it all,' he murmured.

Kitty managed another small portion – but was then relieved to see the men were no longer watching her. They were focused fully on enjoying the honey. Nuru handed out second servings, but there was still plenty in the bag to carry home to the village.

'These bees seem to be hardworking – making lots of honey,' Kitty commented.

'That's bees for you,' Taylor grinned. 'Busy.'

'But I thought African bees were lazy.' As soon as the words were out, Kitty realised how ridiculous they sounded. She hurried to explain herself. 'Have you heard about the beekeeping project that's being run by the Scheme?'

'No – what project?'

Kitty felt a wave of relief – if Taylor didn't know about the bees, then he most likely didn't know about Charlotte. That meant he probably hadn't heard rumours that Lady Welmingham was having an affair with her husband. 'They had problems with the pollination rates, so they got an apiarist from England to bring over some European bees. They're about to install the hives down on the plantations.'

Taylor stared at her. 'Are you sure?'

'Everything's ready to go.'

She told him how the men in the workshops had turned their mechanical skills to the task of constructing wooden hives to Lady Welmingham's specifications. Colonies of imported bees had since been established in them, each with its own queen. Charlotte had brought a container of queen larvae with her and there had been great excitement when they started hatching. One evening over dinner, Charlotte had described to her hosts how she had checked the new queens over, squashing any she didn't like the look of, and painting the others with tiny symbols. The marks corresponded with records in her notebook, and also with matching symbols painted on the hives where each of them would reign. The purpose of this, Charlotte had explained, was that their performance could be measured and only the best bloodlines kept going. The way she'd spoken of breeding had reminded Kitty of Louisa.

'So, right now,' Kitty told Taylor, 'the hives are all stacked up in the middle of the football field, ready to be taken out to the Units.'

'Idiots!' Taylor exclaimed. He jumped to his feet and began pacing. 'Who's in charge, do you know?'

Kitty swallowed. She hadn't expected this extreme reaction. 'My husband.'

The Africans were watching the exchange with interest, but showed no sign of understanding what was being said. If they spoke any English, it was obviously not much.

Taylor was quiet for a moment, standing still, then he shook his head. 'This is complete madness. He has no idea what he's doing.' He waved his hand to take in the scene in front of them – the hive, the bees, the tribesmen in their finery, and the honey. 'Bees are sacred to these people. You can see how they've prepared themselves to come out here today. Honey plays a part in every landmark in their lives: courtship, weddings, pregnancy, the birth of a child, death . . . Many of the Wagogo chiefs already resent the Scheme. It's brought so many new problems. They've watched their traditional way of life being undermined. They'll see this introduction of European bees as an attack on their sovereignty. They'll be deeply offended.'

Everything Taylor said made sense to Kitty. She wondered if Theo had thought all this through, and had decided the needs of the Scheme were to take priority over concerns held by the Africans – or if he'd not even considered the issues.

'They'll also be very afraid,' Taylor continued. 'The lives of the Wagogo are tied closely with nature. In the hills we have the spring water to depend on, but in the rest of the country there's only rain. If it comes at the right time, the people can eat. If there's drought, they starve. If one part of nature is disturbed – like the bees – there could be terrible consequences, from the ancestral spirits and from the land itself.' He broke off, his brow furrowed with concern. 'It simply has to be stopped, at least until there's been some discussion with the chiefs. No offence to your husband, but I need to go straight to the top. I'll see Richard first thing tomorrow morning.'

'Will he listen to you?' Kitty asked. She'd revised her opinion of the man since their interactions over Diana – he'd shown he was someone who could see reason, and was prepared to change his mind if it made sense to do so. But on the other hand, he was responsible for making sure the germination rate of the crops was increased, or else the Scheme could never succeed.

'He will when I explain what's at stake,' Taylor stated. 'The last thing he wants is to have the village people up in arms. He's facing serious problems with the native workers. They still don't have good water; their families are still far away, or else squatting in the slums. There's already been a strike at the wharves in Dar es Salaam. The tension will spread here if nothing's done.'

Kitty nodded – she'd heard about the trouble in the capital. For several days, the women at the Club had been preoccupied with accounts of Africans brandishing spears and clubs, marching on offices, threatening Europeans. In response to the crisis, the Chief Inspector had summoned all the senior staff to Scotland Inch and issued them with pistols. When Theo brought his home, Kitty had been alarmed. People carrying weapons around reminded her of the war years. She was worried about the effect it could have on Theo. But he'd not seemed bothered by the pistol. And he'd played down the threat, saying the firearms were just a sensible precaution. Nevertheless, he carried his gun with him, as instructed, whenever he went to the Units.

'Richard will have to act straight away,' Taylor said. 'I'm just glad you told me.'

Kitty felt a spike of pleasure at the thought that Charlotte's precious project was about to run into a serious hitch. She half hoped the woman would discover it had been Kitty who had, albeit inadvertently, been the cause of the upset. It would almost be worth the trouble she'd get into with Theo . . .

'Looks like it's time to go.' Taylor gestured towards the men who were picking up their spears, slinging quivers over their shoulders. He offered his hand to pull Kitty to her feet. Their palms met, sticky with honey, making them both smile. 'We can wash when we get back to the car.'

Kitty laughed. 'You call that a car?'

'Well, it was once . . .'

Kitty sensed that Taylor was glad – as she was – to change the subject. The tense words they'd exchanged were out of keeping with the beauty of the setting and the relaxed mood of the Wagogo. A man sang to himself as he cradled the bulging bag of honey against his chest. Another picked idly at his teeth with a stick. Nuru wandered over to the fire he'd lit, which was still burning. He looked back at Kitty, appearing undecided for a second – then he lifted up his loin-cloth, letting go a stream of urine, causing smoke to give way to steam.

From the corner of her eye, Kitty saw Taylor checking to see if she was offended.

'We always did that when we left a camp fire,' she told him. 'Better than starting a bushfire.'

They set off, joining the end of the line of men. Now that Nuru was no longer following the honey guide, he chose a more direct route, pushing a path through thick grass. Kitty walked beside Taylor, Gili back in her arms. An Mgogo followed behind them with his spear poised in his hands.

'You've spent time in the bush, then?' Taylor said.

Kitty nodded. 'My family live on a farm, miles from the nearest town.'

'That's why . . .' Taylor's words petered out.

'Why what?'

'Why you are so different to the other Kongara ladies – not that I know any of them, really. But when you helped me with the pipe that day, you knew how to be useful. You speak Swahili. And, I've seen how you work at the Mission.'

Kitty felt warmed by the open admiration in his voice. She realised how much time she spent being subjected to criticism, or trying to avoid it.

'You seem so . . . unlike your husband,' Taylor commented. 'I've crossed paths with him a couple of times, and he's . . . well, very British.'

Kitty could tell Taylor was guarding his words, not prepared to say what he really thought about Theo.

'We are very different,' Kitty agreed. 'We married during the war. We were in love, but we didn't know one another very well.' She was silent for a moment. When she spoke again, it was to herself as much as to Taylor. 'I think we can probably both see now – it was a mistake.'

It was a mistake.

Such a simple statement – and yet its meaning was huge. Part of her was shocked that she'd said the words. And why was she talking so frankly to Taylor, of all people? She looked around her at the thorn trees with their speckled canopies, each the same shape; the clear spaces between the branches; the wide blue sky above. There was something open and truthful about the setting that made her own transparency not only acceptable, but necessary. Social niceties – all the taboos and conventions – were part of another world. 'I don't know if it was the war that changed him,' she went on, 'or if he just grew up and became his true self. And there were other things that happened . . . But whatever the reasons might be, he's just not the man I fell in love with.'

They walked on, their feet following a matching rhythm, swishing through the grass.

Kitty wanted to ask Taylor something about his personal life. Father Remi had once referred to him as a 'single man'. And he'd said Taylor's parents were no longer alive. But that was all she knew.

'I lost my fiancée during the war,' Taylor said, as if reading her thoughts.

Kitty turned to him. Platitudes came to mind but she discarded them one by one.

'I don't mean she was killed. She found someone else. I don't blame her – I was missing in action for years. I was a prisoner of war. She believed I was dead.' Taylor was quiet for the next few steps. 'I often wonder how it would have worked out if we'd stayed together. We met in England while I was at agricultural college. She said she liked the idea of living in Africa. But the truth is, it's not every woman's cup of tea, being out here. Of course, if she'd hated it we'd have moved away from the farm. But I'm glad I never had to do that. The place is in my blood.'

Kitty eyed him curiously as she took in his words. Her father had often talked of being tied to Seven Gums, but he made it sound like a lifelong curse – one that his sons would be saddled with after he was gone. Theo was stuck with Hamilton Hall, as well. In a few years' time, when his work with the Scheme was over, he and Kitty would have no choice but to move back there and take care of it for the rest of their lives. Kitty saw the dark side to the devotion Theo's heritage required, but he simply considered it a privilege. She was amazed to hear Taylor saying he'd move from this place if he had to, for the sake of his wife's happiness. She could see how much he loved living there on the hillside. But she didn't doubt that he meant what he'd said. He was the same person, after all, who had set up a scheme to help prisoners. The men saw him as their rescuer, Kitty knew. Working for him gave them a chance to earn a little money to send home to their families and to learn skills they could use later on; it brought them outside into the fresh air, and they got to eat good food from the Mission kitchens. Bwana Taylor was admired by all – and he deserved it.

Kitty looked sideways at Taylor as they walked along together. He'd said nothing more about his fiancée and she didn't feel she should ask. One thing she knew – whoever the woman was, she'd passed up the chance to marry a man with a kind, strong heart.

Suddenly, it seemed, they were back at the vehicle. Gili hopped down from Kitty's arms and capered about, burning off pent-up energy. Taylor brought out a jerry can of water, and everyone washed their hands. Then he passed around the drinking water. The men drank without letting the bottle touch their lips. When it was her turn, Kitty tried to follow their example, but managed to pour water over her chin. Everyone laughed at her. Dabbing her face with her sleeve, she joined in. Her mistake didn't matter. Nothing mattered out here. She felt freer than she had in a long time, removed from all the troubles of her life. And there was a new warmth inside her – a closeness shared with Taylor, after the talk they'd just had.

Nuru produced a huge bunch of bananas that had been stowed somewhere in the vehicle. Kitty accepted one gratefully, feeling suddenly hungry. Gili stood between her and Taylor, carefully peeling back the skin of his banana, then nibbling delicately at the end.

'Butter wouldn't melt in his mouth.' Taylor said.

Kitty felt a pang of nostalgia at the phrase. It was one her mother liked to use. She wondered if Taylor had also inherited it from his mother. And what was her name? When had she died? What kind of life had she led? Kitty wanted to know so much more about Taylor, and to tell him so much more about herself.

'I've enjoyed today,' she said.

'Me too,' he said simply. But his eyes did not leave hers – those strange, striking eyes with two-toned irises held her gaze. In the sunshine, the blue-green that circled his pupils looked like seawater. The rim of light brown shone like spun gold.

SEVENTEEN

'Are we running late?' Diana asked. 'My watch has stopped.' She was sitting in the front passenger seat of the Hillman; these last weeks she'd finally overcome her fear of being near the driver.

'I don't think so,' Kitty answered. 'We don't have to meet the others until three. That's when the tennis roster ends.' They were bumping along the shortcut track. In the rear-view mirror the bell-tower finally disappeared in a haze of dust. 'It seems such a waste of time.'

The two had promised to join some of the ladies to help decorate the marquee for the Christmas Ball. A lot of the work had already been done. The huge tent had been erected in the open space next to the Club. Men from the Tractor Workshops – the same ones who had constructed Charlotte's beehives – had made giant ply-wood cut-outs of angels and reindeer, and Mary, Joseph and baby Jesus. They'd been installed outside the front of the marquee. The schoolchildren had made yards and yards of paper chains. Now it was up to the ladies to add the final touches.

Diana rolled her eyes. 'I couldn't agree more. I wanted to stay on and talk to Chalula. There's so much I have to do before I go.'

Kitty picked up a tense note in Diana's voice. 'You can leave me a list of things to do, if you like.'

'I expect I'll have to. I've arranged for the post office to let you check my mail. You must look out for something about Daudi's appeal hearing. If the letter comes, make sure the boy's parents are contacted. Chalula knows the name of their village. And if the bail hearing for Ndele comes up, you'll have to act on my behalf.'

'Don't worry. I will,' Kitty said reassuringly. She'd already heard Diana give these same instructions to Father Remi – and more besides. Chalula had written everything down. Kitty understood Diana wanted to make sure everything ran smoothly in her absence, but it was still a couple of weeks before she was due to leave for England. Kitty couldn't help thinking all this forward planning might be Diana's way of managing her anxiety about the trip itself.

Kitty could only imagine how hard it was going to be for Richard and Diana – returning to the town where they'd lived when their son's tragic death took place, and then visiting their families and seeing Phillip's cousins looking older, taller, while their own little boy would only ever be five years old. Kitty wondered if Diana now felt daunted by the journey that had been planned – and whether she should ask her about it.

The pair had become close during the time they'd been working together. They'd shared so much. Not just everyday experiences like changing a flat tyre or picking beans in the vegetable gar-den, but things that had left them exhausted, distressed and even frightened. Only a week earlier, just after lunch had been served, a fight had broken out between two prisoners. Father Remi had been knocked to the ground when he'd tried to intervene.

The assault on the priest had infuriated other prisoners and for a few terrifying minutes the conflict had spread. The *askaris* had responded with heavy use of their batons. By the time the incident had been brought under control, nearly a dozen men needed to be treated for injuries, the Father among them. Diana had had to join Kitty in the clinic, tending the wounds. She'd been helpful and effective, but Kitty had noticed her hands were shaking. It had taken her some time to calm down afterwards. Kitty was worried now that this incident – coming on top of the stress of the trip home – might have been too much for Diana.

'How are you going with making plans for England?' she asked carefully.

'Everything is in place, I think,' Diana said. 'We just have to decide whether to take a train north to Richard's family or arrange to get a car.'

'Are you worried about it – what it will be like?' Kitty felt she could push a bit further.

'Yes, I am,' Diana said. 'Sometimes I wish I could call it off. But I know we have to go.' She was quiet for second, as if reaching inside herself. 'Richard and I need to stand in the street where Phillip was killed. We need to go to his grave and read his name, the date of his death. We have to accept what happened. It's the only way we can face the future.' She put her hand to her eyes. When she spoke, her voice was low. 'But I am afraid.'

Kitty swallowed a lump in her throat. She felt a wave of admiration for Diana. It was hard to believe this was the same woman who'd tried to commit suicide only a couple of months ago. The transformation seemed almost miraculous. Occasionally, there were glimpses of the old unstable Diana. She would become brittle and tense, or else silent and withdrawn. She'd smoke constantly. Sometimes when she was cheerful there was an extreme edge to her behaviour. But Father Remi was a steadying presence, drawing her out or calming her down. And regardless of her mood, Diana was always completely devoted to her work. Whatever was going on around her, she listened carefully to the prisoners who came to her desk, then wrote the appropriate letters in her new neat style. She'd proved to be strong and resilient, Kitty reminded herself. Diana might be feeling stressed, but when she got to England she would rise to the occasion.

'You will get through it,' Kitty said to her. 'I know you will. You are so strong now.' She waited for Diana to nod. 'And I'll be thinking of you,' she added, 'every day that you're gone. And so will the Fathers, Chalula, Tesfa – everyone.'

'Thank you,' Diana smiled, blinking away a tear. 'I'll remember that.'

They drove in silence for a while. The bond of their friendship was a warm cloud in the air between them. As they reached the edge of Londoni, Kitty glanced at her watch again, then drove a bit faster to make up time.

'I have to talk to you, Kitty.' Diana's voice broke the quiet without warning. 'Before we have to deal with the others.'

'Of course.' Kitty rehearsed in her mind some more words of encouragement and sympathy.

'I believe Theo is having an affair.'

Kitty gripped the steering wheel in shock – not just at the unexpected change of subject, but at hearing these words spoken aloud, so blunt and clear. It made what she already knew seem much more real. Her stomach twisted; she felt she might be sick.

'It's that beekeeping woman.' Diana sounded matter-of-fact, rather than outraged.

Kitty nodded mutely.

'So you already know.' Diana sighed. 'Poor you. Everyone's talking, of course. That's one of the worst parts about it. You just have to brave it out, Kitty. Think of it as a storm coming through. Hold up your head and walk straight into the wind. The thing is, it will pass.'

Kitty turned to Diana. 'You sound as if you know what it's like.'

Diana waved her hand vaguely. 'Richard's had his flings. Nothing too serious. It's to be expected, isn't it?' She sounded as reconciled to the situation as Louisa had been, years before. But that was hardly surprising – Diana was the daughter of an earl. She'd no doubt been taught all the rules. Perhaps it was part of the debutante training Louisa loved to describe.

'Are you terribly upset?' Diana laid a hand gently on Kitty's arm. 'Stupid question. Of course you are.' She moved her hand to Kitty's shoulder, giving it a firm squeeze. 'You must always remember, Theo is your husband. He belongs to you. People like Charlotte come and go. They don't mean anything.' Her upper-class accent added a comforting weight to every phrase she put forward. 'That woman will be back in England before long. Next thing you know you'll be reading about her engagement to Lord So-and-So in *The Times*.' She gave a dry laugh. 'Actually, she might be leaving sooner than she planned. Richard's instructed Theo to suspend the honey project until the chiefs have been consulted.'

'I've heard,' Kitty said. Theo and Charlotte had aired their dismay and anger about the decision over the last two evenings while sitting at the dining table with her. 'She still comes over every day, you know,' Kitty went on. She shook her head, at a loss as to what to say about such a bizarre situation: a husband and his lover, sharing dinner each night with his wife.

'That's good!' Diana said. 'You know what they say – keep your enemies close to your chest. If she's there in your home, she's acknowledging your place. Above hers.'

'Should I say something to her?'

'Definitely not. It's beneath you.'

Kitty shook her head helplessly. 'Sometimes I can hardly stand it. I sit there at the table, and I feel like killing her.' It was true. Even though Kitty no longer loved Theo in the way she once had, some primitive part of her felt like a cat whose territory had been invaded. She wanted to scratch that porcelain skin to shreds.

'There's only one thing to do, Kitty. Take care of yourself.'

'What do you mean?' Kitty frowned, puzzled.

'Choose a new hairstyle. A new bottle of scent – quite different to whatever you usually wear. And, of course – lingerie.' Diana clapped her hands. 'Tell me your size and I'll bring you something beautiful from London. Lace. Ribbon. Silk. Those are your weapons . . .'

Kitty almost laughed, but she knew Diana was deadly serious. The woman was applying a strategy she firmly believed in – as rigorously as she did when intervening on behalf of the prisoners. Diana may have changed a lot since Kitty first met her, but underneath she was still an English gentlewoman, just as Kitty was still an Australian farmer's daughter.

Before long, they were passing Head Office. Kitty couldn't help watching out for Theo and Charlotte – but the Land Rover was not in its parking space. They drove on towards the roundabout.

'Now, Kitty, listen to me,' Diana instructed. 'At the Club, everyone will be watching you. You must look happy. If you can't manage that, then lift your chin and look haughty. It's not as good, but it will do. If anyone asks you leading questions, simply change the subject. Be quite blunt about it if necessary. If you need me to help, just give me a little nod. I'll step in.'

Kitty smiled bleakly. She sensed the cat rising up in Diana as well. In the midst of pain and humiliation it felt good to know she had such a strong friend at her side.

'What's that?' Diana pointed ahead.

A thick plume of smoke rose up from beyond the trees that hid the Club from the roundabout. Kitty sped up. She saw flames – leaping flashes of red – along with the billowing smoke.

'Good Lord!' Diana exclaimed. 'The Club's on fire.'

But then the curved outline of the Nissen hut came into view. The fire and smoke were coming from somewhere else.

'It must be the marquee.' Diana's voice was hushed with shock.

As they rounded a corner, the blazing tent appeared. The fire had taken hold; the whole structure was burning – canvas, wooden poles, ropes. Flames licked at the plywood figures standing out in front.

The road was lined with jeeps, trucks and other vehicles all parked hastily at random angles. Kitty left the Hillman half on the road and hurried after Diana, who had jumped out before they had completely halted. The fire engine was parked near the blaze. The crew of khaki-clad *askaris* was hard at work – red fezzes bobbing as they dashed about hauling buckets and hoses.

A large crowd had gathered. The Club must have been emptied of patrons. Kitty ran her gaze over the various groups, relocated from inside but still keeping to themselves. She saw Alice and the other women who held court behind the Japanese screen; the mothers with their *ayahs* and children, standing well back. The men in suits. The staff in their white tunics. Then there was the solitary figure of old Bowie, frowning at the fire as if he could not believe his eyes.

Some distance away stood a much larger number of Africans. Quite a few of them were probably plantation workers – they wore ragged shirts and trousers. But others were in traditional dress: men, women and children, all staring wide-eyed at the spectacle. Moving among them, Kitty saw, was a team of *askaris*. While she watched, they pulled a man aside, handcuffed him, and then dragged him across to where a separate group of Africans were sitting on the ground. The Chief Inspector stood over them, talking through a translator, making notes on his pad. He was grim-faced, his movements heavy with intent.

Diana stopped to wait for Kitty. They stood for a few moments, regarding the burning tent. Sections of canvas fell, leaving the structure standing bare, like the bones of an animal.

'I heard someone say it was arson.' Diana looked anxiously in the direction of the crowd of Africans. 'They're trying to find out who to blame.'

Kitty studied the rows of black faces. Some of the onlookers were still absorbed by the spectacle of the fire, but many had been distracted by the actions of the *askaris*. A shudder of fear ran through Kitty as

she saw in their eyes the smouldering resentment and derision she'd
seen expressed by Alfred and several other members of staff at the
Club, and by the servants in her own home.

'There's Richard and Theo.' Diana tugged at Kitty's arm.

Kitty stiffened as she stared towards her husband. Diana's blunt
statement about his infidelity still rang in her ears. She didn't feel
like facing Theo – or Richard – right now. But Diana was already
leading the way over to them.

The men stood side by side, hands in pockets. They could have
been watching a game of polo, except that their faces were tense
and strained. An *askari* stood nearby.

Richard greeted Kitty and Diana as they arrived, but Theo just
nodded briefly before turning back to the fire.

'Was it deliberately lit?' Diana asked her husband.

'Apparently it was. The fire started in five places at once. Petrol
was used.' He shook his head. 'I assume it's meant to send a message
of some kind to us Europeans. Maybe it's to do with the trouble in
the labour camps. But it could be something else.' He was addressing Theo as well as the two women, but his colleague showed no
sign that he was listening.

'It's a bad time for me to be leaving,' Richard continued. Kitty
saw Diana frown with alarm, and then relax as her husband gave
her a smile. 'Don't worry, Diana. We're still going. But this incident
will have to be handled very carefully.' He turned to Theo, waiting
for a response. A few seconds passed before he got one.

'Absolutely,' Theo said, his attention still fixed on the fire.

'You'll have to make some concessions to the workers. Give
them a pay rise. Do whatever it takes to restore calm.'

As Richard talked, Kitty kept her gaze on Theo. He was mesmerised by the fire – the flames were reflected in his wide, staring eyes. He was not looking at the remains of the marquee – his focus was on the wooden figures. Mary, Joseph, the angel. They looked like real people being burned alive. The top half of Joseph bent forward as the flames devoured him. He could have been writhing in pain.

Kitty put her hand on Theo's arm. She recognised the expression on his face – it was the one he wore when she'd shaken him out of a nightmare but not yet managed to wake him up. 'Are you all right?' When he gave no reaction, she nudged him gently. 'What's happening?'

Suddenly he stiffened, pulling away. He seemed surprised to see Kitty there. He murmured something, then began looking around him, his eyes raking the crowds.

Scanning the faces herself, Kitty picked out Charlotte's red hair – she was standing only a short distance away. Beside her was a man Kitty identified as one of the Unit Managers, Larry Green. Strikingly handsome and single, he was the subject of constant speculation at the Club. The two were chatting excitedly, showing no concern about the situation – the fire could have been put on purely for their entertainment. Kitty examined Charlotte's outfit, the first casual clothes she had seen her in. She wore a tailored safari suit made from honey-yellow cloth instead of khaki. It hugged her figure much too closely to be practical but it showed off the curve of her bottom and her tiny waist. As Kitty watched, Charlotte tossed her long mane of hair. Then she tilted back her head, showing off her teeth as she laughed. Larry's whole body leaned towards her as if drawn by her magnetism.

Theo must have located the pair too. His face darkened as he watched them interact.

'Excuse me,' he muttered. 'I'll be back.'

Kitty swapped looks with Diana as he marched over to Charlotte. Diana gave a faint smile of satisfaction: perhaps Charlotte was already tiring of Theo. But the thought gave Kitty little pleasure. She would almost rather Theo was involved in a real love affair. What was going on here seemed so pointless and tawdry.

Kitty stared at the fire, which was subsiding into glowing ashes. The angel was almost gone; Mary too. The baby was just a smudge on the ground. The bottom half of Father Christmas had been saved by the efforts of the *askaris*, however. The reindeer had survived as well, but without its head. Kitty was reminded of classical sculptures she'd seen at the British Museum: remnants of ancient figures that were no longer whole. She seized on the connection – desperate for anything that would take her thoughts away from Theo. In her mind, she linked the museum pieces to the statue that was needed for the grotto. She would have no qualms now about taking on the task of making the sculpture, whatever Theo had to say on the matter. He'd broken the rules, as far as she was concerned, and had forfeited any right he might once have had to prevent her. Becoming an artist again would be her compensation for having to tolerate his unfaithfulness. Deliberately dwelling on the details, she made a mental list of the materials she'd need for the project. Clay, rope, metal rods, hessian, plaster . . . But Theo's voice kept drawing her attention. He'd reclaimed Charlotte from Larry and was now talking to her about the fire.

'Well, obviously,' he said in his most authoritative tone, 'some fellow burning down a tent is not going to have the slightest effect on anything. One can't give in to such people.'

'Absolutely,' Charlotte agreed. 'Where would it end?'

Kitty moved away out of earshot. She was downwind from the fire now, and smoke brought tears to her eyes. When she closed them, the air felt even hotter, one sense striving to make up for the loss of another. Sweat beaded on her skin, then trickled down. She felt desperation building inside her. She wished she could just run off and hide, leaving Theo and the others here. But that would cause a scene that she didn't have the strength to face.

She forced her thoughts back to the safe subject of the statue. It was going to be a huge undertaking. First, she would have to choose a child model from the village and make lots of drawings. She'd collect careful measurements so that all the proportions were correct. Next would be the task of making the armature – the basic bones of the figure formed from metal rods forged over an anvil. Then she would use rags and pieces of old rope to build up a rough shape of the child. This she would cover with clay. Now came the part she loved most: the careful sculpting, using fine tools and fingers to mould the clay. The challenge was to capture the essence of the child – her life, personality, spirit. Moment by moment, the statue would become ever more alive.

Standing by the fire, picturing the task unfolding, Kitty felt the old excitement about a project brewing inside her. The work would take months; it would fill her days. This, she realised, was how she would survive. She would lose herself in her work – blocking out Theo and all her other griefs. When she finished the statue of the child, she would move on to another. She might even train an assistant, passing on the skills Yuri had taught her. In the calm of her studio out at the Mission, she would return to the purpose in life she'd had when she first travelled to England. Back then, she'd had no plans to become someone's wife. She'd wanted only to be an artist.

Kitty turned away from the fire. Her skin was dusted with ash, her mouth tasted of soot. But she barely noticed. A great sense of relief flooded through her. She had chosen her path. One part of her would go on being Theo's wife, but the other would be devoted to the same quest that had shaped Yuri's existence after he lost his beloved Katya. Like him, she would devote herself to seeking honesty, purity, the perfection of skill. To capturing that essence of life that lay beyond human pain and failure – that would always remain beautiful and true.

EIGHTEEN

The smell of chlorine blended with the oily fragrance of coconut suntan cream. Kitty lay with her hat over her face, protecting herself from the sun. Around her, voices rose and fell as the women chatted idly. The chaos of Christmas week had come and gone. There had been plenty of talk earlier this morning about weight gain and the need for exercise, but now those subjects were exhausted. Pippa was reading out a list of home hints; Alice kept querying whether they would work. Audrey complained that her burnt shoulders were beginning to peel.

Kitty wondered how she was going to manage with Diana away. It had only been a few days and already she was feeling lonely. There was no one to talk to about events at the Mission, or even just to confide in over the latest problem with her house staff. If Diana were here now, Kitty thought, she might even open up the subject of Taylor. She knew Diana had noticed how the two often managed to meet up in the course of their work, and how they always ended up sitting together during tea breaks – yet neither woman had ever spoken about it. The conversation regarding Diana's trip to England, and about Theo and Charlotte, had brought a new frankness to their friendship, but they'd barely had any time alone together since the day of the fire. Diana had been busy preparing to leave, and there had been all the demands of Christmas. Perhaps it was just as well, Kitty told herself. If they did start talking about Taylor, she was not sure exactly what she would say.

Turning her thoughts to a safer topic, Kitty recalled her visit to the airstrip to bid the Armstrongs farewell. Diana had looked stunning, dressed in a new suit the Indian tailor had only just managed to finish on time. The bold orange and brown print was eye-catching and the fabric draped her figure perfectly. Richard was more casual, his jacket slung over his shoulder. Whatever his feelings about what lay ahead in England, Kitty knew he must be relieved that the fire incident had finally been sorted out. Apparently, the blaze had been lit by an employee of the Club who'd been sacked for stealing food.

Neither Richard nor Diana mentioned the fact that Theo was not there, even though according to protocol he would be expected to pay this courtesy to his superior. Theo had told Kitty to give his apologies, claiming he was too busy with his new responsibilities – from that morning on, he was Acting General Manager. But the fact was, he never came to the airstrip if he could possibly avoid it. He said he didn't like the noise, the dust and the smell.

On the runway, with the plane standing ready behind them, Kitty, Diana and Richard had taken turns to shake hands in the formal English way. Kitty had wished the couple safe travel. Then she waited for them to walk away – in this public place she didn't expect any show of emotion. But Diana took her hand again. She looked into Kitty's face. Her own eyes – with their perfect eyeliner and dusting of green – were brimming with tears.

'How can I thank you, Kitty, for all you've done?' Diana's voice faltered; she waved her free hand, unable to say anything more. For a moment the two women stood still, caught between propriety and emotion. Then they moved into an embrace, hugging one another close, pressing their faces together.

When they finally pulled apart, Diana dabbed her eyes with a handkerchief. 'Take care of yourself, remember.'

'I'll try.'

'You will be fine,' Diana said firmly. Now it was her turn to be the one offering reassurance. 'But if all else fails, just run away from home. Join a convent.' She grinned, joking – but once she'd said the words, they took on a meaning of their own. Kitty's lips parted. She pictured the nuns in their blue tunics – the simplicity of their routines. She imagined how it would be, not having to leave the Mission at the end of the day. Not having to return home to play her part in the painful triangle that connected her with Theo and Charlotte . . .

'Give our goodbyes to Theo, won't you?' Richard's voice cut in.

'I will,' Kitty replied. She heard a note of anxiety in his voice. It was not a good time for him to be going away – the arson attack had been dealt with, but there were other issues at hand. Then again, the Scheme was always lurching from one crisis to another.

Kitty stood at the edge of the runway, set apart from the other people who'd come to farewell passengers. As she watched Diana and Richard climb the steps to the same converted bomber plane that had brought her here, she thought back over all the months that had passed since she arrived. So much had happened. So much had changed. She remembered how, on that first day, Diana had greeted her in Theo's place. Back then, Diana had been the stranger. Now her own husband was.

Kitty headed to her car, suddenly keen to get back to Londoni – to avoid being alone. She was almost there when she heard the sound of the aircraft starting up behind her. There was the familiar clatter of the engines firing, the propellers turning. Then a loud, constant roar filled the air. The sound travelled through Kitty, inhabiting every fibre of her body. Without the distractions of people, trucks or piles of luggage, the disembodied noise took her straight back to the airfield at Skellingthorpe. She felt the old fear in the pit of her stomach. Would Theo's plane return safely? Or was this the last goodbye?

She felt a wave of guilt – she'd never taken seriously before now just what effect this sound would have on Theo. Not to mention the distinctive shape and size of the Lancasters that came and went from Kongara (the addition of a few windows did little to change the look of the old bombers). No wonder Theo avoided coming out here. How could he not find himself reliving the horror of those years? Feeling the terror of wrestling a burning plane to the ground? Seeing again the tortured figure of his copilot Bobby being burned alive – becoming lost in the raw guilt of the survivor? Kitty felt a surge of compassion for him, rising up over the feelings of anger and betrayal that were, these days, her constant companions.

Over the years she'd come to see how Theo managed the effects of his terrible experiences through a careful system of engagement and avoidance. He could talk about some aspects of the war – he had to here in Kongara, where nearly all the men were ex-army, navy or air force – but not others. When confronted by something that pushed him beyond his boundaries, he retreated behind a wall of silence. Kitty couldn't help comparing him with Taylor, who'd been literally locked up with his fears and forced to come to terms with them. As a result Taylor seemed strong, free – happy.

Though it hurt Kitty to admit it, since Charlotte's arrival Theo had been brighter and more relaxed than he had been for years. After Charlotte had moved into the Shoebox, tensions between Theo and Kitty had escalated, of course – over his relationship with her, and over Kitty's insistence that she should be allowed to take up art again. He'd become even more irritable and distant with his wife than ever. Yet when Kitty saw him alone with Charlotte, he was light-hearted, even playful. Things had changed recently, though. Since the day he'd watched the marquee burning down, along with the plywood figures, the old nightmares had returned. Kitty had been woken frequently by Theo – yelling to his copilot, 'Get out! Get out! For God's sake, Bobby!', or just shouting incoherently. Kitty stayed with him until he calmed down, then she returned to the main bedroom. The sharing of comfort, the stroking of hair and skin, was not possible between them any more.

Kitty didn't know if Theo's relapse was due solely to the marquee fire calling up traumatic memories, or if he was also being brought down by the dark mood that had descended on Charlotte. The apiarist was still furious about her work being suspended. When she came to the house she either stalked around in cold silence, or spent her time railing at the stupidity of the OFC. Theo always tried to placate her. The problems would blow over. It was just a matter of paying lip service to the local chiefs, he said. Everything would soon be back on track. But Charlotte remained outraged.

Christmas dinner had been a disaster. There had been just the three of them at the table as usual. Most other families in Millionaire Row had arranged to join with their closest friends for the celebration since no one had relatives here. But Charlotte was too angry with the OFC – especially Richard – to want to socialise with any of them. Feeling her responsibility as the hostess, Kitty had attempted to brighten the mood by adding some Christmas crackers to her festive table. She'd found them in Ahmed's *duka*. They were made of red and green crepe paper decorated with silver snowflakes. Theo, Charlotte and Kitty all took turns pulling them, but no one put on the silly hats or read out the jokes. The trinkets lay abandoned among the knives and forks. Silence had settled on the table by the time Gabriel set down plates of roast turkey with all the trimmings. Eustace had outdone himself (Cynthia would have been proud) but no one was very hungry.

Kitty couldn't help thinking of Christmas meals back in Australia. The Millers would go over to Auntie Josie's place where a make-shift dining table consisting of planks laid over sawhorses was set up on the verandah. The women brought plates piled with food from the stifling kitchen, while the men rolled up their sleeves and drank beer. One end of the table was taken over by a whole tribe of cousins. Everyone seemed at their best, relaxed and humorous. Each Christmas since she'd left home, Kitty had been haunted by memories of these good times. This year's bleak company made the contrast between the past and the present even more painful than usual.

Over the plum pudding and brandy custard Charlotte had started talking about how delaying her project was affecting her bees. They were sensitive, she explained; they could pick up negative emotion. What the OFC was doing to them was a crime. Theo could do nothing but commiserate with her. When she snapped at him in response, Kitty felt torn between pleasure at the display of conflict and an odd sense of protectiveness around Theo that she could not understand. She wanted to laugh at herself – she was sorry for her husband because his lover was treating him harshly! It was crazy. And what was she even doing here, sharing her Christmas table with the pair as if it were a perfectly reasonable thing to do? Why didn't she just stand up and leave? Within the hour she could be at the Mission, joining the Fathers for an Italian feast. There would be lots of guests at their table. Tesfa, Sister Clara and some of the other nuns. A novice priest who was visiting from Kenya. Amosi would come in from the kitchen to join in, along with all the other helpers. Taylor would be there too. And Gili, of course, gambolling like a child in their midst . . . Kitty so much wanted to be there. She wasn't even sure what was stopping her getting into her car and going. Did she lack the courage to act? Or was she still bound by loyalty to Theo? Was it a matter of strength or weakness? She had no answer. She could only sit at the table, calm and quiet, and wait for the interminable meal to be over.

After Boxing Day, all the staff of the OFC had returned to work. The Manager of Agriculture continued his visits to the chiefs in the area to talk through the proposed bee project. There was no good news for Charlotte – not a single positive response. The Wagogo felt exactly as Taylor said they would.

Charlotte threatened to pack up and go home. She began spending her days at the Club, abandoning the special desk that had been

set up for her at Head Office. One evening Kitty overheard her
arguing with Theo about her right to have lunch at the Club with
whomever she chose – including Larry Green. Theo had sounded
almost distraught. On top of the stress surrounding Charlotte, he
was now carrying the added responsibility of the General Manager's
workload. Kitty was worried about how he was coping. But there
was such a gulf between them now that she didn't even try to talk
to him about her concerns. The conversation would be cut off
before it even began.

An outbreak of giggles interrupted her thoughts. Pippa was
now reading out a joke – something about a man who mistook his
wife for a car. Even Alice was laughing. Suddenly, Kitty couldn't
bear to stay by the pool any longer. She'd come this morning, as
instructed by Theo, to establish her place as the acting senior
memsahib. She'd made a token appearance, she decided, and
now she could leave.

She stood up and began folding her towel. Pippa lifted her eyes
from the pages of her magazine, peering over her pink-rimmed
sunglasses. 'Are you leaving us already?'

Kitty nodded politely. 'I've got things to do.'

Alice gave her a sharp look. 'But Diana's away.'

'I'm going on my own.' Kitty saw the women exchanging glances,
eyes lit with curiosity. Since the gossip about Theo and Charlotte
had spread, they'd been watching her avidly, as if her life was as
interesting as a radio serial.

'I'd like to come,' Evelyn said, a wistful note in her voice.

'Whatever for?' Audrey sounded puzzled.

'To see what it's like.'

Kitty smiled at Evelyn. 'You can come any time. Just let me know.'

The woman shook her head. 'I wouldn't be allowed.'

'I suppose not.' Kitty gave Evelyn a sympathetic look. Her husband was even stricter than some of the others.

'If you are short of things to occupy your time, Evelyn,' Alice's voice rang out, 'you could do more for the quiz night. We've nowhere near enough questions.'

Kitty stowed her towel in her shoulder bag and hurried to the changing shed.

In the damp, shady room, Kitty dressed quickly in her red-and-white spotted dress, not bothering to shower off the chlorine. She was already thinking of her studio. She intended to do another set of drawings of the little girl who was the model for the sculpture. Tulia had turned out to be a perfect choice. She stood completely still without a word of complaint for much longer periods of time than Kitty imagined a European child could manage. At the end of each session Kitty rewarded her with a bottle of Fanta, which she took half an hour to consume, sip by precious sip. Kitty had suggested paying her as well, but Father Remi insisted it was a great honour for Tulia to model for a statue being made for the grotto. Money could not be involved.

Meanwhile, some of the prisoners had been assigned to collect clay from the area around the spring. It was smooth and pale – almost like the porcelain Yuri had bought from a supplier in London. As Kitty towel-dried her hair then slipped on her shoes, she smiled at the memory of how proudly Taylor had showed a ball of clay to her, pressing it between his hands, pointing out that it was so fine it picked up the print of his skin.

Kitty was about to leave the shed when she heard voices coming from the other side of the back wall.

'*Umesikia habari?*' Have you heard the news?

'Tell me quickly, my brother. I should be in the kitchen.'

Kitty stopped to listen. The speakers were both male. She was puzzled as to why they were standing there: the space had been planted with spiky bushes since one of the pool attendants had been caught peeping through cracks in the flimsy walls.

The first voice continued, but the tone was lowered. Kitty could only hear fragments of what they were saying.

'. . . *nyuki kutoka mbali* . . .' Bees from a faraway place.

'*Yule mwenye nywele nyekunu.*' The woman with red hair.

'*Mchawi.*' The one with special powers.

Then came the words that made Kitty's breath catch in her throat. '*Itauawa.*' She will be killed. '*Itafanyikiwa leo hii.*' It will happen this very day.

Kitty stared at the wall as if she might be able to see through it. Who was saying such terrible things? Surely she must have heard wrongly or misinterpreted the Swahili. But since Kitty had been working at the Mission, her knowledge of the language had been improving by the day. The meanings of the words were quite clear.

She crept closer to the wall, straining her ears and struggling to keep up with translating, as one of the men spoke again.

'They departed for the big *shamba* early this morning. Ahmed's boy told me. He sold them petrol.' The voice was breathless with outrage. 'She was going to hang up her spirit houses. She has already chosen the place to begin – the twin *buyu* trees!'

'She deserves to die.'

'Maybe she is already dead.'

A third voice broke in then, coming from the direction of the pool. This time the words were in English. 'What are you two doing over there? Do you want to get in trouble? Get back to work!'

There was a rustling sound and gasps of pain. Kitty deduced the men were pushing their way out through the bushes. She rushed to the door, just in time to see two Africans hurrying away. They were dressed in plain shorts and shirts, with sandals made from old car tyres, like any number of the people who could be seen around Londoni. Kitty gazed after them helplessly. Should she shout for the pool guards to apprehend the men? They'd just deny what they had said. And it made no sense, anyway. How could Charlotte be setting up her hives today? Alice had only just been complaining that her husband had to hold meetings with chiefs all this week to discuss the plan and wouldn't have time to come home for lunch.

Kitty jogged out to her car – barefoot, shoes in hand – ignoring the curious looks of the Club patrons. She went straight to Head Office, driving so fast she only just managed to avoid hitting a chicken that strayed onto the road. When she pulled into the car park there was no sign of Theo's Land Rover. Even the *askari* who usually kept guard over it was absent. Theo's typist confirmed that the Acting General Manager had left Londoni early in the day, along with Lady Welmingham. As she gave Charlotte's name to Kitty, she suppressed a knowing smile.

'Where have they gone?' demanded Kitty.

'Down to the Units. They took the hives with them – at long last.' She shuddered. 'I live near the football field. I'm glad to see them gone.'

Back in her car, Kitty headed for Scotland Inch. Her stomach churned with tension. Her complex feelings for her husband were overlaid with anxiety. Right now, she just wanted to make sure he was safe.

To her relief, the Chief Inspector was standing outside the main tent, about to jump into a jeep loaded with *askaris*. He listened with an air of impatience while Kitty told him what she'd heard. She translated *mchawi* as 'witch', trying to help him understand.

When she was finished, he said nothing for a few seconds. Kitty clenched her hands in frustration.

'I know for certain they've taken the hives out there,' she repeated. 'They told me at Head Office.'

'I know they have, too,' the Inspector said calmly. 'Theo came here on the way to discuss it with me. I gave him an armed escort. I think they'll be fine. And I've got a lot to do.' He nodded at the men in his jeep. 'There's been a burglary at the Tractor Workshops.'

Kitty stared in disbelief. 'You aren't listening to what I'm saying! The men said she was going to be murdered. *Today.*'

He gave her a condescending look. 'Because the lady's a witch, no less.' He rolled his eyes. 'Mrs Hamilton, if I took notice of every rumour and conspiracy that was reported to me, I'd do nothing but chase my tail. There's a new story every day.' He chuckled. 'But a "witch" – I mean, seriously . . .'

'You don't understand,' Kitty said. 'Bees are sacred to the Wagogo. They would see someone who interfered with them as being a *mchawi* – that's the word they use.'

Kitty preferred the Swahili term – it didn't have that link with tall hats and bubbling cauldrons; make-believe tales for children. She knew the *mchawi* were a real force in Tanganyikan society. Tesfa had described cases where they had used their powers for good – but when they were bent on causing harm, they were terrifying. It was to break a curse, he'd reminded Kitty, that Taylor's friend had gone to retrieve his spear. If he hadn't done so, the man would certainly have died. For a *mchawi* to be accused of using magic against their neighbour was very serious. If they weren't sufficiently feared by their community, they could be driven from their village or even killed. Quite often, accused 'witches' were just old women who had no husband or sons to protect them – they were used as scapegoats, blamed for outbreaks of disease or the failure of the rains or some other calamity. Apparently, there was a Passionist Mission in the north of the country that ran a refuge for these outcasts, but the monks never had enough room for all the women who sought help. There were these sad cases, and then there were the genuine *mchawi* capable of great evil. It didn't matter which group Charlotte was meant to belong to. She was in grave danger.

The Inspector sighed. 'Look, the *askaris* will step in if there's any trouble. So there's really nothing to worry about. I think you're getting a little carried away.' He gave her a pitying half-smile. 'Perhaps you feel personally involved. You'd like Lady Welmingham to be seen as a witch. And who could blame you?'

Kitty just looked at him for a few moments. The words that came to her were ones she'd first heard in the shearing shed. It took all her self-control to turn and walk away.

The Hillman jolted along the road to the Units, lurching from bump to bump. Kitty gripped the steering wheel, only just keeping the car in control. Her eyes were trained on the road ahead most of the time, but when the plantations came into view she snatched quick looks when she could. The peanut seedlings had grown into proper plants, making blobs of bright green against the earth. They were in dead-straight rows running side by side, reminding Kitty of the lines of plaits the village girls wove in their hair. Even at a glance, though, she noticed that the ground was not evenly covered with plants. There were sections where the crop thinned out; in the distance she could see a large patch that was completely bald.

The plantations seemed endless, but at last she reached the outer part of the settlement. From the conditions of the place, she guessed it was the Native Labour Camp. Originally, the accommodation had consisted of rows of army tents like the ones in Londoni, but it had become overcrowded – crude shelters made from bits of old tin, plywood, even cardboard, had been built up against the canvas walls. Along with smoking piles of rubbish dotted here and there, the makeshift structures created a general air of squalor. The camp was empty of people – Kitty assumed the workers would be out in the fields or in the workshops. Their families, of course, were not here.

Kitty sped straight on. The tents gave way to long bunkhouses and mess halls. There was a Nissen hut – a smaller version of the kind that had been converted into the Kongara Club. Outside it was a collection of giant reels made from wood, which had once held steel cable. They'd been placed on their sides to make tables. Crates served as chairs. A cheerfully painted sign erected nearby said *The Contractor's Arms*. A couple of European workers wearing filthy singlets and shorts sat at one of the tables drinking beer. As she reached them Kitty braked, winding down her window.

'Where's the main office?' she called to them.

'And top of the morning to you too,' a man replied sarcastically in a broad Irish accent.

'Sorry, I'm not trying to be rude – it's an emergency.'

The Irishman gave Kitty a sceptical look, then pointed in the direction she was heading. 'You can't miss it.'

The car rolled forward, then picked up speed. Kitty swallowed, trying to quell the anxiety twisting her stomach. Theo was out here somewhere. And Charlotte, with her bees. Kitty had to find them, stop them, before it was too late. The chilling comment about Charlotte that she'd overheard in the changing room came back to her.

Maybe she is already dead.

Kitty felt a wave of sickness. Nothing Charlotte had done – including sleeping with her husband – could even be weighed up in the face of such a horrifying prospect. But there were *askaris* with them, Kitty reminded herself. Surely men with rifles were a match for a crowd armed only with spears and knives, no matter how angry they were.

At last, a collection of large sheds and water tanks came into view. As she drew closer to them, she leaned forward, searching for Theo's Land Rover. There was a line of vehicles parked outside the main building, but all of them were trucks or tractors or massive harvesters.

Drawing up outside, she half ran towards the doorway. She hoped this wasn't the Unit controlled by Larry Green – that would only add to the complexity of the situation. As she hurried inside she planned what she would say. With the Inspector, she now thought, she'd been too hasty, panicking in her desire to make him understand. She had to ensure this man took her seriously. The Unit Manager would have no authority over Theo, but at least he could help find where they were. And then . . . Kitty's step faltered. She'd never been able to make Theo listen to her before – why should it be any different now? But she had to try.

The air inside the building was hot and stuffy. Kitty took in the scene quickly. A couple of Africans were tinkering with an engine that was in pieces on the floor. There was a desk nearby, with nothing on it but an electric fan and a broken pencil. The chair was empty.

'*Wapi bwana?*' she called out to the Africans. Where's the boss?

The men waved vaguely towards the distance. 'He is not here, Memsahib. You may find him outside.'

Kitty spun on her heels, marching for the door. She just managed to stop as a figure appeared in front of her – coming in as she was going out. In the half-second it took to avoid hitting him, she recognised the man's shape, posture. Then they were face to face.

'Kitty! What are you doing here?' Taylor must have read her

emotions on her face. He frowned in concern. 'What on earth's wrong?'

Kitty didn't try to frame her words carefully with Taylor – she knew he'd believe what she had to say. She just blurted it all out. He stopped her as she mentioned the twin *buyu* trees.

'They're on Unit Three. Let's go in your car.'

He raced outside, Gili at his heels.

Kitty expected Taylor to take over the driving but he jumped into the passenger seat. As he folded his long legs into the footwell, Gili leapt about him, excited by the new setting, before crouching on the shelf behind the rear seats.

'Get back on the main road,' Taylor instructed Kitty. 'Then turn left.'

As she drove, she retold Taylor everything she'd heard. When she suggested the armed *askaris* would be able to protect Charlotte from whatever kind of attack had been planned – even if it involved a large number of people – he shook his head grimly. 'They might protect her and Theo, but the outcome will still be a disaster. If there was one thing guaranteed to cause the biggest upset with the Wagogo, it would be to hang hives of foreign bees in the twin *buyus*. They are sacred. Women who are unable to conceive take offerings to them. The people will be about as pleased as the English would be if someone desecrated Westminster Abbey.'

They drove on in silence as if the weight of any more words might slow the speed of the car. In spite of her anxiety Kitty was filled with gratitude that Taylor was here beside her. She suspected he'd failed to talk sense into Theo in the past, but she hoped it would be different out here on the Units. Cut off from Head Office with all its trappings of European power, surely Theo would defer to Taylor's knowledge of the people, the place – and see reason? He had to.

A single baobab tree came into view, standing in the middle of the plantation. The rows of plants veered around it. Kitty wondered whether this had been done out of respect for the tree or because they were so much work to remove. A solitary *askari* stood to attention beside its trunk.

'Looks like they've been at work already.' Taylor pointed to where it was just possible to see a dark-grey shape hanging from a branch of the tree. He gestured for Kitty to turn off the road. She kept the speed up as she drove onto the soft earth; in her rear-vision mirror she saw mangled plants flying into the air behind them.

When they were barely at a standstill, Taylor got out, running up to the *askari*. The exchange of Swahili was rapid. Listening from her place at the wheel, Kitty couldn't follow what was being said, but she could see the African was upset and worried.

Taylor jumped back into the car. 'They began with this tree. There were no problems, but they left the *askari* here as a precaution. He doesn't want to stay. He believes the bees are bewitched. He said the others moved on to the twin *buyus* a couple of hours ago. Let's hope we're not too late.'

The tops of the twin baobabs finally came into sight, rising above a thicket of bush that must have proven too stubborn for the bulldozers. Like before, Kitty turned off the track, driving cross-country towards them.

The lower boughs of the two trees became visible. Kitty caught her breath. A crowd of Africans was gathered around the trunks.

There must have been almost a hundred tribesmen. Not far away stood the Land Rover. Taylor swore quietly.

Kitty drove on, the scene unfolding in fragments as she glanced up from watching the ground ahead. She saw the angled lines of spears. Red-ochre tones of traditional cloths. Sun gleaming on the windows of the Land Rover. Khaki-clad *askaris* bunched together at the centre of the crowd. And in their midst – in the gap between the two trunks – a flash of red hair, a honey-toned shirt. Theo's sunhat, and a glimpse of his face.

'Stop here,' Taylor said when they were about fifty yards away. As Kitty turned off the engine, one of the *askaris* could be heard yelling at the people. A man shouted back, followed by others. A chant began, growing loud and fierce as it spread through the crowd. The noise frightened Gili, who jumped into Kitty's arms and clung there.

'If things get out of hand, Kitty, drive away.' Taylor looked into Kitty's eyes. 'I mean it. I want you to stay safe.'

'Be careful,' Kitty called to him as he was already walking away.

Taylor strode towards the mob, his hands held out a little at his sides; Kitty realised he was making sure everyone could see he was not armed. Before he reached the edge of the crowd, a scuffle broke out as some men from the back began pushing forward, holding up their spears. The *askaris* responded by using the bayonet blades fixed to their rifles to drive them back. There was a tangle of bodies, people yelling and raising their fists, but the soldiers won out. An open space was created around Theo and Charlotte.

Kitty rose in her seat, trying to see them more clearly. Charlotte was cowering behind Theo, her head turning from side to side as if she could not believe her eyes. For his part, Theo just stood there with his arms folded. If he was afraid, he gave no sign of it. He was like a school principal facing an unruly assembly – he was preserving his dignity and waiting for the rabble to settle.

A ripple ran through the crowd as Taylor's arrival was noticed. When he reached the edge of the gathering a pathway opened up, letting him walk through towards Theo and Charlotte. People called out to Taylor as he passed. Kitty saw him nod, taking in what they were saying. He moved slowly, evenly, like someone approaching a bird that might take fright and fly away.

Kitty watched to see how Theo would react when he caught sight of Taylor. But even when the man was right in front of him, Theo refused to acknowledge his presence. The people began pushing in again. One of the *askaris* jabbed threateningly with his bayonet. Taylor turned from Theo to the Africans and back. He was talking steadily – Kitty could see his gestures, though she was too far away to hear his words.

Charlotte called out something then. The strident tone of her voice and the rude way she pointed at the tribesmen roused a rumble of outrage. Taylor held up his hands to quell the emotion.

Kitty looked away as the sound of a vehicle engine came to her. A jeep was approaching, following the tracks she'd left printed on the field. She guessed the mechanics must have listened to the interchange she'd had with Taylor and alerted their boss. As the jeep came closer, she saw Larry Green at the wheel.

She got out of the car and walked a few steps closer to the crowd. Theo still stood there like a figure made from wood, impervious to his surroundings. Kitty's nerves tightened in alarm. The clues were tiny; it was a feeling she had, more than anything, that he was not really here. He was lost in another place, another time. She tried to extricate herself from Gili's grasp, intending to take him back to the car, but he refused to let go. The harder she pulled at his fingers, the closer he clung to her. Something about this scene terrified him. It occurred to Kitty that the commotion could be reminding him of when he'd first been captured, and the torture that followed.

Wrapping her arms over Gili's back, she strode towards the crowd. She kept her eyes on Theo, her heart thumping with alarm. Closer now, she could see the blank look on his face.

Suddenly, Theo started shouting. 'Get out! Get out!'

Kitty recognised the words, the tone, from his nightmares. She broke into a run, jolting Gili against her chest. She could see the Africans were taking Theo's cries as a direct attack on them. Taylor was staring at Theo, unable to make sense of the man's behaviour.

Theo then began shaking his head. 'No! No!'

Kitty saw his hand reach into his pocket. As if in slow motion she watched him take out the pistol, releasing the safety catch.

'Theo – no!' she shouted. *'Stop!'*

The sound of her voice appeared to break his trance. He looked towards her – but showed no sign that he could see her.

'Let me talk to you,' Kitty said. 'Wait!'

He stood rock-still, the pistol poised in his hand. But then Charlotte began screaming. The cries must have panicked him: he swung round to his right, then back the other way, as though searching for a hidden enemy. Taylor ran towards him, pleading with him to lower his gun. But Theo took no notice. He raised the pistol clumsily – barely taking aim – and began firing.

Kitty's eyes widened in disbelief; this couldn't be happening. But in front of Theo, a man fell to the ground. Then another. From behind her, Kitty heard the sound of the car window being shattered, glass falling. Theo was firing wildly in all directions. She ducked, hunching over Gili. Everywhere people were screaming. There was chaos as they tried to run away, pushing one another over, trampling the fallen.

Now Taylor was right beside him. Theo seemed to snap out of his daze. He frowned, shaking his head, struggling towards clarity. But the moment passed. Theo's face became a mask again, darkness returned to his eyes. A scream stuck in Kitty's throat as she saw the barrel of the pistol – a silver streak – swing towards Taylor's head.

Another loud bang – sharp and clear – echoed over the plains. Kitty froze. The air felt suddenly empty, as if the whole world had come to a halt. Then Theo staggered forward, slumping to the ground.

Kitty watched in horror as blood welled from a wound in his back, vivid red invading the khaki. Another shot rang out. Only then did Kitty notice the *askari* standing to her left – his rifle was raised to his shoulder, his body leaning into the aim.

Taylor yelled at the *askari*. Kitty didn't need to translate his words to know what he was saying.

Stop shooting! Stop shooting!

He is already dead.

Kitty screamed Theo's name as she ran to him. He had fallen onto his chest but his face was turned sideways. Blood oozed from a red hole in his temple. His eyes were wide open, his brows raised as though he were still trying to understand what was going on. Kitty stared, motionless. Her brain, her heart, refused to accept what her eyes could see.

Shock travelled through her, emptying her of feelings, thoughts. Her breath came in gasps. Small sensations loomed large as if to distract her from the nightmare – the earth under her shins was rough, hard; the acrid smell of cordite stung her nostrils. The cry of a bird passing overhead pierced her ears.

Moments passed, shapeless, empty. Kitty gazed at Theo's body. His unblinking eyes. His golden hair stained with red. She was dimly aware of Taylor moving nearby. The urgent voices of the *askaris*. She heard Charlotte whimpering, but from some distance away. Then came Larry's voice, sounding shocked and confused, the words unintelligible.

With an effort, Kitty turned her head. Taylor was crouched beside a tribesman lying on the ground.

'*Wapi unasikia uchungu?*' Where is your pain? Let me see.

After examining him quickly, Taylor moved to look at another man who'd been shot in the leg. Not far away, an *askari* was already tying a cloth over someone with a shoulder wound. Two other Africans seemed to have only minor injuries. No one else was dead, Kitty realised – only Theo.

Theo. Dead.

She held the words at bay, refusing to let them be real. She told herself she should be helping with the wounded. Janet had trained her in first aid so that she could be useful when needed. And she was needed . . . But her body was made of stone. She could not move.

Taylor stood up and came towards her. He squatted beside her. 'Oh, Kitty – I'm so sorry. I tried to stop him . . .' He broke off, as if at a loss. Kitty just shook her head. She could not speak. Taylor placed his hand on her shoulder. His touch was firm but gentle. Kitty wanted to collapse against him, to bury her face in his chest – but she knew that if she let herself do that, she would break apart. Instead she just held Gili close.

'Kitty, listen to me.' Taylor's voice was low and steady. 'We have to get out of here.' He looked away, frowning tensely. The tribesmen had regrouped just beyond the baobabs. They hovered there restlessly, the tips of their spears flashing in the sunlight. He turned back to Kitty. 'The trouble's not over.'

Kitty nodded. Rousing herself, she lifted her hand to push back her hair. Then she froze. It was crimson, dripping blood.

She stared at her hand. The red, blurred by tears, was a fog invading her brain. She tried to think – to tell herself Theo had not aimed at her. It was a wild shot, like the one that had struck the car. He'd not pointed the pistol directly at anyone – except, perhaps, the inhabitants of his visions. She felt for the pain that should be there, but numbness had enveloped her body. Gili made no protest as Taylor lifted him from her arms. It was then – in that moment when the creature was still being held by them both – that the source of the blood became clear. It was not Kitty who had been hit, but the monkey who'd been clinging onto her, his body shielding hers.

This new shock drove the haze from Kitty's mind. Her focus returned. Calm strength rose inside her. She took Gili back from Taylor and laid the limp body on the ground. Crouching over him, she put her ear to his chest. She picked up a faint but steady heartbeat. She could feel his shallow breath against her cheek. She looked up at Taylor, meeting his stricken gaze.

'He's alive.'

Kitty searched the blood-sodden fur, finding two wounds. One was small, but the other was gaping wide, leaking a steady stream of blood.

Taylor pulled a handkerchief from his pocket and rolled it into a tight ball. Kitty took it from him, pressing it against the larger wound to plug the hole.

'That's the exit wound,' Taylor said, 'where the bullet came out.' He glanced over Kitty's left side. 'You were lucky it missed you. Must have been the angle of the shot, or the way you were holding him.'

While Kitty held the wad in place, Taylor cut a strip of cloth from his shirt with a penknife, making a bandage to tie over it.

They attended to the second wound, binding it up tightly. When this was done, Kitty stood up, holding Gili against her body. Taylor looked torn – he reached out one hand towards the monkey – but then he turned on his heels, heading for the *askaris* and the injured men.

Left alone with Gili, Kitty moved back to stand beside Theo's body. The first flies were buzzing around the seeping wound. In the hot sun, blood was already crusting on his skin.

She tore her gaze away. Again, she had the sense that if she let reality flood in, she would not be strong enough to contain it. She focused instead on Taylor, who was striding around, giving instructions to the *askaris*. At each step he was shadowed by two tribesmen who were talking loudly and gesticulating. Taylor was responding to the pair in calm tones but Kitty could see that he was worried.

Taylor went to stand beside the *askari* who had fired the shots at Theo. The man was sitting on the ground, his head in his hands, the rifle cast aside near his feet.

'*Umeamua vizuri,*' Taylor said to him in a firm tone. You had to shoot. You made the right decision.

The *askari* lifted his head, looking into Taylor's face. After a little while he nodded, his shoulders sagging with relief.

Taylor organised three of the men to lift Theo's body, grasping him by his legs and shoulders. With Taylor supporting the head, the group moved off towards the Hillman. Kitty stayed where Theo had lain, staring at the dark stain left behind on the ground. The twin baobabs stood nearby, a silent, watchful presence. She peered up into the branches of the one closest to her. She saw pieces of cloth tied around the grey-skinned limbs. Some had been put there recently – the patterns were still bright. Others were old and frayed, leached of any colour. There were small carvings dangling there, too, and leather pouches of the kind witchdoctors made for carrying charms. Kitty was swept by a sense of something powerful and alien. Theo and Charlotte should not have come to this place. The plantation should not be here. Kitty should not be here.

Lowering her eyes from the tree, she found that a group of Africans had moved closer. Several looked at her with open antipathy. Others appeared more curious. Near the front of the group was an old woman. Kitty stared in surprise. Why she was here, among all these men? Kitty met the unwavering gaze – clear eyes in a wizened face. The woman put her hand to her chest, the palm open, over her heart. Kitty recognised the gesture was an acknowledgement – from one woman to another – of the tragedy that had just taken place. The exchange with the old woman made her feel stronger, as if her loss were a part of all the losses that others had endured before her – and survived. Kitty nodded slowly, then stumbled away, following in the wake of her husband's body.

Reaching the Hillman, she saw that Theo now lay on the back seat. His legs had been bent in order for the doors to be closed. Someone had spread a *kitenge* to cover him. The red, yellow and green pattern seemed too bright – too full of life.

As Kitty climbed into the passenger side, Taylor took the driver's seat.

'We can go now,' he said. 'Larry will bring the others.' Before starting the car, he leaned over to check on Gili, who was now draped across Kitty's lap. He cradled the little head in his hand. He swallowed hard as if to control his emotions.

'*Mwanangu gwe*,' he murmured. My little one whom I love.

The tender phrase broke through Kitty's shock, touching her heart. Grief over Theo's death flooded through her. It blended with her fears for Gili and her sympathy for Taylor. The twin strands of pain built up inside her until they became too great to contain. She bent her head, looking down at Gili – a limp shape resting against the red-and-white spotted fabric of her dress. Tears rose to her eyes, brimming over. She let them flow unhindered, streaming down her cheeks, drops falling onto the soft grey fur.

Gili's eyes were closed, his little hands unfurled. A dribble of saliva ran from his slack mouth. The flow of blood had been slowed but not stopped; the handkerchief was a sodden ball of red. Kitty dared not feel for his pulse. At least half an hour had passed since she'd listened to his heart back by the baobab trees – and in that time he'd neither moved nor made a sound. She knew he could be dying, right now as she watched. She willed Taylor to drive faster. But she understood he was torn between wanting to push the car to its limit, and not wanting to jolt Gili by hitting bumps at speed.

All the time, as Kitty watched over Gili, another part of her mind was constantly running back over what had just happened. She kept seeing the image of Theo shooting, the close-up sight of the pistol, the small straight barrel . . . The shouting, the screaming. Then that single, louder shot. Theo falling. It was all so clear in Kitty's mind: every action, every word that had been spoken. One moment the reality was stark and real. But the next, she could not really believe Theo was dead – even when she pictured his body slumped on the back seat, right behind her.

'I can see the others coming now.'

Taylor's voice cut into her thoughts. Kitty turned to look through the rear window. Some distance back along the road, avoiding the dust raised by the Hillman, was Larry's open-backed jeep. Charlotte was in the front passenger seat, her red hair flying in the wind. Behind her, Kitty could see the black heads of the injured tribesmen. There was no sign of the *askaris* with their red fezzes, but she guessed they were in the Land Rover. She was in the midst of turning back around – her gaze skimming past the cloth-covered mound in the rear – when something caught her eye. Theo's arm was hanging out over the edge of the seat. The sight of it there wrenched at her heart. The hand, with its gracefully curved fingers, seemed so fragile, his slender wrist so vulnerable. His watch was too big and heavy. She looked at the pearly watch-face encased in white gold, remembering Theo telling her it had been a twenty-first birthday gift from his father. It meant a lot to him that the watch had been chosen by the Admiral, and not Louisa. Kitty felt a wave of compassion for the old couple, who would soon hear such terrible news. But she couldn't think of them now. Her own emotions were enough to deal with. She shifted her eyes from the watch. Something else drew her attention, then: on Theo's forearm was a small scar – the result of a childhood accident with a penknife. It was this tiny smudge of white that finally pierced the cloud of unreality in Kitty's head. This body lying on the seat – this still, silent shape – really was Theo. The man she had once loved so much. The only lover she'd ever had.

In her mind she looked back, setting aside the Theo of recent years, seeing instead the man he had been when they first met – so full of hopes and dreams. Before the war broke his spirit. Before he slid back into the Hamilton fold. She pictured him in goggles and a civilian flying jacket, standing by his bright-red plane. How he'd loved being up in the air, the whole world at his feet.

Kitty stared ahead through the windscreen. She could feel a tangled mass of thoughts, emotions waiting to engulf her again – but she held them off. She focused only on Theo. He was flying free now. His nightmares were finally over. She imagined his soul rising up into the blue African sky, leaving all the struggles behind – soaring like an eagle over the land.

NINETEEN

Taylor pulled up outside Scotland Inch, sounding the car horn, keeping the engine running. After just a few seconds the Inspector came out, looking affronted. Recognising Kitty in the passenger's seat, he began striding towards her, his bushy ginger eyebrows drawn into a frown. When he was close, Taylor beckoned him to his side of the car.

'I assume you've got an explanation for your appalling lack of manners?' The Inspector stood back from the window, scowling.

'Hamilton's been killed.' Taylor's voice was flat and low. 'He's in the back.'

'What?' The Inspector's head jerked round. As he peered into the rear of the car, his eyes bulged in shock.

'Green's headed for the hospital with three injured,' Taylor added. He gestured towards Gili. 'We're going to the vet. I'll get back here as soon as I can.'

'No, no – absolutely not!' The Inspector put his hand on the car as if to stop it being driven away. He pointed to an area of gravel marked out with white stones. 'Park over there.'

Taylor shook his head. 'We're not stopping now.'

While the Inspector was still trying to absorb his words, Taylor drove off. The image of the police officer's face stayed with Kitty. It was a parody of shock and disbelief. She felt a wave of dislike for the man – the way he'd dismissed her concerns earlier and refused to offer help. She sensed he didn't really care even now about what had occurred down on the plains today – he just wanted to be in charge.

Kitty's thoughts broke off suddenly, her whole body tensing. She thought she'd heard something. Bending over Gili, she listened intently.

'What's happened?' Taylor asked.

Kitty gave no reply, her ears still strained towards the little creature. After what felt like ages, she heard a soft whimper. Then, as she searched the monkey's face, his eyelids fluttered. She turned to Taylor.

'I think he's coming round!'

Taylor smiled with relief, but only briefly. He knew as well as Kitty did that regaining consciousness was only a small step.

Kitty stroked the monkey's back lightly, her fingers barely touching his fur. She let the sensation overtake her, keeping her thoughts at bay.

As they neared the small brick building that housed the veterinary surgery, Kitty searched for Alan Carr's truck. There was every chance the vet would be out in the field: his passion was the experimental cattle-breeding program – ranching was another possible scheme for the area – and he was often seen driving around Londoni with a cow or two in a pen on the back tray. Kitty was relieved to spot his truck parked under a tree. Down the side of the building, where a sign said *Entrance*, a door stood ajar.

Taylor switched off the engine. Small sounds broke into the sudden quiet – the distant crow of a rooster, the tick-tick of the engine cooling, the creak of springs – as Kitty stared at the limp body, willing the legs, the arms, the hands to move. But sprawled there on her lap, Gili could have been dead.

Taylor opened his door, letting in a cloud of dust. 'I'll take him in,' he said. 'I'll be back as soon as I can.'

'No, wait,' Kitty said. She didn't want to be left alone out here. On the other hand, she didn't want to abandon Theo's body. She was still deciding what to do when there was a sudden flurry of dust and noise outside. Two jeeps arrived, one behind the other. The Inspector drove the first; the second was loaded with *askaris*.

As soon as his vehicle came to a halt, the Inspector jumped out. He already had his notebook in hand. Kitty cowered at the sight of him approaching. Facing him, now, was more than she could bear.

'It's all right,' Taylor said. 'I'll deal with him. You take Gili in.'

Kitty waited while Taylor came round to open the door, then she climbed out. She held Gili stiffly in her arms, trying to keep him steady and not crush his body.

'I won't be long,' Taylor said.

Kitty didn't move. She felt suddenly overwhelmed by dread. They would lose Gili, like she'd lost Theo. She tried to take a deep breath, but it sounded like a sob.

Taylor reached out his hand, gently pushing her hair back from her face. He gave her a faint nod. She knew what it meant. Be strong a little longer. You can do it. As he looked into her eyes, she felt his strength reaching her. Lifting her chin, she nodded in reply.

*

424

'What can I do for you, Mrs Hamilton?'

The vet barely glanced up from his microscope as Kitty walked into the surgery. She hardly knew Alan – they'd only met once or twice before at the Club. The man hardly ever went to social events. (The ladies at the Club were undecided if this was due to the scandal surrounding his wife's affair with Cynthia's ill-fated husband, or if he just spent all of his time working.) Today, Kitty was glad of Alan's trademark brusqueness. She didn't have the resources to make small talk or exchange pleasantries. And she didn't want to have to discuss what had occurred – to explain why her eyes were red and swollen. If she let that reality back into her head, she might sink to the floor and not be able to get up again.

'I've got a monkey,' Kitty said bluntly. 'He's badly hurt.'

'For God's sake, put the thing down before it bites you.'

Kitty lifted her head in surprise. But then she remembered, from her years on the farm, that even the tamest animal could be aggressive when injured. Alan wasn't to know that Gili had not responded this way. She laid the monkey carefully down on a stainless-steel examination bench. He looked very small, stranded there – the space was large enough for a big dog or even a sheep. As she took her hands away, Gili moaned. Then he turned his head, as if wanting to escape the glare of the bright overhead lamp.

'Did you see that?' Kitty said to Alan. 'He moved!'

The vet gave no response. He just stood back from the table, eyeing the monkey with a neutral expression. After a few moments, he sighed. 'Look – it's thoughtful of you to bring the poor creature in.' He cast his gaze over Kitty's blood-stained dress. 'But you've ruined your frock for nothing, I'm afraid. In these cases I only do one thing. Quick injection. Put it to sleep.'

Kitty's swallowed. Her throat was clamped up; she didn't think she could speak.

'I can see you're upset – but don't feel too bad,' Alan added. 'It happens all the time. Cars and wild animals just don't go together.'

It took Kitty a few seconds to make sense of what he was saying. 'No – you don't understand. He's not wild. He wasn't run over.'

'Ah, a pet.' Alan pursed his lips. 'Mrs Hamilton, I'll be honest with you. I believe native animals should be left alone, to live where they belong. If you want a pet, you should have a dog or a cat. The very last thing you should have is a monkey. I've seen some bad bites in my time. Rabies is a serious risk – and there's no cure, you know.'

Kitty's hands clenched together. Tears of desperation welled in her eyes. In her mind – still reeling with shock – Gili's fate was tied up with Theo's death. It was as if she thought that by saving Gili, she could bring her husband back, even though it made no sense.

'Please, just do something!'

'All right. All right.' Alan held up his hands as if Kitty had been threatening him. 'I'll take a look at it.'

The vet pulled on a pair of leather gloves before approaching Gili cautiously and untying the strips of cloth. As Taylor had done, back on the plains, he parted the matted fur. 'What happened to it?'

'He was shot. It was an accident.'

Alan glanced up at her. 'People are much too casual with guns out here. They seem to think that just because they're in Africa, they should spend their time hunting.' He turned back to the monkey, continuing his examination. 'Obviously there are internal injuries.

Bowel could well be perforated. Spinal injuries are a possibility. My advice is the same, I'm afraid. It needs to be put to sleep.'

'There must be something you can do,' Kitty pleaded.

'Well, of course there are things I could do,' Alan said patiently. 'I could take X-rays. I could perform complex surgery. I could put on hold the work I am meant to be doing and devote myself to a regime of complicated post-operative care. And the animal would most likely still die.'

'Please save him. I'll nurse him. I'll do anything.'

Alan's voice softened. 'The fact is, Mrs Hamilton, the animal needs to be put out of its misery. If you'd like me to explain my decision to your husband, I'd be more than happy to do so.'

Kitty instinctively leaned over Gili, shielding him. Looking towards the door, she willed Taylor to appear. But what would he be able to do? However inept Alan might be in other areas of his life, Kitty had no reason to doubt his opinion as a vet.

'In a situation like this, it's best to move quickly,' Alan went on. 'Deliberating won't change anything. It just becomes more upsetting.' He crossed to a metal cabinet and opened the door. While he rifled through the contents, he spoke over his shoulder. 'If you'd prefer to hold the animal, that's fine. Or you can leave it with me.'

Kitty's lips moved as she hunted for words. Everything was happening too quickly. She was hardly able to think.

'You can collect the body for burial or I can arrange disposal.' When he turned around, he held a syringe poised in his hands. He stepped towards the table.

'Don't touch him.' Kitty placed herself between him and the monkey.

'Mrs Hamilton, you're being selfish – do you understand that?' The vet spoke sharply now, as if Kitty were a child. 'Think of the animal.'

'I am thinking of him.' Kitty gathered Gili into her arms, holding him against her chest. 'If he's going to die, I don't want it to be here.'

'It's your decision,' Alan replied. 'I can only give you my best advice.'

Kitty barely heard him as she ran from the room.

She was midway down the side of the building when Taylor rounded the corner. At the sight of her there, holding Gili, he stopped dead.

'He wouldn't help,' she cried when she reached him. 'He wanted to . . .' She forced herself to go on. 'He wanted to put him to sleep.'

Taylor's shoulders slumped as her words sank in. A dense quiet surrounded them. Kitty searched for expressions of comfort, but could find none. Finally, he drew in a long breath. 'They've taken Theo to the morgue, over at the hospital. They said you can go there as soon as you're ready.'

Kitty glanced in the direction of the hospital buildings, but then shook her head. She wasn't ready to face Theo's lifeless body again. And she didn't want to leave Taylor and Gili. For a long moment she just stood there. She could feel the warmth of the monkey's body against her chest, the almost imperceptible movement of his ribs as he breathed. Only a miracle could save him. Soon the time would come when his heart stopped beating, his breath died away, and he was gone.

She looked up at the sky as if some comfort could be found there. In the wide expanse of blue no birds flew, no clouds floated.

The sun burned with a merciless heat. She felt at a loss. Then something came to her – a sense rather than a thought. A vision of peace. Of cool, still air and welcoming shade. A shelter, where she would be shielded from the nightmare that had overtaken her. And where by some deep mystery it was possible – just sometimes – to find healing when all hope had been lost.

When the car drew up at the edge of the forecourt, the two Fathers were standing in the shadow cast by the bell-tower, their heads bent close, deep in conversation. The unexpected sight of Kitty and Taylor arriving together – or perhaps the expressions on their faces – caused Father Remi to lift his robe and run across. Father Paulo hurried after him, urgency bringing strength to his old limbs.

'What has happened?'

As Taylor handed Gili through the open window, laying him in Father Paulo's arms, he gave an account of what had taken place. Hearing the facts stated like this brought reality home to Kitty again. She hid her face in her hands. During the drive out here, she'd felt as though her very existence was being held in suspension until they reached the Mission. Now they had arrived, all the emotions she'd held at bay crowded in. Panic rose inside her, the wave of horror building. This time, she knew, it was going to break over her, engulfing her in darkness.

Father Remi almost lifted Kitty from the car, holding her against his broad chest. She was like a feeble child, a ragdoll with no strength. Burying her face against the rough cotton of his robe, she felt the contours of his embroidered badge pressing into her cheek.

The heart. The sign of love, and hope. She heard the murmur of Taylor's voice, blended with the deeper tones of Father Paulo. Then the sounds faded, and were gone.

Kitty had no sense of how long she stood there with Father Remi. When she was ready, he led her across to the arched building. There, in the room they used as a clinic, Father Paulo was already at work washing out Gili's wounds with water. Grim-faced and tense, he moved aside as the younger priest appeared.

Father Remi motioned for Kitty to join Taylor, who was standing near the table where Gili lay.

'Tincture of iodine, Kitty,' he said. 'And my ointment.' Father Remi spoke bluntly, as though this were any ordinary day in the clinic. Kitty took on the tasks gratefully – slipping into her role as nurse. It steadied her, making her feel more connected with normality.

As Father Remi dabbed on the iodine, Gili whimpered in protest. Then the monkey began to struggle feebly, wriggling both arms and legs.

Kitty met Taylor's gaze – a flash of hope running between them.

'Hold him still, Taylor,' the Father instructed. 'Kitty, take his shoulders.' He smoothed on some of his ointment, the musky smell spreading into the air. 'This will help the pain.'

Finally he tied a wide bandage in place over the two wounds, the white cloth standing out against the smoky grey coat.

The ointment worked quickly, and soon Gili was still and quiet again. Kitty tried to work out if he'd lapsed back into unconsciousness or if he was just resting – she knew one of the symptoms of shock was extreme tiredness.

It was then that Father Paulo spoke up. 'Let us carry him to the reception room.' He talked in Swahili – the only language everyone knew. 'We will be more comfortable there. We have a long night ahead of us.'

Frankincense drifted on the slight breeze that blew in through the open windows, blending with the tang of disinfectant and the sweet smell of Father Remi's ointment. Father Paulo's voice seemed to float as well, a soft resonance in the air as he chanted a Latin prayer. He sat in his favourite armchair. Nearby lay Gili, stretched out on a green velvet couch cushion that had been moved to the floor. Grouped around the small, inert figure were Kitty and Taylor, side by side at his head, and Father Remi at his feet, along with Sister Clara. They sat on low wooden stools that had been brought in by Tesfa. The old African now hovered in the background, ready to help out as needed – serving tea, offering glasses of water or finding matches for Father Paulo's beeswax candles.

Several hours had passed since they'd settled in here. Two lots of prayer bells had been rung. Late-afternoon sun slanted in through the windows from low in the sky.

Kitty gazed down at Gili's face, the pale eyelids hiding his bright round eyes. The wrinkled skin around his nose and mouth gave him the appearance of a wise old man, yet he reminded her of an innocent baby as well.

'Do you think he's breathing more deeply?' Taylor's voice, though muted, sounded loud in the stillness.

Kitty watched Gili's chest, wanting to confirm the observation. After a while she looked up. 'Maybe. A little.'

Taylor's eyes were dark pools, the cleft between his brows a deep line. His lips were parted, poised on the edge of a word. He reached for her hand. As his fingers folded over hers, Kitty felt his need to be touched, warmed. She tightened her clasp.

'I'm glad you're here,' he said quietly.

'So am I,' Kitty replied. She tried to imagine what would be happening now, if she had not come out to the Mission. She pictured herself at the house on Millionaire Row with all her neighbours there – clamouring to offer condolences, and pawing over all the details of the tragedy. With Diana far away in London, the other women would be jockeying to step in as 'best friend', soaking up the drama. Maybe even Charlotte would call by, seeking a place in the scene. Perhaps, if Kitty did not manage to remain calm, the doctor would be called and sedatives prescribed. Kitty imagined herself lying on her bed, listening to the hushed murmur of voices from the sitting room, the chink of ice in glasses, the tap-tap of high heels crossing the floor. There would be nothing – no one – to protect her from the complexity of her feelings. If she'd been an ordinary wife who loved her husband, and had been loved in return, her sense of loss would have been acute, but it would have been pure and simple. What Kitty felt about Theo was confused, messy. Her grief was bound by guilt, jealousy and anger. And this would not be lost on others. In the society of Londoni, everything that had been said and done would be laid out, chewed over, and then examined again . . .

Looking around her, Kitty felt a flood of gratitude that she was here and not there. She hadn't weighed up the choice she'd made by seeking refuge at the Mission with Taylor. But thinking about it now, she understood that the implications of her actions were huge. She'd turned her back on English society – throwing in her lot with this mismatched group of Tanganyikans. She'd stepped well and truly outside the boundaries of the life she knew. And there would be no going back. She probed her emotions, searching for apprehension, regret – or even a twinge of doubt. But there was none.

Eventually, night darkened the windows and the air became cooler – the only signs that time had not stood still. Candles sent flickery shadows over the room. Father Paulo dozed fitfully in his chair, his head bowed, beard resting against his chest. Father Remi moved to one of the couches, as did Tesfa; Sister Clara retired to her room. Kitty and Taylor lay at either side of Gili, on mattresses that had been carried in from the guestroom.

Taylor fell asleep eventually, curled up on his side, still facing the velvet cushion as though ready to open his eyes at any second to check on his small friend. Kitty remained wide awake, adrenaline still coursing in her blood. Her mind was buzzing now, trying to keep up with the images and thoughts that paraded in her head. The moment she stopped focusing on Gili or Taylor, her thoughts went to Theo. She found it impossible to picture him laid out in the morgue – she had no idea what the place was like. Did it resemble a doctor's surgery with a stretcher and screen? Or was it a shadowy place of bare concrete and steel? Whatever the reality was, she hated to think of Theo being there alone. She had to remind herself that it was not really her husband who was locked up in the morgue – it was just his body. The person Theo had been was gone. This thought set off another stream of speculation. Had he been simply extinguished, like one of Father Paulo's candles? Or had he moved on to another state? Kitty returned to the vision of the eagle, flying away. Was Theo far off already? Or could he be here, watching over her? Looking down over Gili lying on his cushion, and over the candles and incense burner, the prayer books, the priests, the crucifix on the wall . . . The living Theo would have dismissed the scene as bizarre. But what would he make of it now – coming from the other side of death? Kitty shook her head. She was amazed at the way she was thinking. Only a short time ago she'd been so sure she shared Yuri's belief that death was the end.

She concentrated again on Gili. The bottom half of his body, bound up with bandages, reminded her of the Egyptian mummies she'd seen in the British Museum. But the top half still looked like him – the cheeky little creature who always wanted to be cuddled. Kitty had a flash of memory of the way he liked to put his hands over her eyes when she was carrying him. She could almost feel the rough papery touch of his skin resting on hers.

Don't die, little Gili.

She held the words inside her. She'd lost Theo. She'd lost Yuri too. And her family was virtually dead to her.

Please don't leave me.

She moved her gaze to Father Paulo, snoring lightly in his chair. His face was shadowed with exhaustion. He kept rousing himself, opening one of his books and reading in Latin, or just praying freely. He was fasting as well – he'd accepted water from Tesfa, but had only watched on when the others ate bread and fruit and drank cups of honeyed tea. There was no hint that Father Paulo was taking the situation any less seriously than he would have if Gili were a child, rather than an animal. After all, he had been the one who had hung the picture of St Francis of Assisi in pride of place on the dining room wall, beside the photograph of the Shroud of Turin. In the painting, St Francis was surrounded by ordinary creatures – a rabbit, a lamb, a pair of spotted deer. A bird perched on his shoulder. Written across the green grass at his feet was his well-known saying: *We are all creatures of one family.*

Watching the example Father Paulo set, Kitty wished she could pray too. But she didn't have the faith she knew was needed. On the other hand, she believed utterly in the integrity of the old priest. And she could feel the love that they all had for Gili – especially Taylor, whose bond with the monkey had been formed so deeply during the dark days of his imprisonment. She lifted her eyes to the framed print on the wall above Father Paulo's head – the picture of Jesus with his heart glowing in his chest. Shafts of light poured from his outstretched hands like visible streams of power. Kitty imagined them coming down over Gili, fusing the torn flesh inside him, making him strong again. She fixed her gaze on the image as though Gili's survival depended on her persistence. But eventually her eyelids began to droop, her head bowed. She lowered herself to the mattress and drifted into sleep.

Dawn light shone in through the windows, bringing a golden glow to the room. Kitty stirred, her eyes snapping open as she realised where she was, why she was here. For a few moments she lay still, absorbing the fact of Theo's death. She felt lost and confused as much as grief-stricken – the events of yesterday still seemed like a terrible dream. But her being here in this room was proof that the nightmare was true.

Her thoughts shifted to Gili. She kept her eyes trained on the ceiling – wanting to check on him, but dreading what she might find. She remembered all the times when as a child she'd said goodnight to living animals – orphaned lambs, birds, possums – and returned to discover them cold and stiff in the morning.

She caught her breath, and slowly turned her head.

Gili was looking at her. His eyes were open, shiny and round.

'Taylor,' she gasped. 'Wake up!'

Her words, only whispered, travelled the room. Limbs shifted, eyes opened. Everyone clustered around Gili – except for Father Paulo, who leaned forward in his chair.

'Don't crowd him,' Taylor warned.

Gili's gaze moved from face to face. His amber-green eyes were wide, as if he was puzzled by all the attention.

'He'll be thirsty,' Father Remi said. He quickly brought an eye-dropper from the cupboard in the clinic and filled a bowl with boiled water. Kneeling by Gili's side, he supported the monkey's head with one hand. He placed the end of the dropper near his mouth and squeezed water onto his lips. There was a breathless wait, then a pink tongue emerged, licking at the moisture. A few seconds later, Gili's hand moved up to grab the dropper. Relieved laughter broke out, easing the tension in the room.

When it died away, there was a deep quiet in the room. No one asked the question, no one even breathed the word. But the idea that a miracle had occurred here was an aura shimmering in the air. Kitty could almost feel the hope and joy radiating from Taylor's body. She, too, felt a weight had been lifted from her heart. It was possible, she understood, for dark and light to come together – for grief and happiness to be experienced at the same time.

As if to signal that normal life was to resume, Father Paulo eased himself stiffly from his chair. Ignoring suggestions he should remain where he was until he'd eaten breakfast, he set off for the kitchen. Taylor and Father Remi remained crouched beside Gili, discussing his care. Kitty stood up, stretching her arms above her head. Then she wandered outside, drawn by the gold light and cool air of the early morning.

Birds flitted between the branches of the baobab. The ancient tree was in leaf now, the gnarled twigs softened by foliage. Kitty walked past it to the edge of the yard, looking down towards the plains. *Shambas* made a patchwork of different shades of green, brown, yellow. The wild grass was thick. The arrival of the first rains had prompted seeds to sprout, plants to begin growing. The burst of life was founded on trust that the big rains would soon follow, sustaining the crops until they formed seeds and fruit for the harvest. Sometimes the rains were too sparse, or they failed to come at all, leading to hunger and despair. But the next season, hope rose again. Standing there, Kitty could feel the power of it – the cycle of life and death, and life. The same forces were at play in her own journey, she saw. And the same trust in the future was needed. Closing her eyes, she lifted her face towards the sun, letting its strength flow into her.

There was the sound of footsteps behind her. She turned to see Taylor holding out a tin mug and a slice of pawpaw. As he came close she breathed the fragrance of the fruit, and the spicy steam rising from Tesfa's hot tea. Lifting her eyes, she met Taylor's gaze. There was warmth there, but strength as well. Kitty knew that when she wanted to talk about Theo – to let out her pain and grief and confusion – Taylor would be ready to listen and help however he was able. She felt the bond between them, deeper and more powerful than before. The experiences they'd been through were ones few people ever had to endure. Whatever came next, she felt, would not change the closeness they now shared.

They stood together in silence, sipping their tea, biting into the firm flesh of the pawpaw, licking the juice from their lips. Not far from where they stood a rooster strutted about, showing off his crimson and orange plumage. He lifted his head and crowed loudly, confidently. Another rooster replied from further away, then another. The crowing travelled across the hillside from one rooster to another, as if the good news of the morning were being passed on, from farm to homestead to distant village.

TWENTY

Kitty walked down the hallway on tiptoes. Eustace and Gabriel were expecting her, but she didn't want to alert them to her arrival straight away. She could hear the familiar drone of their voices coming from the kitchen. There were the predictable bursts of laughter. What was missing was the clatter of pans and the smell of food being cooked: the staff were in limbo, in charge of a house where there was no longer anyone in residence.

It had been nearly three weeks since Theo's death. For Kitty, the time had passed in a blur. Everything that had happened felt unreal, disjointed. Ordinary activities – eating, sleeping, talking – were mere echoes of real experiences. Looming above everything was the loss of her husband and all that it meant. And behind that was anxiety about Gili. He'd improved steadily, day by day, but was still very weak.

Kitty had returned to Londoni on the morning after the shootings. She had to give her statement to the Inspector, and she wanted to make a visit to the mortuary to view Theo's body. Taylor had offered to come with her. She had been touched by his offer – the look of concern in his eyes, the gentle tone of his voice. But she'd known it was something she needed to do alone.

On the way into Londoni Kitty had made a detour to the house in Millionaire Row to collect some clothes. She'd only stayed a few minutes. Raw memories seemed to haunt the very fabric of the building. There was no sign of Eustace and Gabriel. They may have been outside in the laundry or in the garden, but she hadn't hunted for them. She was relieved not to have to face them just now – their questions, their shock and distress. She'd just packed a small bag and left.

Her interview at Scotland Inch had been surprisingly brief. Apparently Larry Green had been able to give a detailed picture of all that had happened. And the Inspector made it clear that he didn't think Kitty could be a reliable witness – she was too emotionally involved. He seemed to be trying to wrap up the case as quickly as possible. Kitty suspected he didn't want anyone dwelling on the fact that she had come to him with crucial information about a threat to harm Charlotte and he'd ignored her. Snapping shut his notebook after making only a few brief entries, he'd ushered Kitty from his office. Then he'd escorted her to the room at the back of the hospital where Theo's body was laid out.

The mortuary had revived Kitty's memories of being in an air-raid shelter – there was the same raw smell of concrete walls and lack of natural light. In the centre of the room stood a table, also made of concrete, with a drainage runnel around the edge. A long shape wrapped in dark-green canvas rested there. The Inspector hovered at Kitty's side as she went to stand next to it, bracing herself as the African attendant lifted the canvas away.

She absorbed what lay before her in snatches, the full weight of the sight too much to bear all at once. There was Theo's face, waxy white; his eyes closed. The bullet wound, washed clean of blood, was just a small hole with skin curling at the edges. Cotton wool plugged his nostrils and a bandage ran from under his chin over the top of his head, holding his mouth closed.

The attendant pulled the canvas further open. Large chunks of ice were packed around Theo, pressing into his flesh. Strange to think there were no nerves alive in the pale skin, nothing to flinch from the cold. Someone had removed his clothes; for the sake of modesty a towel replaced his underpants. Around his wrist was a cardboard tag bearing neat handwriting: *Mr Theodore Hamilton*. Under the name were the words *Unit Number, Season, Weight.*

'Is that the best you can do?' the Inspector asked the attendant. 'A label from a peanut bag?'

'It is the best,' the man confirmed. 'It is very strong. It will not tear and become lost.'

It was the pattern of sunburn on Theo's skin that touched Kitty most – the triangle of tan matching the open neck of his shirt, and the brown of his arms below the place where the short sleeves ended. It was so directly linked with life: the seasons coming and going, suntan deepening and fading. And now – no more.

She'd stood there gazing at Theo, her vision blurred by tears. The Inspector had placed his hand awkwardly on her shoulder for a moment, offering comfort. Then he'd stepped away, shuffling his feet and rustling his notebook – making it clear that it was time to leave.

Kitty's next task in Londoni had been to attend a meeting with Theo's assistant, Toby Carmichael. The Inspector had said she could wait a few days before going to Head Office, but she'd explained she preferred to do it now. When she got back to the Mission she wanted to be able to stay there. Inside the solid old buildings, with the comforting sound of bells ringing for prayer times and pigeons cooing from the tower, she felt removed from everything to do with her life in Londoni. The Misson was her place of refuge. Her harbour. And she didn't want to be anywhere else.

After expressing his condolences and offering tea and biscuits, Toby had got straight down to business. He tried to be as diplomatic as possible, skirting the details of 'the incident at Unit Three', while conveying to Kitty that he, for one, had seen warning signs of Theo's breakdown. He even suggested he'd tried to speak to his boss about his concerns, though Kitty found that hard to picture. Toby's manner was sensitive and sympathetic. But as he pointed out, certain facts were unavoidable. With Richard still away, Theo's two positions – Acting General Manager and Manager of Administration – had to be filled immediately. As always, there were crises looming for the Scheme; a new man was needed at the helm. Toby approached the subject of the house on Millionaire Row carefully. Obviously, Mrs Hamilton would have to move out – and soon. Fortunately, the Shoebox was now vacant. Lady Welmingham had left on the first flight out of Kongara – still shaken by the terrifying experience she'd endured. Therefore the cottage could be made available to Kitty for the period of time she needed to arrange her return to England.

When he'd finished his speech, Toby had eyed Kitty expectantly. But she just looked at him. Did he realise he was offering to accommodate her in the house last occupied by Theo's lover? Surely he did . . . Misinterpreting her silence, Toby rushed on, saying how regrettable it was that Kitty should have to lose her home as well as her husband. He wished she could stay on in Millionaire Row, but it just wasn't possible.

Kitty had to break in, stopping the flow of platitudes. 'I'll be living at the Catholic Mission.'

Toby's head jerked back. His eyes widened, his relief almost lost beneath naked curiosity. Kitty wondered what exactly he'd heard about the place. He probably knew about the work she and Diana did there. He could even have been informed about her friendship with that enemy of the OFC, Bwana Taylor.

'So, I won't be needing your help,' Kitty concluded. 'Thank you, all the same.'

She had then stood up, bringing the meeting to a close. Toby had shaken her hand as if to congratulate her, but there had been a doubtful expression in his eyes. Perhaps to make sure she could not change her mind, he'd said he would arrange for her and Theo's personal effects to be packed up, ready for removal – not that it would take long, he'd pointed out, since all the furnishings were the property of the British government.

Kitty thought back to his words as she now peered along the hallway of the house. As promised, the few items that belonged to the Hamiltons – a framed photograph of the grand façade of Theo's ancestral home, a vase that used to stand on the built-in bookcase, a small Persian rug – had all been removed. There was a cardboard box, taped shut, at the far end of the hall.

She reached the door to the bedroom, pushing it open. Inside, she found her suitcase with its faded shipping labels standing in the middle of the floor, along with her brass-studded travelling trunk.

Next to them was her handbag, clipped shut, with the handles sticking up as though waiting to be hooked over her elbow.

Kitty looked across to the window, peering past the *manyara* hedge to the house next door. She thought of Diana – if only she were here, when Kitty needed her so much. Kitty knew that as soon as the Armstrongs got back and heard what had happened, Diana would come straight to the Mission to find her. But it would be at least another two weeks – and at the moment, that felt like forever.

Walking to the wardrobe, she opened the doors. Apart from the bare hangers dangling from the rail, the space was completely empty. Reaching towards the back of the wardrobe, into a crack between the rear wall and the base, she eased out a flat round object.

Kitty looked down at the tortoiseshell powder compact resting in the palm of her hand. As she traced the decorative curls of the initials, she remembered the day when she'd decided it was best to hide the keepsake away, in case Theo made the connection with Katya and became angry or upset. It seemed so distant – that time when she'd wanted nothing more than to be the perfect wife.

She took a deep breath. The air of the room had already changed, the floral perfume of her talcum powder replaced by a rubbery smell coming from the bare mattress. The surface of the dressing table was dull, suggesting a fine coat of dust. At the corner of the mirror a spider had already begun work on a web. It was hard to believe only weeks had passed since Kitty had put on her red-and-white spotted dress and set off for the Club, never imagining the terrible events that the day would bring.

She took one last look around the bedroom, then walked back down the hall into the sitting room. She paused by the drinks trolley, now empty of alcohol – the decanters rinsed clean, the bottles gone. She closed her eyes momentarily, wanting to block out the dark pictures that came to her: Theo pouring himself yet another drink, or shouting at Gabriel, slurring his words. And Kitty having to sit there, watching, all the while shrinking inside herself, trying to reach a place of refuge.

In the dining room, she glanced over Cynthia's collection of Royal Doulton. She wondered how long it would take the new memsahib to discover the set was incomplete. Of course, the woman would most likely arrive with her own set of china – something decorative and delicate; not plain and chunky like the crockery Kitty had chosen.

Crossing to the table, Kitty ran one hand over the velvety smooth surface. She looked up at the sound of footsteps behind her.

'Good morning, Memsahib.' Eustace and Gabriel spoke almost in unison.

'Good morning,' Kitty replied. 'I have come to collect my things.'

'Yes, Memsahib,' they chorused.

There was an awkward quiet. It was as though they all knew that if they began talking about what had happened they would not know where to stop.

'Your luggage is in the bedroom,' Eustace said.

'I saw it. Thank you.'

'The bwana's clothes and his personal items have been taken to the airstrip,' Eustace continued. Presumably due to the gravity of the situation, he pronounced every word correctly – even 'airstrip' had no added vowel at the end. 'The things that belonged to you both are being stored at Head Office. You must divide them according to your customs.'

'That's good. Well done.' Kitty wished she had the energy to thank the pair properly – to show that she appreciated all they'd done for her since she first arrived here. She'd had her frustrations with them, but they had served her and Theo well. 'I'll come back and see you,' she said. It was all she could manage right now.

'Is there something else we can do for you?' There was a new tone of respect in Gabriel's voice. He even lowered his gaze. Kitty thought it could be due to the special status she had acquired as a new widow. But it occurred to her that it could equally be because she'd failed to return home for all this time, and that she'd been at the Catholic Mission rather than seeking the comfort of her lady friends at the Club. She'd acted in a way that removed her completely from all categories of behaviour that Gabriel understood. As a result, he was unsure of her status and was choosing to play safe.

'They have already taken the bwana's body to England,' Eustace said. The look on his face made the statement a query.

'Yes, it happened last Friday,' Kitty confirmed. The Inspector had sent a message to the Mission to let her know about it – 'repatriation' was the word he'd used. 'He will have been buried by now,' she added. The men eyed her intently, clearly wanting more detail. 'His grave will be in the village near the homestead of his parents. He will lie next to his ancestors.'

The two nodded approvingly; what she'd said made good sense to them. But Kitty wondered what they would think of the kind of burial service that would have taken place at St Luke in the Fields.

There would have been no wailing, no tearing of clothes such as Kitty had seen at a funeral held at the Mission. Theo's mother would not have thrown herself on his coffin, giving herself up to her grief. Louisa would have held her composure. The Admiral would have done the same. Theo's words came back to Kitty, from the morning when he'd first given her a full account of his nightmare – when he was insisting there was no need to talk further about his wartime experiences. He'd used his mother's phrase: *No use crying over spilt milk*. No point in raking over pain or trauma. Just keep a stiff upper lip and soldier on.

Kitty knew Louisa would be devastated by the loss of her son. She'd deal with it by blaming her daughter-in-law for what had happened – if Theo's wife hadn't caused an intolerable scandal, he wouldn't have had to go to Tanganyika. She'd blame the OFC as well. The Colonial Service. Africa. One thing was certain, neither Louisa nor the Admiral would ever understand what part they – and their version of a tribe – had played in the tragedy of Theo's life.

'A new family is coming,' Eustace said. 'The bwana is called Major Marsden. They have three children. A special bed has been delivered – two in one.' He shook his head in amazement as he used his hands to indicate how two children would sleep stacked one above the other.

'You'll be busy,' Kitty commented.

'I will show the memsahib the recipe for the polish,' Gabriel offered.

'And I have copied out the menus onto a clean piece of paper,' Eustace said.

Kitty could see their minds had already turned to this new phase in the life of the house on Millionaire Row. She wondered how the Marsdens would fare in this place – what hopes and dreams and secrets they would bring with them.

'Shall we take your possessions to the car?' Gabriel asked.

Kitty smiled. 'Thank you.'

Both men hurried to carry out the task, leaving Kitty standing alone. She turned slowly on the spot, taking in the whole room. Then she moved into the sitting room and did the same. Already the place looked foreign to her. She felt like a trespasser. Suddenly, she needed to get back outside, away from it all.

She walked down the hallway and opened the front door. At the threshold she paused, the stillness of the empty house, the air so dense with memories, pressing at her back. Shutting the door for the last time, she headed for her car. She could feel the past closing up behind her – and the pull of the future, drawing her on.

EPILOGUE

Kitty wandered over to one of the tables that stood next to the pool. There were no chairs any more, so she hoisted herself up to sit on the solid terrazzo slab. As she kicked off her sandals, she gazed down into the empty concrete hole. It was hard to recall how she had once swum laps there, in cool deep water. A stick insect longer than her hand was making its way across the dusty bottom. The pool had been drained years ago. The green and white umbrellas were gone, along with the uniformed staff. The fence had been taken down as well. The waiters' hut and the changing shed – like the Club building itself – were locked up and empty.

Shading her eyes with her hand, Kitty looked over towards the swings and slide. The playground equipment was still shiny and red, untouched by the general air of decay. African children played there – squealing as they launched themselves down the slide, bare legs meeting metal heated up by the sun. They slid head first or sideways; there were no *ayahs* to make them play sensibly. At the top of the ladder, just about to step onto the slide, was one white child – a little girl. She yelled out in Swahili at a boy who was lingering below her, gesturing for him to get out of her way.

Kitty smiled at the sight of her daughter standing there, hands poised to grasp the edges of the slide. Ella wore a simple blue dress, worn through at the hem. Her light-brown hair – as unruly as her father's – hung loose around her sunburned shoulders. The colour of her skin and hair was all that marked her out from the other children. She was probably the youngest of them – only four years old – but she was clearly one of the pack. She was confident, relaxed, happy.

Sometimes, looking at Ella, Kitty could hardly believe this child belonged to her – that Kitty was now part of a triangle of love that made up a new family. She held out her left hand, letting the sun dance on the narrow gold band she wore on her ring finger. Her thoughts turned back to the day when Taylor had first told her he loved her.

She had driven to his farm to deliver a message from Father Remi. Someone from the village could easily have been sent over on a bicycle, but she'd seized the excuse to go there. She was keen to look inside the house she'd seen perched on the hillside. And of course, she wanted to see Taylor, too. She always wanted to see him . . .

Kitty had stood at his front door, trying to adopt a casual expression – she was just a neighbour dropping in. As was the local custom, she called out rather than knocking.

'Hodi, hodi!' Someone is here.

When there was no response, she tried the door. As it swung open she caught a fleeting impression of a large, airy room with cool shadows and flashes of sunlight, and bright spots of colour with restful spaces in between. Her eyes were drawn straight to a row of large windows. There was almost no boundary between inside and out – the edges of the room blended with a vista of earth and sky that stretched to the far horizon.

She called out again, but there was still no response. She knew she should wait on the doorstep – but the house, with its clues to Taylor's life, beckoned her inside.

In the middle of the space, she turned slowly on the spot. She took in a sofa and three armchairs: simple, sturdy furniture like the Fathers had at the Mission. Resting against plain upholstery were cushions covered in pieces of *kitenge*, each with a contrasting pattern. Woven mats made pale circles on the stone floor. There were low wooden stools like the Wagogo used, a couple of cow-skin drums. A zebra skin edged with green felt hung on the far wall, and a collection of ebony carvings – warriors, long-limbed and elegant, interspersed with African animals – marched along a windowsill.

Among the African furnishings were some fine English antiques that would have been at home in Hamilton Hall. Kitty's eyes lingered on a dining table with turned legs that ended in carved lion's paws. One half was bare, as if ready for a meal to be served, but the other was dotted with books and papers and a scattering of pencils. There was a framed photograph standing there as well. Kitty had to go closer. The faded print showed a man and a woman standing arm in arm, laughing at the camera. She could tell they were Taylor's parents: each had passed on a version of their features to their son.

She didn't linger with the photograph – it felt wrong to be studying something personal like this without being invited. Instead she turned to a painting on a wall nearby: a pre-Impressionist watercolour in the style of Turner. The play of misty English rain over a slate-grey river was captured perfectly. Studying the technique, Kitty didn't notice the sound of footsteps until they were close. She spun round, apologies rising to her lips.

And there he was – standing in a pool of sunlight, a look of pleasant surprise on his face. Kitty caught her breath. Time seemed to stop. The air felt charged with tension. It was as if a force had been brewing steadily ever since she and Taylor first met – fuelled by each look that had passed between them, each word and smile, and honed by the hard times they'd shared. Holding the energy in check had only increased its power. Now there was no need to contain it. There was nothing to keep them apart.

They were drawn together, moving in unison. For a few seconds they stood close, just looking into one another's eyes. Then their lips met – tentative, questioning at first, before giving in to a deep hunger. Their arms entwined and their bodies pressed together. The moment seemed to go on forever, and yet was over too soon.

When he pulled away, Taylor kept his hands on her shoulders. 'I love you, Kitty.'

She smiled, joy breaking inside her. 'I love you, too.'

No more words had been necessary. A vision of a shared future spread out before them, clear and endless as the view over the plains.

For her wedding, Kitty had worn a dress made of fine-spun cloth from Ethiopia – a gift from Tesfa, who had been quick to claim responsibility for having brought Kitty and Taylor together. The Rite of Marriage was celebrated in the Mission church, with Father Paulo joining the couple's right hands together and Father Remi hearing their vows. That same day, Kitty had moved from the Mission to join her husband in his hillside home.

It was there – in the very room where Taylor had been born – that Kitty had given birth to Ella two years later. Sister Barbara had been in attendance, along with an African midwife. The hospital at Kongara was not too far away if problems arose, but Kitty was glad she hadn't needed to go there. At home, Taylor was allowed to be present – Sister Barbara had even encouraged it. Kitty had smiled at the thought of what Pippa would have to say about that. Nothing could be more undignified than a woman giving birth! And yes, it had been painful and bloody – but Taylor was concerned only with comforting his wife and looking forward to seeing his child.

He'd been the first one after Sister Barbara to hold little Ella. Kitty still remembered the moment when he tore his eyes from the tiny bundle that was their daughter and met her tired but exultant gaze. The love and wonder that ran between them was so potent that even now, years later, the knowledge of what they'd shared brought tears to Kitty's eyes.

'Look at me, Mummy,' Ella called across from the slide.

'I am!' Kitty replied.

She watched Ella throw herself down the slide, a broad grin on her face. As Kitty clapped her hands, the girl flashed her a triumphant look before rushing round to the steps to clamour for another turn.

Attracted by the sound of Kitty's voice, Gili emerged from the tangle of children's bodies and bounded over. He had a slight limp, which did nothing to slow him down and made his capering gait only more comical. Leaping onto the table, he reached straight for Kitty's pocket.

'No, you can't have it.' She pressed her hand over the letter tucked away there. 'It's mine.'

Shooing the monkey away, she slid the envelope out. When she'd heard there was a letter waiting for her at the *duka* she'd guessed it was from Diana, who wrote regularly from Nairobi, where Richard had taken a government post. But the envelope Ahmed had handed her this morning bore a stamp that had the word *AUSTRALIA* printed beneath the head of the newly crowned Queen Elizabeth. And the address was penned in the careful hand-writing of Kitty's mother.

Kitty pushed her finger under the flap of the envelope and tore it open. As she did so, she felt, as always, a blend of anticipation and anxiety. She couldn't wait to read the latest report from Seven Gums, but she was keenly aware that it could contain bad news as easily as good. Her father had only recently recovered from the pneumonia he'd developed after working outside when he had influenza. Last season a careless shearer had started a fire in the sheds and they were lucky not to lose any sheep. Fear was the inevitable companion of love. Both emotions went with being part of a family – and the more people there were in the circle, the more room there was for worry as well as joy. But it was a price Kitty was glad to pay.

She read the letter twice, drinking in every word. Her mother wrote that Hero's foal had been born healthy and strong. The new farmhand was finally earning his keep, and the Millers had won their usual collection of awards at the Agricultural Show. Jason was stepping out with the Elwood's youngest daughter, while Tim was training up a promising new cattle dog called Bailey. The letter finished with a note of advice, passed on from Kitty's father, about pruning orchard trees.

Kitty's eyes lingered on the final two words.

Love, Mum.

Such simple words – yet how precious they were to her. Though she had grown accustomed now to receiving the letters from Seven Gums, Kitty never took them for granted. For too many years she'd missed out on the lives of her parents and brothers. The painful memory of the long silence was still there.

After Theo's death, Kitty had written to her parents, telling them what had happened, but received no reply. When she married Taylor she'd tried making contact with them again – maybe time had finally weakened their resolve. But this time, too, she was ignored. Kitty wasn't sure if her mother even knew about the letters. It was her father who collected the mail and Kitty could imagine him tearing them up without even opening the envelopes, let alone reading the contents. It seemed that the choice Kitty had made so many years ago had trapped them all inside a cycle of blame and anger that was never going to be broken.

Looking back, Kitty could understand the pain she'd caused her family, and how selfish she had appeared. But she couldn't say she regretted taking her grandmother's money and travelling to England. The decision had shaped her whole life, and while there had been trials, there was so much that had been good. There was Yuri, and all he'd taught her. There was the love she'd shared, at least for a time, with Theo. There was Africa, the Fathers, Diana, and her many friends. But more than anything, there was Taylor and Ella. It was impossible for Kitty to say she should have taken another path, because only the one she'd chosen could have led her to them. Yet, the loss of her family in Australia was a high price to pay.

When Ella was born, Kitty decided to send one last letter. More than ever before, she longed to communicate with her mother – there was so much now for them to share. In the weeks after her birth, Taylor had taken a series of photographs of Ella. When the black-and-white prints arrived back from Dar es Salaam, Kitty sorted through them. She was tempted by one that included Gili but settled on a picture of Ella wrapped in a *kitenge*, her little hand resting delicately on the side of her face. Framed by the picture's white border with scalloped edges, the baby looked even more adorable than she was in the flesh.

Kitty had written in pencil on the back: *Eleanor Miller Taylor, 7 pounds 2 ounces*. Instead of mailing the picture to Wattle Creek post office, she'd sent it to Auntie Josie who lived not far from Seven Gums. In an accompanying note she begged her to deliver the picture to her sister-in-law by hand, without the envelope. That way, Kitty's mother would come face to face with her first grandchild. She would find herself looking into those clear, bright eyes . . .

Once she'd sent off the letter, Kitty tried to forget about it. She didn't allow herself to make unnecessary visits to Ahmed's *duka* – which, in the shrinking economy of Kongara, was now the post office and the chemist as well as the main shop. She tried not to regret that Ella was changing so quickly and Kitty was unable to send an account of the daily miracles to her baby's grandmother in Australia. But then, out of the blue – when Ella was already sitting up – a reply had arrived. Kitty still kept the letter in her bedside drawer, but she didn't need to read it to remember what it said.

She could see the words in her mind – every careful loop and dot, the tiny ink smudge halfway through. It was a short letter, reserved and simple. There was no mention of all the attempts Kitty had made to communicate over the years; the cautious tone of the writing could have been due to surprise, embarrassment, hurt – or all three. There was some news of the family, a few points about the farm and a comment on the weather. But there was one line that brought a lump to Kitty's throat.

What will you call her for short?

It was a question. A beginning.

At first, the interaction was only with Kitty's mother. Then, as Kitty wrote about Taylor and the farm, she began to get comments from her father reported second-hand. That was when she'd started writing to him directly. His replies came in the form of lines added to the bottoms of his wife's letters. Over time, they became longer, and warmer in tone. Her father had mellowed with age, Kitty realised – or perhaps he was just less busy and stressed. There had been some profitable years on the farm – good harvests, good prices – and his sons now shouldered much of the workload. Or could it be that he truly wanted to make up for the harsh silence he'd imposed over so many years? Was Kitty right in her suspicion that he had concealed the existence of her letters? She knew she would never ask. She wasn't sure she even wanted to know.

Kitty explained to her father about the piped spring water on Taylor's farm, and the three harvests that were possible each year. She wrote of how they were now sun-drying sultana grapes as well as making wine, and of how they had plenty of labourers to help, most of them ex-convicts eager to make a new life for themselves.

The farm no longer needed the prison work parties – and the men no longer needed to come there. Her Majesty's Prison Services had a new establishment with a farm attached on the other side of the Kongara mountains, where growing conditions were similar. The Fathers were now able to turn their efforts to working more with the local Wagogo, which had been their original calling.

Kitty wrote to her father about the decline of the Groundnut Scheme. As a farmer, he was interested in all the details. He was not surprised when the OFC was eventually forced to concede that the plains of Kongara were made up of completely the wrong soil for peanuts, and that an adequate rainfall simply could not be relied upon. There were bitter recriminations in the British parliament and outrage in the press. Why hadn't trials been carried out in the very beginning? Why had the OFC employed soldiers instead of farmers? Why had so much good money been thrown after bad? The only explanation seemed to be that idealism had triumphed over practicality. The urgent desire to do something good had clouded all logic. And then, there had always been that gulf between the men in charge – whether in London or in its namesake Londoni – and the men on the ground, with dust in their hair and dirt on their hands.

The collapse, when it came, was quite sudden. Within a couple of months, most of the employees of the OFC were evacuated from Kongara. All the Londoni families returned to England. Only Richard and Diana decided to stay in Africa. Their trip home had been a success – a time of healing and reconnection – but they'd also realised how much they loved being in Tanganyika. They'd moved to Dar es Salaam – close enough for them to visit Kitty and Taylor for holidays. Richard gained a position in the Colonial Service. Diana had spent some time volunteering in an orphanage, but was now setting up a new venture of her own: a home that would provide emergency care for babies whose mothers had died in childbirth.

After just a few years, it was extraordinary how little was left of the settlement and the plantations. Down on the plains the native grasses had grown back, blurring the plough-lines and windrows. Elephants had returned to graze there – their grey bulky shapes set oddly beside the rusting hulks of tractors that had been abandoned where they'd broken down. In Londoni and at the Units, everything that could be moved had been auctioned off and taken away. The Ministry of Food was keen to recoup as much money as possible, having lost such a massive fortune on behalf of the British taxpayer. Generators, vehicles and even small buildings like the ones that made up the Toolsheds were loaded onto trucks and taken away to mission stations, government depots or private farms. The houses on Millionaire Row were listed in the catalogue as 'building materials'. Toilets, baths, roofs and walls had been removed. All that remained were the terrazzo floors and concrete paths, which the Wagogo found ideal as surfaces for threshing millet or laying out their washing.

Life in Kongara settled back into patterns that had been set down generations before, when the first Europeans arrived here. The Anglican and Catholic missionaries worked side by side – spiritual rivals, yet comrades as well. The Colonial Office continued to pave the way towards Tanganyika's eventual independence. And the Wagogo navigated a path between all the different groups, seizing what they saw to be new and good, while at the same time reaching back to the tried and true. It was as if the Groundnut Scheme and the OFC had been just a breeze passing through this remote corner of Tanganyika.

Only recently, Kitty had heard of plans for some of the surviving OFC buildings to be turned into a boarding school for the children of missionaries and Colonial Service officers. If that happened, it had been suggested Ella could be enrolled as a day student. But on the other hand, she could go with her African friends to the little school Sister Clara was just starting up. Kitty was in no hurry to make a choice. For now, Ella was busy from dawn to dusk with no need for lessons and books. She could already milk a goat and knew how to plant beans in a straight row and at the right depth. (She'd grown out of the habit of digging up peanuts to see how the nuts were growing or forcing flowers to open more quickly by peeling open the buds.) She was never bored, even though she had hardly any toys. The ones she did have were mostly gifts from Diana. They were lined up on a shelf – treasured, but rarely touched. To Ella, everyday life was a constant source of fun. She loved joining her dad out on the farm, helping the Fathers at the Mission, or playing with dough in the kitchen at home. She had her own corner in Kitty's new studio where she worked with paints and crayons and clay. Wherever she went, Gili was her constant companion.

Kitty shifted further back onto the tabletop so that the monkey could settle more comfortably on her lap. As she did so, the sound of a vehicle engine drew her attention. Looking past the place where the fence used to be, she saw a truck loaded with people – men, women and children dressed up in traditional finery, though without spears or shields. Black smoke erupted from the exhaust pipe as the driver accelerated. He was headed out of town. Kitty guessed the people were going to the Mission. Today was the Feast of St Paul of the Cross and this afternoon a special mass would be conducted in the church. Afterwards, there was to be a party in the compound. People would begin arriving at the Mission hours early, making the most of the occasion. Amosi was probably already at work heating up huge pots of spiced tea to be handed out by the nuns.

Kitty, Taylor and Ella planned to go out there closer to the actual time of the mass. From past years, Kitty knew how the celebrations would unfold. The focus would be on the old priest, Father Paulo. No matter how often Father Remi preached about the life and work of St Paul, the founder of the Passionist order, the Wagogo remained uninterested. The Italian saint had lived his life too long ago and much too far away. The people preferred to honour their own Father, whose name was almost the same. When the feast day came around they always visited the grotto before entering the church, to give thanks for his gift of healing.

At the appointed time, Father Paulo would be carried to the grotto on his sedan chair. He was barely able to walk these days, and the narrow tyres of his wheelchair, which had been sent from Dar es Salaam, sank into the earth. His friends had taken to carrying him around in an ordinary chair with poles fixed to the sides. The old priest could easily have been lifted by two men, but it was seen as an honour to carry him and Kitty had never seen fewer than four people on the job.

The grotto would be filled with flowers, the air fragrant with their perfume along with the aroma of beeswax candles and frank-incense. The people would receive their blessing from the Father, then stop to pray at the altar.

Kitty pictured the statue in its place on the pedestal. It had been standing there for nearly five years now. As soon as she had left Millionaire Row, and moved to the Mission, she'd begun working on the sculpture. After she married Taylor she'd still returned each day to her studio. Modelling, casting and painting had taken most of the year to complete.

While Kitty was forming the image of the child, she thought of the baby she longed to have. Even though Sister Barbara told her it took many couples around a year to conceive, she was still afraid, as the months went by, that it would never happen. But around the time the statue was finished, Ella had been conceived. It felt like a miracle. Kitty had often stood in the seclusion of the grotto, feeling so thankful that she had finally become a mother. She would gaze in silence at the statue, forgetting she'd been the one who had created it. The little girl seemed so real. Her skin was a rich dark brown. Her hair was black, a mass of tight curls. She wore an ochre robe like an ordinary village child. She held up one hand in the traditional gesture of blessing. But there was nothing solemn about her. Her brown eyes – those eyes of a child who had been born blind – shone with joy and mischief. With pure life.

A flash of fair skin and flying hair caught Kitty's eye. Ella had broken away from her friends and was running towards the car park. From the expression on her face, Kitty guessed who it was she could see. Moments later, Taylor strode into view. He looked preoccupied – the deep furrow was there on his brow. The reason they'd come to town this morning was to find a part for one of the pumps; Kitty guessed the problem had not been solved. But when

Taylor saw Ella, his whole demeanour changed. He crouched down as she ran to him, taking her into his arms and sweeping her up against his chest. Kitty saw their matching smiles – though Ella was fairer, the two were very alike.

Gili scampered over to them, eager not to be left out. Taylor shifted Ella's weight, leaning to pat the monkey's head. As he walked on he waved at Kitty – then he glanced up at the sky, checking the position of the sun.

'Must be time to go?' he suggested. 'We've got to get tidied up.' He glanced down at his clothes, which were daubed with mud from the broken pump.

Kitty nodded. 'I've got to finish my cooking, too.'

At the end of the celebration they were going to join the Fathers for their evening meal. It was like a family gathering whenever they all sat around the long dining table together. Father Remi always served up his homemade delicacies – prosciutto, olives, cheese, salami. The men pretended to argue about who had produced the finest wine. Ella would be spoiled by everyone and given far too much of the Turkish delight that came from Ahmed's store. Kitty's fruit crumble had become part of the tradition. She'd perfected her own version of the dessert, made from stewed mango and passionfruit. It was flavoured with lime juice, coconut and ginger. The fruit and the crumble had already been prepared but it still had to be baked in the oven.

Kitty put her letter back into her pocket, then slid down off the table, pushing her feet into her sandals.

'We're going to wear our big and little dresses,' Ella announced. 'Aren't we, Mummy?'

'Yes, we are,' Kitty agreed.

The two frocks were laid out ready, side by side on the double bed. The Indian tailor had made them both from the length of cloth Kitty had kept aside for so long – the orange silk that had reminded her of Katya. When she'd gone in for a fitting, planning to have a dress made up from the fabric, Mr Singh had informed her that 'mother-daughter' outfits were the latest fashion in London. Kitty had laughed at the idea, but Ella, listening in on the conversation, was entranced. With the tailor joining forces with the child, Kitty could only agree. Today's festival was the first chance that had come up for the two to wear their new clothes. So there they would both be, at the Feast of St Paul of the Cross – mother and daughter in their matching dresses of finest silk, the colour of an African sunset.

'I can't wait to see how you look all dressed up.' Taylor kissed the top of Ella's head, then he leaned close to Kitty, nuzzling his face into her hair. She breathed the smell of grape juice and earth, and felt the warmth of sunshine on his skin. When he spoke again, his lips brushed her cheek. 'My beautiful girls . . .'

Kitty lifted her arms, embracing her husband and her child. Ella's skin was smooth, soft as velvet; Taylor's body was firm and strong under her hands. She rested her head against his shoulder, closing her eyes. What she experienced in that moment was a feeling more than a thought – a current flowing through her. The words to describe it rose from her heart, familiar and extraordinary.

Hali ya kuwa na furaha.

The state of being with joy.

AUTHOR'S NOTE

This novel was inspired by circumstances that arose as a result of the British Government Groundnut Scheme that operated in Tanganyika (now Tanzania) between 1947 and 1951. The scheme had a number of centres, of which Kongwa was the largest. Kongara, the town in the novel, is a fictitious place that bears some similarity to Kongwa but which has its own distinct character and history.

I relied for much of my research into the scheme on the non-fiction book *The Groundnut Affair* by Alan Wood, published in 1950. I also sourced firsthand accounts from people who spent time in the Groundnut settlements during and after the years of the scheme. Glynn Ford and Jean Young, in particular, kindly provided me with much useful information. I was grateful for the opportunity to view collections of archival photographs including those belonging to Edward Bunting, Valeria Gatti, Paul Jackson, Charlie MacDonald, Ray Mullin, Tony Murphy and Jean Young.

For a general picture of life in Tanganyika, I enjoyed reading David Read's memoir *Beating About the Bush* and Joan Smith's *A Patch of Africa*.

As always with my writing, I drew on family memories. It was my father, Robin Smith, who first suggested looking into the Groundnut Scheme as a setting for a novel. He was working in Tanganyika in the late 1950's and drove to Kongwa to buy a diesel generator that was being auctioned by the OFC. In 2011, we returned there together – along with my mother, sister and son – to see the remains of Londoni and discover the seeds of this book.

My father also remembered visiting Bihawana Catholic Mission near Dodoma (now the capital of Tanzania) where the Fathers were experimenting with growing wine grapes from cuttings they'd brought back from visits to their families in Italy. After our research trip to Kongwa we went to the mission and found the old winery still operating and a new one being built nearby. The place became an inspiration for the Catholic mission in the novel. At Bihawana the vines are entirely irrigation fed and three crops a year are harvested. Some of the first commercial wineries in East Africa were established in the Dodoma area, making use of prison labour.

My mother, Elizabeth Smith, studied at the Slade School of Art in London and I drew on some of her experiences there in the creation of Kitty's story. Mum was invited to model for a well-known sculptor who was a Russian prince, and made several weekend visits to his country estate. He had escaped the Red Terror with a carpetbag of heirlooms and was a starting point for the character of Yuri. The sight of my mother at her easel has been familiar to me for as long as I can remember. Her depictions of the various landscapes in which we have lived have done much to shape the way I view the world.

To learn more, visit my website at www.katherinescholes.com

ACKNOWLEDGMENTS

My heartfelt thanks go to all who have helped and supported me during the writing of this book.

Ali Watts for being such a warm, inspiring and astute publisher.

The rest of the team at Penguin Australia – especially Louise Ryan, Sally Bateman, Anyez Lindop, Deb McGowan, Belinda Byrne and Caro Cooper. Thank you also to Saskia Adams.

Fiona Inglis, Annabel Blay, Grace Heifetz and everyone else at Curtis Brown Australia.

Kate Cooper of Curtis Brown London, and all my overseas publishers and agents.

Robin and Elizabeth Smith for lending me their life experiences once again, and for meticulous Swahili translations and comments on the content of the story.

Hilary Smith and Clare Smith for reading the manuscript and offering encouragement and feedback.

Andrew and Vanessa Smith for keeping me supplied with intriguing Tanganyikan tales.

Jonny Scholes for helping with my website and providing patient advice about how to be an author in the twenty-first century.

Hugh Prentice for his ongoing interest in my African writing.

My companions on the Kongwa safari: Alison Talbert, Phil and Barbara Wigg, Hilary Smith, Elizabeth and Robin Smith – and especially my son Linden Scholes, whose presence made the journey very special.

The Fathers and others at the Bihawana Catholic Mission for showing us the historic buildings – including the hidden cells, a grotto awaiting a statue, and even the cupboard where the Italian Fathers used to dry their prosciutto.

Janet Allen of the St Phillips Theological College for a warm welcome during our stay at the Westgate Hostel, Kongwa. (Built in 1914, the building is the model for the Italian Mission in the novel.)

Ned Kemp for his generous hospitality in Mvumi; thank you also to the Mvumi School Trust.

Maura Kerr for sharing insights into Catholic traditions.

My dear friends – including the loyal Curry Girls – and all the members of my extended family who keep me company in a profession that can become solitary.

Lastly, my husband Roger, who is always a true partner in my writing, from the hatching of ideas right up to the last draft of the manuscript. A big thank you, once again.

BOOK GROUP NOTES

1. When Kitty arrives in Africa, she is determined to fulfil the role of the dutiful, perfect wife. Do you think she sets herself an impossible task? Do women today still feel the pressure to become 'the perfect wife'?

2. Is Theo a villain or a victim, in your view?

3. Who, if anyone, deserves the blame for the crisis in Kitty and Theo's marriage?

4. Are the issues faced by Kitty and Theo unique to the time and place in which they lived – or does the same story play out today?

5. Was becoming an artist the beginning or the end for Kitty?

6. How do the different characters in the book deal with past events in their lives? What do you think of the way Yuri uses Kitty as a way of evoking his lost Katya?

7. Do you think that Tanganyika was a tonic or a torment for Diana's condition?

8. When Kitty is with Taylor, she feels that 'social niceties – all the taboos and conventions' fade away. What are the possible reasons for this?

9. In what ways does idealism triumph over practicality in this novel? Discuss in relation to the Groundnut Scheme and to Kitty and Theo's marriage.

10. Father Remi claims that 'Sometimes it's not possible to make a simple choice between right and wrong. Doing good can also cause harm.' What examples of this do you find in the novel?

11. Do you agree with the author that 'fear is the inevitable companion of love'?

12. Discuss the role of spirituality and religion in this and other novels by Katherine Scholes.

GUARANTEED GREAT READ
or your money back

If you are not completely satisfied with this book please complete this coupon and return with the book and original proof of purchase to our Marketing team in your country of residence:

AUSTRALIA – send to:
Marketing Department
Penguin Group (Australia)
PO Box 23360
Melbourne VIC 8012

NEW ZEALAND – send to:
Marketing Department
Penguin Group (NZ)
Private Bag 102 902
North Shore
North Shore City 0745 Auckland

Please allow up to eight weeks for your refund. Refunds are only payable if the book and original proof of purchase are provided.

Name: _____

Address: _____

_____

Daytime phone number: _____

Offer expires 31 March 2014